'Open now the book ⋯
the Eye?' In a candel⋯
sleep, and his apprenti⋯
from human sight and⋯
dust-covered volume. The apprentice turns the key,
releasing Time: the secrets of the past, the present,
and of times to come. He reads . . .

The tale of Eider, Prince of Rhye, dispossessed of his
throne by Zarratt the Usurper. He must win back his
kingdom, but he cannot do so without the mystic
Triad: the gauntlet, the cloak, the sword. And he
must find it before the Dark Lords seize it as their
own: for when Moon and Mercury align, the occult
force ignites, unleashing the power of the Triad for
good . . . or for ill.

Crystal and Steel

Book 1 of
The Eye of Time
trilogy

LYNDAN DARBY

UNWIN
PAPERBACKS

LONDON SYDNEY WELLINGTON

First published in Great Britain by Unwin® Paperbacks,
an imprint of Unwin Hyman Limited, in 1988.

UNWIN HYMAN LIMITED
15–17 Broadwick Street
London W1V 1FP

Allen & Unwin Australia Pty Ltd
8 Napier Street, North Sydney, NSW 2060, Australia

Allen & Unwin New Zealand Pty Ltd with the Port Nicholson Press
60 Cambridge Terrace, Wellington, New Zealand

British Library Cataloguing in Publication Data

Darby, Lyndan
Crystal and steel.
I. Title
823′.914[F]
ISBN 0–04–440159–0

Set in 10 on 11 point Times by Computape (Pickering) Ltd, Yorkshire
and printed in Great Britain by
Cox & Wyman, Reading.

for R. and H.

— 1 —

The eyelashes flickered and the boy yawned. He glanced up from the chess board. The pungent aroma of wood-smoke caught his nostrils and he noticed the misty chamber once again. He watched the delicate smoke curls of the fire mingle with perfumed spirals of the incense sticks and sighed. 'The coals in the grate still flicker fire . . . the candlewax is hardly soft, yet he sleeps,' he complained, watching the snoring Ancient who had been his opponent in the game.

White hair veiled the lined face, the silk cloak was pulled tight about the angular frame, and the long tassel of the velvet cap swung rhythmically to and fro before the pointed nose as he snoozed on.

The boy looked about him, keen eyes eager for the mysteries of the Old One's chamber. First he saw the clocks, of every kind of wood, of every size and shape, ranged about the walls, shelves and tabletops of the room. The boy frowned, for the clocks were silent. So old, he thought, that they had ceased to tick forever. He traced the intricate weave of spider's lace about their stiff hands, reading every hour of day and night upon each old face.

The boy wriggled in his seat, then, casting a glance at the Old One, he rose to his feet. The small white teeth showed in a wry smile and as he moved from the table his body tingled with the freedom to explore. First he stroked the backs of ivory doves, set in static line upon the mantel, then he crossed the cold flagstones to the oak dresser. This was his favourite spot. His eager eyes gleamed as he took in every detail of the shelves: still there, the tiny Harlequin and his Columbine; still there, the twin cats tangled in play before the looking glass. The boy stretched a fingertip to touch, but then withheld. The Ancient One, should he awake, would not approve such tampering.

1

Quietly, the boy moved towards the wall glass, survey-ing himself in its sheen. The new hose were grey, the doublet turquoise, and the wide ruffs at neck and wrist were crisp and white. With a widening grin the boy gave a low bow, linking hands with his own reflection in a comical minuet. Then, suddenly, he saw reflected in the glass a thing of beauty indeed. He gave a gasp of pleasure and turned about. In the corner of the chamber, almost hidden from sight, tall tallows burned either side of a low table. Upon its rosewood surface a great book lay shut tight. The boy moved closer. The cover of the book shone the blackest of blacks, yet as the candles flickered, shafts of silver etched its surface. The boy caught his breath. So great a volume he had never seen. He moved cautiously towards the table. He must be careful not to wake the Old One or he would not have this mystery all to himself. He leaned forward for a closer look. The margin of the book was inset with gold, and such strange inscriptions he had never beheld. The young brow knitted as he tried to read the signs and symbols, finding in their tangled weave a phrase of ancient wisdom, written in the Loric tongue. He spoke it out, knowing nothing of its power: 'Walk forth,' he said. 'Scribe all you see within the book.'

The boy stroked the silk black sheen, his bud-red lips parting as he tried to prise open the cover. It did not yield, and his heart sank at the book's refusal to share with him the mystery of its pages. Yet suddenly he discovered the lock, and then the silver key. He frowned, for the key had no handle to turn it by. Instead there were at each end identical locking mechanisms. Which of these should he slot into the cavity? A final glance towards the Ancient and the boy had made his choice, slotting the key into the lock and turning it anti-clockwise, once, then twice, then once again.

The sudden and resounding clank and dropping of the metal latch set the boy's teeth on edge. He saw the dripping candles flare and felt compelled to turn lest the Old One had awakened. But then, the soft insistent pressing of cool metal on the back of his hand drew his attention, and the boy gasped, for the key turned of itself within the lock. Moving his hand away allowed the key to spin full circle, yet even as he watched it his fascination turned to panic as he saw the book's great cover start to rise. The boy retreated. A new sound met his ears and he whirled about, his small face whitening as he saw the clutter of pendulums swinging to and fro, marking with their metal rods and discs the frantic beating of his own heart. The twisting of the key had started up the tooth-and-ratchet scratching and turning, and soon the chamber's peace was lost to the ticking and tocking of every tone and speed.

The boy shrank back from the great book, its turning key and the room of clocks, to hide safely in the shadows. Yet still he could not take his eyes from the unfolding sight, except to glance at the Ancient One who slept on oblivious. He tried to think. How could he repair what he had done? What he had undone? He glanced at the book again – too late, the cover was almost vertical and showed no sign of halting there. He gulped hard, for now bright light was pulsing from the widening gap, soon the cover would drop to the tabletop, the book would fall open, the light would be brighter, the clocks would tick louder, and the Old One would be woken for sure. As the boy's heart raced with the fear of these things, the fingers of the clocks, once poised, now clanked in unison to strike the middle hour. 'Midday or midnight?' The boy sobbed aloud, clasping his ears as the chiming and the clanging began; a curtain of sound meant for this moment alone, as the great book's cover came finally to rest and its luminous pages lay outspread.

Only then, in all the light and all the noise, did the water-grey eyes of the Old One flicker open, and, as the tapered fingers stretched, the Ancient saw the open book, its virgin parchment exposed upon the wood.

By now the boy was hiding beneath the chair, and from that position he heard the Old One groan, saw the ill-shaped feet move out across the room, and knew the Old One moved towards the book. He craned his neck to see what the ancient man would do. He saw the pure white hair and beard illuminated by the shimmering light. He saw the

3

trembling fingers brush the parchment's edge. The boy frowned, for as the Old One touched the page, the chiming of the clocks ceased.

It was within this sudden stillness that the small one felt the need to sneeze, and the Ancient turned, old eyes blinking against the dark in search of him. Knowing that his hiding-place was lost, the boy stood to his feet, his head hung low for shame at all his mischief. But the Ancient did not chide him, only clasped the small hand in his grip to draw the boy towards the virgin page. 'Child,' the Old One said sadly. 'While ever these bright pages lay outspread, we are compelled to read.'

The boy, suddenly aware of the Old One's wisdom, obeyed, looking for the first time upon the magic script.

'On what page does the book fall open?' the Old One asked.

The boy scrutinised the parchment for some moments. 'Upon the page of Kings,' he said at last, looking up into the shining face. 'The Time of Crystal, it is written.'

The Old One gave a mournful smile. 'Indeed, my son, but this Time was also one of Steel.'

The boy frowned as the Old One scrutinised the page, the wrinkled lids lowering until they closed to all sight.

'Read on,' the Ancient said. 'Flow with the black and the white, for from it comes the Vision.'

The boy did not respond but gazed perplexed at the open page.

'Come, boy,' the Old One gave an impatient sigh. 'What sees the Eye?'

The boy's brow creased as he gulped the hot air of the chamber, but then upon the page he saw it. 'A castle,' he said, gripping the Old One's hand a little tighter. 'Its walls pitted with the marks of Time.'

The Old One nodded encouragement as the boy continued. 'About its towers shrill cries pierce the air. There! Battling crows rise and fall upon the draught . . . They hover above a secret place – a garden space, where ivy coats the walls, keeping all without.'

'Good, good,' the Old One breathed into the small ear. 'And the circles? The three rings ... where are these?'

The boy frowned again. 'Master? There are but two ... the ring of trees within the ring of walls.'

'Yet the third,' the Ancient insisted. 'There has to be a third.'

The boy could only shake his head. He glanced at the anxious face. 'Old One,' he said, 'I see one such as yourself. He points at the earth with a stave.'

The Old One nodded.

'And there is one other,' the boy breathed. 'One such as I. He kneels upon the earth.'

The Old One's lips quirked in a weak smile.

Sudden understanding flickered across the boy's face. 'Yes, Master! There it is!' He cried. 'The third circle ... he scrapes it out within the dust.' The boy tugged at the Ancient's silken sleeve, 'Old One, I grow dizzy,' he gasped. 'We draw too close ... I am afraid.'

'Fear not,' the Old One assured. 'The shield of the Eye is fine as crystal, yet separates us and protects as would a shield of steel.' As he spoke the Old One turned the great white page of the book. 'Read on,' he said.

The boy began again: 'Tapering fingers brush the velvet earth. Abundant curls frame the crescent face. The circle is completed at his feet. Yet, the tap of wood on stone brings him back to his task ... the whining voice of age gives him command: 'No, no, no ... not circles, boy,' he says, 'but squares ... the magic square gives all.'

'The willow trees shiver in the bitter wind and the properties of Ancient Lore are put aside, replaced by talismans of the Dark. The sky becomes heavy as the square is traced afresh upon the earth. The youth lacks willingness to do the deed, and old age predicts another failure. The ageing wizard stamps his foot and the youth braces himself, raising the stave as he whips it through the air shouting out the incantation: "Hagdarth Horam!" he cries and the garden echoes on and on ... "Hagdarth

Horam ... Hagdarth Horam ... Hagdarth Horam ...
Hagdarth ...""

'Wait, wait!' the ageing wizard cried pointing angrily at the soil.'The seals, Nairb, do you forget so soon?' The youth's hazel eyes gazed blank reply. 'At each corner of the square,' the wizard groaned taking up the discarded seals and setting them with his own hand at each corner of the design. Carefully he measured the distance between each corner, then the position of the sun from the centre of the square, and finally he gauged the angle of the sun in relation to the whole. Certain that the youth could not fail, the wizard gestured to him to perform the rite once more.

Nairb gave a nervous smile and grasping the staff in earnest, he raised it high above his head, 'Hagdarth, Horam, Hecate and ...' He closed his eyes for the words of the incantation had escaped him. The young brow creased and he began again, whipping the staff harder with every turn and with each remembered word: 'Hagdarth, Horam, Hecate and ...' He opened his eyes, still the words evaded him and the square remained a void.

The aged wizard shook his head in disgust as the youth took his stance afresh and prepared to begin again. Nairb nervously fingered the talisman about his neck, surely the power of Ancient Lore would come to his aid? He gripped the staff, beads of perspiration dripping from the tip of his pointed nose. Amid the frenzy of incantation, a sudden screech pierced the heavy air and the youth glanced up at the three black rooks as they alighted atop the stone wall. Their presence gripped him with fear and he cried out loud, 'Hagdarth, Horam, Hecate and Harath!' Centring his whole being on Ancient Lore and urging All-Power to grant him deliverance from the dark omens of the deed. The sudden friction of great force halted his flight and he stood stock still, eyes closed tight until at last he heard the wizard cry out.

6

'Orchid? Orchid!' he screamed, unable to believe his sight.

Nairb opened his hazel eyes, his thin lips curving upwards in a wide smile, for there, at the heart of the square, an abundance of rare orchids had sprung from the dust.

The wizard charged at him, his old face white with rage as he turned upon the square. With one glancing motion of his hand the blooms had vanished and in their place a squirming mandrake oozed its syrup dew. The youth shrank back repulsed.

'The King,' sneered the wizard, 'I told you boy, think only of him. His needs, his wishes ... his terrible power!'

'But wizard,' Nairb began, 'I thought of a King, should I be blamed for the honesty of the square?'

'Honesty of the square?' the wizard exclaimed grasping the talisman at the young man's neck. 'You think only of the old Lore,' he cried, breaking the slender chain and throwing the talisman to the ground. 'The Ancient Lore is only that, 'tis myth, 'tis dead! If ever it lived, it nurtured only the minds of fools.'

'Not so!' Nairb protested.

Hairb Horatious turned on him anew. 'No kinsman of mine shall be called fool. No kinsman of mine be put to death for heresy.'

Nairb's eyes filled with sorrow as the wizard raised his powerful hand.

'None shall hear of this!' he swore. The point of his forefinger directed at Nairb's solar plexus, 'Be sure your gross ineptitude brings shame upon our art and henceforth be gone, return not until your mind holds reason over fantasy.'

Nairb's breath was snatched from him as the force of the wizard's anger raised him from the ground and transported him up towards the zenith. His ears rang with the speed of his flight and his anguished cries were lost to the swirling clouds as they crashed and rolled about him.

'Be gone!' he heard the wizard cry, as he sped higher

7

through the thinning air to the point where sky and spire met and his eyes closed in sorrowful submission.

When next he woke, his heart sank at recognition of his plight: once again he was alone, imprisoned behind the cold grey walls of the castle's highest tower. Once again he was disgraced and left to waste amid the chaos of ancient books, there to ponder upon his failings and his Fate.

Suns rose and set while Nairb continued his exile, heartbroken with despair as once more he watched the sundial cast full shadow on yet another summer day. He sighed, cupping his head in his hands as he knelt upon the window seat. On the sill white doves sat snoozing in the sun. How he wished he could have their ease, instead he was forced to struggle from one dust-laden volume to the next. The scripts were indecipherable, stunting any magic that he might perform. How he wished he could make this hot day vanish and with it the Arch-wizard, his dark alchemies, his books, his phials . . . and his doves! 'Give it up,' the youth sighed at last. 'I give it all up.'

Mournfully he looked out across the heat haze and beyond to the distant horizon where brooding crags were etched against the bright sky. How he longed to know what lay beyond the boundaries of his tower. Was there indeed a world beyond? He remained before the window until the colours of afternoon had changed to evening mauves and greys, musing on as the night came down and he saw the watchfires glow upon the ridge. His heart grown heavy, he lay down upon his meagre bed and submitted himself to the mysteries of sleep.

The tower bell punctuated an endless night, until upon the hour of three Nairb rose from his bed, his limbs aching with fatigue. He rubbed his sore eyes, his thin lips quirking in a sad smile as he recognised the dust-veiled portrait which hung on the wall before him. From the holy alcove, the kindly face gazed out at him, its features etched white in the moonglow. Nairb's heart was wrenched with grief.

'Horatious Thor,' a sob caught in his throat. 'O much

loved kinsman, I wish you here in this time of dark.' Nairb wrapped his arms about his own thin frame, memory his comforter as he recalled the ancient man and childhood lessons learned at his knee. He shook his head dejectedly, 'By now I should be following his line and keeping Ancient Lore alive.' He looked once more upon the gentle face, 'Instead I tamper with spells, urged to raise Dark above Light.' Nairb gave a heavy sigh, 'The mysteries of Time are within my grasp, the power for good is strong within, yet Dark Lore forces me to fail.'

The desperate apprentice hung his head in sorrow, 'Grandfather's bones entombed. He that names me son, lost all faith in me ...' he sobbed aloud, raising both hands in heartfelt supplication. 'And if not I, then who will save the secrets of the Ancient Lore?'

As the cold chill of night crept through the chamber, the doves on the sill snuggled closer for warmth, blinking as Nairb padded to and fro. He stopped abruptly before the window: in its frame the moon hung full and bright. Nairb sighed, 'Eye of night, illuminate my path amid this Dark,' he whispered and felt the shafts of luna light as cool as a maiden's hand upon his brow. He raised his arms in invocation, the floating orb seeming to rest in his cupped hands, 'Mother goddess weave my fate, show me this night what kind of wizard I shall be.'

In that instant he turned about, the hazel eyes set upon the unyielding wood of the chamber door. Yet before his hand had stretched out to clasp the handle, his trust had released the latch and the heavy wood of the door swung open of itself.

Nairb's thin frame cast no shadow along the twisting corridors, his quiet footfall marked only by the brief flicker of torches where he passed. On and on he paced, climbing the narrow spiral of stone steps to where a maze of passages met then stretched away in every direction as far as the eye could see. Beyond, none but the chosen ever ventured to glimpse the solitary torch puvvering ochre in the blackness. The fragile flame cast little light upon the carved wood door before which Nairb halted.

9

'The chamber of Hairb Horatious and of Horatious Thor before him,' he breathed solemnly and reached for the ring of the latch, its cold iron yielding to his touch. The door creaked open and he stole within.

Inside the candles flared at his presence, their ghostly shimmer veiling all in shifting vapours. Nairb blinked hard, trying to adjust his eyes to the murky glow as the chamber took shape before him. Piles of books stood in tall columns stretching almost to the ceiling, held safe by the slender threads of the spider's craft. Benches and shelves bowed beneath the weight of bowls and beakers, parchments and phials. Time-worn receptacles layered with dust perched on warped racks, or lay in scattered heaps on the chamber floor, their multicoloured contents oozing in the dim light. Along the length of every wall ran endless shelves crammed with bottles and jars, each one containing its own specimen, some dried, some pickled ... all acrid with age. Nairb took up a jar, its strange colours drawing his curiosity, yet the shape and texture were of mortal remains and he threw down the container. Such gruesome contents were not the stuff of Ancient Lore.

He looked about, amazed at the length and width of the place. 'So narrow a tower ...' he whispered. 'Yet so vast a chamber.' For many moments he traced the chamber's murky dimensions unable to define its boundaries within the impenetrable dark. He shook his head, it seemed that the chamber stretched far beyond the confines of the tower. 'Yet to where?' he mused.

Sudden movement upon the tressel drew back his thoughts and he glanced down as a spider darted across the back of his hand. Nairb snatched his hand away and the spider stopped abruptly, then sprang forward in attack, its hairy body slung between raised legs. He watched it as it waited, then with silent speed sprang from the camouflage of the black bound volume to clamber up a silken strand to the safety of its crevice. Nairb's hazel eyes narrowed in thought, could this poor creature be enchanted? Bound by some dark spell to remain a spider forever?

He turned back to scan the chamber, saddened by the sight of his father's folly. The demands of the King had debased the noble art and sacred Lore was reduced to nothing more than evil sorcery. Nairb kicked at the scattered relics of the black arts, his heart lamenting the Arch-wizard's craft put to ill use. 'O father,' he sobbed, 'am I to be named failure by your fault?'

He looked about him at the place where in childhood he had felt the air charged with the purity of celestial force. Now all lay fettered beneath the weight and stench of deadly enchantments. Fungi crept underfoot, and the fruits of the hemlock thrived amid the shrivelled remnants of diabolical tamperings. Gone the shimmer of white candles, the sweet aroma of the healing herbs. In their place, the impure glow of tallow, the mandrake's yellow fruit and the deep purple of belladonna.

Nairb shuddered at the sight, 'If being a wizard is the legacy of my kin then this I surely am, but of Dark Lore I shall have no part,' he vowed sweeping the tressel clear of its debris. The sudden clatter as the dark accessories scattered shook vermin from their lair. In an instant, Nairb was plunging after them through the gloom until, stumbling in the chaos, he caught the drape of a workbench, upturning it as he fell headlong. Yet as he struggled to his feet, his eyes glimpsed the edge of something silver within the dark.

The tallow's flame cast its dull glow upon the ornate latch of a box, lacquered and carved in wood of the deepest red. Nairb eased the box out into the light to find etched upon its lid a succession of mystic symbols. 'Pentacle, triangle ... circle, and square,' he breathed. 'Uriel, Raphael, Gabriel, Michael ...' he uttered the names associated with the signs. He stroked his chin as he gave the inscriptions further thought. 'Rulers of the Sun, the Moon, of Venus and of Mercury,' he whispered, his eyes softening as he recalled the stories his grandfather had told. Nairb smiled, seeing in his mind's eye the skilful fingers as they carved the marks within the wood. With a sudden gasp of realisation Nairb clasped the box to him as if it were the ancient man himself, 'Horatious Thor, thy box is safe with me,' he vowed.

He fumbled with the latch and as the lid fell open the magic treasures hidden there awoke. Tenderly he embraced each object as it emerged, his eyes wide with joy as he recalled the ancient rituals to which they each belonged: talisman and compass, gemstone, ring and rune. He caught his breath, for the ancient's presence emanated from them still, even though these mystic properties, all so pure, had so long been hidden from the light of day. Nairb examined the items now strewn upon the floor, conscious of the ghostly light which hovered about them like a fine mist. Soon his brow creased, surely there was something missing?

He delved once more into the endless depths of the box, pulling out more phials, more gemstones and yet more jars filled with glittering powders. Finally, his fingers caught the edge of something cool and smooth. He tugged at it with calm insistence until, at last, the box gave up its greatest treasure: the silken garment rippled from the depths like a stream of silver, folding itself about Nairb's frame in shimmering cascades. 'The gown of Horatious Thor!' Nairb gasped, running his slender fingers along its folds. The gown sparkled with the purity of crystal, being at once white and silver, draping from his outstretched arms in a myriad of tiny pleats, its sleeves trailing the floor in identical points of silver. Upon the silk, in thread as fine as spider's yarn, were traced the same mystic symbols as upon the box itself. Nairb felt his spirit soar as he whispered each of the names, then spreading his arms in invocation he turned first to the east, 'All honour Horatious Thor, Grand-Wizard of the Ancient Lore, I conjure thee!' He turned to the west, 'Forthwith cast evil from this place and make of your true kinsman worthy servant of the Lore.'

The tallow flames flared as Nairb turned south and then north: 'Honoured kinsman, bestow on me your Vision, that I may work for good. Desiring neither wealth, nor hurt to any living thing, I shall bring light and the wisdom

12

of the Lore to this place.' He took up the pentacle and hung it about his neck, then he slipped the ancient ring onto the last finger of his right hand. This done, he returned each of the relics to the box and clutching it tightly to him, he left the chamber.

Dusts of Time spiralled in the wake of the grand-wizard's gown as Nairb sped the corridors past the guttering torches and on towards his silent tower. He glanced about, nothing had been disturbed. His face was set with determination and he entered in, closing the chamber door with a resounding clank.

2

The dawn sky flooded with colour as the downpour subsided, and soon the dancing trickle of water ran from the gutters in pleasant counterpoint to the chirping birds, who flitted from their shelter after the storm. In moments, weak sunshine had washed the cobblestones silver and the monotonous rumble of cartwheels echoed in the market square once more. Here the bustle of the day began in earnest with the clattering of wood and iron as stalls were sited and decked with wares. Water showered the cobbles as canvas was unfolded and stretched to form a patchwork of uneven shelter over all. Soon the market was full spread. A curious array of stalls rambled the length and breadth of the square, weaving in drunken lines upward through the alleyways to splash the rain-drenched day with jangled colours. The noise of the marketeers rang like a clarion call throughout the town as fishmongers, grain merchants, potters and wax-makers filled the air with their cries, and the hammering, spinning and bartering of their neighbours provided rhythm for their incantations.

As the sun reached the zenith, the whole town hummed with the excitement of the market fayre and rich displays wafted their temptations upon the warm air: cheeses, ripe and rare, ranged against the sweetest fruits, their delicious aromas mingled with fragrant blooms and the earthy damp of root produce. On makeshift spits the cooking meats were turned and basted, whilst close by the confectioner spun his sugar-webs, spreading sweet and sticky spores upon the breeze. In the midst of the buying and selling, sprightly mountebanks plied their trade, their clumsy pirouettes and cure-all potions a curious distraction from the stiltmen who strutted between the stalls, raising their hats and proffering stolen blooms.

14

In the russet light of afternoon, a wandering minstrel paced the uneven streets, his lute casting notes of harmony upon the noisy scene. Settling himself at the heart of the square he gave voice to the tune and the people drew close, caught by the mystic air and eager to hear its meaning.

The minstrel raised his voice, his look engaging every face as each one marked his youthful frame in turn. Clothed in silks of white and black, he took his graceful stance, brushing the lute with slender fingers, midnight hair cascading down the straight shoulders, the swarthy features strained until, as the last notes ebbed away, the dark-edged eyelids were raised to reveal globes of liquid black.

With the crowd's applause the fine-cut cheekbones tinged pink, and as the coins bounced at his feet, the minstrel straightened his back with proud acceptance of his reward. As silence fell, he found new notes upon the strings while his eyes measured all, caught now within the music's flow as it weaved its spell upon the air.

Suddenly within the crowd, the minstrel glimpsed a golden head and pointed ears, then soon after, the winking of an elfin eye. Nodding with the rhythm of the song, the minstrel acknowledged him, casting a glanced reply. The lute song charmed all within its range and the elfin gave a sly grin, for as the minstrel began his tale, so the crowd did sway and roll, then the eflin ducked and weaved – then the eflin fingers stole.

Catching the darting elfin shape, the minstrel's ebony pools glinted, and with one flourish of his silks he bound the happy faces of the crowd to him. 'Friends,' he said, 'you have heard my songs, and blessings on you all for my reward.' He directed a courteous hand towards the silver coins spread at his feet then strummed the lute gently as he continued, 'And in return, I give you dreams, for there is much truth in dreams.'

An appreciative mutter ran through the crowd as the minstrel placed his hand against his breast. 'Friends,' he insisted giving a low bow, 'you see before you a humble minstrel, wandering these lands with songs of joy . . . and songs of woe.' He lowered his eyes as the audience groaned mock sympathy. The minstrel raised a hand for silence and smiled sadly, 'Or, could it be you see before you . . . a prince?'

A roar of disbelief rose from the crowd as the handsome songster went through the courtly paces of a monarch. 'Perhaps 'twas not low birth made me as I am today . . . but some thief!' As the audience voiced mock concern, the minstrel cast a glance into their midst seeing again the blond head as it moved amongst them, a flash of steel glinting in the shadows as each purse was severed from its thong.

'Yes!' the minstrel raised his voice. 'A royal child, cast out upon the waters of time to grow to manhood in distant climes and vow revenge.' Cries of 'shame!' rose from the crowd and as the eyes of the farm women moistened at the tale, the menfolk leered their disbelief. 'For truly I am no minstrel,' the stranger carried on against all odds, 'but I am a son of Rhye and rightful heir to the throne of that realm.'

A unified gabble of sympathy and abuse rose up once more and the minstrel strummed at the lute strings, his voice falling to a theatrical whisper. 'And so a vagabond I am, forced to roam the lands until I find the realm of Dream . . . ' his eyes had grown distant.

A scarred hand was thrust high above the sea of faces, 'My fist will help you on your journey there!' the gruff voice mocked.

'Aye!' yelled another. 'If you be a prince, then so must I be.'

''Tis all but idle dreams, say I!' another groaned.

A unified 'Aye!' rang out above the crowd's mirth and the minstrel shook his indigo mane. The dark eyes flashed.

'Believe, for it is so!'

'Come now,' provoked a woman in their midst, 'do you tell dreams or true?'

The minstrel smiled persuasively, 'I am a minstrel – I

sing of dreams, but dreams must be believed or will never be.'

The yokel's fist thrust up once more, 'Aye, minstrels sing their songs and tricksters spin their yarns!' Laughter spread the crowd but the minstrel took his stance anew, and strumming gentle chords upon the lute he began his tale:

Horses race with speed of light
In the seelie realm, where faces bright
Sing songs of joy, forever.
There the river's sweetest wine
Flows on and on, forever.

Yet while elders sleep
This son of Rhye sees all
And now to champion right he knows
The sons of night must fall
And vows it will be so.

For from the darkness fear did steal
And put to sword who would not kneel,
And by his hand all life turned sour,
Spilled the blood royal, the land did spoil.

Then the seven sees did churn
And seelie charm did ebb away
Its colours drained from night and day
While evil darkened all.

But see, the prince now grown a man
And none can halt the master-plan
For darkness now must fall
And light flood colour over all.

For when dreams become reality
Rhye blooms again with victory
And when my vow has been upheld
Then this, my dream, will be fulfilled.

The minstrel's keen eyes scanned the silent crowd – the elfin form had vanished from sight. As the songster brushed the final chord, the magic tale that had held

17

simple folk enrapt came to a close, and in the streaming light of sunset the crowd let out a cheer of joy. The minstrel gave a humble bow. Yet as he scooped silver coins from the ground, a solitary voice cried, 'Thief!' and panic broke. The minstrel's eyes blazed as he glanced round the fray, yet all had forgotten him. In the blink of an eye the market square had become a chaos of arms and legs, as first one, then another of the townsfolk found himself made lighter by the loss of purse and valued possessions. Unnoticed, the minstrel watched their panic, then with one last and unseen flourish of the silks, the lute was slung across his back and he paced away up the narrow alley to the waiting alehouse.

Upon entering the smoke-filled tavern, the minstrel scanned its occupants. Before the blazing hearth farm-workers drew upon their pipes, silver tankards glinting as they supped their brew. Soon he caught sight of the familiar blond head nestled between the heavy bosoms of serving wenches, and moving briskly forward, the minstrel ordered ale.

The gold-headed elfin turned at sound of the minstrel's voice. 'Aye,' he said rising to his feet. ' . . . And so would I have more ale had I the coins to buy it.'

The minstrel glared into the impish face. 'Then stranger, let us sup, for this day brought good fortune to my side.'

The elfin grasped the newly filled tankard. 'Good fortune be celebrated!' he laughed aloud raising it to his lips.

The minstrel's eyes narrowed, his deft hand gripping the elfin wrist. 'Come friend,' he growled below his breath and darted a glance towards the alcove by the fire.

Reluctantly the elfin did as he was bid and followed the minstrel into the shadowed recess. Once seated, the elfin leered into the swarthy features. 'A fine and fortunate day indeed, my friend!' he sneered.

The minstrel glared annoyance. 'I warn you, Regor,' he swore. 'Your roguery will be the end of both our lives!'

Regor gave a short laugh. 'Come now, when did your honest warblings ever earn our bread?'

The minstrel made to bang the wood of the table, but then withheld. He leaned forward. 'We agreed, no thieving be done.'

The elfin sank back in his chair and sneered. 'No friend, you agreed, not I.'

The minstrel moved closer still. 'I coax silver with my songs, there is no need of more.'

The elfin darted a quick look about the room before meeting the minstrel's glare full on. 'Look about you . . .' he insisted, lowering his voice almost to a whisper. 'How soon shall we find another place as prosperous as this?'

The minstrel shook his head. 'We gather all we need to live, it is enough,' he said adamantly.

Regor gritted his teeth. 'Live you say? Well, I would thrive and where it is to take – then take say I!'

The minstrel's face grew dark with rage. 'Steal today and hang tomorrow, friend, you have no understanding of the price.'

Regor fell silent, but then with a slow grin he drew the bulging purse of booty from his jerkin and casually placed it before the minstrel at the centre of the table. 'These spoils shall see us through this land and on to where you say the boundaries lie,' he said with a wink, 'No need of empty dreams . . . or empty bellies!' The minstrel's eyes narrowed as the elfin continued. 'Eider, I know your heart is in the work, but surely . . .' he gave a low laugh. 'You cannot really think that they believe a word . . .'

Regor's breath was stopped as Eider seized the collar of his shirt twisting it as a knot about his clenched fist. 'And this?' Eider swore, sweeping the purse from the tabletop. 'You think this all of life?'

Regor snatched at the purse in time to halt its fall. As quickly as he had caught it with his left hand so he snatched at his dagger with his right, but before he could unsheath the blade, the door of the alehouse was flung open. In the door's gape stood two hefty dwarfs, axes gripped tightly in their gnarled fists. All eyes in the tavern

19

turned upon them, and the elfin features froze in terror as the dwarfs entered in, clearing the way for a well-rounded farmwoman. The fat red face shone like a beacon as she scanned the room, her gaze falling finally upon the guilt-ridden Regor. The wind-chapped finger pointed immovably in his direction.

'Thief!' she bellowed. 'There be he!'

Regor swallowed hard as Eider growled into his pointed ear. 'Well, friend Regor? A fortunate day indeed!' Casually the minstrel gathered together his belongings and nodding towards the door he rose quietly to his feet. Regor followed suit.

'Good lady,' Eider smiled as he moved towards her. 'What panic is this?' he soothed, flourishing a hand in courtly manner and offering a polite bow.

'I'll show you what panic, minstrel,' the woman snorted, refusing courtly charm. 'Tis gone!' she said, indicating the severed purse strings.

'The purse . . . gone!' echoed the stone-faced dwarfs.

'And there the thief!' the woman bellowed like a sow as she tried in vain to side-step Eider and tackle the villain.

Regor cringed in Eider's shade as his accuser moved closer.

'He walked up and he took it – under my very nose!' she glowered, pushing a tankard-strewn table out of her way.

'Under her nose,' echoed the dwarfs in unison.

Eider gave a carefree laugh. 'Surely, there is some mistake?' he said matching the woman's every movement in protection of the elfin at his back.

'No mistake,' the dwarfs assured him.

'There I stood, a-listen' to your songs . . . ' the woman stopped abruptly, sudden realisation spreading across her face. 'Why, 'tis the both of 'em!' she cried. 'the both of 'em be thieves!' she told the room and the gathered crowd rose as one, moving in upon the strangers even as she spoke. By now the first dwarf had made ready with his axe and the second had blocked the doorway with his awesome bulk.

Eider turned to Regor. The elfin gave a nod and with a sudden war cry he threw the bag of coins at Eider's chest, flinging himself at the dwarf like a battering ram, the blond head thrust firmly into the rounded belly. Eider, meanwhile, ran at the farmwoman, spinning her about until her skirts billowed out and she flew from him in dizzy chaos on into the heart of the noisy crowd who tumbled backward beneath her weight. As the second dwarf lurched towards him, Eider threw the purse to Regor, landing the distracted dwarf a hard blow upon the jaw. The axe clattered to the floor and Eider snatched it up, slipping through the turmoil towards the tavern door. He turned to search for the elfin.

'The purse ...' Regor hesitated, stretching for the trampled bag of coins.

Eider forced the door. 'Leave it!' he ordered, brandishing the razor-sharp axe at the pursuing farmworkers, forcing them to reel back as the blade scythed the smoky air and Regor darted through the half-open doorway. Quick as shadows they slipped into the darkness, Eider slamming the door against the baying crowd and jamming it shut with the axe stave. A low whistle echoed at his back and Eider spun about, following Regor over the rough stone wall.

Manically they ran through the winding alleyways of the town pushing each other on when first one then the other began to flag. Once clear of the gates they pounded on along the country lane, scaling briar and stone fences, finally to collapse exhausted within the shadowed safety of woodland. From the camouflage of trees and tangled ferns Eider listened intently for the sound of footfall, but no sound came save the moaning of the chill wind. He turned to the panting elfin. 'What do you hear?' he whispered.

Regor caught his breath, his pointed ears twitched slightly. 'Not a sound,' he grinned into Eider's anxious face. 'No one follows.'

As they struggled to their feet the force of the ice-wind

hit them full on, snow flurries whipped their faces and they ran on in search of shelter for the cold night. Soon a meagre fire flickered within a low cave and the two sat close to its flames for warmth and comfort.

Regor shivered. 'Leave the purse indeed,' he scowled but his companion paid no heed to the comment.

Eider gazed steadily into the flames, their amber dance reflected in the shining globes of his eyes. Within the rippling coals he watched images take shape and quietly gave voice to his vision. 'Robes of white . . . circles . . . and . . . a star.' The dark brow knitted in a frown. 'A red box . . . a box of delights . . . ' he turned a bright smile on the sulking elfin.

Regor poked at the fire with the toe of his boot. 'Dreams and visions,' he growled. 'Such games are for infants!'

Eider turned back to the flames and said nothing.

'A waste of time and energy!' Regor provoked. He leaned forward. 'Such games do not fill the belly,' he shouted into Eider's distant features.

Eider glared at him through the flames. 'They have their place as well as silver, my friend.'

Irritable, the elfin stood to his feet and paced towards the mouth of the cave. He looked out across the twinkling expanse of the night sky then shrugged once more. 'So what now say I?' he sneered looking back at the impassive minstrel.

'We move on,' Eider gave a heavy sigh and tossed the remaining sticks of wood upon the fire.

'Move on?' Regor kicked at the dusty floor of the cave. 'Move on and starve while cold and ice scrape at the bones?'

Eider pulled the rough cloak close about him. 'At the next town we earn our bread and shelter as before.'

'More songs! More dreams!' Regor flared, snatching his fingers into a fist. 'With that purse we'd have had an easy winter.'

Eider shook his head wearily. 'The purse was already lost.'

Regor strode back towards the fire, his teeth clenched. 'Then with this . . . ' the dagger blade gleamed in the firelight. 'This could have made it easy.'

'Then go! Use it! Kill for gold!' Eider exploded with anger. 'But count yourself no friend of mine.'

With a snarl, Regor backed away and reluctantly sheathed the naked blade. In the silence he thrust his hands deep into the pockets of his jerkin. 'Then we go on walking. Walking and starving.'

'There is no other way in these lands for us,' Eider's tone was one of resignation.

The elfin's eyes glinted. 'There is another way,' he insisted and crouched down at Eider's side. 'Friend, we struggle to survive, we are grown thin,' he persuaded. 'I say to you again, sell the Firestone, let us live.'

Eider's anger woke fear in the elfin as he pushed him roughly away. 'Enough!' he swore. 'Firestone has no worth in gold.'

'Not so!' Regor spat, 'And if it is so, such simpletons as those would know only that it gleams and would give any price we asked!'

'No!' Eider shouted into the taut face. 'Firestone has worth for none but I, and it remains with me.'

In the silence that fell between them Regor wrapped his cloak about him and stood to his feet. 'I will check the snares,' he scowled, pacing from the cave and out into the dark night.

Alone, Eider reached inside his jerkin and withdrew the smooth leather pouch. He tipped the contents onto the palm of his hand: the gemstone lay like a bright red tear, its facets sparkling in the fireglow. He looked at it for long moments, Regor's argument echoing in his ear as he returned the gem to its pouch and tightened the thongs with an emphatic snap.

—— 3 ——

Regor groaned and halting he slid the sodden pack from his aching shoulders. He kicked at the stony earth and glared into the colourless sky, seeing nought ahead but the fog and the faint outline of the minstrel tramping on, oblivious of his discomfort. Eventually Eider stumbled to a halt, aware of the eflin's absence.

'What ails?' he frowned, barely able to speak the words.

'That which ails you, friend,' Regor groaned again. 'My belly plays a tune upon my backbone. I am weary and frozen with cold.'

Eider stared dejectedly into the murky distance. 'Come, Regor,' he urged pushing himself on. 'Soon we shall find shelter and some food.'

Regor spat at the churned earth. 'I would we'd stayed closer to the townships, here is only mud and trees.'

Eider adjusted his pack wearily. 'The people of these climes are hospitable, here they shall take pity on us, here we shall find help.'

'People?' Regor fumed, spreading out his arms to the wide sky. 'There are no people!' he shouted even louder at the minstrel's back. 'I would have warm alehouses, wenches and all their comforts. Here is nought but dung and turnips!'

Eider turned angrily upon the elfin. 'But for your greed we need not have wandered so far afield,' he reprimanded the sullen-faced elfin awaiting a quarrel. When none came he turned and walked on. 'Let us be about the business,' he ordered, gouging out fresh footprints in the sludge.

They trekked on hour after hour, hoar-frost clinging to their boots, their cloaks wrapped tight about their numb bodies. At sight of the shadowed outlines, Regor turned to the minstrel. 'Dwellings,' he gasped in relief.

Eider nodded, his frost-whitened hair hung with tiny ice-droplets.

They pushed on with renewed vigour, stumbling across the half-frozen furrows of ploughed earth towards the promise of warmth and food. In their desperation Eider cried out, falling on the ice-packed soil and Regor turned to help him to his feet. 'On friend, soon we shall have bread and rest,' he encouraged with a weak smile.

Eider's dulled eyes flickered with the pain of hunger. 'I have no songs left in me to earn it,' he breathed, his dry throat rattling against the cold.

Regor clung to him. 'Fear not, where bread is not freely given, I shall take it for you,' he vowed.

Their faltering steps quickened as the glow of a bright fire took shape ahead of them and they glimpsed the small dwelling, low and roughly crafted, set apart from the homesteads which squatted in a shadowed ring some distance beyond. Eider's eyes danced at sight of the fire. Before its warmth a group of people crouched, and as the two companions drew closer Regor's keen eyes caught sight of food strewn out upon the ground. He gasped, pulling Eider along as he quickened his pace.

Eider tugged at the ragged sleeve and halted him. 'Careful friend, these people gather here for wisdom not for bread.'

Regor tilted his head, a frown creasing the dirty forehead.

'Here is knowledge,' Eider whispered hoarsely. 'We must show the proper respect.'

They moved closer, Eider motioning Regor to crouch down with the rest as the lilting tones of the curl-haired teacher wafted towards them on the pulsing smoke.

'And blended with the hawthorn flower it eases the bones.'

'A medic,' Regor whispered to Eider as the teacher distributed dried herbs and powders to eager hands. One awestruck landsman pressed forward:

'Master, what of the remedy for faerie-stroke?' he pleaded. 'That which you told us the first day.'

'Yes, and the cure for maladies of the mind!' first one and then another insisted.

While Regor crammed his mouth and then his pockets with food, Eider craned his neck to catch sight of the man who sat at the heart of the gathering. Between the heads of the listeners, he saw dark brown curls cascading about a crescent face, saw heavy eyelids shading hazel eyes and traced the finely chiselled nose. The half moon of the jawline was strong while the lips were softly curved. As the teacher turned to answer questions, Eider glimpsed the long and graceful neck, and the straight shoulders and long limbs indicated a tall and wiry frame. Eider watched slender fingers stroke the air and the noisy gathering fell silent. With a shudder the teacher wrapped the heavy cloak about him and gave a weary smile.

'The day is bleak,' he breathed in a soft, tear-drop voice. 'My light flickers, I can teach no more this day.'

None protested although their eyes reflected disappointment; instead the gathering rose as one, and bowed respectful thanks before leaving the circle of fire and moving off in the direction of the homesteads.

Eider felt a tug at his sleeve as Regor pushed bread into his grimy hand with a rueful smile, but the minstrel could only look at it, distracted. The halfwit boy who had held the teacher's hand throughout now left his side and was taking up the gifts that had been left for them. He gathered up all that he could find to carry it within as his master pushed back the sackcloth flap and entered the makeshift dwelling.

Eider turned a reproachful look upon the elfin. 'You should not have taken the bread,' he said, barely able to speak. He rocked unsteadily for lack of food and Regor gripped his arm. Eider's dark eyes met his in silent thanks, but the elfin looked elsewhere.

The halfwit boy stood in the doorway, his feral eyes drawing Eider's glance. Sensing their need, the child proffered bread in his small outstretched hand. Eider turned to Regor. 'Friend, here is wisdom indeed. We must partake.'

Within, a small group of children sat, plum-cheeked and smiling, happy at the return of their teacher whose soft voice coaxed them in their tasks. One child played gentle tones upon a pipe, another mixed herbs in a bowl before the hearth. A third scratched his alphabet upon a rough slate whilst his companion spread out sand, drawing geometric shapes in its fine grains. The halfwit boy, meanwhile, crouched in the hearth's recess, lost in a twilight realm, wild eyes intent upon the sharp knife as the cedarwood he held yielded up a crude face. He giggled demonically as long twists of wood shavings fell into the hearth, flaring as they were consumed by the hungry flames.

The teacher moved quietly amongst them, brushing the boy-child's head as he beckoned to the bedraggled strangers to warm themselves before the fire. Together they sat cross-legged before the rippling heat and with trembling hands Eider broke the bread in two, sharing it with the elfin. As he did so he felt the eyes of the teacher upon him and looked up. The kindly smile that met him warmed Eider's spirit to the core and he smiled in gentle reply. Quick as a flash Regor took up the discarded bread as Eider stood to his feet and gave a bow of silent respect.

Before he could speak the teacher raised his hands, sensing Eider's weakness. 'Friends, you starve,' he said softly. 'Be seated, warm yourselves and eat.'

At that moment, a girl-child moved towards them through the woodsmoke bearing bowls of steaming broth. While they ate their fill, they watched on as the gentle teacher sat himself before the hearth, gathering the children to him. From the folds of his gown he took a sphere of smooth wood and this he balanced on the palm of his hand for their inspection. Eyes grew large as saucers as the children watched his bony fingers dismantle the mysterious object. Soon it lay upon the floor in a dozen strange and irregular shapes. Young, eager hands stretched out to grasp the sections of wood, fumbling and

27

twisting, turning and forcing the pieces until in exasperation they were cast down upon the ground in as many fragments still. In the silence, the girl-child stepped forward, her amethyst eyes shining with the confidence vested in her as the teacher beckoned her to him. Soon caution was replaced by joy as with speed and determination her deft fingers worked the wooden wedges into a sphere. With one final snap of wood against wood, the puzzle was complete and she smiled triumphantly, she who had watched all and looked unsure, the owner of the perfect sphere once more.

The cheers and protests of the others were soon silenced by the sweeping motion of the teacher's skeletal arms. 'What would you have now, more sums?'

'No, no,' the children cried. 'A tale!' they insisted of one accord.

'The Ancient Tale,' the halfwit boy grinned from his place beside the hearth.

'Yes,' the children shouted out. 'The one you spoke on the first day – tell us again, master, tell us the Ancient Tale.'

The teacher raised his arms for quiet and Eider shuffled closer, enchanted by the scene of harmony accentuated by the wistful strains of pipe and the rhythmic fluttering of the amber flames. The children's eyes grew wide with wonder as the teacher leaned forward, his hands upon his knees.

' 'Tis a story without end or beginning, neither written, nor forgotten,' he beckoned them to him as if sharing a confidence. 'An ancient tale of a time and place where the beauties of every season never faded, where no darkness was and no poison thrived.'

The girl-child snuggled closer to the master's knee, eager for every word that would be spoken by the wise one.

'In this realm, Rhion ruled all. A goodly monarch, with justice and humility. Even the lowliest tribes of the kingdom, and that included the unruly spriggans, were welcomed at his court.'

The teacher scanned the bright-eyed faces before him. 'Rhion's courage and wisdom met no match in all the realm, and his parents were hard put to find one suitable to be his bride.

'Yet,' said the teacher, 'a maiden was found, white as the new moon and delicate as spring. Soon they were married and very happy, except . . . ' the teacher's brow knitted. 'They were not blessed with babes.'

The children listened intently as the teacher pressed forward. 'None knew why, except Rhion's father, the old king.'

'He had a secret?' prompted the halfwit boy.

'He did indeed,' the teacher agreed, surveying each small face in turn. 'In his wish for the perfect bride, the old king had made a great error. He had rejected many a beautiful girl in his search, and among them had been one they called the Black Lily.'

'A Black Lily?' frowned the girl-child. 'What kind of creature is that?'

The teacher cupped his hands together until his long arms formed the stalk and his tapered fingers formed the bud of a monstrous flower. 'She was the daughter of the dark perimeter. The pride of her father, the Elder of the Edge who was deeply insulted by the rejection of his offspring and cast an enchantment upon the old king's son.'

'That they should have no issue,' the girl-child interrupted.

'Indeed, and other things far worse,' the teacher drew them close to him. 'It was said that Rhion's young queen died of an unknown malady, and on that day the eternal blue of the kingdom's skies momentarily darkened and Rhion fell into a deep melancholy.'

'What did they do, master?' asked a tousled-haired youth with a dimple in his chin.

Nairb shrugged. 'They could do nothing . . . until, one day the Elder of the Edge arrived at court bringing his daughter with him.'

'The one they called the Black Lily?' the youth gasped in realisation.

29

Nairb nodded. 'Yes, it was she, and at sight of her Rhion fell instantly under her power. 'Tis said their marriage completed the Elder's enchantment, for soon Black Lily had conceived a child.'

'And the kingdom was saved!' the children cheered.

Nairb raised a calming finger. 'It was not so simple, for the egg was split and Black Lily brought forth two children at once: a girl-child they named Rhia and a boy-child titled Rhys.'

'Two in one?' the girl-child breathed, amazed at her imaginings.

'Good fortune!' another nodded.

'Not so,' the teacher shook his head sadly. 'It was as if the strange princess's tasks be done, for as the twins first cried aloud, Black Lily's life did ebb away.'

The children caught their breath as their teacher spread his arms out wide. 'Yet the kingdom rejoiced for the offspring were healthy, strong and beautiful, and though they briefly mourned the loss of a queen, soon all celebrated the happy future of the kingdom and the king's new born.'

The girl-child played absently upon her pipe as the halfwit boy fed his wood parings to the fire. The teacher sipped at a beaker of tea, casting a half look at Eider who by now was as engrossed in the Ancient Tale as were the children. He sat upright amid the infants and adolescents at the teacher's feet and smiled with relish as the tale was continued.

'Celebrations were in haste!' the teacher said with a frown. 'For soon great trouble stirred, for though Rhia had been first born, the Elders designated Prince Rhys heir to the throne.'

' 'Twas as it should be!' the eldest youth cried petulantly.

'Aye,' said his brother. ' 'Tis so, boys are always heir to a throne.'

The teacher nodded patiently. 'But even though it was as tradition dictated it should be, the moment of the Elders' decision brought forth cries of terrible rage from the infant Rhia.' The teacher lowered his voice to a whisper. 'And the tears she shed were black.'

'Black tears?' the girl-child exclaimed in disbelief.

The teacher nodded. 'No one could explain it, and the Elders, fearful of such omens, vowed to watch her close each and every day of her life.' His eyes met Eider's in a penetrating stare and the minstrel shuffled a little closer, his face taut with concentration as the teacher continued.

'Such watchfulness was not in vain. Soon it was clear to all that Rhia and her brother were opposites in every way.' The teacher held up both hands to depict the two children. 'Rhys was gentle, reflective and kind. His sister, wilful, strong and cruel. From their first days they were in competition and fought at every opportunity.'

'But boys are stronger than girls,' one male-child argued.

The teacher turned a gentle look on him, 'Not so ... and Rhia fought as hard as Rhys in every game they played, and as they grew, she made her brother's combat lessons a danger for him, being his match in all things.'

'In swordplay too?' Eider asked enrapt.

The teacher smiled at him. 'Indeed, and her sharp intellect made many nervous in her presence.' He took up the beaker of herb tea and closed his eyes as he drank, replacing the beaker to keep warm upon the hearth. The teacher looked Eider full in the eye. 'In time Rhia drew to her all those who thought her claim to the throne was just. Quiet schemers, seeing in her rancour an opportunity to seize power for themselves.'

'They would plot against the gentle Rhys?' the girl-child breathed, half afraid.

The teacher nodded. 'With adulthood the rivalry between the two had grown to great enmity, and with the death of their father this enmity turned to feud and finally to bloodshed.'

Silence fell upon the group of listeners as the teacher described the scene. 'Kin fought kin in the madness and

31

thus began the cycle of discord and bloodletting which lasted many long years.' The teacher lowered his eyes as the fire crackled in the hearth.

Eider leaned forward, his black eyes reflecting the glitter of the flames. 'Tell me, what happened to these two?' he urged.

The teacher raised his serene face. 'One day Rhia met her brother upon the battlefield. At last the time had come. They fought long and hard amid the blooded earth, until the sword of Rhys took his sister's life. The loyal faction ran to meet their victorious king, but alas found him mortally wounded.'

The children gasped in unison as their teacher gazed at the earth floor, his voice grown distant. 'Dying of his wounds and of his grief at the fate of the kingdom, Rhys uttered his final wish: that he and Rhia be united in death.' The teacher's young face seemed suddenly older than the ages and Eider gasped, prompting him to awaken from his silence.

'And so they were buried together?' he questioned.

The teacher nodded. 'Laid together in the burial mound of kings, and with them the gauntlet of Rhia, the cloak of Rhys and the great double-edged sword of the great king. Their bodies were consumed in the pyral flame and the tomb was sealed forever as a symbol of the kingdom's new unity.'

The teacher fell silent and the tiny faces about him turned their attention to the crackling fire, imagining the mystic pyre and the smoke-draped ancient vault.

Eider too watched the flames, their flickering tongues changing to rippling figures in the glow. Quietly he raised the lute and soon the muted rhythms of the fire became the gentle strumming of strings.

The children turned from the flames and the teacher's face spread with a warm smile. 'Such gentle harmonies are rare in these dark lands,' he breathed.

Eider nodded modestly. 'And so I earn my bread, warming the hearts of men from end to end of this cold place.'

' 'Tis wonder you survive,' the teacher mused. 'Your touch seems far too light for mortal ears.'

Eider darted him a cautious glance. 'Music touches those who have the heart to hear it,' he shuffled with irritation. 'And for the rest, I care nought,' he frowned.

The children and their master sat entranced, listening as the final notes melted away on the warm air and were lost to the resounding snores of the elfin who had tucked himself up for sleep in the warmest corner of the room. Eider laughed aloud, and so did the teacher and all his young friends. At their sudden uproar the elfin stirred, then sat bolt upright, unnerved by the sea of staring faces that surrounded him.

The teacher called the girl-child to him. 'Bring them wine,' he said. 'Be sure it is well mulled.' He turned to Eider. 'Minstrel, you and your assistant take your ease, while we prepare for night's warmth and comfort.'

Regor squirmed. 'Your assistant?' he echoed the teacher's tone beneath his breath, glowering as he watched the man lead the children in their tasks. He glanced at the hearth where Eider sat cross-legged before the fire. The elfin scowled and, rising to his feet, moved towards the window. He pressed his face against the leaded glass, straining his eyes to focus in the fading light beyond. He saw the snow flurries and the boys as they trudged off into the falling darkness. Turning back to the room, he observed the teacher as he ferried silently back and forth, preparing sleeping quarters for the night. Regor's eyebrows knitted in a deep frown. What was this man? Teacher or medic? Regor could not tell, yet he was sure that in some way he weaved strange enchantments over young and old alike.

Nairb paused to collect the chalk-inscribed slates that had been stacked beside the hearth and Regor bristled with new attentiveness, for the light of the fire had reflected momentarily upon silver. Suddenly the elfin saw the star-shaped talisman that dangled about the teacher's neck and he shifted for a closer look, the azure eyes narrowing as he measured the intricacy of the object, weighing up its value . . . should it ever come to be sold.

Nairb carried the slates away and Regor shoved both thumbs into his belt, sauntering over to where Eider sat deep in thought before the hearth. Casually, Regor took out his pipe, seating himself beside the silent minstrel. He filled the bowl with tobacco. 'Fortunate day, indeed,' he whispered into his companion's ear, but Eider was distracted still.

Regor firmed the tobacco with his thumb. 'Food . . . shelter . . . ' he added drawing so close to Eider that their shoulders touched. ' . . . and rich takings for those with the wit to recognise them,' he finished with a smile of roguish contentment.

Eider flinched as if shaken by the comment. He turned a quizzical look upon the elfin. 'What do you mean?'

The teacher re-entered the room and Regor drew sharply away to snatch up a taper from the hearth. Nairb caught his eye and the elfin, eager to deflect the wise man from his dark thoughts, offered up a broad grin.

Nairb set a flagon of mulled wine upon the table and filling two cups with the fragrant brew he proffered a cup to each in turn. Regor took up the wine with an awkward smile, whilst Eider graciously acknowledged their host and raised his cup in a gesture of thanks.

Regor nodded as the teacher wandered off to gather blankets and pillows. 'Simple soul, kind-hearted . . . generous,' he surmised, downing the wine and wiping his mouth on his sleeve. 'Not one to begrudge those in need,' he smirked leaning forward to catch a spark from the fire.

Eider caught Regor's arm roughly. 'Friend, what scheme is this?' he demanded under his breath.

Regor lit his pipe and sucked hard at the flame. He exhaled the smoke with a curious arrogance. 'Look on,' he said, the small face gashed with a savage grin. 'This sage cares not for goods. He barters knowledge . . . ' As Eider watched the elfin features, Regor plucked the pipe stem from his mouth to make the point. 'See . . . ?' he cocked his head in Nairb's direction and drew a line across his own throat with the stem of the pipe. 'About his neck ... there dangles our salvation.'

As Nairb paced across the room Eider's dark eyes took in the shining talisman. Realising Regor's plan, his face flushed red with anger but before he could admonish the elfin, he saw that Regor was raising his cup in a gesture of thanks towards their host. 'Continued health, good friend,' Regor nodded in Nairb's direction.

The teacher waved a dismissive hand, spreading the open palms wide. 'Friends, it is my joy to give. Welcome to you both and the Gods aid you on your way.'

'They will,' Regor breathed through the clenched teeth of his smile, nudging Eider as he watched the unsuspecting man set once more about his tasks. 'See?' the elfin said with a smirk. 'He would aid us on our way.'

Eider tightened visibly as the elfin chuckled to himself.

'The embers fade,' Nairb's patient voice cut between their murmured conversation and both turned to meet his penetrating gaze. 'Nights here are long and chill,' he gestured towards the dwindling flames. 'The boy and I must seek out fuel for the night fire.'

As the sackcloth of the door flapped at their backs, the elfin's face beamed with possibilities. 'A most fortunate day,' he repeated to himself.

Eider glared into the self-satisfied countenance. 'What dark plans are these you weave?' he questioned.

Regor spat into the flames. 'This,' he began, reaching inside his jerkin, 'I found it in the teacher's cupboard.' He held up fibrous roots and blunt, serrated leaves for Eider's inspection.

'Well?' Eider demanded.

Regor's face broke into a sly grin. ' 'Tis fragrant valerian,' he said triumphantly. 'Mixed with balm and hops ... it brings on sleep.' He rolled the lemon-scented leaves between his fingers. 'By the blood of my ancestors, this brew shall see a long sleep made.'

Eider inclined his head as Regor shuffled closer to him. 'Only a little of the stuff induces deep slumber ...

and we leave this place with full bellies, full purses and assurance of their replenishment.'

In a second Regor's gloating words stopped in mid-flow, snuffed out by Eider's iron grip about his throat. The impact jerked the clay pipe from the gaping elfin mouth.

'None of this!' Eider commanded. 'I will have none of this!' he growled again.

Regor gripped Eider's forearm with both hands but could not struggle free. 'A joke ...' he spluttered, the blue eyes bulging with terror and pain. 'I meant no harm, minstrel, no harm ...'

Eider's mouth tightened and his fingers pressed hard against the elfin's larynx.

'A joke, no more,' Regor's voice was barely audible. 'I swear!' He gasped and retched as Eider thrust him away. Shaken by his sudden outburst, the elfin scowled, setting his garments straight as he watched Eider turn away and poke at the fire with the last stick of wood. Silently they watched the slender wedge flare until Regor could bear the silence no longer. 'Then what are we to do?' he pleaded.

'We work the villages as before,' Eider said simply.

' 'Tis madness!' Regor started up once more. 'We shall starve to death. Friend, winter is already on us, we are spent.'

Eider's eyes flashed daggers. 'I shall not steal from those who freely give.'

'Then do as I said before, or I shall do it for you!' Regor snarled, snatching at Eider's sleeve.

Eider pulled away, his brow raised in defiance.

'Sell the Firestone!' Regor insisted into the unmoving features of the minstrel's face. 'Sell it, let us live.'

'I shall never part with it!' Eider swore.

The unyielding look forced Regor's hand to dagger-hilt, yet as he raised the glinting blade, Eider snatched at his wrist, forcing the weapon from his grip. The two of them tumbled to the dusty floor, Eider wrestling to take the blade while Regor pulled at the minstrel's jerkin, searching with rapid fingers for the gem.

'Give it to me!' the elfin growled, his busy fingers weaving through every fold of the jerkin until finally he uncovered it and snatched it up in his grubby fist. Eider lunged at the dagger-blade, forcing Regor off balance and sending the shimmering gemstone rolling about the floor. Regor scrambled after it leaving the unwanted dagger in Eider's grip.

'Brother, you would steal from me?' Eider cried aloud as Regor fell upon the gem.

'Hold!' Nairb's gentle voice broke between them.

Quickly, Eider concealed the blade whilst Regor looked up, his wide eyes scanning the towering frame of the teacher at whose feet he crouched. Nairb bent down and taking up the gemstone, he held it out to Eider. Upon the smooth white palm the stone gleamed deepest red, its facets etched silver in the firelight. Eider reached for the stone and as the teacher dropped the gem into his square palm, their eyes met in mutual respect.

The shame-faced Regor, resenting their silent alliance, rose to his feet and planting his cap firmly upon his head, made for the doorway. Eider watched him go before pocketing the Firestone and bending to pick up the chairs and cups upturned during their brief fray.

Nairb moved closer to him and rested a calm hand upon Eider's taut shoulder. He nodded towards the doorway. 'I heard you call the elfin "brother" – surely 'tis not so?'

Eider shook his head. 'Not so in blood, but in race. We are of the same realm, that which mortals call "seelie".' He scanned the passive countenance. 'But mark, the distinction between us is strong defined. There are as many ranks as races in that realm.'

The teacher nodded, his eyebrows raised in question. 'Yet he would commit unseelie acts, would steal from you and do me mischief with his schemes.'

Eider gave him a guilty glance. 'It is the trait of his roguish ancestry. He means no harm.'

Nairb scrutinised Eider's swarthy features. 'What brought you so far from your own borders?

Eider tightened at the wise man's gentle quizzing. 'I could say Fate,' he shrugged. 'Or could ask the same question of you.'

The teacher smiled at him. 'I am Nairb Horatious, like you a traveller of the lands.' He gave a bow. 'Teacher, wise man, healer, seer . . . these simple folk would make all these of me.'

'Traveller?' Eider frowned. 'To where do you travel?'

Nairb's smile broadened. 'As far as the eye can see, my friend.'

Eider gave a sigh of exasperation. 'Wise men have wise answers. Friend, that journey has no end.'

Nairb gave a slow smile. 'Indeed,' he agreed. Their eyes met in sudden friendship and respect as quietly he led Eider towards the tressel. At its centre an ornate box had been set down. 'This is my box,' Nairb explained. 'I cannot travel without it. Come,' he said, drawing Eider closer still. 'I have a gift for you.'

Eider hesitated, suddenly suspicious of the stranger and his box. He watched Nairb rummage inside until finally the gentle gaze met his once more. 'Friend, will you not relieve me of this burden?' he held out that which he had extracted from the box, a heavy bag of coins. Eider's dark eyes widened, yet though he longed to take the purse, he felt a deep unease within and hesitated. Nairb shook the pouch. 'Take it, please. I have no use of such stuff. 'Tis yours now.'

Slowly Eider stretched out his hand but as he did so Nairb withdrew the purse slightly. 'There is but one condition,' he whispered. Eider's eyes narrowed abruptly. Nairb smiled at the suspicious face. 'That I also travel . . . with you.' With a nod he pushed the bag of coins at Eider's chest and the minstrel was forced to clutch them before they fell to the floor.

'With us?' Eider repeated, testing the weight of the pouch. He looked hard at the fragile form before him and with a sudden shake of the head he pushed the purse of coins back at Nairb. 'I cannot accept this,' he stated.

'Take the purse,' Nairb insisted quietly, offering it to Eider yet again.

Eider moved back, pushing Nairb away, both his hands raised in defence. 'Old man, you could not walk so far!' he said dismissively, yet even as he spoke, he frowned for the firelight illuminated the youthful features of the stranger's face. 'You are too frail,' Eider insisted, but the unwavering smile that met his stern look seemed to break down his fears.

Nairb pressed the pouch into Eider's strong hands once more. 'Here is money for every need, and for horses. Yes, minstrel,' he nodded, 'you shall buy horses for our ease.'

Eider made to speak but in that moment the door flapped open and in with the windrush came the laughing children, Regor in their midst, his cheeks bright red with the cold. His eyes sparkled with merriment as he raised the dead hare by its back legs. 'Good meat and gathered firewood shall make a supper to be remembered long,' he grinned.

With a laugh, Eider moved to greet him, slapping him on the back as together they piled the wood beside the hearth and set about the cooking of the meat. Nairb smiled as he watched their busy preparations, pleased to see how quick the rift between them had been healed.

Soon the gathered bread and fruits of Nairb's earnings were cooked and spread beside the open range where meat sizzled and spat, filling the humble dwelling with the sweetness of the roast. The children fell silent, their faces glowing as they readily devoured the fare. Nairb ate well of the wild fruits and bread, while Regor, eager that no morsel miss his lips, chewed on the brittle bones.

Eider licked his fingers. 'And so ...' he turned a quizzical look upon Nairb. 'You would journey with us still?'

Regor's pointed ears twitched at the news but he said nothing.

Nairb smiled graciously. 'The choice is yours, my friends.'

Conscious that they both looked at him for answer, Regor flourished a careless hand. 'As far as the next town or village and welcome, friend,' he said, swigging happily at the mulled wine. 'There once more to sell the tuneful dreams of the minstrel bold.' He grinned as Eider gave a low bow to his jest.

Nairb smiled at their playful antics. He nodded towards Eider. 'A minstrel indeed,' he said and turned back to Regor. 'But what of you?'

'A rogue!' Eider interrupted slapping Regor hard upon the back.

'Aye,' Regor laughed, throwing his arm around his comrade's shoulder. 'Rogues and scoundrels both, plying our trade across the land.'

Nairb watched their laughing faces, illuminated by the roaring flames. 'There is joy in music, and much good 'tis said,' he stated quietly. His hazel eyes set on the minstrel once again. 'Yet . . .' he mused aloud. 'In your face the whirling seas do ebb and flow. The mountains' mighty shadows loom.'

Eider lowered his eyes, unnerved by this new tone.

Regor wiped his greasy chin. 'Good friend, you speak true,' he laughed, oblivious to Eider's deep unease. 'This minstrel-prince sings daily of his land.' Eider gave Regor a secret kick, but the elfin was already in full flow. ' 'Tis of just such a place he sings, where rivers overflow with wine and there are rulers of seven sees . . . ouch!' Regor clutched his ankle and Eider snatched the wine-skein from his grip. The elfin scowled. 'Go on, friend, sing your songs once more,' he urged sarcastically. 'Pray do not deprive this good man of the tale.' Eider's smouldering look silenced the elfin at last.

Nairb looked again into Eider's determined face. 'I never heard of such a place,' he whispered. 'Yet I see 'tis your dearest wish there to return.' Embarrassed, Eider rose to his feet and as he paced away from the fire, Nairb turned his full attention to the rippling flames. 'Your journey has begun,' he stated simply.

40

Eider turned abruptly. ' 'Tis so,' his brow creased. 'Yet there is no sign for me, no route.'

Regor's pointed ears twitched at the familiar words. Had he not heard the minstrel describe this dream a thousand times? He grinned to himself. The wistful look on the teacher's face was proof of Eider's persuasive tongue. So, they were to trick him yet, leave him light of his possessions? If this was the ruse to gain the wise man's trust, then Regor admired his good friend's stealth from the bottom of his rougish heart. But the elfin musings were halted abruptly as Eider returned to crouch before the fire, his dark eyes dancing with the rhythm of the flames.

' 'Tis Rhye,' Eider said distantly. 'The wondrous kingdom, framed on every side by seven sees.'

Regor frowned, he knew well and did not like the look of rapture which spread across the minstrel's face. Yet before he could manoeuvre the conversation back to its old course, Regor blinked worriedly as he saw Eider extend both hands in supplication towards Nairb. 'You see it? In the fire?' he urged.

Nairb looked up into the anxious face and though he did not speak, Eider understood the meaning there. 'Then journey with us,' Eider nodded emphatically. 'At least until you reach your destination.'

Nairb clasped Eider's hand in his own. 'It shall be so, we all have need of company along the way.'

'Shake on it, friend,' Regor interrupted, anxious that no one should forget his presence, for whether such a kingdom thrived or not, Regor could ill afford to be left out. With a wry grin, Eider clasped the elfin hand, and there, before the fire, old friendships and new unions were sealed.

They settled themselves for the night. The children huddled in their tiny groups for warmth, Regor nestled in the corner of the hearth and Eider with Nairb stretched out before the grate. As all slept on, Nairb watched the embers far into the night. He had travelled far in flight. Tenderly he stroked the lacquered box, his anxious

41

thoughts tumbling to and fro with the flickering pulse of the fire, until at last the heavy lids shuttered and he drifted into sleep.

—— 4 ——

Cries of the starving fox echoed in the early hours and Regor woke, cold and uncomfortable. He sniffed the smouldering coals; his mouth was dry and he reached for the wine-skein. Catching the white square of the window, he realised that dawn was close, its spectral light hovering just beyond the glass. About him all slept: Eider with his hand upon the dagger-hilt, the children breathing as one amid the soft furs, and the teacher, his hands crossed upon his chest. Regor scanned Nairb's sleeping form.

'What manner of person is he?' the elfin murmured to himself. 'No common traveller 'tis certain.' He climbed quietly to his knees, scrutinising the silk-draped figure in the half-light. His eyes glinted longingly as he caught sight of the silver talisman once again. Regor sniffed, remembering the quarrel he had had with the minstrel and averted his eyes, transferring his gaze to the carved box of red wood that lay unattended at the teacher's side. The elfin nose twitched with fresh curiosity and he rose slowly to his feet to get a better look. 'I wonder . . .' he whispered, the tips of his fingers skimming the highly polished lid. The slightest contact was enough, for in that split second Nairb blinked open an inquisitive eye.

'What is it?' he breathed, barely awake at all.

Regor had snatched back his hand. 'Indeed,' he laughed, agitated. 'That is what I should like to know,' he added, feigning desire for honest knowledge.

Nairb's placid face broke into a smile, as thin fingers turned the ornate key in the lock. 'This is my box,' he said with great deliberation. Gently the heavy lid was eased open and Regor sniffed the air. Whatever was inside was certainly not edible he decided.

Sitting upright, Nairb delved deep into the box, casting a frown at the shame-faced elfin and though Regor felt uneasy he could not resist drawing closer still, as a bright array of strange and wondrous objects was brought forth and placed with tender care upon the floor before him. Nairb named them each in turn. 'Here, magic stones,' he brushed a fingertip over each one. 'Carnelian to guard against evil; moonstone to grant sleep . . . red coral to heal all wounds, lapis lazuli to take the fever . . .' his eyes smiled into Regor's awestruck face as the slender fingers drew further gemstones from the depths. 'One small jasper to find water, topaz to soothe the eyes . . . red ruby to guard against lightning . . .'

Regor's eyes grew hot and greedy as the glittering array continued, until finally the brightest of them all was extracted. Within the slender hands a sphere of purest gold was held aloft and at its centre a globe of perfect crystal gleamed, celestial symbols finely traced about its frame. Regor watched the spangles of crystal light weave to and fro as the dawn glow cast them dazzling about the shadowed walls.

'Eye of Time,' Nairb whispered reverentially. As the elfin frowned with curiosity, he added, 'Earth mirror . . . for the art of scrying.' Regor nodded, concealing both his ignorance and awe, for whatever it was, an object framed with purest gold, and its whereabouts, was well worth remembering. As Regor pondered upon such tempting thoughts, Nairb began unravelling string upon string of colourful beads which snaked from the box in a dazzle of hues. The elfin screwed up his nose, what use or meaning did these hold?

'I like them,' Nairb shrugged reply to the silent question, irritated by the elfin's ignorance.

'Of course,' Regor murmured, confused, as he watched the teacher delve further into the recesses of the strange box. 'So many treasures . . .' the elfin mused. 'So small a box.'

Soon Nairb thrilled with joy and he cast down among the gemstones a large black book, decorated with symbols of gold and silver. Regor watched on as he flicked the pages, each one crammed with the same indecipherable writing and strange diagrams scratched out in the margins. Nairb glanced up into the confused face but before he could explain anything, the elfin's attention was distracted as Eider roused from sleep. Soon his eyes focused on the scene and he frowned to see the open box, the gemstones sparkling in the early light, and the ancient book spread out between the two. He shuffled towards them reading Regor's awestruck face.

Nairb smiled benevolently. 'You return to us safe from sleep.'

Eider yawned as he drew closer to the grinning elfin. 'Look, friend ... so many objects from so small a box,' Regor enthused.

Eidor gave a wry smile, he knew only too well the thoughts on which Regor dwelt and watched with close interest as Nairb returned all to safe keeping. 'A wondrous trick indeed,' Eider coolly agreed before moving off to gather up his bed-roll.

Regor followed close upon his heels. 'Friend,' he whispered urgently. 'Did you not see the things I saw?'

'I saw them,' Eider frowned intent upon his task.

'Gold,' Regor prodded his shoulder. 'Real gold, and gems of every kind.'

'I saw all,' Eider glared folding up the blankets and stacking them beside the hearth.

'What are you doing?' Regor scowled at him, snatching the bedding and throwing it to the floor.

Elder turned an impatient glare upon him. 'I am packing, there is much to do this day.'

Regor merely frowned into Eider's stony face.

'Come, pack your things,' Eider urged.

'Where are we going?' Regor argued.

'We take the trackway towards the village yonder,' Eider snapped, pulling tight the leather thongs of his pack.

Regor watched, dumbstruck, as Eider paced out into the morning light. He heard the icy water splash and saw the minstrel wash beneath the pump. In moments the elfin had joined him and together they raised the heavy packs

45

to their backs. As Eider gathered up his cloak and stave, Regor gave a sly grin, 'So . . .' he nudged his friend, ''tis hello to the road and a fond farewell to the wise man.'

Eider's dark eyes met his. 'Not until you return the things you took from him.'

Regor's smile disappeared.

Eider pulled him close. 'Brother, you have stolen from the man,' he said through clenched teeth. 'Return all to him . . . now!' he glared.

Regor raised his hands defensively. 'Eider . . .' he tried persuasion. 'He has so much, and we have no . . .'

Eider was furious. 'Are you so blinded by his wealth that you cannot see the mystic nature of the man?' he swore, as anger overtook him at last. 'Here is no hermit teacher or medic – can you not recognise a wizard when you see one?' he insisted into the frightened face.

'Wiza . . .' Regor began, his mouth suddenly frozen half agape. He swallowed with difficulty. 'I know of wizards,' he tried bravado. 'Have heard tell, but never thought . . .'

Eider caught his sleeve. 'Well think now,' he growled. 'He has the power to make of you what he will.'

The darkening look sent Regor hurrying back to the dwelling, hands dug deep within his pockets, in pursuit of stolen goods.

Eider turned and scanned the horizon, the sky lay flat and grey, its yellowing tincture threatening snow. He felt the weight of the pouch of coins in his jerkin pocket and smiled, turning back towards the dwelling in time to see Regor and Nairb stepping out into the light. The wizard stood silent in the doorway as Regor paced away.

''Tis done?' Eider questioned as the elfin drew close.

Regor nodded, aggrieved.

Eider waved to the wizard and the children who had gathered about him. 'We shall return soon,' he cried, and together he and the elfin set off along the narrow pathway.

They marched for several miles in silence, past the thickets of bushes and sinewy trees, the elfin whistling contentedly to himself. 'Farewell and good riddance, say I!' he offered his thoughts to his solemn-faced friend.

Eider kept his even pace. 'There is a good ostler in this place, he will have sale stock.'

'Horses?' Regor stopped abruptly, his sullen face breaking into scornful laughter. 'You force me to return the gold, then talk of buying horses?' he glowered.

Eider drew the pouch from his jerkin and held it up for Regor to see. ''Tis a gift from the wizard.'

Regor scratched his head, incredulous. 'Eider, brother,' he enthused. 'Why even with all my greatest schemes, I will never be a match for you.'

Eider smiled into the awestruck face.

'You prised it from him as you would take honey from a bee,' Regor ranted on in admiration. 'So . . .' he shouted aloud pulling on his cap. 'It is goodbye to the teacher, or wizard, whatever he may be!'

Eider gave a short laugh. 'Not quite.'

Regor halted and caught his friend's arm. 'No?' he quizzed.

'We buy horses and provisions,' Eider said casually, 'then return for Nairb as agreed.'

Regor let out a laugh of disbelief. 'Eider, if the man is fool enough to part with his wealth, let us take it and flee.'

They stopped on the brow of the hill. Below, the low thatched households clung to life at the edge of bleak moorland and the wind blast blew full into their faces.

'Take it and be gone!' Regor yelled into the wind. 'What good is he to us?'

Eider said nothing, only wrapped the tattered cloak about him and pushed on. Regor began to run, desperate to keep up with his friend's quickening pace. The sound of the gusting wind drowned out the will to speak until, as they climbed the rough hewn fencing of the first homestead, their sore eyes met once again.

'Tell me, friend,' Regor began hesitantly. 'What does it mean, to scry?'

Eider narrowed his eyes. ''Tis some art of wizardry,' he said.

Regor grimaced. 'The stranger, Nairb, he has a crystal orb,' he explained, adding with a wink, ''Tis pure and framed with gold.'

'He showed this to you?' Eider quizzed.

'Aye, "earth mirror" he named it. Said that he would scry this day,' Regor gazed into Eider's distant features. 'It was framed with gold, I say, real gold.' The elfin mouth shut tight at Elder's admonishing glare.

The minstrel paced from him, on towards the stone-grey homesteads clustered so close at hand. The elfin swore quietly to himself and clinging to his cap, he followed on, chasing short of breath in Eider's wake. Together they crossed the walled fields and soon were following the stone-scattered path towards the heart of the sleepy hamlet. Regor stopped for breath as they neared the open door of the alehouse, but Eider did not heed him, keeping his pace until he sighted the ostler's yard ahead.

Regor caught up with him. 'Eider, where to in such a hurry?'

'To buy sale stock,' Eider frowned sharply.

Regor turned about and catching up Eider's sleeve, he made to draw him back to the alehouse. 'No more need of play-acting!' he laughed.

Eider pulled away and turned a quizzical look upon him. 'We have the purse, we buy horses and provisions as agreed.'

'No, my friend,' Regor laughed. 'There was no bargain made, the fool parted with his purse willingly and so we vanish!'

Eider gave a sigh of exasperation and turned from him to pace on to the ostler's yard.

'But why not?' Regor cried after him. Eider made no reply and continued his pace. The elfin threw down his pack in a show of rage, but the gesture went unnoticed and he was forced to take it up again. 'Why use silver to buy horses?' he shouted making fresh pursuit of his determined friend.

'There is need,' Eider replied, not even looking back.

'Eider, we are wanderers,' Regor insisted. 'Entertainers! We cannot waste good fortune on such things.' The elfin fumed as Eider's taut back remained turned upon him. 'How shall we keep them fed when winter's hard on us?' Regor reasoned.

Eider stopped and drew the elfin to him. 'Only yesterday we learned how far the journey is between the settlements.' He scanned the round face of his disagreeable companion. 'Do you not see how much greater the distance will become in time?' Regor gazed at him blankly. Eider threw up his hands in frustration, 'Clearly you do not!'

Regor screwed up his face in disgust. 'But horses ...' he squirmed at the thought. 'Elfins never will like horses! Not one of my kin ever rode such a beast, of that I'm sure. Never, in all my born days ...'

'Good horses will ease the arduous paths ahead,' Eider interrupted.

Regor stopped abruptly, the word 'arduous' certainly did not fit his scheme of things. 'But Tourhon lies ahead, two days trek at most!' he argued.

Eider sighed, his patience wearing thin. 'The journey does not end there.'

Regor shrugged. 'We then move full circle, return to the lands through which we came.'

Eider shook his head. 'The lands stretch endless miles beyond Tourhon, of that I am certain.'

Regor grew uneasy. 'Beyond Tourhon?' he echoed, noticing again the distant look on Eider's face. 'Friend, those lands are harsh,' his frown deepened. ''Tis said those lands are hostile!'

'Then we shall have double need of sturdy mounts!' Eider insisted, slapping him hard upon the shoulder.

Regor gripped his forearm as he turned, 'Eider, see sense! We know nothing of that place. Not even the way the winds blow!'

Eider's face was resolute. 'We journey east!' he stated, pacing into the shadow of the ostler's barn.

Regor followed on, unwilling to let go of the quarrel.

49

'Friend,' he pleaded. 'This is madness. Buying horses, wandering uncharted lands! We shall be lost! Attacked by bandits! Murdered even!'

Eider remained unmoved. 'The place we seek lies east.'

Regor bristled with sudden realisation. 'You would risk our lives for that idle dream?' he sneered at Eider's back.

Eider spun about. 'Then, fearful friend, we part at Tourhon!' he said, stepping into the barn.

Once beneath the great wooden beams of the ostler's stables, Regor fell silent, watching on as Eider showed the ostler his purse of coins and bid him display his best sale stock. Together, his friend and the honest man inspected the steeds, checking the evenness of equine teeth, the shine of coat, the strength of hoof and fetlock. By noon, the minstrel had made good choices for his friends, but then stood back, deliberating long upon his own purchase. The ostler's big face creased in an anxious desire to please.

'Sir, you have before you my very best,' he stated.

Eider scanned the remaining stock but remained unimpressed. 'I had wished a horse of noble stance and character. One with more spirit, more intelligence . . .'

'More expensive!' Regor muttered to himself as he eyed the dwindling bag of coins.

Eider took the ostler's arm. 'Do you not have one other?'

The ostler grew uneasy, unnerved by the piercing look that Eider turned upon him. Finally he gave way, shuffling as he nodded. 'I do have one other . . .' he said reluctantly. 'But I be loathe to sell it, sire,' the ostler insisted unable to conceal his deep unease.

Eider frowned impatiently. 'Your living is in selling horses, is it not?'

The ostler nodded with a look of embarrassment. Eider slapped the good man on the back. 'Then come, show me this horse you will not sell?'

The ostler raised a finger. 'No sir, 'tis a horse I dare not sell!' he explained. ''Tis a demon mare.'

'A wild mare?' Eider enthused, gripped by the thought.

The ostler shook his head. 'More than wild, sir ... she was took from the seelie folk!'

Eider stiffened at the man's words. The ostler drew Eider close and pointed out towards the horizon, his finger tracing imaginary riders. 'A-fightin' and a-plunderin' them seelie-folk did come on a dawn raid! Stealin' salt and flour. Stoppin' the clocks and turning the milk sour!'

Regor cast a secret grin into Eider's solemn face as the honest man told his tale, his face lined with memories of that night.

'Why, it was so bad, the wise man of these parts had to carve new talismans! And he had to set the boundaries round our dwellin' afresh!'

Eider shook his head in feigned disgust. 'And the wild mare?' he drew the ostler back to the matter in hand.

The ostler's face broke into a proud smile. 'Oh aye, why she was captured by my own hand and not a wink have I slept since! But such beauty, such beauty I never 'ad seen afore. White as snow and fleet as the wind she is, with large eyes that see all that would approach un-noticed. Yet she shall have no low-born rider! All as have tried to tame her 'as been maimed or lost his life! She is a beast of fire and flame, I tell thee!' The ostler fell silent seeing Eider's shining face. 'Sir, why not decide upon the bay?'

Eider gripped the ostler's shoulder. 'Come, honest man, let me judge your demon mare for myself,' he insisted.

Reluctantly, the ostler led Eider and Regor from the stables and out towards a strong and high fenced pen. Within its bounds, the white mare stood, her long arched neck and silken mane shimmering in the misty light. As they approached, the equine neck grew taut and her fierce eyes flared. With an angry cry, she rose to her back legs, stabbing the air with lethal hoofs.

The ostler halted and urged Eider to keep well clear,

but the minstrel frowned at him and moved closer to gain a better look.

'Eider!' Regor called, standing well back. 'Leave the creature be.' But the minstrel was already pushing through the rough-hewn gate.

He entered the confines of the pen with caution, softest whispers falling from his lips as he moved towards the twitching mare. As their gaze met, she shook her head and whinnied, watching him intently as he dared draw closer. 'Whoah, lady,' he soothed. 'Here is no harm,' he assured, his dark eyes appraising her noble stance and qualities: the finely carved head, the strong, broad chest and quivering nostril. 'Have no fear of me,' he whispered moving to within three paces of her. 'I shall not break your spirit, but shall match it with my own.'

The mare whinnied low reply, her silver-shod hoofs pounding rhythmically at the dust. Yet even as she trotted away from him, her taut, erect head nodded to the measured flow of his speech. Once again, Eider vowed his intentions, coaxing and reassuring her until at last his fingers were within touching distance of the velvet muzzle. Gently he smoothed the snow white head and flanks, saw the wild eyes begin to soften.

'Rare beauty,' he breathed, reaching then to stroke her silken neck. She reared violently and Eider was thrown off balance. 'Whoah, be calm!' he urged, climbing to his feet, his palms outstretched. 'No harm is here.' Again he approached her, felt her warm breath upon his hand as he caressed the smooth muzzle. She neighed and tossed her head, but did not attack him and Eider snuggled close against her warm belly, smiling as she steadied with his touch. He caught his own reflection in the brown orb of her eye and there too he saw her spirit shine. This horse was not of dull earth, but one of blood and passion and in that moment he came to know her. In that moment too she came to know him and sank low upon her forelegs as if in reverence of him. He took her silken mane in his grip and eased himself into the hollow of her back. The mare twitched nervously but as he took his place, she calmed, her keen ears flickering to the gentle rhythms of his voice. Soon Eider's legs were gripping her firm about the belly and she responded to the gentle digging of his heels.

Eider felt himself relax to her proud motion, as with head held high she carried him the full circumference of the pen much to the astonishment of the fearful onlookers. Soon horse and rider moved out into the yard where, at Eider's command, the white mare halted before the open-mouthed ostler.

The minstrel grinned triumphantly. 'See? The faithful mare has claimed me for her own! I shall name her Zephyr, fleet as the west wind!' he nodded to Regor. 'Pay the man his price and let us be on our way.'

Regor sulked, digging deep into the near-empty purse.

The ostler took his price, the ruddy face still set with disbelief as he watched the mare obey the stranger's every command. He hurried towards Regor, helping him to secure the reins of the chestnut to his own dappled steed, then providing a leg-up for the elfin. Still scratching his head in puzzled awe, the ostler bid them farewell and watched them safely on their way.

Eider led them out across the yard, eyeing the unsteady Regor as he clung to the dappled mount, the elfin face lined with unease. As the grey sky seeped with the coloured strata of sunset, the two companions made their way beyond the boundaries of the settlement, zigzagging the lanes towards the good wizard's dwelling place.

Sliding on the grey-white back, Regor gave a sullen scowl. 'Buying nags!' he swore into Eider's happy face. 'I never shall be 'customed to such a beast!'

Eider laughed at him and put on a spurt. The white mare flew the hilly expanse with the chestnut and the dappled grey following at rapid pace. By the time Eider had halted them, the elfin had learned much about staying aloft the shiny back and he grinned at Eider, elated at the thrill of the race.

'Eider . . .' Regor began cautiously as they trotted at even pace. 'Why return to the dwelling place, why not simply move on?'

Eider tightened. 'It was agreed.'

'But what good is such a man to us?' the elfin insisted. 'With silver and speed, why burden ourselves with a seer?'

'We have need of him.' Eider pointed a warning finger. 'Do you forget so soon the Lore? The respect due to those who have the Sight?'

The elfin bowed his head, well chided by the minstrel's stern warning.

Eider paced the mare on whilst at his back Regor shrugged his shoulders and gave a resigned sigh. 'At least I shall not have to walk,' he mused. 'No more shall my feet ache at close of day.' This new thought brought the smile back to his face. 'In fact, Regor my friend, they most probably will never ache again!' he laughed aloud.

Eider turned with a smile as the elfin cast him a friendly wink, then conjuring a Loric tune they rode on, singing their way through the falling mists of late autumn in anticipation of the humble dwelling and the warming fire.

— 5 —

Alone within his dwelling place, Nairb paced to and fro, his heart uneasy all the day, his mind filled with the constant flow of visions. Soon he found himself seeking out the red-brown flowers of the mugwort and taking pestle and mortar from the carved box of Horatious Thor, he crushed the dried blooms, burning their coloured powders as pure incense. Then, from the box he extracted twin candles, both white and decorated with the symbols of the Ancient Lore. Next he took from the depths a copper jar, and then an ebony pedestal.

Carefully, he draped the pedestal with a square of black silk and placed it in a position due east, setting the candles on either side. Gently he lifted the crystal sphere from the box, his bony fingers trembling as he balanced it at the centre of the pedestal. With the tip of the wand of ebony, Nairb traced invisible circles in the dust, enclosing himself and all the magic properties within. He whispered the words of Ancient Lore, then he sat himself cross-legged before the sphere, blessing the crystal with clouds of the potent incense. Next, he lit the candles and then into the copper jar he poured three perfumed liquids. These he ignited, watching their colours change and flare as they fused as one heady vapour.

Nairb drew deep breaths and focused all energy upon the shining sphere. Silently, he passed his right hand across its surface, waiting brief moments before making the same motion with his left hand. These things done, his eyes closed in solemn invocation. 'The gods of Light consecrate this ground and let no Darkness enter in,' he breathed.

His flickering eyelids fixed the sphere with a steadying gaze. 'Being clear and of the nature of air, I ask that all things moving and unmoving to be seen in the air, be shown to me, humble servant of the Eye.'

Nairb's look penetrated to the core of the globe as slowly it began to cloud. Soon upon the opaque surface, pinpoints of light sparkled towards the limits of the dome. His gaze intensified and soon the pulsing mists gave way to a flood of serene blue light which formed a stark backdrop to the visions being born within the confines of the crystal.

Nairb smiled, for there had appeared before him the face of a small boy with eyes of liquid black and midnight hair cascading from a shining helmet. At the child's shoulder the loving couple stood, clothed in robes of majesty. In their likeness the child was cast and Nairb nodded recognition. 'The one of noble blood who smiles out often from the glass. Again I say, what of this boy?'

Within the orb, castle spires rose up, their tallest turrets lost in swirling clouds. Below, the patchwork fields of rye grass spread far and wide, rolling as green waves towards the dark horizon. Yet soon the wizard's gentle smile dissolved with the vision itself as the mists inside the sphere gave way to blackness once again. Within the shadows blurred shapes had begun to crowd the globe and Nairb watched them long and hard until his head began to spin with the sounds of battle, and the outlines of soldiers finally became distinct. From their gaping mouths silent battle cries were caught as savage combat raged within the granite confines of the castle keep. There again Nairb glimpsed the dark-eyed monarch caught within the fray, rallying his troops whose arrow-shafts flew in glinting showers of attack. Straining for air, Nairb blinked momentarily – did not both armies wear the same livery? 'Divided?' he breathed, sweat moistening his brow. 'And the child?' he asked of the sphere.

At his words the vision of battle ebbed away and a new scene emerged from the pulsing smoke and vapours: a sailing ship bobbed in strong currents and there, huddled amid the tarpaulin, sat a small boy his hand clasped in the tight grip of a wizened servant. The boatman cast off and the child turned to look back, his face gazing sorrowfully out from the window of the sphere, crystal tears streaming from his eyes. Nairb's heart lurched wishing the child could see him in return, yet their eyes did not meet and he could do nothing to comfort him. He watched the flapping canvas of the sail grow smaller against the dark horizon and felt the keenness of the child's grief well up within his own heavy heart. The wizard closed his aching eyes and when next he looked into the sphere, new images were unfolding.

A torch-lit chamber had spread across the glass. Within the shadows, two flower strewn biers were set. Nairb watched the guttering candles cast their reflections on the gemstones of a crown nestled among the fragile blooms. Now he felt a deeper grief and had no need to question further. Suddenly he started, for there before the bier a black-draped figure stood, almost concealed within the gloom. 'La morte?' Nairb questioned. The figure turned and the wizard's blood ran cold as he saw the strong hands take up the crown. Nairb shook with rage, knowing the sinister smile that spread across the tight, narrow mouth. Yet he could not avert his gaze as the colours within the orb pulsed red and he saw the figure of a man step out onto a balcony of marble. Below, the waiting crowd cheered mechanically and Nairb shook his head in sorrow.

'A king buried. A new king crowned,' his heart had begun to race. 'A kingdom lost – a kingdom won?'

He cried aloud his anger and the images within the sphere ebbed away as the crystal clouded over once again. Exhausted, the wizard closed his eyes, his heart grown heavy with a sorrow that was not his own. The silence of consultation was soon replaced by the jangle of bridle and stirrup as riders drew close. Nairb heard the horses whinnie and urged himself back from trance, shaking his tousled hair and focusing his energies on the physical. He moved unsteadily to the door feeling the ice-edged air suck at his clammy skin as he took in the

sturdy mounts halted before the well, hot breath spiralling from their nostrils.

At the sight of the minstrel and his companion, Nairb's
face broke into a weary smile and he moved out into the
spreading dusk to give them welcome. 'Good friends,' he
greeted as they dismounted, his eyes widening at the
beauty of the white mare. 'Such horses!' he smiled into
Eider's happy countenance.

'Such prices!' Regor scowled, sliding the packs from
the mounts.

'Worth every coin we paid!' Eider insisted, fondling the
mare's velvet muzzle. 'This is Zephyr! She is faster than
the west wind!' he enthused. 'And look . . .' he gestured
to the remaining steeds. 'A sturdy dapple for the elfin and
for you the strong chestnut mare.'

Nairb looked long into the minstrel's eyes as Eider
recounted the ostler's tale of the demon-mare and how
she had claimed him for her master. But the wizard's
smile began to fade, 'And these?' he frowned, eyeing the
pristine swords and daggers that Regor had spread at
their feet.

'A precaution,' Eider said lightly, sensing the wizard's
unease. 'We cannot know what is ahead. It is wise to be
prepared,' he assured.

Nairb made no remark, only turned and led them
inside to the dancing fire. As they passed across the
threshold, Eider saw the gleaming crystal and halted, his
keen eyes appraising its shifting veils of colour. Suddenly,
he frowned, seeing Nairb move rapidly towards the
sphere, his silken sleeves spread out as a protective
shroud. Eider watched on as the slender hands took up
the crystal and returned all to the depths of the carved
box.

A sudden tug at his sleeve and Eider turned, finding the
elfin close behind him. Regor's acquisitive eyes glinted,
for he too had seen the sphere. He made to speak, but
Eider raised fingertips to lips gesturing he keep his peace.
They moved together to the glowing hearth, eager to hear
the wise man's speech, yet though the evening passed and

good food was partaken no mention was made of the sphere and soon within the dying embers' light, all three were sharing wine and dreams.

Eider took up the newly bought sword and polished at the blade, a look of pensive concentration spreading across his face.

'Fine weapon!' Regor enthused, his tiny pointed teeth glinting as he smiled his approval.

Eider nodded. 'And one more worthy of my swordskill,' he turned dark eyes on Nairb. 'Though I wish it were the blade owned by the great King Rhion, then none would be my match!' He whipped the sword through the air in a dramatic gesture of triumph.

Nairb frowned. 'Speak not lightly of the myth. His was a sword never tainted with the stain of blood.'

Regor screwed up his nose. 'Myth?' he prompted, taking a long draught from the wine-skein.

'The Ancient Tale,' Eider explained with a frown. 'That which the wise man told to the children as you slept.' He sheathed the blade and drew closer to the fire. 'There is more to tell?' he turned a questioning look upon the wizard.

The thin line of Nairb's mouth eased into a smile. 'It is a tale of ancestry, of history, my friend.'

'Whose ancestors?' Regor sneered. 'Not mine, you can be sure.'

Nairb laughed. 'No, not yours, small friend.'

'Quiet, elfin!' Eider snapped and turned again to the wizard. 'Tell the tale, good Nairb. I would hear more.'

Regor shook his head and comforted himself with the wine, ever more puzzled by the minstrel's constant desire for idle fantasies.

'Rhys and Rhia were buried as one,' Eider reminded him.

Nairb took a moment's silence to focus upon the scene within his mind's eye. 'With them the cloak of Rhys, the gauntlet of Rhia and the old King's ceremonial sword.' His gentle eyes searched Eider's distant look as he continued. 'Their bodies burned within the pyre, a symbol of the new unity bestowed upon the kingdom.'

'Surely that is not the end?' Eider insisted, eager that the tale should not finish there.

'Indeed, it is not,' Nairb agreed. 'For while brother and sister were consumed by the fire, the artefacts remained untouched by flame or smoke and when the elders looked within they saw them gleaming still among the ashes.'

'Mystic force!' Eider breathed, captured by the vision.

'Tanterabobus!' Regor swore beneath his breath, unimpressed by such tall stories.

Nairb looked hard at Eider. 'None doubted that the artefacts had been preserved by the power of a magic hand.'

Eider's face broke into a grin. 'But how?'

'The elders had built the tomb according to Ancient Lore, at a place where all paths met, a sacred place of times long past.'

'But surely hallowed earth alone could not work such a spell?' Eider frowned.

Nairb smiled slowly. 'You speak now of the equinox.'

Eider's frown grew deeper. 'I do?'

'The fire had been set at the time of cosmic motion, a time henceforth called by the elders the Time of Change, when the planets newly aligned fused their power and charged the artefacts with mystic properties.'

'The force of the planets! Of course!' Eider gasped with realisation.

'Thus from generation to generation has it been voiced that the mystic fire transformed the amulets into a Triad of All-Power.'

'All-Power . . .' Eider echoed the words.

'Mercury in the moon's shadow transmuted cosmic energy into mystic power.'

Eider frowned. 'But what is All-Power?'

Nairb leaned towards him. 'It is that which the believer has.'

Eider could not understand.

'To believe is to have All-Power,' Nairb insisted into the awe-struck face.

'A truly wondrous gift!' Eider whispered as one inspired.

Regor scowled. 'So wondrous, friend, it does not exist!' he dug the minstrel in the ribs. 'Eider, wake up! 'Tis but dreams, no more!'

Nairb shook his head. 'It is the history of the Ancients.'

'Continue,' Eider urged him. 'Tell me what happened then.'

Nairb sighed deeply. 'It is sad to recollect, for Rhys's wish was never honoured and the offspring of the twin-starred pair quarrelled on ever more bitterly than before.'

Regor spat at the hearth, impatient with this tale of woe.

Eider's look of scorn silenced him once more and the wizard continued anew. 'Battles raged between the black and the white, each faction more desperate than the last to seize the Triad for their use. Yet the elders never lost sight of the chance for good.'

'They kept the Triad safe?' Eider's racing mind prompted Nairb's words.

'Indeed. Through it all they safeguarded the realm, keeping the Triad secure though many lost their light to dark of death.'

'When did the warring cease?' Eider frowned, engrossed in the tale.

'Never,' Nairb whispered. 'For even with the victory of one faction, another would rise in opposition until the kingdom was in fragments.'

'Nothing was ever resolved?' Eider asked.

The wizard nodded. 'One lunar eve, the elders turned as one towards the east and together they trekked across the dry lands and the moor in search of the ancient burial place. Once at its heart, their desperate rituals began and as thunder raged about them they cast the amulets to the four winds. This done, they evoked their mystic vow.'

Eider leaned closer, his face meeting the wizard's in the

firelight as Nairb shared the secret with him. 'Their invocation guaranteed that he who finds the amulets will set all things right!' As he spoke Nairb saw his own intense gaze mirrored in Eider's face.

Regor belched, having guzzled the wine-skein dry, and Eider turned a dark glare upon him. The elfin duly admonished, Eider touched Nairb's sleeve asking gently, 'Where did these amulets fall?'

Nairb smiled, strangely pleased by the minstrel's question, yet he gave no immediate answer.

'The amulets,' Eider insisted into the distant face. 'Where did they land?'

Nairb shrugged the narrow shoulders. 'Who can know?' he said simply.

'Rantera-tantera!' Regor scoffed. 'I told you, friend, 'tis all lies!'

'An ancient tale,' Eider corrected. 'A wise man cannot tell lies.'

'A tale then,' Regor frowned. 'But all the same . . . not real!'

Nairb turned to the elfin. 'It is a story still told . . . for many believe that the amulets exist.' He gave a wry smile, continuing with his line of thought. 'Their worth is more than mere gold to he who finds them first!'

Regor brightened at the thought of such worth.

'And the wars?' Eider asked, drawing the wizard back to the tale

Nairb frowned. 'They continued through time. Endless conflict, within and without.' He moved from the fire, leaving the two companions to flounder in a mass of questions and contradictions.

'Wars through time,' Eider mused, unable to comprehend.

'Priceless to him who finds them first,' Regor muttered into the rippling flames. Each met the other's look of puzzled awe as Nairb returned with the wine-skein refilled.

'Come, friends,' he offered with a slow smile. 'Let us sup to journeys new.'

Eider nodded. 'And to friends new,' he smiled into the placid face.

'And friendships old,' Regor insisted, taking the newly filled cup from the minstrel's hand.

They laughed together and drank on in the dappled firelight.

At length, Nairb shook the abundant curls of his hair. 'How did such ill-matched fellows come to be friends?'

'Friends?' Regor screwed up his nose in distaste.

Eider gave the elfin a playful kick. 'Who but I would ever befriend a halfling such as he!'

Regor took off his cap, hitting Eider with it as he stood to his feet. 'This creature here is a lowly minstrel, whilst I ...' he gave a solemn bow. 'I am elfin-kind, on my father's side, of course.'

'Of course,' Eider said with a yawn.

'My mother,' Regor continued unperturbed, 'was golden haired. A mortal of blue blood, so 'tis said. They met in the bluebell wood one summer's day and married in the elfin way.'

'A likely tale!' Eider laughed aloud. 'Your mingled blood makes you a rogue, no more!'

'Mingled ancestry serves me well!' Regor retorted. 'For I can live among fay folk as well as mortal kind.' He winked at the wizard. ''Tis useful, mind ... for I know much of mortal and seelie Lore.'

Nairb smiled. 'Of that I have no doubt.'

Regor's face crumpled into a frown. 'For example, take that crystal sphere you keep yonder in the box ...' The elfin's speech was brought to an abrupt end, for Eider had kicked his legs from under him and Regor sat on his rump with little grace and an embarrassed smile.

'And yourself?' Eider asked of Nairb.

Nairb waved a casual hand. 'I have travelled far and wide,' he replied softly.

'Alone?' Regor asked between draughts of wine.

'Quite alone, until settling in this chosen place.'

Regor wriggled closer to the fire. 'I wonder then you have the will to follow such as we through unknown

63

climes.' He drank long from the wine-skein. 'I would not have wandered, but for him,' he grinned, slapping Eider on the back.

'Not so!' Eider insisted. 'Your wanderlust brought you to me. I merely followed on.'

'That I cannot believe,' Nairb smiled, and the three of them laughed on as the cups were filled to the brim with the ruby wine.

'But in honesty, friend,' Eider said to Nairb at last, 'you do seem frail. Is it wise to travel on?'

'Indeed. It must be so!' Nairb's passive brow creased. 'The time has come, my work here is all finished.'

'Then we three go as one!' Eider nodded emphatically. 'Good companions, good steeds and my honest map – what more could I ask?'

'Honest map?' Regor echoed with a frown. 'That rotten parchment barely shows the route to Tourhon.'

Much annoyed at Regor's tone, Eider pulled the tattered chart from the pack at his side. 'See?!' he protested, pointing to a red stain on the map. 'It shows Tourhon! There it is!'

Regor shook his head. 'It shows where Tourhon ought to be – there is no route!'

'No quarrel, friends,' Nairb placated. 'It cannot be so far away.'

Disgruntled, Eider returned the parchment to the pack and Regor gathered up the empty cups, refilling each of them before settling himself down before the fire.

Throughout the long night Nairb watched them sleep, patiently awaiting the first glimmer of the dawn when together they would leave this peaceful place, each carrying within his dream of things to come.

——— 6 ———

Now the days grew short, long gone the season of warm fruitfulness, in its place the bitter chill of winter had settled upon moor and man alike. Soon rain would swell the rivers and snow devour the contours of the land, making them stark and uniform in their whiteness.

Against the brooding skyline, their slanted bodies were etched as the trio pushed on towards the homesteads of Tourhon. In the leaden light the melancholy wail of the winds ebbed and flowed, orphaned leaves scattered the frost-edged wastes and those forced to travel the night-scape cursed winter's inhospitality.

Eider drew Zephyr to a halt and pulled the battered parchment from his jerkin. His hooded eyes scanned the map's faded scrawl and looking up he took in the mist-clad trackways, the sentinel trees and the shadows speeding across the rising moon. Regor drew alongside him. 'Night comes down,' he shivered, wiping ice-cold water from his eyes. Eider folded the parchment with his numb fingers and returned it to the safety of his jerkin.

Regor sniffed and pulled the rough cloak tight about his trembling bones. 'What price a well-fed fire,' he murmured as their eyes met in an exchange of sympathy. But as quickly Eider tightened and turned away, setting his face to the bitter wind as he spurred Zephyr on. Regor spat his disenchantment to the elements, whilst at his back the wizard watched on saying not a word.

Mile upon mile they trekked in the relentless cold, their bodies taut against the howling winds, their eyes dulled by the monotonous dark of night. It had begun to rain and yet the air about had a strange clarity. Storm clouds had gathered and cast their dark veil across the moon's placid face.

Nairb was the first to see the pale yellow light blinking

out from the darkness ahead and he stretched out his thin arm like a slender arrow pointing out the threading trackway.

Eider narrowed his eyes, seeing first the snaking path washed silver in the moonlight, then finding the small glowing orb of the lantern winking out against the blackness. He stood in the stirrups trying to ascertain the nature of the light and its distance away. At one moment it seemed to flicker at the farthest point of the track, then as if it were just within reach of them. As he looked on he realised the form that was emerging before them: a stone house, set beneath the shadow of great rocks, shielded from the cruel winds, yet isolated from the comfort of humanity. The solitary homestead was at once embraced by its awesome host then threatened by the brooding wall of stone and earth at its back.

Eider shivered and turned to the wizard who nodded reassurance. Through rain and ice they coaxed their weary mounts on, winding their way down the uneven hillside, skirting long derelict dwellings towards the stone house, its light a beacon of hope to any who sought respite from the winter night.

Eider's knock was loud and firm. They waited uneasily in the dark until finally a thick shaft of light fell upon them as the door creaked slowly open. Before them the sturdy figure of a man, head and shoulders haloed by the fireglow at his back. He was tall and strong of limb, dark hair hanging long about his shadowed face. At his waist, the hilt of a dagger glinted. He did not speak.

'Friend, we seek hospitality,' Eider extended a hand of friendship. The offer was declined.

'Travellers are we, and much weary this night,' Nairb said softly.

Eider stiffened, and visibly annoyed by the continued silence of the house's occupant, he flourished a hand towards his companions. 'We come in good faith, a little food and shelter would earn our gratitude and payment.'

Regor sneered at the mention of silver being paid away, yet the prospect of a night without shelter prompted him. 'A barn or else some makeshift store would suffice, nothing fancy for our needs.'

The figure in the doorway did not yield to conversation.

Eider fidgeted impatiently. 'Come, man, winter's chill has frozen us to the marrow.'

Nairb took a step forward, his eyes pleading. 'Much are we in need of a warm heart,' he said quietly.

'And warm bellies!' Regor muttered to himself.

The figure in the doorway hesitated, then slowly stepped back into the room and beckoned to them. Eider followed briskly in his wake, closely attended by Regor anxious to feel the heat of flames upon his numb fingers and find food for his stomach. Nairb closed the door at their backs, his quick eyes surveying the dwelling and its inhabitants in one brief glance.

'They are travellers and would sup,' the man said in a slow, nasal voice, laced with local dialect.

He had addressed an old woman who carried vegetables towards an iron pot slung above the open fire. She stopped abruptly and turned to look at the visitors, her charitable smile dissolving into a dark scowl as she tossed the vegetables carelessly into the cauldron, splattering the crouching Regor with hot broth. Worriedly, she grasped her kinsman's arm and in the bright fireglow Eider and his companions realised that it was not her husband to whom they had spoken, but her son whose stature and silence had belied his youthful years.

Nairb gave the youth a sideways glance. He was muscular with a quiet but assertive demeanour made more acute by his unusual calm. His pale face was long with straight brows accentuating tolerant, deep set eyes, whilst his mouth was wide, the lips thin and compressed. 'The guardians of secrets,' Nairb mused.

The old woman had drawn her son away from the fire and was whispering agitatedly, wringing her apron with anxious hands. Though he could not hear their conversation, Eider grew increasingly uncomfortable as the old woman turned fleeting glances upon him, her face at first taut and vexed, then pale and fearful. The youth placed a firm hand upon her arm, his voice dropping to a low, sonorous tone at which his mother's face grew pained and she moved away, snatching up bowls from their place beside the hearth.

At the centre of the room stood a rough crafted table, scrubbed white with the years. Eider watched as the old woman placed the wooden dishes and spoons upon the smooth surface, muttering the rhythmic incantations of prayer and curse alike. Turning back to the fire, she snatched the ladle from Regor's eager hands, swearing anew as she stirred the steaming broth with so much gusto that the cauldron swung violently to and fro, its contents hissing upon the hot coals.

Regor glanced at Eider who nodded to him to move away; this he did, but only as far as the table where he eagerly seated himself, taking up a bowl in readiness. Uncertain of their welcome, the wizard had moved quietly to the window, peering through the shutters to be sure that their mounts were tethered fast and safe without.

'Seat yourselves and eat,' the youth gestured while his mother grudgingly set bread upon the table.

Nairb smiled into her careworn face. 'Blessings and much welcome,' he thanked.

Her icy stare chilled him anew and Nairb turned away, seating himself beside the minstrel who watched the youth with unflinching eyes. Their host stood on the opposite side of the table, silently observing them. Eider took in the mane of hair framing the long face with sombre brown, the large almond-shaped eyes were steadfast and green and the gaze impassive. He made to address the youth but before he could do so, the old woman had slammed a second bowl upon the table.

Eider turned to her. 'Good lady, our presence offends?' he questioned.

She scowled, violently tearing the bread into chunks and resentfully proffering them to the travellers. 'Here, take the offerings demanded of us by your kind, then leave!'

Eider stiffened, his face betraying visible anger.

The old woman backed away. 'Cast no curse upon our goodly dwelling!' she shrieked nervously.

'Mother, you bring curses upon yourself with your foolish words,' her son admonished, marking well the reaction of the strangers in their midst. He extended an open palm to their guests. 'Please, we would have you eat.' At his invitation, the elfin grabbed a chunk of bread and tore it in half, but before he could cram his mouth, Eider's hand had caught his wrist and his solemn expression bid him wait.

'Why such coldness to those who seek but brief comfort?' Eider questioned the old woman, his eyes softening in a gesture of friendship.

'If that be all you seek then we will indeed be blessed!' she snapped. Her son placed a calming hand upon her shoulder and whispered silence. With a shake of the head, she turned away and took up the steaming cauldron from the fire, setting it firmly down at centre of the table. Angrily she slopped the contents into the wooden bowls.

Regor reached for the warming stew, his nostrils twitched at the delicious aroma and he licked his lips in greedy anticipation.

'Woman, speak your mind before we take your offerings,' Eider demanded, staying Regor's spoon-clasped hand afresh.

The old woman stopped abruptly and putting down her ladle she nervously glanced at her son, unsure of her reply. He shook his head but she straightened her apron adamantly, eager to have her say and protect her kin. 'Is it not the proper custom to placate those of your race who cross a mortal threshold?' she demanded, folding her arms in defiance.

Eider placed both hands upon the table. ' 'Tis so,' he nodded proudly.

Nairb, who had remained silent throughout, leaned forward. 'Good lady, what know you of us?' He looked into her eyes with the intensity of telepathy.

She backed away, unnerved. 'Spirits who wander by in

the moonlight,' her voice faltered as she turned her wide eyes first upon Eider. 'Some calls you fays, or seelie-kind . . .' she added, looking directly at Nairb. 'Others calls you demons, yet all know the trouble that follows in your wake!' she finished quickly, casting a sneer at Regor whose eyes had never once left the bowl of stew set before him.

Nairb nodded calmly and bid her continue. 'And what trouble would this be?'

The old woman stuttered, flustered by the wizard's question. 'Why, there are those whose crops be blighted, and those left with changeling babes,' she stopped, adding bitterly, 'And some be lost to madness.' Her voice trailed off to a quiet sob and clasping the neck of her dress she closed her eyes in memory, whispering holy prayers amid the silent tears. Her son stood to his feet and moved to console her.

'My mother is dogged by times past,' he explained, smoothing the old woman's silver hair with his gentle fingers. He turned to the travellers. 'We are humble folk, we know nought of your lands and are fearful of wicca ways,' his strong arm protectively encircled the old woman's shoulders. He nodded to the food set before them. 'I bid you eat and leave when you are done,' he said, leading his mother away.

Regor gave a heavy sigh. 'Now that's settled, perhaps we can fill our bellies!' he scowled, snatching up his spoon and plunging it into the stew bowl.

Nairb caught his wrist. 'Friend, it is not wise to eat that which is given in bad faith,' he warned.

Regor pulled away. 'Wise or not, my belly knows only that it must be filled!' he gulped the victuals heartily, leaving Eider and the wizard to muse upon the offerings and the inhabitants of the dwelling place.

Eider pushed his bowl away and taking out his map, spread it flat upon the table and beckoned his companions to look at it. The strong forefinger traced faint contours from Tourhon to the waterline. 'See, the port lies here,' he prodded the map emphatically. 'A day's journey at most.'

'But what lies between, friend?' Regor sneered, scooping broth and vegetables into his mouth. He pointed at the chart with his spoon, indicating an expanse devoid of markings. 'Valleys? Rivers? Mountainous climes? The chart is worthless and will lead us into the mire, say I!'

Eider pushed his hand away. The elfin laughed and filled his mouth once more.

'This map . . .' Nairb leaned closer to gain a better view of it. 'From whence did it come?'

Eider flushed. 'A gift,' he said slowly. 'A lady in Elmdor, she gave it to me.' Ignoring, as best he could, the elfin's snigger, he continued. 'A dark-eyed gypsy . . .' he said wistfully.

At this point Regor gave a loud belch and then an even louder guffaw. 'A wench dull of brain and very short of sight!' he laughed, mopping up the remaining morsels with a wedge of bread.

Eider said nothing, dismissing the elfin's jibes as he leaned closer to Nairb, happy to recount the tale. 'They were a troupe such as we, performers of mime, tellers of tales, explainers of dreams . . .'

Nairb raised a quizzical brow as Eider talked on.

'She read my hand, told the story of my destiny,' his voice quickened with excitement. '. . . of battles to come . . . and of triumph!'

There came a sudden clatter as Regor slammed down spoon and bowl. 'Tell the wise man the truth!' he chided and turning to the wizard, smirked. 'My good friend, the minstrel here, parted with much hard-earned silver to receive these worthless tidings!'

'Worthless to those who would believe them so!' Eider countered, his expression darkening as he glared into Regor's grinning face.

'A tale told to all before you, and all after!' the elfin insisted, flicking the parchment provocatively. 'A handsome price for such a well-marked chart!' he taunted.

Eider leaned towards him. 'It was a dream, meant for me alone!' he said through gritted teeth.

71

'Aye!' Regor snorted with laughter. 'Those dreamt between ale and the morning in her bed!'

Eider seized his collar tight within his fist, their playful banter turning to quarrel. 'The map is true enough.'

The threesome turned at the sound of the low voice and certain opinion. 'It is rough-crafted, yet still gives good direction,' their young host explained in the flat regional tones of the mortal's dialect. The youth traced imaginary markings across the surface of the chart. 'Here grasslands spread, and here give way to rugged climes ...' At realisation of his guests' silence, the youth fell dumb, though his keen green eyes remained intent upon the map. Eider gestured for him to continue.

Hunched over the map, the youth drew a vertical line with his fingertip. 'The land here becomes steep with little shelter from the north winds,' he added quietly. 'And beyond, two days by horse, an expanse of brine water ... the tides there are difficult, yet they have been mastered.' Aware that all eyes were upon him, he fell silent once again.

Nairb touched his sleeve. 'How know you of all these things?'

The youth shrugged modestly. ' 'Tis knowledge common to my kinsfolk.'

'Then you must be blessed with a chart of your own?' Eider prompted. The young man nodded warily.

'Then friend, let us compare them here and set right the markings for our mutual use.'

The youth hestiated before moving to a small wooden chest set in an alcove beside the fire. Pulling open the top drawer, he extracted a sheaf of ragged parchments. With these he crossed back to the table and spread the charts out upon the smooth wood.

'Lehon!' his mother sobbed, as she entered the low room and glimpsed the maps over which her son stood. She glared at each of the travellers and then turning to her son, she shook her head. 'Have you no sense, or shame?'

Lehon lowered his eyes. 'Mother,' he breathed as she

turned her back on him. 'Mother, would you have them lost and perish?' he pleaded.

The woman wrung the edge of her apron. 'Many have been lost, and many more by their enchantments!' she cried, pointing towards the silent visitors, her eyes wet with deep and sudden grief.

Lehon shook his head and turned back to the charts, tracing with masterly precision the rivers and valleys, the narrow trackways and the peaks beyond. Eider stood over him, his eager eyes widening with the possibilities for the maps were truly astonishing, their infinite detail charting routes and villages, indicating terrain, places useful for encampment and areas most abundant in nature's food.

The ebony eyes flashed with sudden realisation. 'This chart, it goes beyond the waterline?' he asked, pressing his forefinger upon the expanse marked as brine.

Lehon looked to his mother whose eyes were awash with tears, but Eider had caught his arm.

'Show me!' he insisted.

The youth flattened out one final length of parchment, and Eider's face shone with new excitement. He beckoned his two companions to draw closer. 'Look on,' he enthused into their puzzled faces. 'The lands that lie to the east are marked here!' His hand smoothed the surface of the chart as if it were a sacred raiment. Noting each mysterious landmark, Eider gasped for joy. 'Friend,' he gripped Lehon's arm. 'I must meet the man who made this record.'

Lehon shook his head and hearing his mother's quiet sobs he gathered up the rolls of parchment. 'None knows his resting place,' he murmured. Eider stiffened at Lehon's sudden refusal to co-operate, but it was the wizard who pursued the questioning.

'Your father taught you much, for you have great knowledge for one so young,' Nairb prompted gently.

Lehon gave a thoughtful sigh. 'He was a great adventurer like my grandfather before him . . .' he flourished a hand towards the alcove of the fireplace. There in the shadows sat a frail old man, silent and unseeing. At sight of him all three companions frowned, for until that moment none had been aware of his presence.

Eider caught Lehon's sleeve. 'The lands beyond the waterline, it was your father who mapped them?'

Lehon nodded with youthful pride. 'To the peaks and beyond, even to the Great Forest.'

'Lehon! Heed me!' his mother's voice had grown distraught and she pulled him to her. 'Have no part of this, it bodes ill for us simple folk.'

Eider spread both hands on the table. 'This map. I will buy it from you. Come, name a price!'

The youth's placid face met Eider's full on. 'Whose price?' he demanded.

'Eider, son of Rhye!' he announced emphatically.

Regor gave a sniff, unimpressed by the minstrel's bravado.

'Rhye?' the creak of aged wood echoed from the shadowed alcove as the old man wheezed. 'Rhye is but legend, my son ... ' he said hoarsely. ' 'Tis lost ... lost long ago ... ' the old man grew silent as memory carried him away to times long past.

The flames of the fire blazed in Eider's eyes. 'No, old man,' he smiled to himself. 'Rhye is not lost, only shrouded from the sight.' He turned to Lehon. 'Good Lehon, take my price in exchange for the memorial of your father's great skill, for we shall put his charts to good use and prove the mastery of his work.'

Lehon turned from him. 'I cannot,' he said simply.

In an instant Eider's hand was at the sword-hilt, but there it halted. The elfin, however, sensing his friend's decision, had acted on impulse and the dagger was immediately unsheathed. The old woman screamed and the face of her son had begun to pale. Lehon's steady eyes scanned the intent on the faces of the travellers and quietly he pushed the charts to the centre of the table.

'Eider, this is not the way,' Nairb whispered. 'You cannot steal from those who freely give.'

Eider ignored the comment, studying for himself the

look on Lehon's face, then eyeing the parchments lying at his fingers' touch. In moments he had scooped them up and shoved them inside his jerkin. 'Pay the man,' he commanded Regor. The elfin tossed coins upon the table, keeping firm grip upon the blade should any try to halt their exit. The wizard shook his head with silent contempt as all three moved towards the door.

'Hold!' Lehon called out. 'Stolen or bought, those charts will be of no use to you.'

In the open doorway Eider stopped, his face flushed with sudden anger.

'You see but scratches of the quill,' Lehon taunted. 'Worthless routes. You cannot know the father's ways as does the son!'

Eider's brow knitted with frustration as he glanced at Nairb. The wizard nodded solemnly. 'The word is handed on,' he explained, casting a look at Lehon's grandfather, then to the empty chair which faced the old man, and finally to the youth himself. 'These charts are useless without the knowledge known to kin.'

Eider gave an exasperated sigh as he extended a hand to the youth. 'Then, good Lehon, bring your knowledge with you,' the dark eyes met the young man's impassive features. 'Join us on the journey to Rhye.'

'No, my son!' the woman cried aloud enfolding Lehon in her arms and rounding on Eider and his companions. 'A thousand curses on your kind!' she swore.

Eider wheeled about. 'Come,' he nodded to his companions. Before he crossed the threshold he cast a final glance at Lehon. 'Upon the ridge, in shelter of the copse, you will find us. Join us before first light, or we shall have your answer.'

As his mother wept bitter tears, Lehon watched their unexpected guests vanish into the indigo night, leaving the soup turned cold upon the table.

The cottage fire flickered on into the night as Lehon paced the square room. Carefully he filled the leather bag, while the old man murmured in his sleep and his mother watched in tearful silence. She moved close to him once again, her face creased with love and sorrow.

'Take no heed of their madness, my son,' she pleaded. 'They do not know the things they will find, or if they do, then they belong to that place.'

Lehon frowned into the soft eyes. 'Perhaps I belong there too?' he said.

'Lehon, you are mortal and will perish with their kind as your father did!'

'We cannot know that to be true,' Lehon protested, but seeing the tear-streaked face he softened. 'Mother, you know that I must follow on.'

The woman glanced towards the aged man sleeping by the fire. 'Then go! Perish! Or else lose your mind as he has done!' Unheeding, Lehon fastened the leather thongs of the bag, then from the drawer of the chest he took up a small compass.

'My son,' the woman cried at his back. 'You would leave me with nought but memories?' She watched as Lehon moved silently through his tasks. 'Them folk work ill in their enchantments! Once within their realm your fate is sealed!' she warned, her voice desperate.

Lehon shook his head. 'My father had safe passage,' he reminded her, tucking the compass into the pocket of his jerkin. 'His maps are both a proof and a memory of that fact.'

'Aye,' his mother sobbed, ' 'twas the memories called him back . . . never to return to his own!'

Lehon took the finely carved staff from its nook beside the hearth. As he appraised its strength and the intricacy of design, he saw his grandfather's face turned upon him. For a brief second their eyes met in the glow of the flames but the old man said no word. Lehon looked to his mother. 'Why did he leave the rowan staff, if not for me and for my protection in that place?' His mother saw the echo of her lost love and merely wept, knowing she could not deny her son's words. Lehon's arms encircled her and held her close. 'Mother, the staff will protect me from enchantments.'

The old woman shook her head sadly. 'My son, you are already enchanted.'

With a gentle smile, Lehon kissed the tear-stained cheek, then taking up the bag he moved towards the door. Stepping out into the night he made ready his mount, securing leather pack and climbing gear to the saddle. Once mounted he turned back to take a last look at the homestead. He raised the rowan staff. 'I shall return,' he vowed.

'Nevermore,' his mother breathed as her fearful face gazed into his.

Lehon cast her a look of farewell, yet he fancied she saw nothing. As he dug his heels firmly into the mount's flanks and moved off along the winding trackway, he heard the iron bolts slide solidly against the wood of the door. Suddenly the track was dark and he felt his body tighten as the shutters of the stone house slammed hard at his back.

Before the campfire the elfin watched Eider flatten out the brittle parchments. He moved closer and peering over his comrade's shoulder, saw the interlacing lines of the aged charts and made no sense of them. 'So,' he gave a yawn. 'What does it all mean, friend?'

Eider gave a sigh of exasperation. 'I know not.'

Regor's laugh was edged with contempt. 'Take gold! Silver! Steal bread! At least then you know exactly what you have in your hand!' he slapped Eider hard on the back. 'But maps?' he laughed aloud, casting a wink at the wizard.

Eider snatched up a chart and shook it in the elfin's face. 'With these we have more than fills the hand and belly!'

'Indeed?' Regor sneered.

'Yes!' Eider insisted. 'Here we have the future. We have hope!'

'Hope?' Regor glowered. 'Give me none of those mortal lies.'

Eider brandished the chart anew. 'The maps are good I tell you.'

'Good for what?' the elfin argued kicking at the charts. 'Why, that simple map you call your own is of more use than these.' He stood up on his feet. 'Worthless!' he said insolently. 'Like the mortal fool you stole it from!' The elfin paced away towards their mounts, anxious to have the final word and making heavy work of taking down the packs and bed-rolls.

'Think not of it,' Nairb smiled as he moved nearer the dark-faced Eider. 'He is tired and hungry. Elfins cannot see far beyond immediate needs.'

Eider rolled up the parchments. 'Yet I fear he is right,' he shook his head. 'I can make no sense of these maps . . . and the old man – he said that Rhye is lost.'

Nairb placed broken wood sticks upon the fire. 'The elfin and the old man, both fear the things they cannot understand.'

Eider ran weary fingers through his hair. 'I too have fears,' he confided.

'And I,' Nairb smiled gently as the campfire flared and hungry flames consumed the new wood.

Eider gave a heavy sigh and looked up at the clear sky. 'Let him join us,' he whispered his plea to unseen gods.

Nairb made no sound, only watched as Regor placed their packs within the circle of light cast by the crackling fire. The wizard smiled as Eider stretched, pushing his strong arms high towards the velvet canopy of the night. 'So many stars,' the minstrel breathed at last.

Nairb looked at him with kindly eyes. 'A star for every soul that ever lived.'

The newly returned elfin sniffed the air. 'I'm cold!' he scowled, turning to grimace at his star-struck companion. 'How much longer must we wait?'

Eider looked at him irritably. 'We wait for Lehon to decide.'

'Mortals!' Regor gave a cursory sniff as he untied his bed-roll. 'What good are they to seelie-kind?'

'Regor! Enough!' Eider gave his final warning.

The wizard placed a calming hand upon Eider's forearm and they shared quiet amusement as they watched the sulking elfin wriggle beneath the blanket, curling up to sleep before the fire.

Eider's face had grown taut as he scanned the constant flicker of the flames and the wizard felt compelled to ask the question. 'What thoughts?'

Eider gave a sigh and shrugged dismissively. 'Dreaming ...'

'Wishing you were a thousand miles away?' Nairb concluded.

Eider gave a weary laugh. 'It could be so far!' he said, prodding the crumbling embers with the dagger's tip. 'Who can know what lies ahead? So few are gifted with the sight.'

Nairb uncorked the water-skein. 'True enough,' he answered unflinching.

'Yet ...' Eider mused, turning dark eyes upon him. 'One such as yourself possesses many skills.'

Nairb's eyebrows arched slightly as he offered the skein to his astute companion. Eider declined and leaned forward to press the question. 'Do you ever see the future?'

Nairb flourished a dismissive hand. 'My friend, you are able as I to see what lies ahead.'

Eider shook his head. 'I see but fire visions,' he turned keen eyes upon the wizard. 'But you have gifts, special power ... and the crystal orb, does it not see beyond?'

The wizard's continued silence prompted Eider to provoke. 'Cannot the wielders of the Lore see all?'

Nairb stiffened at Eider's needle-sharp perception. 'You seek advice? Opinions?' he asked quietly.

Eider stretched out an open palm. 'I seek truth. I seek the Sight!'

The wizard avoided Eider's desperate gaze. 'How may I assist?' he said.

Eider sat upright and pointed to the carved box close to Nairb's side. 'Look within, the crystal shall reveal my destiny.'

Nairb shook his head adamantly. 'Upon unhallowed ground? You would make dull the Eye?'

Eider delved into the pockets of his jerkin, snatching the Firestone out into the dappled light. 'Then with this!' he demanded thrusting it at the wizard.

Nairb's thin hand covered the dazzling gem. 'Friend, return the gem to safety,' he said with a patient smile.

Eider clawed at his arm. 'It is clear, as pure as any crystal sphere.'

Nairb frowned into the desperate face. 'Friend, return it! This is not its use!'

The immovable hardness of the crescent features brought Eider's whim to nought and he looked at the deep red gemstone upon his palm as if considering its value and its use for the first time. Yet the anger turned to curiosity as he watched Nairb draw closer to the campfire. The pulsing flames cast strange shadowplay upon the impassive face, and soon the slender fingers were etching designs upon the dusty ground that lay between them. Eider watched on as Nairb performed silent ritual, tracing out three perfect circles within the ash and dust. 'Adonay, Shaday . . .' the wizard breathed reverently, his eyes never once relinquishing their gaze upon the churning flames. 'Minstrel be warned, from flame comes fair and foul alike.'

Eider nodded his understanding. 'I am prepared for what the gods dictate,' he whispered.

Nairb watched the flames ripple, fanned by rogue winds. 'Look on,' he said, the intensity of his gaze harnessing the fire once more. 'If your heart be true, you shall gain knowledge of your fate.'

Eider placed a hand of allegiance to his breast. 'My heart is true,' he affirmed solemnly.

The wizard bowed his head and silently manoeuvred himself into a lotus position before the fire. He closed his eyes and prepared himself, repeating incantation and the rites of purification.

Eider sat hushed as the wizard drew back the silken sleeves of his gown and stretched his skeletal arms towards the fireglow. Now the hazel eyes were wide and unblinking as Nairb fixed the molten coals with a penetrating gaze, causing firebrands to spit defiance. The tapered fingers did not waver or resist but moved closer still, absorbing the searing heat yet remaining unscathed. With a harpist's motion, Nairb drew forth jets of rubescent flame which he circled on the smoky air until they flared together as a shimmering sphere of fire. Eider caught his breath as the blistering fireglow dazzled him and the wizard's distant voice weaved amid the veils of smoke.

'The powers of light and darkness are with us.' The thin hand thrust out like a dagger, cleaving a passage to the fire-sphere's heart.

Eider was stricken with fear, yet he drew close to see visions forming at the pulsing core. Soon he was smiling.

'There! I see myself . . . a small boy!' he laughed. 'And on my head, the Helmet of Courage!' he turned to look at the wizard. 'My first trophy!'

Nairb's features were without expression. 'So small a boy for such great prizes,' his voice ebbed and flowed like the night wind.

'It was expected of me,' Eider nodded. 'However small.'

The wizard drew his hand across the smoke vapours. 'You see the fortress?' he prompted.

Eider smiled slowly. 'Not a fortress,' he corrected. 'It is Rhye, throne of the seelie-kingdom.'

The wizard's breath was slow and heavy like one infirm. 'And the bier? The dark one who clutches the royal crown?'

Eider had stiffened. 'Loth am I to call him kin,' he said with contempt. 'Though such he was.' His fingers tightened to a fist. 'Zarratt! the dark lord who sacked the realm and seized all for himself!'

The wizard rocked quietly to himself as the questioner looked on, the fire visions prompting memories afresh. 'The warlords sold their honour for his coinage,' Eider's voice had grown strained. 'Rhye's noble king was slain . . . his queen lost to grief . . .' A solitary tear glistened on his cheek, then conscious of the wizard's silence, Eider tightened. 'And I, no more than seven years, was smuggled from the land, my life and heritage no more than a bundle in my hand. The gemstone is all that remains of that old life, yet it is my inspiration. The folk who raised me kept all safe, returning it to me the day I left their home to find my own.' The flames leapt in the draught as Eider shook an angry fist. 'My birthright was stolen! My belonging! I shall not rest until revenge is mine!'

Nairb touched his arm. 'Speak not so! Dark as well as Light is present here, fear for your soul.'

The look was steadfast. 'My heart is true, I shall have my right!'

'The price may be your life,' Nairb warned anxiously.

Eider gave an exasperated sigh. 'With Rhye lost, for

what does my life count?' He flourished a hand, bidding the wizard to look on and reveal to him his fate.

Nairb conceded and with a patient nod of the head, he fixed his gaze once more upon the crackling flames, slender hands weaving a tapestry of psychic visions amid the smoke coils. 'Ask what you will.'

Eider leaned towards the glowing coals, his lips trembling slightly as they formed the words. 'How shall I regain my birthright?'

Nairb's spatulate fingers traced careful designs within the ash dust yet the motion seemed involuntary and the wizard oblivious to all but the seething fire. 'The House of Cancer,' the words hovered upon the air as a whisper, though the finely carved lips barely moved. 'From crystal depths pure waters flow ... there burns the solar fire, creator of individuality.'

Eider nodded into the serene face understanding nothing yet desperate to hear more.

Nairb's straight forefinger etched the second glyph. 'House of Leo, sustaining force of dreams.' He traced a third glyph within the dust. 'Earth, the sphere of Virgo,' he smiled mechanically. 'The combination gives birth to the grand plan of your destiny.' The heavy lids closed and the wizard spoke on, his fingers busily etching new shapes and signs. 'The triangle: Leo at the apex, Cancer and Virgo at the base.'

Eider's face changed from puzzlement to a smile of sudden realisation. ''Tis us, our zodiacs are told!' he cried. 'We shall journey together.'

Nairb nodded but the forefinger was now raised in warning. 'Mark me. Without the power of the Triad, Rhye is lost!'

Eider hesitated at his words. 'The Triad? But?'

'The three keys of your destiny,' Nairb insisted hearing no argument.

Eider shook his head. 'Wizard, that is but an ancient tale. Nothing more than a dream told long ago.'

The distant look remained upon the wizard's stark white face. 'Not a dream ... but forged within the mystic fire and cast to the four winds . . .' he turned keen eyes on Eider. 'The amulets of All-Power await your command!'

'I?' Eider gave a laugh of disbelief. 'Friend, I am no wielder of All-Power,' he shook his head sadly.

The wizard's gaze was certain and the smile on Eider's face soon faded. The minstrel extended a hand to the diviner, 'Even if such things were real,' he said defensively. 'Who knows where they lie?'

The wizard's face now bore a look of bitter contempt. 'The Dark Lords stole them throughout the mists of Time.'

'Dark Lords?' Eider echoed with sudden interest. 'One such as he who stole my heritage?'

The wizard nodded impassively. 'Such thieves exist throughout all time.'

'Then I must seek out the thieves!' Eider declared impulsively.

The wizard's look was one of premonition. 'Be assured, good friend, they seek you out.'

'All to the better!' Eider growled, snatching his fingers into a fist of allegiance. 'I shall save the Triad! In return, the Triad shall grant me the throne that is mine!'

The wizard gripped Eider's shoulder. 'Friend, none bargain with the Lore,' he whispered.

Unheeding, Eider clung on desperately to the vision that Fate and the wizard's hand had conjured. 'The amulets, where are they to be found?' he insisted.

Nairb's fingers moved now with speed and vigour, spirals and squares merging in the smouldering ash. 'Moon and Mercury align and the Triad gains its strength,' he chanted, oblivious of Eider's panic or his questions. 'Mercury gives speed and stealth, the Moon gives power and Dark is overcome.' Lucid once more, the wizard raised a sharp brow of warning. 'Mark this – with the passing of the planets, Triad power is defused. The kingdom lost.'

Eider hunched closer to the fire, eager to see all that the Sight granted. 'But how shall I find the way?' he pleaded.

'The way finds you . . .' the wizard said simply.

Silence fell between them as these final words echoed and re-echoed through Eider's reeling mind and he scanned the wizard's motionless features, craving more, yet knowing nothing would be given.

At last Nairb rallied as with one deft motion he thrust a trembling hand towards the dying flames. 'Man of Earth! He comes.'

Seconds later the brittle crack of undergrowth forced Eider to his feet and the elfin's acute sense of self-preservation saw him wide awake and at the minstrel's side. Whilst Regor marked woodland to their left, Eider took his stance to the right, their twin dagger blades glinting in the firelight.

'Who goes?' Regor demanded.

''Tis I,' came quiet reply as the mortal's sturdy frame moved into the light. ''Tis Lehon.'

Eider paced to meet him, his hand outstretched in welcome. 'Come friend,' he grinned leading Lehon to the fire. As they drank together, all took careful stock of the young mortal though it was left to Eider to state the terms afresh. 'And your price?' he questioned.

Lehon shook his head. 'I cannot name it.'

Eider glanced darkly at the wizard.

Lehon frowned at their silence. 'Just as I cannot guarantee arrival at your chosen destination,' he added flatly.

Regor flashed a worried look at Eider, then glowered into Lehon's honest face. 'You said you could be our guide!' he reminded insolently.

Nairb caught Regor's sleeve. 'The young man is wary, he knows the path we take has dangers.'

Lehon's steady eyes met the elfin's full on. 'The route is one from which few have returned,' he said simply. Regor swallowed uncomfortably and did not press the point.

Eider drew closer to the mortal. 'Lehon, we know we face danger on this trek.'

'Then turn back now,' Lehon advised. 'If you are not prepared.'

'I say "aye" to that!' the elfin muttered pulling the cork from the wine-skein and drinking long.

'I must go on, there is no choice for me,' Eider insisted into the youthful face.

Lehon cast a glance at Nairb, who nodded whole-hearted agreement. 'Most definitely.'

Regor frowned, feeling all eyes upon him. 'I go where the minstrel leads,' he shrugged. 'Hasn't it always been so!?' he gave Eider a nudge as he grinned into their solemn faces.

'The maps,' Lehon gestured and they watched as Eider spread them out before the fire. Lehon looked at them long, then stretched out a strong arm to trace their route from the Tourhon valley, over uneven terrain and on towards the port. They watched the patient finger slide across the blue stained boundary. 'This is not fresh water, but salt,' Lehon explained. 'A treacherous expanse, set between that world and this.'

The wizard stroked his chin thoughtfully. 'It is some distance across?'

Lehon nodded. 'None has ever agreed the distance, or the time it takes to ferry.'

'We shall need a sturdy craft,' Eider considered.

The elfin had screwed up his nose. 'What need have we of crossing waters?' he groaned, ready for argument.

'To get to the other side!' Eider glared.

Lehon smiled tolerantly and once again he pointed to the map. 'Here, rough dwellings perch among the rockscape and simple folk make living from the tides.'

'They will supply the sailing vessel?' Eider quizzed.

Lehon rolled up the charts. 'They are a clannish folk. Yet people have been well served by them.'

Regor shuffled irritably. 'A body could be washed away in such seas, never to be seen again!' he insisted under Eider's implacable gaze.

''Tis so,' Lehon agreed. 'Yet I have well drawn maps of all upon the opposite bank.'

Eider grinned into the elfin's anxious face. 'Fear not, good Regor, you shall survive the waters. No danger shall be met with a sturdy craft and a guide as knowledgeable as this.'

Regor gave an uneasy laugh, not certain such assurances included all that they might encounter upon the distant shoreline.

Lehon's expression was uncompromising. 'To master such lands requires great fortitude,' he lowered his eyes, his voice falling to a whisper of regret. 'My father is long-lost among those climes and it is for his sake alone that I take your part.'

Eider grasped his forearm. 'Be assured, we have the courage and the will to master all that fate demands ... for your good and for our own.'

With sudden decision, Eider thrust a clenched fist into their midst. 'Together, or never!' he swore.

In their turn Regor and Nairb joined their hands to his whilst Lehon searched their determined faces, until, smiling, he laid his wide palm over theirs.

'Together or never!' all agreed, their friendship affirmed and the pact sealed.

— 8 —

With first light they broke camp, cantering the wooded ridge, their silhouettes sharp black against the grey sky. About them trees bent in the wind, their boughs crashing with the force of a storm-wrenched sea, whilst beneath their tread, the first scattering of leaves splashed the black earth copper and yellow.

Their cloaks wrapped tight about them, the small company wound its way down the dirt track and on into the spreading grassland below. Here twitch-grass ranged itself flat and coarse upon the hillocks and beyond their tiny spears could be seen the taller grasses flurrying first pale then deep green, a rolling verdant ocean powered by the north wind.

By midday the horses were chest-deep in brittle stalks, gorse barbs snatched at cloaks and rattled stirrups. Soon with the rising of the sun the cold sky softened and as the air warmed, Lehon drew them to a halt. They each felt the force of the grass-tide, watched the speeding clouds and the deepening blue of the sky. As Lehon unrolled the parchment maps, Eider's keen eyes scanned the rugged contours of the distant steeps, marvelling at the puvvering mists which hovered about the tree-capped pinnacles. He followed the thrust of the mortal's arm as it cut a straight line towards the horizon, and nodded agreement at the chosen route.

They resumed their journey, dipping down into the rolling landscape towards the sun until its fiery colour seeped across the skyline changing the contours from gold to bronze as it lowered in the afternoon, finally to splash the threading trackway with the deepest of crimson hues. Lehon halted them again, his windblown features perplexed as he raised himself in the stirrups and sought out familiar landmarks.

'I'll wager he has lost his way!' Regor murmured under his breath.

Eider pushed Zephyr forward and drew alongside their guide. Together they scrutinised the charts, Eider narrowing his eyes in concentration but making no sense of the faded markings.

Regor reined in his horse alongside the wizard. 'He is lost and we with him.'

Nairb made no reply but strained his eyes against the shifting light to focus upon the crags, their endless line now almost obscuring the horizon.

Lehon turned and gestured for them to stay put, then urging his mount forward he galloped ahead, tufts of earth scattering in his wake. They watched him negotiate the rugged steep and halt atop the ridge, wheeling his mount about and with bold gesture summoning them to follow on. Once alongside their guide they saw the coastal formations that Lehon had previously described to them. The steeps dropped sheer to pebbled flats and at the base thick sea mist rose up from a dark expanse of water far below.

Eider raised himself in the saddle, his eyes wide with excitement. Regor in his turn sniffed the briny air, whilst the wizard watched the intermittent glimmer of lamps from the homesteads nestled among the rocks. Nairb smiled to himself. 'Such beauty in so rugged a place.'

'Wait on me,' Lehon said firmly as he buried the charts in his jerkin once again. 'Build your fire in cover of the rocks,' he instructed, tightening his grip on the reins.

'Wait?' the elfin face wrinkled in annoyance. 'Shiver here in the elements when yonder there are ...'

'I make the way alone,' Lehon glared.

Nairb turned to the disgruntled Regor. 'Here is no welcome for us, friend.'

Eider scanned the distant cliffs, heard the desolate calls of sea birds. 'It is better the mortal makes barter with his own,' he told the elfin.

Lehon nodded, intent upon Eider's face. 'I shall seek

provisions and a sailing craft. We meet at sun's rise upon the shoreline below.'

Eider grasped his arm. 'Be careful, friend,' he urged.

The threesome watched their guide set off along the uneven track until he was nought but a small speck weaving among the rocks.

Regor gave a groan of discontent. 'We starve and freeze up here, whilst he finds food and a warm dwelling for the night!'

'Yonder is dangerous for seelie-kind!' Eider growled in the elfin face and wheeled Zephyr about. 'The mortal makes all things right, ensuring our safety in these climes and upon the waters!'

Regor sneered at Eider's back. 'Seelie-kind trusting to a mortal,' he shook his head. ' 'Tis unnatural!'

Eider doused the last embers of the nightfire and looked out across the land, seeing the sweep of the cliffs down to the shingle coastline. Climbing to Zephyr's back, he led them down the rock-strewn pathway, eager to be gone. Yet the wailing wind haunted their every faltering step and the shifting mist seeped up from the icy water to obscure their route. About them watery sunlight filtered through the heavy clouds, glinting gold on the surface of the brine-bleached rocks. Here reed grass lay battered flat against granite and the twining stonecrop clung fast to the smallest crevice.

Soon the mounts slid from the base of the steep into soft, yielding sand, scrambling the uneven range of dunes where tall grasses sprang up like coarse hair atop each crown. Eider found the highest sandy brow and brought Zephyr to a halt, narrowing his eyes against the gritty wind as he judged the height of the sun.

No word passed as they waited, searching out the slightest sign of movement on the deserted shingle. The deafening crash of the sea sharpened their senses and the rushing wind robbed them of breath, coating their lips with bitter brine. Suddenly all eyes caught the shift of black at the farthest point of the shoreline and they scanned its shape for likeness of their guide.

Eider dug his heels into Zephyr's flanks and led her at a canter through the straggling gorse and arcs of sand towards the hard-packed shingle of the beach. Once upon the flats, the cross-winds raged unabated and now their cloaks billowed at their backs and the stinging brine air lashed their cheeks. They galloped the chiselled stones, hoofs scattering the multicoloured shingle to the seaspray.

In the distance, Lehon thrust a hand against the grey skyline and in that moment Eider felt the breath snatched from him as Zephyr leapt forward, seeming to fly faster than the speeding winds, towards the waiting mortal. Regor and Nairb gave chase and soon all three were racing across the shingle, splashing the white rush of the waves.

'Friend, what news?' Eider gasped as Zephyr halted at Lehon's side.

The guide nodded. 'The night was long,' he said with a weary smile. 'But the clansfolk grant us passage from their harbour.'

Eider slapped him on the back. 'You have done well; then we set sail this day!' As he spoke Regor drew the dappled grey to a halt at their side.

'Well?' he frowned into Lehon's white-cold face.

'We depart, soon as we are able,' Lehon gasped to the sharp wind. 'The clansfolk gave, yet grudgingly.'

Nairb offered Lehon a hand of welcome. 'These folk are as hostile as their lands,' he surmised.

Regor watched the rise and fall of the waves, sensed their awesome strength and speed. He scowled at the icy wash and turned his face away. Lehon had read the elfin's anxious thought. 'The craft is sturdy,' he assured. 'We shall be safe enough.'

'Let us lose no more time this day,' Eider ordered and they pushed on along the tide line, following its frothy trim to where the giant hills were cleft apart and they could see rock-hewn dwellings clustered from cliff to shoreline.

Regor noted the shuttered windows of the harbour dwellings. 'Surely it is no great thing to ask? A warming cup, a few morsels?' he moaned thrusting his chin into the warmth of his cloak. As they drew closer to the small harbour, they glimpsed the crowd of clansfolk standing motionless upon the granite jetty. Confused, the elfin frowned. 'They give us welcome?'

Nairb shook his head, reading mistrust in the simple faces. 'Not so, Regor, they wait upon our leaving.'

Eider beckoned them close ranks. 'Stay together, yet show no fear,' he instructed.

Lehon led them cautiously to the harbour mouth where the sailing vessel lay moored in the shallows. Within sight of the harbour wall, Lehon dismounted, marking their worried faces in turn. 'Do not speak to anyone,' he warned.

Eider took Zephyr's reins in his grip and walked her on. 'What is it they fear?' he questioned.

Lehon looked about him warily. 'Rumours and tales,' he shrugged. 'It takes little to frighten such folk as these.' Grim-faced they followed him, dragging their mounts up the makeshift ramp of the vessel that bobbed at the water's edge.

Once aboard, Regor led the horses to the stern, while Lehon and Eider hauled up the anchor and cast off. As they worked, Nairb stood silent, scanning the belligerent faces of the crowd. They in turn watched on, as hostile as the sea-thrashed cliffs that they inhabited. The wizard swallowed hard, saddened by their impenetrable ignorance. He lowered his eyes, wishing them peace as the gusting winds sent the small vessel surging from them on the tide.

'To sail!' Lehon commanded as they scrambled along the creaking boards.

Eider grinned into the wizard's face. 'Come, follower of stars!' he said offering the charge of the tiller. Nairb moved briskly to the stern while the others set to unfurling the sails and harnessing the mighty cross-winds. With a creak of the yardarm the canvas billowed out and the vessel lurched forward, slicing the swelling waters as it flew upon the winds.

For two long days they were swept along, skimming the foam-flecked waves, pitched and rolled in changing currents, plunged to the darkest troughs, then raised to the curled white trim. Nairb withstood the roaring winds of storm, legs apart and arms stretched taut as he held the tiller fast. Meanwhile, the elfin pulled tirelessly upon the ropes, his golden hair blown flat against his skull as Lehon directed the rhythm of their work.

'The rain,' Eider pointed to the blackening sky. ' 'Tis upon us.'

As the squall hit the vessel they worked in unison, and as the icy brine lashed the timbers of the decks they raced the sodden planks, port to starboard, salt-spray stinging hands and eyes, their clothes grown heavy with the wash. Through black of night and on into new day, each fought thus against the windrush, urging their fragile craft through the eddying waters, storm-tossed to the summit of the waves then plummeted to the darkest green of the depths.

At dawn on the fourth day, deafening silence fell, the rolling motion of the waters halted and the vessel's sails slackened and fell useless against the mast. Exhausted, the four companions greeted one another with uneasy smiles. The dull groan of drenched timber echoed in the stillness as one by one the threesome frowned into the placid features of the wizard. Yet the good man shook his head seemingly as mystified as they. Regor gripped Lehon's sleeve, 'Storms bate, then slowly pass. Yet such as this?'

Lehon shrugged. 'We can but wonder, friend, and be mindful of changes,' he said, taking the steps to the quarter deck, there to scan the horizon.

They watched the endless calm until darkness fell and Regor lit the taper, pacing the deck to ignite glass lanterns. As he passed the silent wizard, Regor shuttered the last of the lamps and saw Nairb's eyes flicker anxiously. The elfin looked out to sea and shuddered. Not a star shone in the night sky and the wan moon was obscured by thin veils of mist. Regor moved closer to the wizard, watching in silence with the good man as the mists began to thicken until they hovered sickly yellow above the becalmed waters. Soon the lamps began to dim as vapour weaved like moths about the flame and the candlelight within glowed violent green, then eerie blue.

'What kind of fog is this?' Regor wiped the sticky damp from his skin. The wizard looked on but kept silent counsel with his thoughts.

Eider searched the uniform stillness. 'We could circle for days and nights in this stuff!' he frowned at the wizard. 'These mists dropped quickly,' he bit the corner of his mouth in consideration of the signs. The wizard nodded, yet still did not reply. 'We could lose much time if they persist,' Eider coaxed, yet could raise no response from the gaunt face.

Eider turned irritably to the others. The elfin shook his head, 'He is lost to trance and we lost to mists!' he scowled. As the mists congealed to a dense fog, they wrapped themselves in cloaks and blankets for warmth, watching the amorphous vapours with deepening distrust.

Unmoved, Nairb held fast to the tiller, seemingly entranced by the pulsing colours, shaking droplets of the glistening damp from his tousled hair. He shivered involuntarily and Eider, ever watchful, draped his blanket about the wizard's skeletal frame. Yet Nairb's face never changed expression, his eyes riveted upon the encroaching fog. Eider shuddered with a cold unease, sensing the strange detachment of the wizard which had set a spark of fear in their hearts.

Lehon filled the round bowl of his pipe with tobacco as the elfin drew close for company. 'So, does such a thing as this appear well marked upon your map?' Regor provoked at last.

Lehon struck the tinder box and drew upon the pipe. 'These waters are shown,' he answered calmly.

Regor sniffed the sweet tobacco as he spoke. 'And of mortal's making?' he asked resentfully.

Lehon shook his head. 'Nay, friend, 'tis no way connected with the things we have left behind us.'

'This 'tis unseelie!' Regor decided. 'For my kin never led good folk astray in murky mists!' He took out his own pipe, tapping it gently against the palm of his hand.

Lehon smiled to himself and pointed a forefinger at the elfin. 'Your kin make sport with travellers! Most especially mortals!' he offered the tobacco pouch to Regor with a wry smile.

'Aye,' Regor gave an apologetic grin as he took the pouch. 'But for jest alone. Such deception as this never befell a mortal in seelie lore.'

Lehon watched as the elfin filled his pipe. 'Seelie or unseelie,' he said at last, 'I can see no differences between such folk!'

Regor frowned annoyance. 'Why, 'tis the difference 'tween good and bad!'

They glanced up as Eider paced towards them. His eyes blazed. 'Speak no word of Dark Lore here, lest the unseelie claim us all!' he reprimanded.

Regor turned to Lehon, but the guide was already on his feet. 'The wizard,' he motioned. 'He speaks!' Together they moved up to the haggard-faced man who held the tiller. Together they watched the bone-white profile etched against the spiralling mists and listened hard as the thin lips moved in speech. Eider frowned, hearing no word. He moved closer, his ear pressed almost to the wizard's lips as Nairb breathed the faintest of whispers.

'What does he say?' Regor questioned anxiously.

Eider's face was perplexed. 'The waters of Time . . .' he repeated quietly. 'He said, "the waters of Time".'

'Riddles!' Regor fumed and turned away.

'That must be where we are?' Eider offered looking to Lehon for agreement.

Lehon took out the charts. 'But the maps show the waters,' he frowned.

Eider mused. 'Then the words must have some other meaning,' he decided.

'Why must they?' Regor scowled. 'Can he not say simple words like everybody else?'

'It is the name of the place,' Lehon interjected.

'Then how does he know it?' Regor retorted.

Eider raised his finger to his lips for silence and withdrew his companions to a more respectful distance. 'Soon he may return from trance,' he said in a hushed voice.

'And give us explanation of these mists!' Regor growled.

'And of his words,' Lehon frowned still trying to fix reason to the wizard's speech.

Regor shrugged and buried his chin deep into the folds of his cloak. ' 'Tis all the work of the unseelie! That's what I say!'

'I said speak it not!' Eider commanded. 'Respect the initiate in our midst, do not put him at risk with your unruly talk!' As he spoke Eider's eyes flashed, his skin flushed blue-green in the ghostly light.

For many long hours the vessel rocked and creaked, drifting blindly on through tide and time. Together they squatted on the deck, huddled close for warmth, seeing nothing but the shifting vapours, hearing nothing but the insistent groan of the timbers and the shuffling of their mounts made restless by the terrible calm. At length they drifted into sleep, leaving the wakeful wizard to his silent task. Only he knew how fragile was the thread that anchored them to life. Only his eyes were granted sight of the treacherous dark and of the nightmare precipice of water that overhung the known world, and fell away into the immeasurable void of Time.

Regor shivered and opened his eyes. He blinked hard, then blinked again, for he could see clearly the spent lanterns and the spreading light of day on the horizon. He scrambled to his feet and roused the others. 'Friends,' he cried aloud. ' 'Tis dawn, and see, the mists have vanished!' As his two companions rallied Regor leapt to the quarter deck. 'Land ahoy!' he pointed as they ran towards him.

Eider clasped the mortal's forearm. 'We are safe!' he grinned and gestured to the slow rhythm of the clouds. 'See, a fresh breeze rises and soon we shall be on dry land!' He paced along to the wizard, seeing him blink hard in the brightening daylight. 'All is well,' Eider breathed, taking the tiller from the frozen hands. 'Time has turned the tides anew.'

The wizard gave a weary smile and together they looked out at the spreading horizon, yet neither gave voice to their darkest thoughts.

Regor rubbed his hands in anticipation. 'Land,' he grinned into Lehon's face. 'There to light a fire and eat fresh meat!' he enthused, pulling with him upon the ropes.

Lehon shook his head. 'We rest not upon that shore, but ride the distance.' Securing the yard-arm, Lehon beckoned the others to him and spread out the charts for all to follow. 'These are called the Flatlands,' he announced grave-faced as he traced the expanse with a grimy forefinger. He looked up from the map to glance at the line of land growing more distinct on the horizon.

'Speak on,' Eider prompted. 'We would all know that on which you brood.'

Lehon cast a long look into the wizard's face before turning back to the maps. 'Most be tales,' he gave Eider a sideward glance. 'Though the wastes have claimed many, travellers like ourselves.'

'Wastes?' Regor echoed, his eyes now fixed upon the deep red line that divided sea from sky.

Suddenly the heavy canvas flurried in the rising winds and Lehon looked to the mast. 'Direction!' he commanded, racing along the decks. 'Man the ropes!' he ordered and in an instant all were grappling with the knotted ropes and heaving timbers as the vessel lurched into motion. Frantically they worked, steering the boat from one swirling vortex to another, on and on, between sharp pronged coral and banks of shifting sand until with a hollow knock and mighty jolt, the vessel scraped ashore.

The mounts whinnied as they swam the frothing water to the shoreline, their masters urging them on as they struggled beneath sodden packs and across the unstable shelf of sand and pebbles. Once on dry land, the sombre look of the place silenced all, for here no dunes separated shoreline from land, only shingle, flat and putrid orange, which spread upwards to a plateau of deep red clay. It was as if the sea had simply halted there, obeying no natural tide or motion, as if the land obeyed no law of climate or contour.

Eider narrowed his eyes at the copper sky, the unrelenting flatness, but soon he was stumbling with the others upon uneven stones, splashing through brackish pools which lay inert amid the rocks. There upon the shingle they made ready the horses, falling silent as they worked, aware of the hovering winds and the spiralling red dust which flew up against the brooding sky.

'Make haste,' Lehon urged as he mounted his black steed and scanning the flats he tried to judge direction. 'Flatlands,' Regor muttered as he viewed the spreading clay and spat its dust from his clogged mouth.

Nairb too had observed the curious environment, seeing neither grass, nor tree, hearing no birdcall and sensing no beginning and no end to its deadly dimensions. 'The place is bereft of life,' he judged.

Lehon turned to him. 'Do not be deceived by apparent slumber,' he warned.

The minstrel raised a brow. 'Cannot the eye clearly see if danger arises?'

They all looked out upon the dust-clad plain. 'A place such as this tricks the eye and makes mockery of the senses,' Nairb surmised.

'Remember,' Lehon added. 'We too are clearly visible in lands as flat as these.' He traced a horizontal line far into the distance. 'How far think you to the border?' he questioned Eider.

The dark eyes narrowed. 'Several miles,' he said confidently.

'Or several hundred,' the wizard added quietly.

Lehon nodded. 'Just so. The nature of this place makes the charting unsure.'

Regor screwed up his face. 'Good thinking, friend,' he sneered. 'Now none shall ever know if your maps be true or false!'

Eider darted him a look.

'One mile or one hundred,' the elfin rounded on him. 'We are all lost forever, of that I'm sure!'

Nairb ignored the disagreeable tones and returned his gaze to the brooding plateau. 'And beyond this red dust?' he asked their guide.

'Peaks,' Lehon stated calmly.

'Mountains?' Eider voiced his surprise.

'Such a land is at odds with Nature!' Regor insisted into their weary faces. 'Eider, forgo this madness. Let us return to the vessel and seek out gentler climes!'

Eider ignored his plea, tightening his grip on Zephyr's reins as if steeling himself for whatever might come.

Regor glared his discontent into the sulphurous sky but aware that none took notice, he returned his attention to the wizard who had dismounted and was searching within the depths of his valued box. 'Now what talisman will he find to aid us,' the elfin glowered.

Nairb laughed aloud as he snatched a string of bright stones into the light and scrutinised them long.

'Beads?' Regor scorned and cast Eider a sideways look. 'He is mad,' he pronounced.

Nairb carefully unravelled the string of sparkling stones. 'We must travel with the utmost speed!' he announced, moving to each of the horses in turn and threading several of the gemstones to their bridles. 'Turquoise!' he grinned up at Eider. 'For speed and sure-footedness!'

Remounted, the wizard moved off across the crunching shingle, leaving Eider and Lehon to consider the mystic protection bestowed and the elfin to motion 'madness'.

At the edge of the plateau they had halted and Eider's hooded eyes scanned the spreading vista of inert red dust: the colour of old blood, it lay flat and interminably the same. No trees or vegetation, no change of colour or of contour to break the rigid monotony of hard baked earth. He breathed the heavy air and traced the copper sky to the point where its fiery tongues licked at the line of the horizon. He shivered. The elfin was right, this place was at odds with Nature, for though the sun's bright orb throbbed in the molten sky, it emitted no warmth. The plateau, though scorched and sterile, was the battle-ground for bitter crosswinds that snatched up the dust into dizzy spirals. Again Eider tried to determine the distance to the boundary, but as the nebulous dust clouds rose and fell, so his perception was blurred.

Regor drew alongside him. 'What stuff is this that clogs the lungs?' he coughed.

Eider rubbed the gritty particles between finger and thumb. 'Of clay, and others like,' he surmised, looking to their guide for confirmation.

Lehon nodded. 'A meeting place for the elements,' he frowned, pulling his neckerchief over his mouth for protection and bidding the others do the same.

Eider glanced at the wizard who scrutinised the landscape with a calm, pensive gaze. Feeling himself watched, Nairb turned, his brow etched with a frown. 'Strange, a place where the sun shines chill and casts no shadow.'

Regor had heard the comment and now looked about him anxious to sight his dark reflection but nowhere was it cast. He cleared his throat of the dust, 'Return to the boat, I say!' he urged, catching Eider's arm. 'Friend,' his voice had dropped to a whisper. 'We have travelled far, done many things together ... yet I am more fearful of this than any other.'

Eider nodded silent understanding. 'Is there no other route to sail?' he questioned Lehon.

The guide took the parchment from his jerkin and traced the route for Eider to see. 'These flats intrude on all sides. To sail the coastline would still lead to such as this,' he explained grimly.

Eider tightened with resolve. 'Then we have no choice but to go on,' he declared, looking to the wizard for reassurance.

Nairb smiled calmly into his worried face. 'One always has choice, my friend,' he pronounced, securing a string of turquoise to the bridle of his own mount. 'Make your own and leave others to make theirs.'

Eider looked to each of them in turn but none spoke out against him. 'Lead on!' he commanded their guide and they moved as one body across the border between the shingle and the hard packed clay.

From tentative trot to anxious canter their horses sped the parched earth, carmine dust bloodying their hoofs from the very first. The pounding rhythm of the chase echoed the empty wastes in counterpoint to the ice-laced windsong. Soon the dust had become a screen obliterating all but that which lay only feet ahead. It flew about them in manic dance, battering their faces, clogging their eyes and settling inches deep upon their clothes. It was not long before it blurred distance and direction, not long before their mouths were caked with the choking dust, not long before they were separated as each struggled to maintain the pace.

In the lacerating wind, the wizard wrestled to control his nervous mount as she veered hopelessly left and right, her pace quickening as she panicked. Nairb gave out a worried cry, seeing nought but red grit from floor to sky and fearful of the consequences; yet suddenly Regor was there at his side, his strong hands snatching up the mare's reins and steadying her. 'Blessings on you,' Nairb thanked, a-tremble with sudden fatigue.

The elfin spat the clay dust from his lungs. ''Tis madness!' he swore. 'Madness!!' he shouted to the gritty wind.

The wizard wiped his sore eyes and wheeled his horse about. 'The others?' he said anxiously.

Regor turned his mount. 'There!' he pointed, catching sight of a dark blur just ahead, but as the dust flew hard into his face so the shape vanished from sight. He frowned as he lead them on, unsure of their direction and the location of their comrades.

Ahead, veiled from Regor's sight, Eider had drawn Zephyr to a walking pace, his eyes streaming as he called out against the biting wind. His voice was deadened by the density of the atmosphere. Eider tightened abruptly: from the east a fleeting wave of sound had brushed his ear. No fellow greeting but a dark, disembodied cry, as if the earth itself had groaned in a final death-throe. Eider shivered, aware that his teeth were chattering against the cold. Yet in that moment his keen eyes narrowed, for he had glimpsed a solitary shape to his left. He whirled the mare about. 'Regor!' he cried out. The dark, undulating mass gave no reply. 'Lehon!' he cried anew, but the mass transformed into a sudden spiral and when Eider looked again he could see nothing but the shimmering curtain of dust.

'Hallo!' The cry came from the west and Eider spun Zephyr about as Lehon cantered into view, his hair and face smeared red-brown from the dust storm. As he halted he wiped the grit from his mouth, 'Friend, I thought you lost!' he gasped at last, white teeth flashing against the new pigment of his skin.

'Have you direction?' Eider shouted against the stinging wind. 'And the others, where are they?' he coughed, as together they searched the pulsing dust clouds once again.

Lehon pointed ahead to where a series of low mounds rose gently from the flat earth. 'We must follow on, these mark the route we must ride.' Eider nodded but the landmarks had as quickly diminished in the raging wind.

102

They looked at each other with anxious eyes. Lehon frowned. 'All is change,' he shouted and stashed the charts away.

Eider drew closer, his dark eyes flinching against the windblast. He glimpsed the compass which lay flat upon Lehon's palm and watched nervously as the needle of the instrument spun in all directions. 'You mean we are lost to this place?' he gave voice to his fears.

Lehon gave no sign of his feelings. 'Nought to aid us now but the sun's course . . . if that be true.'

Eider marked the blurred distance with determined eyes. 'Lead on and trust to fate!' he swore through gritted teeth.

'Ho! Friend!' Regor's voice flew to them on the wind as he and the wizard raced into view, their anxious faces lined with veins of the bloody dust. Eider gripped their hands in turn, relieved to see them safe.

Nairb gave a shudder. 'The place heaves with strange life.'

'With strange sounds, and sights,' Regor agreed turning nervously about.

'We must close ranks,' Lehon told them and they did as they were bid, careful to follow closely as he pushed on into the thrashing dust, each aware that the hostile flats could be the gruesome resting place of their young bones.

Onward they rode, bent low against their mounts, trapped within an ever diminishing space until none of them could determine how far they had come, nor how far they must yet ride to reach the boundary and safety. At length the dust veil had grown so dense that Eider was forced to raise himself in the stirrups and seek out the reassuring figure of their guide. Against the ever shifting powder curtain, Lehon was little more than an indistinct outline and Eider quickened Zephyr's pace, eager to keep them all within sight of their guide lest they be lost for good.

Upon the cruel wind a sudden hollow crack resounded, like the shattering of brittle bone. The mounts whinnied their unease and Eider turned anxiously about. Beneath him the ground shuddered violently, and he gasped as the hard earth was shot through with a network of deep fissures. From the depths, clouds of acrid dust belched forth and Zephyr faltered, rearing back onto her haunches and almost unseating her master. The earth had begun to heave and buckle all about them and Eider clung to her as she recoiled in horror. 'Flee!' he cried out as Regor galloped towards him.

The elfin's face had drained to white. 'We shall be buried alive!' he screamed into the gusting winds, his mount rearing as it slithered across the fractured earth.

Lehon had hastened back to them. 'Keep moving!' he cried, urging them on despite the chaos of groaning earth and shifting clay.

The ground beneath them was wrenched slowly apart and hot rivulets of foul liquid spread like blood from the oozing clay. With every sickly groan of its motion, the surface ruptured, spewing dust then soft, cloying clay from its throbbing depths.

Eider ordered Zephyr on and she scrambled along the quaking surface, reeling as the clay crazed and burst open to drag her into the chasm. The mare leapt clear, dust billowing as she stumbled to firmer ground, yet safety was barely won before the earth was torn by fresh tremors and bloody gashes spread nearer to them on all sides.

'Ride on I say!' Lehon commanded, circling his companions and slapping wildly at their horses' flanks.

At that moment there came an awesome shudder, followed by a sickly succession of cracks like the tremulous splintering of ice. From the savaged clay spectral cries broke forth, hideous moans of torment carried upward on the gritty wind. Eider's senses registered panic and he backed Zephyr off, instinctively drawing his sword in readiness. The wails ebbed momentarily but then raged anew and the soft clay beneath Zephyr's hoofs began to ripple. A violent shudder tore apart the very fabric of the earth and from its bloody depths a fearsome creature burst forth.

Newly formed and glistening wet, it was a creature of

clay itself and at sight of it Eider cried out in fear. The head, large and ovoid, turned slowly on the thick neck to form a jagged profile, whilst the face bore no constant features only shifting planes and fluctuating angles. Momentarily, the gouged out slit of a mouth was glimpsed, then the scooped hollows of eyes. The bull neck was fused to broad, clay packed shoulders, while the moulded arms and thighs cleaved to the thick torso like unwanted appendages.

'Mother of Hecate!' Regor screamed as he turned the dappled grey in desperate retreat.

Behind them the wizard shouted warnings seeing several more of the earth-formed creatures emerge to encircle them. First the bulbous head eased from the fissures. Then the clay-smeared shoulders pushed through. Soon arms, and then fingers thrust upward from the mire to snatch at equine forelegs. The horses reared, then in panic circled wildly, their frightened riders flailing the air with sword and staff.

'Flee for your lives!' Eider cried out, struggling to remain seated as Zephyr recoiled. Before him the oozing clay brought forth more of its offspring, the scattering dust settling on the glistening limbs, hardening the rough-crafted joints and caking the eyeless sockets.

'On! On!' Lehon urged his floundering companions as again and again he whipped the rowan staff through the air, smashing the grasping fingers and charging the clay hulks into their holes. He glanced back seeing the white mare stumble as slime-clad hands wound themselves about her legs.

Eider swept the sword in an arc of flashing steel, hacking at the clay manacles and severing malleable hands from wet forearms.

'Friend!' the wizard's frantic cry drifted through the chaos and Eider saw the chestnut mount flounder belly-deep in the quagmire. Nairb had been dragged from the saddle and now clung for his life to the mare's long mane, his foot caught fast in the pulsing clay.

Eider urged Zephyr towards them and with one strong

leap she cleared the mire while her master rained blows east and west in his frantic haste to release the good man. He severed the creature's head yet the sticky hands clung on, then with new-found strength he lopped the muscular arms, casting them to the depths. In haste, he snatched at the chestnut's reins but his trembling fingers missed their mark. 'Hold on, friend,' he told the ashen-faced wizard and lunged again at the dangling reins. The white mare had begun to slither as the fissures fell in upon themselves, sucking riders and steeds into the growing chasm.

'Aksharat!' Eider swore, making a last desperate attempt to retrieve the reins of the wizard's mount. In that moment the reins were in his grip. Eider urged courage and speed into his faithful mare and Zephyr's eyes blazed as she reared forward, muscles straining with raw power. With a guttural cry she leapt forth, the speed of her sudden flight dragging them from the mire, while Lehon and Regor fought the ever growing army of claymen, hacking arms and hands as they tried to prevent their escape.

Zephyr whinnied and reared again, pounding the gritty air with her strong legs, her nostrils flaring as she wheeled about, forcing Eider to cling to her as she turned upon her hind legs in a frantic circular motion. Eider's head began to reel as he glimpsed his companions rush by in a blur of movement, heard their fearful cries grow faint and distorted. The mare bounded forward again and Eider's breath was taken from him as the wind beat with all its force against his face. His cloak billowed at his back and his hair flew in wild black ribbons upon the draught. His stomach tightened, now they were racing the red earth and on either side the malevolent flats were shrinking away. Eider felt the throbbing strength of the mare as she fled on with a speed he had never known, the sudden acceleration made the windsong whistle in his ears and he glimpsed his companions caught up in the turbulent wake of her flight. Zephyr blazed across the flats like a dazzling comet, the magnetism of her fiery hoofs drawing them on to safety. Now in close formation the foursome flew the swirling wastes, hearing snatches of their own laughter as they raced the spectral winds. Faster still they sped, a fleet black line carried eastward in the white-heat of Zephyr's demon power, towards the dark horizon and the boundary.

Eider glanced at the sky, its sulphurous glow seeping now to the mauve of cleaner air. He wiped the dust from his eyes and could see clearly the way ahead and the horizon where the deeper hues of nightfall had begun to spread. Yet his eyes widened not at the prospect of dark but at the sweep of awesome crags whose jagged pinnacles were splashed vermillion in the setting sunlight.

On they galloped until the clay wastes were far behind them. They were conscious only of the howling wind, the flapping of their cloaks and the clatter of hoofs on firmer ground. Soon they were wearily stumbling the boulder strewn base of the crags and taking stock of the pitted torsos of rock that loomed above them.

'Three-Peaks!' Lehon declared as they halted in the ice-cold shadows and traced the outline of three identical spires of granite that attacked the skyline like a trident. Silently Lehon led them on, picking a track among the slithering hollows of the shale. Gradually the lower level of the steep flattened out to form a smooth shelf of rock and here they halted, shivering beneath the brooding crags. In unison they turned to view the treacherous flats from which they had fled.

The shifting dust spread below like a bloody tideline and in the sun's dying rays the clay wastes lay silent and inert. No dust spirals flew. There was no trace of ruptured earth.

Only the wizard dared speak the words. 'Were we ever there at all?'

Their silence and their fear-strained eyes gave him reply.

'It was real enough!' Lehon frowned, sliding from his mount's back to examine the weals and bruises left upon its forelegs.

'Aye,' Regor croaked. ' 'Tis a seelie blessing we survived!' The elfin soothed his mount with a gentle hand.

'The white of Eider's mare led us to safety through the dust,' Lehon said, extending a strong hand towards Eider. 'You and she saved all our lives.'

Eider took the firm grip in his, yet he said nothing. He glanced at the silent wizard who stroked the white mare in gentle appreciation.

'A wondrous beast,' he smiled into Eider's weary face.

At their backs the elfin drank deeply of the water-skein and coughed the red dust from his lungs. 'Here we rest!' he said, wiping his mouth upon his sleeve.

Lehon gripped tight the rowan staff as he nodded towards the sky. 'Look on, storms gather and we must find shelter before night comes down.'

Regor viewed the sky with anxious eyes. 'Aye, you can be sure 'tis no natural kind of storm! Nothing in this place keeps step with nature!' he scowled, following Lehon's careful path upwards to the overhangs of rock that would provide their refuge for the night.

Eider's dark eyes met Nairb's placid gaze. 'It is as if the land puts obstacles in our way.'

Nairb frowned. 'Or traps?''

'Traps?' Eider questioned. 'Who would set such traps?'

Nairb looked towards the sharp outline of the crags. 'Dark eternally encroaches upon light,' he mused, then turned to Eider, his face calm again. 'Come, let us to shelter.'

Eider sensed there were many questions left unspoken, yet followed on as he was bid.

— 10 —

The weary mounts snorted against the cold as they stumbled along the narrow track, which meandered upward from the moss-clad base to the wind-flattened ridge that trimmed the crags. Throughout the ascent the chill bit hard and the crosswinds battered down the tangled gorse until it could do no more than claw at the face of the crag in bitter retaliation. The higher they climbed, the colder the ice-winds blew and soon they were forced to stop and gasp for breath in the thinning air.

Now sheer walls of rock stretched up before them and they stood in silence watching loose stone and shale trickle from the wind hewn fissures, listening to the frenetic scrape of clinging briars. Lehon looked about, 'There!' he pointed. 'There is shelter enough.'

In the fast fading light they followed his direction to the narrow cave which slashed the granite face with its shadow. The jagged roof hung low and before the entrance gorse and briar stood firm rooted, providing a natural defence against the elements. Having tethered the horses in the shelter of the overhang, they gathered roots and woody debris for a warming fire.

Though cramped, the rock dwelling provided shelter enough and they settled down to share their meagre food and the comfort of the crackling flames.

Nairb shivered, clasping his knees to his chin as he crouched before the fire. 'Soon the storm will break,' he breathed hearing the distant thunder roll.

'It will soon pass,' Eider reassured.

Lehon looked to the cave mouth and the darkness beyond. 'My father spoke of constant storms about these crags.'

Regor spat into the flames. 'He left you tales then, as

well as maps?' The small mouth rippled in a disgruntled sneer. 'He left you stories of these crags? Of mists and of storms?' The elfin pushed his angry face closer to Lehon's. 'Yet no word of the gruesome tribe below and their chasms!' Lehon's face coloured as Regor raised his voice. 'He told you of the coast dwellers and of the sea, yet not a word of the treacherous fog!'

Eider pulled at Regor's sleeve. 'Do not provoke!' he warned.

Regor shrugged away. 'Provoke?' his eyes grew wide with rage. 'This mortal leads us into danger with his half-truths, and I should not provoke?'

Eider met the round face with a steely look. 'Silence, I said! Lehon cannot know all things in this place.'

Regor gave the parchments a kick. 'Then what use are these to us?'

Eider pushed the elfin back on his haunches. 'It is better to be with them than without!'

'To lead us where?' Regor shouted. 'To wastes? To sheer peaks where boulders could fall and strike us dead?'

Eider shook his head in silent exasperation.

'Avalanche!' Regor insisted. 'That's what it is called!'

Nairb shook his head as Regor ranted on, disparaging all of mortalkind with his elfin logic.

'Enough!' Eider cried at last. As he raised his hands to silence the elfin, a mighty thunderclap ricocheted from sky to earth and lightning filled the mouth of the cave with an electric blue shimmer. Regor dived to the gritty floor as the others instinctively ducked. A second flash, and Eider saw the wall of the crag lit brightly, the smallest detail etching long shadows in the searing light. His eyes narrowed. How like the profile of some grotesque face the boulders seemed, set in stark relief against the lightning dance. How like wisps of hair the clinging flora seemed, pinned flat against the granite by the speeding winds. Yet even as he watched, the threat of storm vanished and the night was calm indigo once more. No

110

rain fell, and soon even the forceful drumming of the wind had dropped to a distant moan.

Nairb glanced at their watchful guide. 'There is nothing. Not even a downpour.'

Lehon nodded. 'These are not natural storms.'

'And this is no natural place,' Eider added with a frown. He turned back to look at the charts. 'These crags are hazardous indeed.' The black eyes flickered as he traced the snaking line of the route they were to follow, noting its sudden turn southward and back on itself. He turned to Lehon. 'The route your kinsman drew,' his tone was diplomatic. 'It seems the longer and more arduous.'

'Aye,' Lehon looked over his shoulder at the charts. 'Yet, it is the safer course.'

Eider retraced the route with a deliberate forefinger. 'Your kinsman's route can be trusted?' he said at last.

Lehon stiffened at the question.

Eider nodded, folding the maps abruptly. 'Let it be so. We ride at first light.' He handed the charts back to Lehon with an apologetic smile.

As they settled before the flames to sleep, Eider glanced from the mouthslit of the cave. Outside, the shield of gorse tossed fitfully, resisting the new-sprung winds. Beyond it, the sheer dark wall of the crag stared ice-cold and impenetrable. Eider felt its monolithic presence and shivered, turning back to the meagre warmth he wrapped the rough cloak about his weary bones and settled down to sleep.

The embers of the fire lay like rubies amid the ashdust and from the blackness without a deep, insistent rumble echoed and re-echoed among the crags. Regor's pointed ears amplified the sound and soon he was awake. The earth beneath him had shuddered momentarily and the elfin stiffened, holding his breath until all was still again. The sensitive ears were now so finely attuned that they missed no scrape of briar, nor rustle of gorse. The embers of the fire shivered and Regor felt a new tremor beneath his bones. Winds flurried about the low cave, yet what the icy draught carried to the sensitive nose turned the elfin stomach. Regor found himself retch involuntarily, yet the earth had stilled once more and the gusting winds had sped away. Confused, he shook his head, but the vile stench lingered and he knew it had not been a dream.

'Eider!' he urged, his desperate whisper filling the silent cave. 'Good minstrel, wake I say!'

Eider growled annoyance beneath the warmth of the blanket but the elfin's insistence drew him from sleep.

In a flurry of garbled speech and wild gestures, Regor told about the strange echoes, the fitful winds, the shuddering earth and the hideous stench.

Eider shook his head, recognising only the smell of the woodfire. 'Friend, you made yourself afraid with talk of avalanche. Go back to sleep,' he yawned, settling himself down again.

'But I heard it all!' Regor insisted. 'I felt the earth shake! Smelled that awful smell!'

'I smell nothing!' Eider mumbled from beneath the blanket.

Regor's face grew taut. 'That stench . . . it is not new to me.'

'An elfin dream!' Eider assured unable to keep his mind upon the mystery. 'A smell from the world of imagine!' he chuckled, burrowing deeper into the folds of the blanket.

Regor gripped Eider's shoulder in an effort to keep him awake. 'Not a dream!' he insisted. His protestations went unheard and once again he found himself alone within the uneasy dark.

With first light the wizard woke to see the elfin already making firm the packs and Eider arming himself for the day's trek.

'All is well with you?' Eider whispered into Regor's sullen face.

'Aye,' the elfin sneered. 'Though I did not sleep a wink.'

Eider cast him a warning look. 'Regor, no more

112

imagined fears,' he placed a hand upon the elfin shoulder. 'We knew this would be no easy trek.'

'Aye,' Regor agreed gruffly. 'Still, I do not feel at ease.' He kicked at the earth floor of the cave. 'This place is bad! And the way ahead leads to worse things yet!'

Eider gritted his teeth. 'You fill your own head with fears and would have us all do the same!'

'Yes, I am afraid!' Regor admitted petulantly. 'The things I heard and felt last night made me more so. Those signs give good warning, take some other way, I say!'

'Then you lead us!' Eider prodded him in the chest. 'Take us all this other way!'

Regor fell silent and turned his attention to the packs. 'You know I cannot,' he conceded.

As he spoke, Lehon stirred from sleep and Eider drew Regor close. 'No more distrust. No more fear of thunder, nor of things that may not come!'

Regor's mouth opened to give further quarrel but Eider's dark look silenced him.

'Friends, look yonder!' Nairb's voice drifted to them from without, drawing them all to the mouth of the cave and into bright daylight. The bony arm stretched skyward and the wizard's fingers pointed to the red disc of the sun, encircled by two vibrant bands of amber and of gold.

'A ringed sun?' Eider frowned, his eyes drawn to slits. 'What sign is this?'

' 'Tis not natural!' Regor chimed.

Lehon said nothing, yet with sudden purpose he took up his pack. 'Come, we must be moving on,' he urged them to their tasks.

Regor strapped his belongings to the dappled mare's back. 'What knew your kin of ringed suns?' he growled into the mortal's ear.

Lehon glanced at the elfin but made no reply as he raised himself into the saddle. At his command they moved off, riding in silence, listening to the distant windsong and nervously glimpsing the strange eye of the sun.

By the time the fiery orb was at its height they were

resigned and weary having followed Lehon across the crag's great girth, clinging to its bulk like mites. Soon cloud shadows veiled the sun and the crags about them changed from vibrant blue to slate-mauve, cracking like old bones as they cooled.

Ahead of them the crag wall split in two and an expanse of metal-grey sky spread out to fill the chasm. Lehon lead them on through the wind-made arch and now the individual peaks could be clearly seen pushing up on either side like the joints of giant fingers thrust out against the flat sky. Shale scattered beneath their careful tread and soon single raindrops splashed to earth. Here the rock walls were sheer and offered no welcome retreat from the downpour.

Regor screwed up his nose. The air was sickly and the juices of his stomach had begun to curdle anew. He turned about, catching sight of the sleek black outlines perched atop the rocky spires. 'Carrion crows!' he yelled his anger to the heavy sky. The sound of his voice reverberated through the gully and scattered the feathered observers, their shrill cries echoing on and on among the silent crags. The foursome watched the shadow of the flock pass overhead, circle and then return, hovering in giddy dance as one by one they came to roost atop the granite heights. Before any could voice his thoughts, a sudden deluge broke forth, saturating riders and rockscape alike.

Bent low against the cloudburst they turned their mounts about, desperate for cover in this inhospitable place. Eider had galloped on ahead. 'Over here!' he cried aloud, pointing down to the lower levels where the debris of past rockfall had been wedged into angled dwellings and windbreaks. Most were inaccessible by horse and the route down narrowed abruptly, the path growing unstable if the scattered stones were evidence of its treachery.

Lehon halted them. 'The path is unsure, the charts say this way!' he thrust his fist due south. 'We shall be rid of these crags before nightfall.'

Eider shook his head. 'We are spent and this weather will finish us!' he gasped, wheeling Zephyr about and leading them down towards the precarious wedges.

Water streamed down the face of the crag like a giant's bitter tears and they pushed on with grim determination, eager to find shelter from the storm, however meagre. At last, Eider had discovered the half-hidden hollow amid the slabs and soon they were bending low as their drenched mounts carried them inside.

Lehon was the last to enter, and all three read the anger in his face. Yet the call of warmth and food was uppermost in their minds and soon they were sharing their tasks and their comforts. Eider cupped his hands about the pile of dry lichen and broken twigs, while Regor struck the tinderbox. The sudden spark made the debris flare and Eider hurriedly placed the remaining wood upon the fragile flame.

'This will not last long,' he frowned as they crouched about the crackling fire, peeling off their sodden clothing and hanging them from flimsy structures of bent twigs to dry.

While they worked, Nairb rummaged in his box retrieving candle stubs which he lit and set down in rough cleft niches. Eider watched him search the shadows for firewood, his thin frame bobbing in and out of the light until suddenly he slipped, dislodging shale as he fell. Eider ran to him and helped him to his feet.

'I am safe,' Nairb smiled. 'But look ...' he pointed ahead. 'There is an opening, a drop very deep, I think.'

Eider felt his way along the rough wall. 'Yet feel,' he said, reaching inside the jagged gap, 'there is also a ledge.' He held up the candle to the slit. 'Above, it looks like a low tunnel.'

Together they explored the oval-shaped opening, testing the dimensions with inquisitive eyes and fingers. 'Perhaps more caves or larger chambers lie beyond?' Eider mused, pushing himself further into the cavity.

'Friends,' Lehon moved towards them. 'Do not take the risk.' He pointed to the mouth of their dwelling. 'The rains do not abate, if there are tunnels beyond this they could flood quickly.'

'The mortal speaks true for once!' Regor said. 'Once the storm is past we can be away from this place!'

'Not until I see what is within!' Eider glared.

'To enter would be foolish!' Lehon warned grabbing Eider's sleeve. 'It wastes time and we would be wise to leave these crags behind before night falls.'

'Nights in this place are cold,' Regor agreed beneath his breath.

Eider stiffened and pushed Lehon's hand away. 'Then I shall see what is within whilst you remain!' he frowned, turning to Regor. 'Give me your candle stub,' he commanded. Reluctantly, Regor handed him the largest source of light and Eider pushed himself through the opening and into the dark beyond.

As he vanished into the secret blackness, Regor grew uneasy. He turned to the wizard. 'Wise man, stop him!' he pleaded.

'I cannot,' Nairb said simply.

For the first time panic showed itself on Lehon's face. 'We must. Elfin, go too, we have to fetch him back!'

Regor moved fearlessly into the dark, calling out the minstrel's name, gaining new confidence as he felt Lehon's sturdy frame close at hand. Then, within the spreading blackness both heard the gentle shuffling of the wizard's sandled feet and knew all three of them were now committed to the unknown dark and the fragile flicker of Eider's flame.

— 11 —

Eider fumbled along the rock wall of the tunnel, his senses growing more alert as the indistinct blur of light grew in dimension, finally to fill the wind-carved exit.

Regor caught Nairb's arm. 'Can this be so?' he asked fearfully as they moved out into the nightscape.

Moonlight spread ice-blue, lighting a vast arena of chiselled rock, the debris of avalanche and weather having fashioned a curious amphitheatre of stone onlookers. High above, the death-black sky seemed held aloft by craggy spires, while the horned moon cast a dramatic shadow across the grey floor of the arena.

'Strange,' murmured the wizard, his brow creased in quizzical unease.

Regor looked to their guide. 'How so?' he demanded.

Lehon looked warily about. The floor of the rock bowl was shelved with wind-blown shale, scattered with huge stones and slabs of pure granite. Toppled monoliths lay prostrate and crumbling. He shook his head at Regor.

'This was not the chosen route, come let us return the way we came,' he turned to the dark mouth of the tunnel. Yet none followed him, too intrigued by the shadow-play of awesome silhouettes, the fitful howling of the wind about the rocky towers.

Nairb drew him aside. 'Oh, it was indeed chosen, friend,' he whispered.

Eider heard his words and stepped out into the brooding arena, picking careful route amid the static carnage of stone. The shifting light lent a sinister quality to the place. Eider wrapped his cloak tight about him, sensing far more than the night's damp chill upon his skin. The darkness was acute, primal, and in its depths a sense of dread close enough to touch. Suddenly he started as lightning shot from the brooding heavens, ripping the blackness with its silver claw. The fearsome roar of thunder shook the boulders and scattered ravens from their hides.

'What place is this?' Regor gave voice to thought.

Lehon scrambled up a giant slab, watching lightning tracers arc the indigo backcloth. He shook his head. 'I am not sure,' he frowned, examining the curious stone structure on which he stood. He glanced at the premature shadows of night, ' 'Tis a place found by chance, not design.'

Regor screwed up his nose. ' 'Tis wracked with that same stench!' he pronounced.

The crags trembled beneath the thunder-voice as the four stumbled across the granite layers towards the centre of the arena. Ahead of them, Eider halted and turned back to Lehon. 'This place ... it is not marked upon the map?'

Lehon shook his head emphatically. 'The map led us south, 'twas the rain and need for shelter led us east.'

'Then your map would have us bypass this place?' Nairb breathed.

'It would look so to me,' Lehon agreed.

'For once I'd say the map was right!' Regor muttered to himself. He glanced up at the night sky and spat into the chill wind. 'The smell of the place ... it raises the bile!' he sneered, turning to Eider. 'Friend, can your senses be dulled to it?'

'I sense it sure enough, elfin,' Eider nodded watching the sky and the shadows of the monoliths. He half turned, catching in his glance the wizard's crescent face washed spectre-white in the storm-shock.

'This place bodes ill,' Nairb shuddered, gathering the flowing sleeves of his gown as protection against the creeping chill.

Eider turned his companions back to the safety of the cave, yet they had moved mere paces when the sky was rent by the power of lightning force. They halted, their hands pressed to their ears as the thunderbolt fell to earth, shaking the towering crags anew. All scrambled for cover, covering heads and faces against the dust fall as the great slabs toppled with the tremor. In silence they watched the quivering peaks, listened to the menacing rumble and felt the sting of granite slivers that rained in upon them like arrow-shafts.

'The senses shiver,' Nairb gasped, clutching at the shifting rock for balance.

'Be calm, it is a storm, no more,' Eider assured him.

Lehon scanned the flat sky and shook his head. ' 'Tis too clear,' he surmised.

' 'Tis an avalanche!' Regor swore beneath the dust fall. 'Let us be gone from here!'

They ran for the open mouth of the tunnel, but the warning had hardly been spoken before a calamitous roar echoed round the amphitheatre, wrenching boulders from the heights and hurling them to the earth below. In their wake rushing thermals laced the rock towers with gusts of foul air. Eider gripped Nairb's arm and together they dodged the flying shale, following hard upon the heels of the frantic Regor who had stumbled in his desperation to be gone. Eider offered a helping hand, but as the elfin climbed to his feet, his face drained of all colour.

'Friend!' Eider pulled at Regor's sleeve. 'To cover!'

The fierce winds blew and Regor could do no more than stand transfixed, pointing skyward. The others followed his gaze and as they scanned the granite's rugged contours their faces stiffened in terror. They stood, barely the size of rock slivers, in the shadow of a leviathan. Thrice taller than a man, the giant creature with legs thick as ancient oaks stood at centre of the stone arena, an awesome wall of scarred flesh and rippling muscle. A thick neck rose from the bulging, fur-clad, torso and the compressed features of the face showed no expression as he thrust the iron-toothed stave towards the zenith, stating his presence and his supremacy to the skies.

Eider gasped. They had stood beneath him, taking him for rock! Lightning had been the glint of his weaponry, and the hot winds the rhythm of his breath! Earth had shaken beneath his step, and the thunder was his voice!

'Impossible!' Nairb trembled as they watched the awesome motion of the massive frame.

Regor caught his breath as the beast-man rose to his full height, the great chest heaving in a mighty roar. In that split second they decided to bolt, scrambling for the relative safety of the cave mouth as first one, then another of them was sent sprawling with each new tremor. Boulders were ripped from their crevices and sent crashing to the ground in clouds of dust and shale.

'What creature is this?' Eider cried, as Lehon pulled him clear of the stone-fall. The mortal led them into the shelter of three huge slabs that had long lain wedged, forming a moss-coated table of rock. From the shelter of its low arch they could see out, though were themselves hidden from sight. Lehon's face was white and taut as all three turned to him for explanation.

' 'Tis what men call Giant or Ogre,' he said at last.

'Ogre?' Nairb repeated, peering out at the creature from the rock slit.

'Cannibal!' Regor added in a frantic whisper. He shifted from the slit, pressing his back against the slabs, his face sickly pale. 'That persistent stench!' he choked, eyeing the quiet Lehon. 'I know it now . . . 'tis death.'

All three turned from the fissure, hands clapped to their ears as the creature raged anew, shaking his great fists at the heavens, the sheer volume of his battle-cry pinning briar and thorn to the face of the rocks. Behind their barricade, Eider watched on from the jagged slits. 'It does not rage at us,' he said thoughtfully. 'I think we stumbled on its lair, quite unseen.'

Lehon shook his head, 'The cave is too small, and the cavern ill sheltered.'

'Lair or not, we could soon be dead!' Regor growled into their guide's placid face. 'Eaten alive!' Eider's look was dark, but the elfin ignored it. 'Were my warnings heeded?' he reminded sarcastically and prodded his own chest. 'I heard this creature's roars, and smelt its breath nights ago!' He cocked his head at the silent Eider, 'Dreams he said! Why, this is worse than nightm . . . '

Regor's complaints were silenced by the wizard's hand across his mouth. As their eyes met, Nairb pointed upward through the rectangular gap between the slabs. Within its frame could be seen an area of weathered crag, fashioned by the winds into balconies of sculpted stone. As lightning struck the rocky heights it was no tower of granite they beheld, but the haloed outline of a second ogre, etched upon the jagged ledge.

The elfin stiffened and hid his face as slowly the creature began its descent. The rest watched dumbstruck as the ogre took the massive contours of the crag in its stride, scattering loose shale in his wake. Soon the slabs of their hide were shifting and scraping one against the other as the creature passed within feet of them. Seconds later its vast black shadow threw their hide into darkness, until, as he moved on towards the centre of the arena, the light returned. The creature roared and all four pressed against the jagged fissure to look.

'Perhaps they search for food among the crevices?' Nairb whispered.'

'Us!' Regor trembled, wiping the sweat from his upper lip.

Lehon shook his head, 'No. These creatures tend to some other, more important task!'

'Battle!' Eider exclaimed beneath his breath. Eagerly he adjusted his position to get a better view from the rock slit. He saw the ogre pace forward to the centre of the stone circle: strong of stature, yet more youthful of gait, the second of the two creatures lumbered to where his kinsman awaited him. Soon only yards apart, they circled one another, exchanging no greeting. Eider beckoned Lehon to him, 'Look,' he whispered. 'They shall do battle!'

Growls escaped the knotty throats, the thunder rumbled long and loud while lightning arched, reflecting in its searing glow the silver of the axe-head and the streaming tresses of giant combatants.

121

'I'll wager the one that roared the louder will be the one to lose!' Eider grinned into Lehon's worried face.

Lehon did not smile. 'Come, this is no time for wagers. Let us away.' Stealthily he moved towards the widest fissure in the wedged slabs. He pushed upward, peering out and trying to determine the quickest route back to the cave opening, now partially blocked by scattered debris. He glanced at the threatening ogres caught up in their ritual of challenge and counter-challenge and frowned, his mind examining every possibility until, at last, he ducked back into the safety of the hide. Within, his three companions waited on his words, 'The tunnel head is obscured by shale-fall. We can get back, but must pay heed!' He cast them all a solemn look, 'If we are seen, we are lost!' The three gathered close at Lehon's heels as he eased himself up through the gap. 'Mark my direction,' he commanded. 'Watch for the signal, then come after me one by one keeping well in shadow.'

The elfin nodded and as Lehon climbed quietly out, he took his place, watching him clamber across the debris to the opening of the cave. Several times Lehon was lost from sight, slipping into the long shadows cast by the stone monoliths only to reappear as a dark blur against the moonwashed rock. Soon the elfin saw the flutter of the mortal's neckerchief and knew Lehon was safe. He nodded to Nairb, then climbing out onto the moss-covered wedge, Regor followed in Lehon's steps, careful to keep low against the rocks lest he distract the ogres at their sport.

Nairb saw the green cap flash colour against the rock as lightning gashed the flat black sky. 'Regor is safe,' he whispered to Eider. 'I shall be gone. When you see my sign, follow on,' he urged.

Eider nodded and watched the wizard negotiate the first jagged section of rock, silken robes clutched to his frame to prevent them rippling like a battle standard on the fitful wind. As he watched, Eider heard the thunder roll, it was then that the growls of the vicious ogres turned to roars, and he could not resist the spectacle of ogre battle about to begin within the vast arena. He watched them circle closer, saw the axe, and then the stave begin to rise then fall in warning. Heard the growl of territory, then of supremacy, saw the strident stance and heard the roar of challenge once again. The dark eyes widened as Eider's heart pounded, eager for the fray. It was then he saw it: the victor's prize! There about the neck of the older brute, a strange talisman hung upon a leather thong. From where Eider crouched the thing resembled a blackened claw tipped with silver. Why it captured his attention he knew not, only that the sight of it made his heart lurch with sudden desire. Desire to have that talisman within his grip, no matter what! As he watched, the ogre fingered the talisman provocatively, signal for battle to begin. The youthful adversary made the first move, lunging forward with a blood-chilling roar. A flurry of heavy blows followed; yet when the two retreated, no wound had been cleaved.

By now, Nairb had reached the safety of the opening and amid the thunder of ogre feet and fists had signalled to Eider with the flourish of the white-robed sleeve. All three turned their faces in search of Eider and to their horror saw him perched upon the slab roof of the hide. They saw him crouch low, not following the route that they had taken, but clamber down towards the heart of the battle-ground!

'Mother of Hecate!' Regor swore, as he watched Eider dash over the rocks like some frantic spider. 'What madness is this?' He moved to the edge of the cave. In fearful silence they all watched on as step by step Eider was swallowed by dense shadow.

From his new vantage point, Eider could clearly see the nature of the two combatants as they took fresh stance: the older of the two, and wearer of the talisman, Eider named Claw, his leathery face ravaged by time and battle alike. He had a massive, bulbous head, made more pronounced by the glistening bald pate. At the temples, long wisps of coarse black hair fluttered in the wind like tattered flags. His was a face more unsightly than fearsome, with a heavy brow that met in a 'V' above the broad, pear-shaped nose. The mouth was fleshy and what teeth remained were green-black, chiselled square, yet still able to rip flesh. Claw's good right eye rolled manically in its socket, whilst the left sagged white and unseeing, the corner of the socket dragged in a deep scar and drawn white across his cheek to the jaw-bone. The disfiguration gave him an unchanging scowl, a grimace caught between pain and demented glee. The fleshy jowls and heavy jaw were stubbled, while about the brawny shoulders of the brute, animal fur was draped showing a torso run more to fat than muscle. Claw moved with a heaviness, an awkward lethargy that stated his age more distinctly than the mighty roars which issued forth with every movement of his adversary. He gave out a bellow of warning, saliva flying onto the ice-wind like crystal spores.

The challenger was smaller in stature yet his comparative youth made up for this in agility of movement and speed of reflex. He was square of shoulder with a muscular upper body that bristled with fibrous veins. Like his kinsman his head was large, with flowing pale hair which fell past his square shoulders. A beard of similar colour clung to the determined jaw and there was a terrible, unremitting cruelty about the deep-set eyes that was reflected in the utterly impassive expression of the face. The challenger wore deer hide which permitted swift movement, unhampered by the weight of heavy furs as was his opponent. He took firm stance, his calloused hands gripping the axe stave as he swung it aloft.

'He has waited long for this moment,' Eider breathed, unable to avert his eyes as the creatures stalked one another in the hardening cold of the peak.

Arcs of razor steel sliced the black sky as they lunged towards each other in their barbarous, yet seemingly time-honoured ritual of combat. Time and again blade met stave as they clashed, the force thrusting one or the other off balance. Yet the challenger was always the quicker to recover, the faster to respond, his lethal blade sighing with blood desire.

Claw's chest strained with uncontrollable fury as first one then another wafer of his skin was sliced away as prize for his adversary. He threw himself upon the challenger, his weighty stave flailing the air yet hardly landing a solid blow.

In the safety of the cave Regor paced irritably. 'What can have possessed Eider so?' he fumed at the bloody combat below. 'We should be long gone, but for his madness!' He glared at his companions, distraught with anger and fear, well aware that without Eider none would leave the place. 'And you!' Regor swore at Lehon. 'How much of this place did you know?'

Lehon stiffened at the accusation, 'I have told you all that the charts record!'

'Charts! Pah!' Regor spat. 'As worthless as the tales you tell!'

Nairb calmed the anxious elfin with a scornful look. 'We must not quarrel here but deal with that which threatens our safety, and that of our companion!'

The elfin pulled away from the wizard's grip and pointed out to where the battle raged on. 'Deal with that?' he cried incredulous, and rounded on Lehon again. 'Scheming mortal! You told us only half the tale!'

Lehon flushed with anger, 'I told you true! I cannot know all! I feel brooding, wait for signs, like any other man!'

'Signs!' Regor swore, glaring at Nairb. 'Signs are we should be gone from this place!'

Lehon moved to the jagged rim of the opening. In silent agony he watched the dust and shale fly where the ogres fought on. 'Let dawn come quickly,' he muttered casting a pleading look at the night sky.

The wizard looked to him. 'Why so?'

' 'Tis folklore,' Lehon explained. 'Dawn and dusk for the seelie-folk. Night for demons and ogres, and day for man and all his works.'

Regor growled annoyance at their backs.

'Our folk-tales state it plain,' Lehon insisted. 'These creatures cannot survive the daybreak!'

The wizard touched his shoulder. 'Then we wait for light!' he smiled into Lehon's sombre features.

'Light shall ever triumph over dark, my grandfather did say,' Lehon added.

'Let's hope it is so,' Nairb breathed.

'But that was back there!' Regor pushed between them. 'Here nothing is so certain!'

The wizard turned his face to the mouth of the cave. 'What of our errant friend?'

All three looked anxiously towards the blood-stained arena.

The mighty creatures battled hard, and as the long hours passed, the powerful limbs had begun to grow weary, their stamina almost sapped. Now ogre challenge and ogre rage had changed to the sheer will to survive.

Atop the wedges of the hide, Eider lay flat on his belly, mesmerised by the ferocity of battle, and the curious attraction of the talisman that swung back and forth about Claw's neck.

Claw gave out a deep laugh of scorn as once again he thrust his stave into the challenger's stomach, waiting, as he doubled up, to land a lethal blow to spine or skull. Yet he could not match his opponent's youthful speed, and the challenger did not yield but simply rolled clear of the plummeting head of the stave. As it thudded to the arena floor it cleaved a deep furrow in the shale, and remained wedged there. No matter how he tried, Claw could not retrieve it from the flinty grip of stone and rock dust. Seeing his opportunity the challenger snatched up his once lost axe, and smashed at the stave, splicing it in two and casting the broken weapon skyward and out of sight.

Eider gripped the rock on which he lay, sensing that the moment of truth had arrived.

Claw had backed off as the challenger moved towards him, jabbing at the exposed paunch with the axe-blade and forcing his adversary to stumble backwards out of reach. Yet the cold eyes of the younger creature narrowed and a strange smile played about his lips. Could it be the challenger hesitated in a moment of compassion? Eider lowered his eyes, his mouth turning dry with aweful expectation, but no, when he next turned his eyes upon the scene the smile had vanished from the challenger's face. There was no mercy in the steel-coloured eyes. The death-blade fell. Sharp and swift, it embedded itself in Claw's sinewy neck and he staggered back in the blood rush. Eider pressed the palms of his hands to his ears against the agonised roar that split the air. He felt the bile rise to his mouth as he saw the creature crash to his knees, fountains of blood gushing from the ragged neck wound.

Eager for his victory, the challenger moved closer to him, whipping the axe-head in ritualistic motion before swiping at the nape of Claw's neck and severing the massive head. It rolled like a giant boulder towards Eider's stone-wedged lair, and as he watched it he saw the talisman clinging still to the skin and hair of the remaining neck muscle. It had not deserted its master even in death! Eider's body tightened as the rock beneath him shuddered to the vibrations of the challenger's mighty roar of triumph.

From the safety of the cave Regor tightened with fear. 'Eider, my good friend,' he gasped and turned anxiously to Lehon and Nairb. 'He will be discovered!' All three watched Eider's shadowy form and wished him safe beneath the hide.

'We must do something!' Regor cried.

'Do nothing,' Lehon frowned into the anxious face. ' 'Twould be foolish against such might as that!'

Regor broke free of the wizard's grip and clambered out onto the wedge of rock, yet even as he gained his balance a violent shudder ran through the crags as the ogre gave a second roar of victory. Regor teetered on the edge of the vibrating slab until Lehon's strong hands snatched him back to safety. 'We cannot leave him to be taken!' the elfin implored.

127

'Our discovery will see all lost!' Lehon insisted.

The wizard had said nothing, his distant gaze fixed upon the ogre and the plight of their comrade.

'He may yet find a way,' Lehon whispered into the elfin ear.

They watched Nairb's face crease with concentration as he sifted the words and signs of his mind's eye, muttering the rhymes of incantation, pondering the mysteries of the initiate.

Regor turned a sorry look upon the mortal. 'Pray the brute may wait upon his plan!' he scowled.

Now, within the hide, Eider caught his breath, for the serene features of the severed head drew his gaze and he could not escape it. Now he saw too the full beauty of the talisman, for it was not as he had thought the wizened claw of some ill-fated beast, but the smooth black leather and finely woven silver thread of a majestic glove. The unfortunate and late wearer must have been some seelie kind thought Eider, for against the massive chest of the ogre it had been no more than an adornment. His dark eyes flashed as they appraised its strange beauty. Its mysterious light-lustres brightening beneath his intense gaze. He felt himself compelled to move towards it, to reach out, to take it up.

'The gauntlet . . .' he breathed entranced. 'This is the Triad amulet . . . the prize!' As his mind raced with possibilities he felt ice-cold air hit his face as he eased his way out and over the flat rock, his dancing eyes caught by the gauntlet's mysterious lure, his body obeying its silent call. He crawled from the flattened wedge to boulders close by, slithering over the cold stone like a snake, conscious of nothing but the pulsing desire to touch the gleaming amulet. Yet suddenly he halted, aware of a gentle trickling . . . rivulets of melt-ice seeping the blackness? Seconds later he felt the rush of hot air and saw the victor shake the sweat-drenched head, the mane of tallow hair casting droplets of water on the wind. He saw the ogre lumber to where Claw's torso lay, the giant bulk sinking to its haunches over the stiffened corpse.

Eider clenched his teeth. 'He seeks the talisman,' he whispered to himself within the dark. He heard the beast grunt, saw the great hands search the lifeless body. Still Eider could not long avert his eyes from the precious glove, yet he knew he dare not ignore the rippling strength of the ogre. The dark eyes flickered, glancing first at the gauntlet, then at the beast. He saw the great bulk rise and impatient hands search the shale, first in the shadow of the corpse, then about it. At last the beast had turned his back, and Eider stood full height, leaping the final gap between himself and the gleaming amulet. The gauntlet shimmered and he reached out to the leather thong. Still it clung to its bearer and Eider was forced to tug at it like a rope. He glanced up seeing the living beast still searching through the dirt and dust. One final yank of the thong and the talisman came away, dragging with it see-through skeins of flesh and scale from the dead Claw's neck. With a gasp Eider seized his prize, the glow of the glove's gems illuminating his awestruck face with a myriad of spangled colours. Yet the uneven shale caused him to slip and in that moment he saw the ogre turn. The spreading features flickered realisation and Eider's body froze to the spot unable to retreat. The beast staggered forward, the bulging eyes focusing on him as they had once focused on Claw.

Eider watched on, his mouth dried out, his limbs trembling, but still he could not make retreat. He gulped, surely those bulging eyeballs could not have picked out his tiny form against the blackness of the rocks? Instinctively he crouched low, yet he knew the ogre saw him, knew there would be no mercy.

In that moment the massive head lolled back upon the strong neck, and the vast black orifice dropped open to release a blood-curdling roar. The heavy fists were raised, sounding a tattoo of warning and of challenge upon the taut drum of his chest. Eider sank lower still, clasping the gauntlet to him. Now kneeling in the rock-dust, the shimmering gems of the glove caught his eyes anew, its light-clusters dazzling him with their intricate display. The earth-tremor as the beast took its first step towards him forced him to lurch, and he stumbled again in the dust. It was cold and wet and, as he tried to save himself, he gave thanks he had made no sound, yet the amulet had dropped to the shale and in its spreading diaphanous light he saw the tincture of blood on his clothing and on his hands. He retched, knowing that the stream in which he crouched was the corpse's blood.

The ogre fell silent, and Eider saw a spark of light ignite in the limpid eye. In that moment the creature raised its great arm, the scaly hand extended its five razor claws.

Eider felt the earth shudder as the beast surged forward, the great eye focused not upon him but upon the gleaming talisman. 'So . . .' Eider breathed. 'You would have your prize?' He glanced again at the oscillating gem-lights of the glove. 'Well, so would I!' he growled through gritted teeth, driving through the bloody shale towards the waiting gauntlet. At the moment of contact, Eider felt the gauntlet's power, felt it clasp his hand like a long-lost friend claiming him from the dust. Eider's heart leapt for joy as he held the gauntlet aloft, releasing it from the leather thong. Transfixed, he appraised its magnificence, for that moment oblivious of the beast as it loomed ever closer. With meticulous care Eider pulled black leather over the fine bones of his hand and wrist, flexing his fingers beneath its touch. The light-spark of its gems reflected on his pointed teeth and he cast the silent stones a victorious grin. But the smile vanished as he felt the tenacious grip of the gauntlet tighten, and as its leather and silver melded with the cold flesh of his hand he cried out. He felt the searing pain of fusion, felt the stinging heat and shock of the gauntlet's power, saw the vast shadow falling towards him through the rock-dust.

Regor seized the wizard. 'Do something!' he implored the gentle man.

Nairb swept from the elfin's grip, silken robes billowing with the sudden speed of movement as he climbed from the safety of the shadows, out onto the granite wedge. Once atop the jagged platform the dark curls streamed out on the ice-wind, and Nairb turned his face to the brooding heavens. Momentarily his profile was etched against the night sky, but then was lost to shadow as storm clouds raced the horned moon. Slowly he raised his arms in silent invocation, his voice a wisp of warm air carrying

131

the mantra of the Ancients. His placid brow creased as he concentrated on the deed, patiently seeking union with the elements and the Lore.

'Hurry!' Regor winced from the crevice. Yet at Lehon's bidding he was silent, the two of them frozen in anticipation as the cold winds blew.

Nairb stretched out the tapering fingers, stroking the black pitch of the sky, drawing down strands of luna light from the ghostly orb of night. Soon his mantra could be plainly heard above the moaning wind. 'Luna,' he cried aloud above the roar of the beast. 'Luna, turn the tides of water . . . and of time!' As he spoke he traced invisible circles on the night sky, swaying with the rhythm of his incantation. 'Luna . . .' he urged the glowing sphere once more. 'Silver eye of darkness . . . bring forth new life . . . give birth to day!' As his cries grew louder so the motion of his hands turned rapid circles on the air. 'Turn!' he cried, his hazel eyes fixing the moon. 'Turn!'

Regor caught Lehon's arm, seeing the ogre raise his glinting axe.

'Eye of night . . . give way to day!' Nairb's trembling voice flew to the heavens. 'Eye of day!' he cried again, shaking with the force of his command. 'Eye of day . . . I conjure thee!' Suddenly his head fell back and he raised his hands to the zenith, 'Solar!' the bony finger shot eastward like an arrow. 'Sol invictus!' he commanded, staggering back beneath the churning sky. From the east it came, a rebel spark of gold, striking the first flame. As it flared it rose to the zenith as a ball of fire racing the night sky, swallowing blackness as autumn fires eat the earth.

In that moment Eider felt the draught of the axe-blade, felt the fear of blood-gush, caught the sight of sun-rush and as the blade fell, dawn struck the ogre to stone. Frozen in time he stood transfixed, a monument of ravaged stone looming over its diminutive deceptor, petrified by the wizard's lore and the awesome power of light.

The spark of dawn had been conjured as quickly as the fall of night, and Regor and Lehon embraced the wizard, and all looked with new eyes upon the curious army of scattered stones and boulders, now keenly aware of their textures and shapes . . . their origins. Lehon shivered and turned away, extending a hand of heartfelt joy and thanks to the wizard.

Regor pointed to the amphitheatre where Eider scrambled across the shale away from the shadow of the stone-changed axe. The two companions watched as he trod the stones oblivious of the graves over which he passed, his face alight with joy. Upon his right hand the gauntlet shone and he raised it in greeting. 'My prize!' he cried. The prize that Time afforded him, the gauntlet of the Ancient Lore, the Triad amulet.

Nairb stumbled towards him, arms outstretched. 'Friend,' he gasped, 'I feared you lost!'

Eider laughed, raising again the gauntlet-clad hand. Together they appraised its beauty, its diamond clusters dazzling in the dawn-light, the tip of each finger gleaming with a sharp talon of silver.

Nairb gripped Eider's arm. ''Tis begun,' he breathed. ''Tis the gauntlet, the first amulet of Triad power.'

Eider's eyes flashed as the wizard spoke and his body trembled with the mingling of fear and joy.

'In claiming this, you have accepted the challenge of Triad Lore,' Nairb drew him close. 'Others will follow . . . each one a trial for you alone.' Eider made to speak but Nairb's voice was urgent. 'If you succeed, All-Power shall be yours, for good or ill.'

Eider's face tightened with firm resolve. 'For good!' he swore. 'It will be a force for good!' he insisted into the faces of Regor and the mortal.

The wizard said nothing but raised a hand to Eider's forehead, where with the tip of his forefinger he traced the symbols of Ancient Lore, and encircled them with the ring of Oneness. 'To protect,' he said simply, as Eider bowed his head in reverence of his seelie blessing. 'The Ancients brought you to this place . . . have chosen you to wield the power . . . yet with it you must wield the knowledge, and the conscience of the Lore,' Nairb said quietly. 'Should you fail, then Rhye, your friends and you, all shall be destroyed, lost to the endless void of Dark.'

Eider's eyes were steady as he looked at the wizard. 'I shall not fail,' he pledged.

'Eider!' Regor's voice shattered the moment, and soon the elfin was clambering towards them. 'Such madness!' he grinned, hugging Eider to him.

'Such prizes!' Eider laughed, proudly displaying the gloved hand.

Regor's eyes widened with possibilities as he inspected the glittering gems.

Eider flexed his hand, 'Taken from the Devil himself!' he laughed.

'Nought is worth the risk you took!' Lehon's voice was laced with reprimand as he reached the group.

Eider frowned into the concerned face. 'Did not Fate aid me?' he gestured towards the petrified leviathan. 'There is nothing to fear, Fate brought the dawn and we are safe!'

Lehon eyed the wizard, but Nairb said nothing of his deeds.

The elfin shivered, glancing once again at the stone-littered arena. He sensed the uncanny in his bones and his keen nose carried the hated stench to the pit of his stomach. 'Let us be gone,' he frowned at last.

They moved together to the cave-mouth, and Lehon mused upon Eider's happy demeanour, his apparent unawareness of the sudden dawn and its stark illumination of the uniform monoliths that lay about them, transfixed by the power of daylight. 'Perhaps mortal lore means nothing here,' he murmured to himself.

'Praise the gods you are safe,' Nairb smiled into Eider's blood-speckled face.

'Praise the gods indeed!' Eider repeated clasping the wizard's arm.

Ahead of them, Regor clambered onto the table of rock and looked for the last time over the rugged amphitheatre. 'Say a prayer, Regor, my friend,' he muttered to himself, 'that we meet no more such things along the way!' He offered a hand to Eider as he climbed the wedge, seeing in the dark eyes a look he had not seen before and knowing in his heart there was far worse to come.

— 13 —

Throughout the day they travelled taking neither food nor rest, keen to put safe distance between them and the brooding crags. The narrow galleries of bleached rock gave way to straggling walls of uneven stones and finally to monotonous shale. Lehon paused frequently to gauge direction, confused by markings of the chart and their contradiction in the reality of the landscape.

'The lands lie bleak and endlessly the same,' he said, halting them at the sun's height. 'We risk returning the way we came.'

Regor spat into the wind at the mortal's words though he said nought.

Lehon's brow creased. 'We best bear south and track the edge.'

Eider leaned against Zephyr's neck, deep in thought. 'To retrace our steps will lose us time,' he said at last.

Lehon shook his head. 'We return only in part, then move due east with the levelling of the land.'

Eider gestured irritably towards the uniform contours. 'To edge the crags is to take the longest route!' he said tightly.

Lehon sat back in the saddle. 'To struggle along our present course loses more time all told.'

Eider braced himself for quarrel but the wizard eased his mount between them. 'Our guide offers good advice,' he told Eider quietly. 'Look to the land. Time is not always gained by choosing the shortest route.'

Lehon traced an invisible line across the chart. 'The route is old and the land much changed, tracks have disappeared and rivers altered their courses.'

Regor gave a sniff of contempt. 'More excuses, friend?'

Lehon ignored the comment. 'Bearing south we trek to the lower level,' he bid them observe the projected route.

'From here we ride east, through grass plains and on to woodland beyond.'

The wizard smiled into Eider's determined face. 'Be patient, Eider,' he urged. 'We shall make good time,' he reassured.

Eider gave neither look nor word to the idea as he scanned the map, shielding his eyes from the raw wind.

Slate grey clouds had begun to blot out the sun and a curtain of fine drizzle issued forth to drench them anew. Regor scowled. 'The land is against us, and the elements,' he glowered into Nairb's patient face. 'Tell me wise man, who are the fools? Those who quarrel over useless maps, or those who sit soaked to the skin watching on?'

Nairb shook his head, half smiling at the elfin's cruel wit as he watched him curse and burrow deeper into the folds of his cloak.

Eider by now had looked up from the parchments and gave a sudden and emphatic nod. 'So be it. South will be our route.'

At his words they turned their mounts and pushed on into the blustery wind and drenching rain. By the time the downpour had subsided, the landscape had changed from jagged stone to the softer tinctures of dark earth and battered grasses. Here and there the tangled boughs of solitary trees wrestled with the windrush, their leaves showering the multicolours of the season. Soon the thick veil of cloud broke open and the sky showed flint-blue, seeping to lilac with the movement of the sun. By late afternoon they had halted atop the gentle steep to view the land.

Below, the grasses flurried and rippled like emerald tresses over the crests and hollows of the meadow and dappled pastures spread towards the horizon in every shade of green. Lehon pointed to the thread of silver which embroidered the grassland ahead. 'Fresh water,' he said, 'and our night's resting place.'

Soon the campfire crackled, set with the abundant twigs and flame-coloured leaves fresh blown from the spinney of trees among which they sat. All were cheered at the sight and sound of the bright water and as night fell they crouched about the fire to recount the events of recent days with horror, and with zeal.

As his companions slept, Eider stared moodily into the flames. He leaned closer to the fireglow and extended his gauntlet-clad hand. How its gems sparkled . . .

'A powerful amulet,' the wizard whispered at his shoulder.

Eider started. 'I thought you asleep.'

Nairb drew near and bid Eider offer the gauntlet for inspection. 'Quite beautiful,' he mused, his gaze lingering upon the menacing talons of the fingertips. 'And cruel,' he noted.

Eider pulled his hand away. 'Enough to rip out Zarratt's heart!' he swore.

The wizard raised a critical brow. 'You could show no mercy?'

Eider clenched the spangled hand into a fist. 'I would show that same mercy given by Zarratt to my dearest kin!'

Nairb read the hatred in Eider's eyes and made no quarrel with his words.

Solemnly Eider returned his gaze to the fire. 'As my time comes closer so shall his!' he vowed. 'And he shall die a thousand times before it is done!'

Nairb shook his head. 'To incur such enmity in a noble heart . . .' he met Eider's smouldering look '. . . this man must be a tyrant of the darkest lore?'

'He is evil!' Eider growled, snatching up a twisted root and snapping it in two. 'Regicide the least of his deeds,' he threw the splintered wood upon the fire. 'He deflowered the king's most precious bloom . . .' his voice trailed off to grief. 'From Rhye's tallest tower my mother leapt,' he said at last. 'It was told that where she fell a flower sprang that wept crystal tears for the kingdom lost.'

Nairb clasped his arm in silent sympathy. 'A kingdom soon to be regained,' he said firmly. 'Eider, know that the Triad will not fail you.'

Eider flexed the leather-clad fingers. 'This hand shall one day wield the Sword of All-Power!' he swore, his sadness turned again to cold revenge. 'Will sever Zarratt's head . . . and make me King!'

Nairb nodded, unnerved by the bloodlust in his friend's eyes. 'But first, you must win favour of the gods. The Triad marks the acquisition of three amulets!'

Eider gave a savage grin and stretched out his arm until the gauntlet clad hand was at the centre of the leaping flames. The fire blazed about the leather and the flesh of Eider's hand, yet he showed no trace of pain. As shafts of light sprang from the gemstones, he revelled in the mystic protection afforded him and drawing his hand away, Eider grinned triumphantly into the wizard's face. 'Let fate dictate my course, for here already is the power to vanquish Zarratt! With two more amulets I shall have All-Power and the strength to wield it . . . then shall no dark lord take my heritage from me! Here is power!' he said with a final clenching of the gloved fist.

'Power indeed,' Nairb echoed quietly, fire-shadows accentuating the deep creases of anxiety etched upon his brow.

With the dawn Eider rose quietly, leading Zephyr down to the fast-flowing stream which shimmered cold silver in the morning light. As the mare drank, Eider knelt beside her, entranced by the patterns spreading out across the water's surface. He leaned closer, smiling at his own reflection caught in the clear mirror of the stream, then dipping both hands into the cool flow, he scooped up the sparkling water, marvelling as it dripped through his fingers like a shower of crystal jewels.

Zephyr shook her flaxen mane, nuzzling her head against his shoulder and waking him from thought. Eider caressed her noble head, the gauntlet-clad hand stark black against her velvet white, then turning from her he spread out his arms to encompass the breadth of his vision. 'How beautiful the land is!' he enthused. 'Soon we shall find Rhye,' he whispered, pressing his face against her smooth neck. 'Then we shall see the rarest beauty of all!' The mare nodded rhythmically to the sound of his speech.

Eider took down the skein, kneeling at the water's edge to refill it and catching once again his own reflection as it danced amid the watery swirls. Yet as the ripples ebbed away, the mirror of the stream held within it another image, a fleeting glimpse of blackest silk which hovered momentarily about Eider's reflection. He turned. He was quite alone, and though he listened for long minutes, only the gentle lap of waterflow met his ears. He stood to his feet, dismissing the watery vision as the last remnants of sleep. Recorking the water-skein he tied it firmly to the saddle, then taking up the mare's reins he led her back to the camp. They had reached the brow of the grassy incline when Eider's face broke into a smile as the elfin paced towards him.

Regor's face was taut, his eyes wide with concern. 'The wizard,' he said gesturing to the campsite. 'We cannot wake him!'

Eider threw down the reins and ran with Regor to where the ashen-faced Nairb lay motionless in Lehon's strong arms.

'We were making ready the mounts,' the guide explained. 'He fell faint and could not be roused.'

Eider brushed the sweat-streaked brow, yet though the heavy eyelids fluttered the wizard did not wake. 'There is fever,' he frowned, gesturing for Regor to bring water.

Regor knelt beside him. 'Perhaps it is fatigue,' he suggested as Eider administered refreshment. Nairb swallowed mechanically, the water seeping from the corners of his mouth as his body jerked suddenly in a paroxysm of pain.

Lehon wrapped his blanket about the shivering frame. ''Tis more than that, I fear,' he whispered as the wizard moaned beneath his touch.

Eider sat back on his heels, distractedly rubbing a hand over the gauntlet's gems. 'We need a medic,' he frowned.

Regor gave a sigh. 'The wise man is he,' he gestured hopelessly. 'There can be no other for miles.'

Lehon shook his head dejectedly. 'Fever must burn of itself 'til it be done,' he offered. 'That I do know.'

Eider grew agitated. 'But we cannot wait on this!' he said coldly. 'To stay means to let the moment pass!'

Lehon gripped his arm. 'There is no choice, he cannot be moved. We must stay or leave him here alone.'

'To tarry here is no hardship,' Regor grinned and looked about him. 'Nature provides ample for our needs.'

Eider gritted his teeth. 'Time passes!' he declared into their uncomprehending faces. 'And with it victory.' He turned his desperate face to the horizon.

'Such love of speed!' Regor stood to his feet and pointed at him. 'It was your impatience led us to this impasse!'

Eider rounded on him. 'It is destiny that cannot wait on this, not I!'

''Tis one and the same!' Regor flared.

Eider moved towards the elfin, his fists raised. 'Press no quarrel with me!'

'Hold!' Lehon moved between them. 'This is no time for dispute!'

Eider extended his palms to the mortal. 'Whilst we dwell here, Rhye's throne slips from sight!' he offered anxiously.

'Then be gone, noble prince!' Regor baited. 'Dreams are of more worth than friends!'

Eider snatched at his sword but before he could unsheath the blade, the wizard's voice rose in an agonised moan and Eider's anger was dulled to sudden remorse.

Throughout that day and the long night they sat in vigil beside the ailing wizard as he tossed and turned in feverish sleep. Agitated, Eider stabbed the coals of the fire with the sword-tip. How cruelly fate had intervened, wrenching from him the taste of triumph before it was hardly won. Yet as he bathed the wizard's jaundiced features his heart grew heavy with the deepest sorrow.

In the darkness, a short distance from the fire, Lehon

sat out his vigil. Quietly he drew upon his pipe, watching the fiery trail of starshot arc across the black sky. He glimpsed the tobacco smoke curl upward into the leafy canopy of the arbour and mused upon the nature of the place. Autumn had not yet settled here. Birds sang on, oblivious of the approaching chill, and ripe fruits and blossoms still cast their heady perfumes to the winds. It was a place where time moved to its own rhythm, though had they not travelled with the turning of the seasons, seen the last of summer days and felt the damp chill of autumn morns? Lehon shook his head, there were many things he could not comprehend: the awesome and illogical landscapes, the sudden dawns and blinding duststorms, the bloody deeds. So many things that made him wake in the dead of night drenched in a cold sweat that only fear can produce. Yet the beauty of this land drew him on, a beauty more alluring than its colours and constant changes. It was something far more powerful than the curiosity of the traveller that called to him. Perhaps he had been enchanted, and now was compelled to follow on, thinking it to be his destiny, yet fearful it was his doom.

'You brood, friend?' the elfin said, sitting down at Lehon's side and reaching for the water-skein.

Lehon drew thoughtfully upon the pipe. 'There is much I do not understand about this land and perhaps never will.'

Regor drank deeply to quench his thirst. 'Think not on it,' he warned, wiping his mouth. 'It is a mystery will drive you mad in time!' he shook his head seeing the mortal's furrowed brow. 'Know only what I know myself, 'tis a strange journey and the land we make it in is stranger still!'

Lehon smirked into the elfin face. 'A land hostile and beautiful at once.'

Regor nodded. ''Tis true, friend, and who can tell the one from the other!' he gave him a side-long glance. 'What say we quit it?'

Lehon gave a heavy sigh. 'It is a temptation sure, for I

142

am sick for home and those I love . . .' his voice trailed off.

'Yet something keeps you?' Regor prompted.

Lehon sat upright proffering the worn tobacco pouch to the elfin. 'Pride maybe . . . or perhaps the madness has begun?' he smiled sadly.

Regor lit his pipe. 'Yours seem a folk touched by madness,' he nodded to the rowan staff at Lehon's side. 'For your kin to go off leaving such goodly protection behind is proof of it!' He silenced abruptly, suddenly aware of his tactlessness.

Lehon smiled patiently. 'The rowan protects its charge whoever it may be.'

Regor's face split into a grin. 'Eider would follow if we turned back.'

Lehon shook his head. 'You are mistaken, elfin.'

Regor's mouth stiffened as Lehon gave a short laugh. 'He will not give in, it is his destiny!'

Regor sneered at the mortal. 'You believe that old dream? A dream is all it is!'

Lehon turned a searching look upon him. 'All have dreams. Mine is to follow my father's line so that his dream was not in vain!'

'Pah!' Regor spat. 'This talk of dreams spreads like the pox!'

Lehon nudged him. 'Then what of you? Do you have no dreams at all?'

Regor's eyes lit up. 'Aye, I dream of wenches and of ale! Good food to fill my belly and a life that is long and happy!'

They laughed together at his words until the elfin stopped to pull his cloak about him for warmth. 'I dream of the days when Eider and I did trick and sport together,' he said quietly. 'Days when we laughed together though we had nought to our names but friendship.'

Lehon clasped his shoulder. ''Tis said that friendship is the richest gift of all.'

Regor nodded. 'Aye, there can be no price put on that,' he said with certainty.

143

Lehon frowned and pressed the point. 'Yet you would quit this place without that you value most?'

Regor turned upon the mortal, suddenly aware of the truth he had made him speak.

Lehon smiled and gripped the elfin's shoulder. 'Come, friend, sleep on it,' he urged, climbing to his feet. ''Tis time for Eider's vigil and soon for yours.'

Regor watched their guide move off towards Eider and the ailing wizard. The elfin eyes widened abruptly as they caught the fragments of starfire chase across the indigo sky. He made a silent wish and smiled to himself: such was the stuff of dreams!

— 14 —

The new day broke and with its first rays a scrambling in the undergrowth heralded Regor back to the heart of their camp. He grinned, his cap bulging with fungi and wild fruits, and crouching down beside the newly woken Lehon, he spread his collection of flora on the ground.

Lehon gestured to the wizard. 'The fever grows,' he said. 'Neither I nor Eider know how to aid.'

Regor rummaged inside his jerkin, extracting a handful of earth-clogged roots. 'These I found!' he said triumphantly, rubbing his fingers through the contents of his cupped hand. 'Herb of mercury,' he explained, sniffing the crushed fragments, and raising his palm to Lehon's face.

Lehon sniffed at it warily, an aroma of aniseed wafting to his nostrils.

Regor blew away the husks and dried earth, then held up bulbous roots for closer inspection. 'A rare and precious find!' he grinned into the puzzled face. 'St John's wort!' he explained, extracting new roots and flowerheads. 'A plant of wondrous healing!'

Lehon shook his head dumbfounded. 'I know nought of seelie cures,' he confessed.

Regor grinned proudly. 'Yet one amongst us holds such knowledge,' he whispered and took up a cleaned root to sniff it appreciatively. 'My kinsfolk taught of herbal brews and though short on memory, some of their magic still prevails in their wayward son!'

Lehon clasped Regor's arm and grinned. 'Then call upon such works of magic if you think they would aid.'

He watched Regor prepare his brew, crushing root and flowerhead between smooth stones and transferring them to a pot hung above the fire. Carefully the elfin added small measures of water until all within the pot bubbled and cast pungent vapour upon the morning air. Regor's cheeks shone bright and red as he worked, prodding the soon pulpy substance with his dagger. When all was ready he took a small blue gemstone from the pouch at his waist and held it up against the flames. He winked at Lehon. 'Borrowed from the wizard's box,' he whispered. ''Tis lapis lazuli . . . to take the fever.'

Lehon frowned unsure, yet dare not dispute it, watching solemnly as Regor dropped the gemstone into the steaming brew. It sizzled on impact and sent forth waves of colour, its blues and gold agitating the surface of the brew. When finally the liquid had stilled, the elfin took up a small wooden bowl and scooped out a measure, watching its colours change as it cooled. He knelt down beside the wizard to administer the potion.

Nairb swallowed wearily, the liquid trickling from his thin lips, yet he managed to grip the elfin's arm and tried to speak. 'Be gone,' he urged breathlessly. 'I am of no help to you now . . .'

Eider shook his head. 'Drink the elfin's cure, then rest,' he said, pulling the blanket about the wizard's shoulders.

Nairb frowned as he swallowed the potion. 'Time . . .' he said desperately. 'Time passes . . .'

Eider cupped Nairb's head in his hands and gazed determinedly into the death-white face. 'The pact is sealed, do you forget?' he said softly. 'Fate brought us all here and we shall wait on your recovery.'

Nairb's face softened as he drifted once more into a comatose sleep.

Eider looked sheepishly at Regor and Lehon. 'Together or never!' he stated.

Regor gripped his arm. 'So it shall always be!' he grinned.

The wizard's recovery was a slow struggle but with every passing dawn faint colour tinged his cheeks as Regor's healthful brew subdued the fever's rage. Daily Eider went in search of the healing roots and flowers, while the elfin tended Nairb and Lehon fixed his thoughts on the route ahead. In the evenings all sat about the fire, the gentle tones of Eider's lute bringing a happy smile to the wizard's face.

On the seventh day Eider rose early for it was his turn to gather the herbs and scout the path ahead in preparation for the renewal of their journey. En route he checked the snares, then rode on well pleased with the catch. Carefully he guided Zephyr through the undergrowth towards the wildwood where Regor had located the medicinal properties so important to Nairb's recovery.

Above, spindle pines and silver birch stretched up, their proud heads tossed black against the clear blue of the sky. As the mare stepped patiently through the tangled ferns and bracken, Eider marvelled at the filtered sunlight and changing hues as they danced upon the velvet moss. He dismounted, enchanted by the birdsong and wildwood delights. Finding trace of the useful herbs that he had come to recognise, he knelt upon the soft turf, plucking the colourful heads, cleaning choice roots and tucking them away into the leather pouch. His keen eyes softened at the delicate white bells of lily of the valley bobbing among the moss. Eider cupped his hands about their clean white blooms, breathing in the gentle fragrance and touching the fragile petals with his lips. At his back, the crack of old wood tightened his senses and he reeled about. There were only vistas of layered green and shafts of sunlight filtering through the gaunt trees. He turned back to Zephyr who was nibbling at tender scions of grass; with a shrug Eider resumed his task, depositing the sweet white blossoms among the healing herbs. Yet as he worked, the fine hair at the nape of his neck began to bristle, as if touched by an icy finger. He sensed a sudden closeness and turned abruptly to catch the fleeting glimpse of black as it disappeared through the sombre trees.

'Who goes?' he cried, leaping to his feet and drawing his sword. He scanned the silent woodland for the slightest shift of branch or leaf but nothing stirred save the fitful wind.

147

Zephyr gave a low whinny as he moved to her side. 'What did you see, my lady?' he whispered, gripping her reins and leading her quietly through the ranks of dark pines. Eider marked the wood on every side, there came a shift of bracken to his left, then as quickly a rustling of ferns to his right and just ahead, the crack of brittle wood and the rhythm of running feet. He narrowed his eyes and waded on through the tangled undergrowth finding frond and bracken that had been flattened by movement. A coldness was at hand, a presence he could not name but before he could raise his sword in defence he was felled from behind.

Sent sprawling, Eider watched the weapon fly from his grip and out of reach. He felt hot breath upon his neck and glimpsed the blackest of shadows at his shoulder. The mass flew at him but Eider rolled away avoiding the lethal claws yet meeting the beast head-on as it leapt at him again. The wide mouth of the she-wolf gaped in a vicious snarl, saliva dripping from the chiselled fangs as she stalked him, wild green eyes fixed to his form.

Eider edged towards his sword but the wolf raved anew, her throaty growls rising to a crescendo as she pounced. He fell back, the sheer speed of attack, the crazed strength of her neck and back pinned him to the ground and though he raised his hands in protection the sharp grille of teeth sank through his jerkin and deep into his flesh. He grappled with her as she savaged and shook at him, eager for blood as the first taste ran across her tongue.

Eider wrestled her to the ground, pulling her over onto her back and attempting to break her hold. The coarse grey hair bristled as she clawed him and Eider kicked out frantically, trying to land blows to the beast's head with his free hand. Her hold was broken momentarily and gasping for air he threw himself forward to grab his sword. Demon howls spiked the still air as she pounced again, pointed ears flat against her head as she locked powerful jaws about his leathered hand and dragged him away from the weapon. The raw power of her muscular

148

body shook him off balance and Eider felt hot needles of pain sear his flesh, felt his forearm stiffen and numb. Desperately he seized the drooling muzzle, straining to part the rigid jaws, until, as his nails ripped the flesh of the rabid mouth, she released a yelp and the hold was broken. Eider clutched at his savaged arm and staggered to his feet releasing a terrible cry of pain. A bolt of energy had pulsed through him and as the she-wolf slavered in preparation for fresh attack, his gauntlet-clad hand seized the beast, its leathered fingers locking about her throat.

The green eyes blazed, yet the armoured hand yielded not. Eider winced feeling the heat course through him, the tremulous blood-pulse, the welding of iron and flame. The veins in his forearm bulged as the strength of his muscles grew and energy flooded to every nerve and sinew of his hand. The leathered fist locked tighter about the feral throat and the beast struggled so violently that both were dragged to the undergrowth once more.

Eider felt his body stiffen as he tried to steady himself, for now the gauntleted hand was a force unto itself and he watched his fingers tighten involuntarily, strangling the creature with systematic force. He felt the bile rise, sensed the stoppage of air in the canine throat, felt the crack of bone and sinew as the neck was broken. The armoured hand clung on like a vice.

Eider rocked unsteadily, the gauntlet's unremitting power had made him weak and now its studded gem-stones blazed in victory, dazzling him with their mystic light. When breath and vision returned, he found himself alone among the flattened undergrowth. The beast had gone. He looked to his savaged arm, the shirt was torn and dirty yet no wound was there. Eider trembled with disbelief, had he not felt the beast's claws and razor fangs? Had he not witnessed the cruel power of the gauntlet, seen the she-wolf expire before his eyes? What had become of him in this place? Had it somehow worked enchantments on him? He fell to his knees exhausted and confused, every fibre of his body aching from the strain of a combat he could no longer prove had taken place.

A chill draught tossed the ferns and Eider shivered, nervously snatching at his sword, but the breeze had vanished, the foliage stilled and before him only the quiet tranquillity of the wildwood. He wiped his face and moved towards the faithful mare whose wide brown orbs had watched him patiently. Easing himself into the saddle, he took up Zephyr's reins and saw the gauntlet's gemstones pulsing still. He watched their shimmer gradually ebb away and vowed he would make no mention of this day. None must know of the she-wolf, nor the true power of the gauntlet, at least not yet. He dug his heels into the mare's flanks and together they retraced their path to the safety of the camp and its welcoming fire.

With next day's light Nairb rose from his bed and smiled as he breathed in the sweet aroma of willowherb and forget-me-not. High above, the swallows dipped and soared, testing the currents in preparation for their winter flight. In the pale sunlight his sharp eyes caught the fleeting shimmer of the dragonfly hovering above the crystal stream and as its wings blurred in a myriad of rainbow hues, the wizard's gentle features shone in healthful joy of life. Now like the swallows they must be gone, must make preparation for dark days and the hope of spring to come.

Eider crushed the campfire's charred embers underfoot and climbing into the saddle he turned a final glance upon their makeshift dwelling, secretly reluctant to leave its peaceful shelter.

At the head of the party, Lehon cried, 'Onward!' and off they trekked picking their way through the heather and bracken and out into the rolling meadowland. Beneath them the rich dark earth was spread with the flickering blue of harebell and speedwell, whilst above the colourful tapestry the polished black spikes of the hedgerows glistened, their twiggy fingers strung with delicate necklets of morning dew. As the sun burnished the landscape, the woody perfume of autumn rose up in misty spirals upon the frost-laced air. Through long

150

autumn days they travelled on, seeing the season mellow and marvelling at each vibrant sunset as it seeped from fiery vermilion to moody indigo, finally to vanish into the jet-black cloak of night.

This night was clear and sharp with frost. The sky was radiant with the white disc of the moon whose crystal purity washed all beneath in ghostly silver. At his back Eider heard the wizard's heavy sigh and he turned to see Nairb's crescent features smiling up into the placid lunar face. Did he muse upon her regal grace, the sad dark hollows of her eyes, the ink blackness of her tresses woven with stars? Eider smiled to himself, how well that heavenly face spoke of the earth, its untold secrets written in her gaze. She who had watched Nature's willowgreen far into the mists of time, her gentle eyes watching still and knowing of all time into eternity. Eider watched entranced, knowing that in that moment the wizard was at peace with the earth, in love with the silent goddess of the night. As the soft breeze placed a moon-kiss on his brow, the wizard turned to meet Eider's thoughtful gaze.

'Dear friend,' Nairb whispered beneath his breath.

— 15 —

'Bethalon!' Lehon cried, and all eyes turned to look upon the spreading tangle of mist-clad trees that stretched ahead of them as far as the eye could see. Above them, ravens' cries pierced the cold air and Lehon halted abruptly, scanning the forest's edge with narrow eyes, seeking out shelter amid the dripping foliage.

Eider walked Zephyr closer to the giant trees. They stood in dark battalions, great knarled pillars holding aloft the grim sky. From their capitals, leafy boughs trailed, knotty forearms akimbo like some woodland wraith. About their solid torsos, nettle and bramble competed, wrapping cruel fingers in a cloak of barbs. From the jointed bark, fibrous stems draped and wefts of dew-strung gossamer fluttered in the wind, clinging to the weather-grooved trunks. Beyond the trees, mist-webbed vistas braided the wildwood. Soon the dark allure of sylvan mysteries had drawn Eider within the forest's shadow, his fascination caught. Then he saw it.

'There!' he gasped. The black shape darted through the chequered light, slipping away among the sentinel trees. Eider tightened his grip on the reins and held Zephyr stock-still as he scanned the brooding towers. 'Again!' he swore, his keen eyes tracking the fleet edge of a black cloak as it vanished into the forest dark.

'Eider!' Lehon's cry echoed at his back and he turned to see the guide and his companions dismounted. Lehon called to him again and beckoned, but Eider only frowned.

'Closer!' he gestured to the arboreal heart.

Lehon looked anxiously to his companions: the wizard shook his head and the elfin glowered at the darkening sky. Ahead of them they saw Eider wheel Zephyr about and push on into the woody tangle of Bethalon.

'Eider!' Regor called out, pacing forward in angry strides. 'We shall be lost within!'

Eider halted the mare, yet remained straight-backed in the saddle. 'To circuit the forest wastes our time!' he yelled as they drew closer.

Lehon frowned into the determined face. 'We agreed to stay clear of this place.' He pointed an insistent finger. 'Last night, before the fire, the route was stated plain.'

'Aye!' Regor echoed, siding with the voice of safety.

'We trek to the forest edge and follow its perimeter to the ranges,' Lehon repeated the conversation of the night before.

Eider glared into his solemn face. 'Time is of the essence!'

The wizard drew close, his hand held aloft in a gesture of peace. 'Friends, hold against this impulse. Where no light shines, dark and fear await.'

'No light and no way out!' Regor complained eyeing the treacherous mists that spread out from the forest's heart.

'Then make light!' Eider snarled into Nairb's passive gaze.

The wizard's eyebrows arched at the angry tone. 'Friend,' he replied quizzically, 'I thought you not afraid of Dark?'

Eider shrugged uncomfortably. 'Nor am I!' he stated, turning Zephyr about and kicking hard upon the stirrups.

As they watched him push on into the lengthening shadows of the forest, Lehon and Regor looked to the wizard, but sudden wrath had marked the gentle face and Nairb raised a long forefinger, its tip directed at Eider's disappearing form. 'Be gone!' he cried aloud. 'Your courage be your defence!'

'Have you forgotten the pact?' Regor frowned at Nairb, making a move towards his mount. The wizard held him back and gestured for Lehon to stay his pursuit of their impulsive friend. 'Wait on this!' Nairb insisted, glancing at the rolling mists. 'The pact is not forgotten, yet stay – all is as it should be on this day.'

Eider pushed Zephyr on at a canter, following the mossy path which wound from the frond-layered threshold and on into the damp twilight of the forest. They raced between the avenues of trees and Eider's heart leapt with anticipation of woodland secrets, his keen eyes aware of every contour, every twisted bough and fluttering leaf. Yet as he drew Zephyr to a walking pace he frowned, for there was something in the mouldering leaves, the dank curtain of mist and the seeping green of the arboreal light that brought to him a deep unease. He pulled Zephyr to a halt and in silence watched the gentle rocking of the boughs, heard the dripping rhythms form uneasy counterpoint with the creaking of ancient wood. He tensed and looked about him; darkness had almost swallowed the narrow track and the army of trees had closed ranks to bar his retreat.

Sensing her master's anxiety, Zephyr whinnied and Eider turned to calm her. As he did so he caught the ripple of black among the foliage. 'On!' he commanded his steed, seeing the inky trim vanish into the stratas of mist. He urged the mare on into the tangle, growing uneasy as the fresh-sprung breeze took up the silken hair of Zephyr's mane. Eider caught his breath as the new winds flew together and he was forced to lower his head against their manic flight. In their wake, shrubs were tossed and broken and forest debris scattered in a whirlwind about his head. The regiments of trees were solemn and rigid, save for the insistent creaking of their aged boughs which echoed on until the treacherous mists had risen to consume the meagre light.

Eider ordered the mare on, threading the darkened corridors of trees towards the heart of the night forest. A new sound, like the snap of virgin wood! Zephyr faltered, tossing her head as Eider scanned afresh the deepening dark. He saw nothing and though he drew the cloak about him, the cold of panic had gripped him and he dug his heels into Zephyr's flanks, eager to be gone. At first the mare refused his command, then hesitantly she paced forward among the clasping leaves and trailing roots that coiled themselves about her hoofs. The trees tossed and roared above them, a jagged finger of light thrusting down through the crashing sea of branches. Eider held the mare still, it was a substance not of lightning nor of bone, yet even as these thoughts were racing through his mind, the raging boughs flurried and in their midst the knotted silver trunk of a towering birch tree took shape, tall and straight it blocked the path ahead with its immovable bulk!

Eider glimpsed the elongated torso which stretched skyward to form a long, twisted neck. Heavy leafed upper branches formed tresses of flame, while the lowest and longest of its boughs became a knotted arm and spike-tipped hand. As the great tree tossed and fell in the squall, the jointed arm flailed the air with woody groans, then caught in the downward thrust viciously towards the leaf-strewn ground.

Eider watched the forest's guardian intently. Its motion was as fitful as the wind itself and he could perceive no pattern to its erratic dance with which to gauge safe passage. Then slowly, horrifically, the tree revealed itself – first, he saw the deep-cut eyeslits and then the scored features of an ancient, baneful face carved amid the slats of bark. At the centre of the ravaged face, a jagged orifice had broken open – a deep, black gash into which the icy wind flew, echoing the hollow and granting the birch an eerie voice. 'Who goes ...?' it rasped.

Eider tightened with alarm as the birch's finger-staves lunged down at him on the bitter draught. 'Zephyr, on!' he urged, determined to gain passage, but his command was lost to the rushing winds and the cracking of aged joints.

The lethal prongs thrust earthward and Eider clung desperately to the mare as she recoiled. He willed her on, but the knarled gateman spread out spectral fingers, the echo-whisper of the wind giving it voice once more. 'Who wakes the mighty birch?' The windrush rattled in the splintered wood of the throat.

Gripped by panic, Eider halted the faltering mare at safe distance as he saw the tree heave its branches skyward in preparation for the down-draught and new attack. Eider narrowed his eyes, seeing the agonised features of the slatted face made taut by its knotty motion. The windrush came, the muscular boughs arched and plunged forth as the charge was whispered again. 'Who goes forth?'

Seated upon the strong mare's back, Eider allowed himself no show of fear as he cried to the frenzied wind, 'Eider, true King of Rhye!'

At sound of his voice the great tree wailed and hurled its silver boughs in a torrent of leafy rage, the echo-whisper reverberating through the twisted trunk in the ebb and flow of arboreal speech. 'The Birch knows no such king ...!' the spiked fingers thrust earthward with the fresh gust.

Eider braced himself to shout command. 'None deny me what I ask! And so the lowly birch will let me pass!'

The great boughs shuddered and the five staves of the woody hand scythed the air about Eider and his brave mare, the razor tips almost finding their mark. 'A king ...? True born ...?' the ice breath hissed. 'Yet ill-prepared for war ...!' The lethal birch coiled its silver fingers like a whip and, as the mare retreated, lashed out to shred Eider's heavy cloak and score deep red weals in Zephyr's haunches. The mare cried out, weaving right then left beneath the stinging fingers. With a rush of wind the tangled boughs stretched skyward once again, and Eider held the white mare firm as he growled defiance. 'King I am, and one well trained for war!'

The echo-song flew through the silvered boughs and the great tree moaned, the black gape of its twisted face stretched in savage mockery. 'None shall pass ...' The flame tresses flew on the gusting winds in frenzied expectation.

Eider jerked violently as his leathered hand snatched at the sword-hilt and freed the weapon of its scabbard. He had exercised no will over the action and watched on involuntarily as the gleaming blade was raised upright, obeying no command of his but that of the gauntlet. 'Let me pass!' Eider yelled, his heart beating fast in his chest. 'For trees, my Lord Birch, may be felled!'

The warning went unheeded as with the down-draught the fearsome staves plunged again, its anger rallying with every lethal swoop. The eye-slats narrowed and the deep orifice of the mouth had twisted in cruel contempt of its adversary. 'The Birch obeys none ...!' The heaving boughs clawed and flailed, their knotty joints creaking as they reached for him. 'One touch ... makes madness!' the ferocious staves plummeted.

Tossing her flaxen mane, Zephyr reared, her fiery eyes alight as she sprang from the forest tangle, bearing Eider to safety once again. Terrified, he clung to her, his grip upon the sword unrelenting as he hurtled forward in an attempt to wound the malevolent tree. Gritting his teeth with determination, he weaved Zephyr between the scything talons, cheating them of victory every time, but the taunting rasp of the wind-rush had surrounded him again. 'One touch ... is death!' With a terrible wail the birch attacked again, lethal arm and fingers launched like forked lightning towards the victim's heart.

Zephyr railed, tossing Eider back in the saddle and out of reach, yet though the birch had missed its mark, the flow of blood trickled red across her flanks as Eider groaned. At sight of the wound, the crazed birch flexed its fatal spikes, eager to deliver the final sting. It roared throaty delight and shuddered with the promise of victory, tossing its wild tresses to the rushing winds and summoning the elements to aid its final attack.

Eider trembled with the sting of the wound, pulling Zephyr around to face his attacker head on. He felt the gloved hand pulse with heat, felt the iron grip of his fingers about the sword-hilt, saw the glinting blade jerk

157

upright. Sweat trickled down his face and neck as he waited for the moment to come.

The birch attacked, wailing wind rushing from the orifice as the death-staves bore down upon their victim. Each cruel talon stretched out, eager to drag their ragged tips across the youthful face, to touch the heart with sudden death. As the boughs plunged, Eider released a cry of attack, feeling brute force pulse his veins, feeling his finger-joints lock as he brought the blade scything down upon the knotty arm.

Severed, the demon forefinger, and then another! The forest shook with the hideous birch-scream. The tree reeled, thrusting its remaining staves at the dark sky, shuddering from base to crown in woeful convulsions. As quickly, it rallied in wild, instinctive attack, bearing down on Eider with new-found strength. Though Zephyr's frightened cries echoed on the wind, the gauntlet-clad hand did not relent, landing one solid blow after another. One by one the trembling staves fell and the birch screeched with each newly inflicted agony. The awesome trunk shuddered and threw its wounded boughs to the sky. In that moment, Eider felt the irresistible pull of omnipotent power as his leathered hand thrust the blade straight and deep into the blackened heart of the birch. Eider gritted his teeth determinedly, the sinews in his arm were as taut as bowstrings, and he felt as if the bicep would explode as the sword hacked on relentlessly, slivers of bark showering the forest floor like an autumn windfall. He saw the great tree topple, glimpsed the writhing black roots clawing the undergrowth in a final death throe. Eider let out a throaty roar of victory as he kicked upon the stirrups, his dark eyes ablaze as he sheathed the sword and saw the gauntlet's flickering gemlights ebb away. With such power as this, all would bow before his might!

He urged Zephyr on and on, elation blurring fear and caution as they streaked through the endless corridors of trees. Eider's face ran with sweat and grime, his blood-speckled shirt gripped tight against the pain of his wound.

Fixedly he watched the track ahead, panic chasing at his back, his mind reeling at the fate that had almost befallen him, while fear of what he might yet face raced on before, luring him ever closer to the forest's heart.

The further they pushed into the jade depths, the more tangled the undergrowth became, and soon Eider paced the mare anxiously this way and that, the track having dwindled to nothing. Briar spikes tore at his clothing and scarred the flanks of his steed and soon Eider grew too weary to hack at the tangle. He drew Zephyr to a halt, the light was dimming rapidly and the damp mists had erased all sign of pathways. 'I shall not be trapped!' Eider cried in steely defiance at the sentinel trees. They stood together, silent and overcome, Zephyr shaking her knotted mane as Eider sank low in the saddle, his head heavy with exhaustion.

The trampling of bracken to his left alerted him once again and his grip tightened afresh upon the sword-hilt. He made no move nor sound as softly he slid the blade from its scabbard, seeing reflected in its argent sheen the edge of silk-black slipping away through the brindled light.

''Tis there again!' he growled into Zephyr's ear. Gently he persuaded her on in pursuit. The yearning for sight of that elusive black trim had grown to frenzied desire and by now he had banished all else from his mind. He did not heed the lost pathway, nor the direction in which he trod. He did not heed the dwindling light, nor the puvvering mists of night, and when at last Zephyr halted, Eider found himself boxed in by briar and thicket.

'The gods help us,' he realised his folly. 'We are lost!' He flinched as the ice-wind sprung up afresh and glared up through the tree towers at the last remnants of light. The forest echoed with a rushing like the sea, a ghostly tide of greenness scattering about its rooted inhabitants. Debris flew in barbed spirals from the forest floor, forcing Eider to shield his face against the mare's neck as the fibrous wreckage savaged all in its path.

Crazed and exhausted, Eider clung to Zephyr for

warmth and comfort. The mare whinnied low, swaying beneath his weight as weariness overcame him and he drifted into sleep.

Darkness patterned the forest with nightmare shadows as the raging winds finally blew themselves out and Zephyr shook the debris from her tangled mane. Eider's eyes flickered open, then widened with realisation. How long had he slept? He gripped the reins. It had been a foolish act!

Now the forest had thickened and closed in about them. Now strong roots had forged solid barriers and the light was all but gone. Eider looked anxiously about, frantic for the sight of that silk-black trim among the trees. He lowered his eyes in self-contempt, for the sake of his wild imaginings he might be lost forever to this dark place! He shook his head in despair, tightening as he glimpsed the strong green tendrils that had grown up about the mare's hoofs, their thorny manacles gripping her fast. Incensed, Eider snatched at his sword and leapt into the tangled undergrowth.

'The King of Rhye shall have passage through Bethalon!' he cried aloud as he slashed at the twining cords with the glinting blade. The task begun, he hacked away like a man possessed, venting his rage upon the malevolent woodland, releasing his venom on the savage briars which dared prevent his progress.

'This forest be damned to hell!' he shouted to the watchful tree towers, but the vigour of his anger was soon spent and he was forced to lean upon the sword, hands bleeding, his face and limbs dripping wet with the effort. As he gasped the dank air, he heard the mare call to him and turned to find her drinking steadily from a shallow pool.

He knelt beside her, dipping his hands into the tepid water and splashing his face with the greasy droplets. His senses calmed, he gave a deep, mournful sigh. 'Zephyr, we are truly lost!' he groaned, tying the soaked neckerchief about him. The mare nuzzled him as he stared down into the shimmering film of the pool.

'Lehon and the wizard spoke much of stars,' he mused aloud. 'Yet here they afford us no direction.' He frowned, for the deep purple sky was void of moon and starglow. Eider looked about him, every branch and briar was clearly defined and there within the pool his own reflection shone.

'No heavenly light, and yet we see all.' He gathered up Zephyr's reins, tearing away tendrils fresh grown about her forelegs as he lead her on through the network of branches and stems. Patiently they negotiated the wood spikes and fleshy leaves, Eider grown certain that their route was now no more than a pattern of circles. Now ochre damp rose up as a veil before them and Zephyr halted, snorting as she shook her mane. Eider gripped his sword anxiously and searched the brooding trees. The sound of running water met his ears. ''Tis a stream, lady, no more,' he coaxed and parting the meshed branches saw the bubbling water just ahead of them. It ran layered brown and green and upon the fern fronds heavy droplets glistened like celadon jewels.

The mare's nostrils flared and she pounded the black soil, refusing to walk on. Eider tried to steady her but as he did so, he brushed against the tangled foliage sending gaudy globules cascading to the forest floor. They slid like honeydew, their bitter stench clouding the air as they melted in a wisp of smoke. Zephyr backed off, shaking her head in agitation. Eider covered his mouth as he knelt beside the sulphurous flow, 'The source of life tarnished by dark alchemy,' he sighed.

The rustle of undergrowth at his back forced Eider to his feet, catching sight of the black-cloaked wraith as it darted on through the trees. 'Now I have you!' he swore, giving immediate chase, determined that this time the artful wearer of that cloak would not evade him. Stealthily he threaded through the greenwood pillars, severing the waist-high ferns and grasping roots with the merest touch of the blade. Now he was running, his manic pursuit leading him deeper into the mire. Now the towering trees had arched above him, linking their

161

spidery joints as a dense canopy which enveloped the forest in shadows of deep malachite. He saw the layered mists and coils of woodsmoke spiralling towards him like beckoning hands. Slowly he followed the corridor of trailing roots and leaves nearer to the smoke-veiled mass of giant ferns. He parted the leafy curtain.

In the midst of the wildwood a ruined edifice loomed up, its crumbled stones and rotten timbers half hidden among the tall grasses. Eider marvelled at the hollow shell of the central tower, its gaping window coated with velvet moss, its broken masonry held intact by the green-grey of lichen and ivy. Intrigued, he moved towards it. The closer he drew the deeper his curiosity grew and he gasped at its dark majesty, the tracery of its arched windows, the grimaces of its gargoyles, the broken bell of its tower.

Now the smoke seeped in his direction in flat blue planes, folding and unfolding upon the heavy air. He heard his boots scrape the granite steps as he moved, entranced, into the ruined structure. Once upon the threshold he saw long grasses and hardy tares ripple within the drifting layers of smoke. In wonderment he passed beneath the dark arch and felt the chill shadow of the tower consume his own. His eyes met emptiness . . .

He fell away from sight . . . and sound . . .

Falling . . .

  Falling . . .

    Falling into darkness . . .

      Into ice-coldness!

His limbs were as heavy as lead. His hair spread out as a silken net. He gasped and water seeped between his lips, between his fingers. Above him faint green light shimmered and he cried out, his voice lost to a myriad of bubbles. He followed their upward flight, seeing them burst against the surface film. Frantically he kicked out, thrusting his cumbersome body weight up through the cold green depths. Panic gripped him, for the surface did not yield. Rock or ice, he could not tell, as desperate for air he flew at it with the gauntlet-clad fist, ramming it with all the force that he could muster. It stretched like thick green skin across the water and as his fist met it, Eider felt the slimy texture give. With the force of the full blow it tore apart and he surfaced, spluttering as the warm air filled his spent lungs.

Treading water he looked about him, confused by the sight. The barrier that had kept him from light and air had been the flat green leaves of giant water-lilies, the beauty of their blossoms spreading the blue-green water all about him. He stretched to touch their delicate petals, but at that moment the lilt of gentle laughter caught his ears and he glanced up, his black eyes wide with wonder.

She reposed naked upon an island of lily-leaves, her stature that of a young child, slender legs caught up beneath her chin, her long brown tresses tucked behind her pointed ears. Moth-like wings fanned out at her shoulders, their delicate gossamer stretched between slim veins and joints in a rainbow of colours. As she flexed in the warmth, the intricate designs ebbed and a low humming patterned the still air with mesmeric rhythms.

Eider watched her intently, afraid to move in case he frightened her away.

Her skin shone like silk, yellow in hue and marbled green. Her nut-shaped head bore a smiling face and as her laughter rippled on the air, tiny teeth showed silver, their sharp points matching those of her ears. She watched Eider with slanted eyes that glinted like the blue-black fruit of blackberries. There was a wantonness about her demeanour and as Eider swam towards her, she fell onto her back, covering her small, firm breasts with coy hands. Her wings spread flat, she kicked her tiny feet, splashing water in his face as she laughed on. Bemused, Eider reached for her, then hesitated as the sound of twin-laughter echoed at his back.

At the water's edge, two nymph-brethren stood, giggling at his plight. Sisters in face and stature with large wild eyes, the taller had golden hair, its fine strands decorated with lily blossoms. Her wings were pale pink gossamer, shaded green-mauve and interlaced with purple veins, whilst her skin was stippled green and pink from the webbing of her toes to the webbing of her pointed fingers. Her sister's hair was auburn, her slight body draped in the gloss of lily leaves whilst the tracery on her red-mauve wings shifted from circles to spirals in the ever-changing light. With a child-like smile she held a lily blossom out to him and Eider reached to take it. He breathed in its heavy perfume and in moments the calm pool was alive with the harmony of tiny voices as they chanted their mysterious song of welcome.

Enchanted by both sight and sound, Eider felt his muscles relax and giving in to the warm waters, he drifted on among the gentle ripples. Closing his eyes, he was unaware of the nymphs as they slid silently into the pool closing in upon him as the water lapped at his skin. Soon they were all about him and Eider gave a sudden gasp as he felt them flocking to his side. They frolicked like wayward children, splashing him with their darting hands and feet, their high-pitched giggles filling the air as he twisted and turned to escape their playful taunts. Soon their wings were buzzing on the thin air as they laughed and sported, pulling him this way and that, in an effort to remove his clothes. Eider protested weakly, feeling their sharp fingers work on him with unrelenting speed, finding every sensitive spot of his anatomy, forcing laughter from him though he gasped for air and fumed at them, begging them to halt their play.

Soon they were dragging him down to the cool green depths, nibbling at his unprotected skin with needle-sharp teeth. They twisted his hair, pulling silk-black strands out at the roots, until certain that he ached all over with their torments, they hauled him to the surface.

Eider gasped for air and swam for the bank, his body a riot of pleasures and agonies as one by one they overcame him, their rose-bud lips turned down in sardonic play. Soon sharp fingernails had drawn blood from his chest and thighs, while the pointed teeth chewed at the leather thong of the gauntlet about his hand. The nymphs turned pale with rage when the glove did not submit, kicking the water into a foaming mass. Desperate to be free of them, Eider flailed the water but the torments stopped abruptly. The pool had suddenly calmed and he found himself floating free. Weak and trembling, he cleared his eyes of the water veil, seeing other woodland creatures pushing towards him through the reeds.

These two were older in face and figure. Wood nymphs with skin of yellow ochre mottled mauve. Their brown hair fell to sagging breasts, their large nipples having the colour and soft texture of fungi. They moved towards Eider, their gaze unflinching as they gripped him fast within their twiggy fingers, and though he tried to struggle free, his body-weight floated with them to the water's edge. Above he saw brown woodfolk gathered on the bank, their dour faces intent upon his progress. Eider's heart raced with fear, the flattened noses and coarse features revealed them as spriggans, the lowest and most cruel of woodland creatures.

Helplessly he drifted in their direction, feeling his arms seized from above as they hauled him onto the grassy bank. Though he struggled against the muscular legs and wart-marked hands, he found himself dragged on through the twitchgrass. Grass spores rose about him in yellow clouds and looking up Eider saw the strong backs of the spriggan youths who gripped him fast. Heads bent low, their stocky bodies bore his full weight as they dragged him on through the lines of onlookers. Almost senseless, Eider felt himself raised high into the air and passed, like an effigy, along endless queues of woodland brethren to the heart of the clearing. Drifting in and out of consciousness, he was aware of the steady rhythm of clasping hands, and then of the burnished flames of a great pyre.

'I am to be burned alive?' the thought hit him like a blow and as his head began to spin he felt the breath squeezed from his lungs as he fell into unconsciousness once again.

165

—— 16 ——

He opened his eyes to pitch blackness, not certain if he still slept. With his hands he explored the confines of the narrow cell and trembled against the mildewed walls. Shafts of amber light flickered through the door slats and Eider climbed to his feet, his fingers searching for the latch. Both lock and bolt were without and he could not bring his strength to bear upon the heavy door. He felt the rough back of the gauntlet and clenching his right hand into a fist, he beat at the stout wood but it remained unmoved beneath his efforts. In a rush of fury he threw himself at it but it did not give and he slid its damp length to the floor.

'I am Eider!' he cried out against the dark. 'True King of Rhye!' His protests echoed in the cell, old cries merging with new until his throat grew hoarse with effort. As his shouting ebbed away, he ran trembling fingers over the studded gauntlet. 'Amulet of power,' he pleaded, 'do not desert me now.'

Even as he spoke the smell of incense seeped to him on the heavy air and soon the flickering torchlight grew brighter between the door slats. At the echo of footfall, Eider backed away from the door, his body tensing with the sliding of the aged bolts. In a blaze of bronze light stood the spriggans and Eider rushed at them gallantly. They seized him with cruel delight, seeing in his rage an opportunity to taunt and to abuse him as they went about their allotted tasks.

'What place is this?' Eider demanded as they man-handled him. 'What is happening?' His frantic questions went unanswered as the spriggans jeered, fingering him until he wept bitter tears unable to withstand, yet fearing he may have their cruel sport to endure forever!

Within the dappled light, time had stilled as his tormentors bathed him in heady perfumes, dried him with rush fans and then daubed him with the vibrant colours and designs of their clan. On and on they toiled, singing their scratchy songs of magic oils and sugar-coatings until their work was done. Then the bright-eyed nymphs trod softly through the dark, laden with pots of colour and brushes made of squirrel hair. 'Black on every fingernail! Black on every toe!' they sang, their busy brushes dipping into the gleaming pitch. 'On, on, our work is only just begun!' their high-pitched voices weaved amid the gruff spriggan tones as they varnished every fingernail and toenail with the blackest dye. This done, they showered his silken hair with poppy dust and lined his almond-shaped eyes with kohl. 'Shimmer him and shine him! Shimmer him and shine!' they sang, dusting eyelids and cheek bones with glittering gem dust. Satisfied, they raised him to his feet before a giant salver, its lustre providing a reflecting plane in which to view their crafts-manship.

Before it, Eider gave a stifled gasp, for he could neither speak nor move beneath the weight of silver and gold lacquers. He felt himself flood with joy and repulsion. Gem dust lay heavy on his eyelids lowering them in a sultry gaze, and the painted red of his lips folded now like rose petals over the pearl-white of his teeth.

The spriggans offered gummy smiles at the sight of their handiwork, ushering in the chattering nymphs who draped their captive in vestments of silk black. Eider noted the gown's edge, embroidered with rippling flames which leapt upward in bold red and gold across his chest. Soon necklets draped his throat as chains of majesty, while at his wrist and ankles, gaudy spangles were clasped tight. Eider shuddered. Was this finery the ritual prepar-ation for his death? Caught in the salver's reflection he saw the gauntlet tight-wrapped about his hand, strong and immovable. His heart gave silent thanks that it remained so.

The spriggans moved in upon him, carrying him like a silken doll up the crumbling steps to where his fate awaited. The air above hung with smoke and the fumes of incense. Now the sky was black matt and so was the clearing, save for the violent dance of the blazing pyre at its heart. The shock of the firelight and ferocious heat took Eider's breath and he stumbled as his captors set him down upon the stone floor of the ruin. There he was forced to wait, surrounded by the hollow shell of the edifice. Directly before him the steps descended to the clearing and the leaping fire where the busy woodland creatures haggled over cauldrons and crackling spits, pouring glistening liquids into regiments of pewter goblets.

'A funeral feast!' Eider whispered beneath his breath, yet the sudden, savage silence drew him back from thought. He could not turn quickly beneath the weight of his adornments and so glanced left then right to determine the reason for the deathly quiet. It was then that he caught the flicker of torchlight in the corner of his eye. The light grew, rippling in long shadows across the walls of the edifice as two, four, then six swarthy goblins clambered like apes from the darkness below. In the magenta light these companions to the dead were hideous and Eider cringed as they scuttled past him on both sides, their fire-filled eyes intent upon the crackling pyre. They moved in solemn procession down the crumbling steps of the edifice towards the hypnotic glow. Some carried torches, others incense sticks as together they chanted their dirge-like song, their hoarse voices joined in one continual prayer.

Now the nymphs circled the lily pool, their vampire fangs glistening as they chanted their measured replies, whilst the spriggans too gave voice to song, and soon the clearing was a cacophony of musical enchantment as their endless lines marched single file to form a semi-circle about the pyre.

Eider's heart leapt at sight and sound of flapping wingskin. From the unburned apex of the pyre sprang a riot of bats and with their manic flight the black of the sky intensified. Now the pulsing energy of the fire dominated the clearing, and soon Eider's gaze was riveted upon its dancing patterns as they rippled and interlaced in a myriad of images. Slowly the mesh of lines and spirals began to merge until a fully formed figure writhed at the white hot core of the flames. Its limbs, like charred sticks, flailed the air, the bony forearms wielding a molten rod amid the hot coals.

Eider swallowed hard, closing his sweat-veiled eyes against the aweful vision, he swore beneath his breath – the torments of this place had warped his mind! Now he was lost forever! His ears rang anew as every creature gave voice to the vision: 'Here comes the Black Queen, dancing in the pyre!' The spriggans sank to their knees, their chant accelerating to a fever pitch. 'Fie! Foe! The Black Queen!' they sang on, their foreheads meeting the mossy ground in homage.

Eider felt compelled to look once more upon the fiery spectacle where now the writhing shape was more distinct. At once male and female, the figure was shrouded in the flowing black silk of a voluminous cloak. Eider shuddered. Was he at last in the presence of that which had evaded him for so long?

Now he could see the head, sheathed in a tight black cowl which fanned out at the nape of the neck to frame the shifting features of the face. Eider winced, for the skin of the visage was soft as tallow, dripping and congealing in the heat. Then, at last, the hooked nose took shape and the sharp cheekbones set to form dark hollows above the strong and pointed jawline. Within deep sockets, the eyes flickered like green globes floating as separate moons in liquid silver. As the flames sprang to the leafy canopy the thin scarlet lips curled back, showing an ivory grille of pointed teeth which railed the pitch-black gash of the mouth. With a sudden cry the Black Queen leapt from her pyre, the bone white arms attacking the smoke-filled air.

The spriggan guards tightened their grip on Eider as their monarch brought the iron rod down hard upon the coals, her unintelligible curses scattering with hot cinders to the jet sky. At the rapping of the rod on the slate grey steps, spriggan, goblin, nymph and all, ran helter-skelter to their allotted tasks, while the monstrous Queen turned about, halting on the first step of the edifice as the ape-goblins took up the endless train of her cloak.

Eider trembled as she made her voluptuous ascent towards him. His mouth was dry with panic. Perhaps his death would come quickly. Yet, surely such an elaborate trap was meant for more than this cruel sport?

Her sticky body heat wafted to him as she drew close, red lips rippling as she spoke: 'So . . . ? Here is a King?' she breathed warm and acrid breath into his face.

Eider rallied. 'I am Eider!' he exclaimed into the fiendish face. 'True heir to the throne of Rhye!'

The scarlet mouth twisted in a spike-filled grin as the Black Queen strutted to and fro before him, tossing the folds of her capacious cloak and cackling her crude laughter to the night sky. When the laughter ceased, she drew close to him again, twisting strands of his midnight hair around the tip of her taloned finger. Eider saw the endless cloak gleam with highlights of ink blue and mauve as she swept from him towards the ivy-clad throne at his back. As she seated herself, the spriggan guards led Eider across the platform to stand directly before her. At their Queen's command they unclasped his robes, leering as billowing silks fell about his ankles. Now he stood naked of all but the delicate designs of bodypaint, his limbs a network of figured spirals and glittering dust, of jewels and glamorous enchantments.

The Black Queen's gaze was impassive as she appraised his gaudy beauty. She sighed, pleased that his ebony eyes, so heavy with gem-dust, were lowered in respectful homage to her majesty. Rising from her throne, she extended the black talons. 'Now,' she breathed. 'My little King shall reign!' She reached to touch him and Eider closed his eyes as she explored him, drawing a sharp fingernail from his nipple to the inside of his thigh. He groaned, meeting her hunter's gaze as she breathed her evil passion into his face. Eider gasped

170

beneath her sadistic touch, her caresses more potent than any the nymphs had laid upon him, the danger of her fangs and talons more fearsome to him than theirs. He had begun to sweat, for repulsive as she was, he knew he must fight to keep grip upon his senses or be forever lost to her unseelie realm.

'I am Eider!' he swore through gritted teeth, desperate not to submit.

The Black Queen smiled sweet poison, her attention drawn by the gleam of the gauntlet about his hand. She took up his hand in her spectral fingers and stroked the rough gems. 'Fine embellishments,' she oozed. 'A trophy of some . . . little war?'

Eider caught his breath as she toyed with the leather thong and prayed that it would not be undone. The gauntlet did not yield.

'It matters not!' she gave a hollow laugh as her greed for his beauty overcame her and she covered him with kisses from waist to neck.

Eider tightened. 'I . . . am . . . Eider,' he gasped beneath his breath, desperate to maintain control as she forced him to his knees. 'True King of . . . Rhye,' he groaned as his sweat-streaked face was smothered by the heat of her body. 'In search . . . of a . . . vision,' he whispered.

'Vision?' the Black Queen purred, pressing her waxen thighs against his lips.

Eider moaned, his senses strained to breaking point as she scraped the dye-paint from his back with eager talons. 'The cloak,' he managed through the pain.

'Ah!' the Black Queen murmured into his ear. 'My little King would have his Cloak of Light?' she lifted his midnight hair as a skein of silk.

Eider clenched his teeth expecting pain, but the deadly nails stroked the nape of his neck gently.

'Well then . . . ' she oozed. 'He shall have it!' Her back arched as she encircled him, the grille of her teeth barred as she spread the cloak out before him. 'Behold! Your cloak!' she laughed hysterically. 'Behold . . . your rightful

Queen!' she commanded, straddling him. Her green eyes grew wild. 'And Rhye?' she spat. 'You shall never see it!'

Entwined in the infinite black folds, Eider's heart raced within the silken dark and he fell onto his back, feeling her bear down upon him, her writhing form pulsing in rhythmic spasm. Voraciously she fed upon his nakedness, fondling then wounding him, her appetite demanding all strength and vigour from him. She screamed with sudden delight as finally he submitted to her will, enslaved by her iron embrace, the senses of his body lost in the frenzy of her heat.

In his head the constant pounding of his own heart, the rise and fall of the spriggan's chant, the screech of violent ecstasy. Eider saw her throw back her head, the ivory grille clenched in hatred of him and delight. In the moment of climax their eyes met, her teeth showing in a cruel grin. 'Now 'tis done!' she gasped. 'Now shall he never be free of Bethalon! Nor of me!'

Drowned in exhaustion, Eider fell back upon the velvet moss as the Black Queen rose above him, her silken cloak billowing as she strutted back and forth over his lifeless body.

When he awoke, the clearing was quiet, save for the nymph song drifting upward from the lily pool. Eider sat up, seeing the ivy-covered throne where the Black Queen preened before the giant salver. In silence he watched her. He had been lured here by this ink black vision, by the very trim of that cloak she wore. Yet, had she not called it a Cloak of Light? His thoughts were riveted as her wild eyes met his. In one motion she swept away the reflecting silver and raised in its place a goblet. 'To my King!' she cried, and the creatures of her domain returned her victorious toast.

'To our Queen! Her King! And All-Power!'

Straightening her proud back, the monstrous Queen swept towards Eider, pressing a wine-filled goblet into his gauntlet-clad hand. Her eyes glinted as she rapped the iron rod upon the flagstones. Their wedding feast had begun!

In the beat of a bat's wing, the clearing was a giddy chaos of sound and colour, and Eider was ordered to his knees before his demon Queen who force fed him upon sweets and kisses. As their goblets met, she glanced at the gauntlet again and bid Eider drink with her in celebration of their bond. Though he held the goblet to his lips, he took none of the syrup wine it contained. The Black Queen's pointed teeth meshed in a grin of malign content as she bid her spriggan youths make a couch for him at her side. As they worked in the shadow of her throne, the revelry of her subjects grew into hysterical abandon. Eider watched all, his thoughts colliding.

'To our Queen, her King, and All-Power ...' he murmured to himself and frowned. 'The cloak gives her power, and yet is it incomplete?' His musings were interrupted as the spriggans lifted him in their strong arms and carried him to the couch where the Black Queen had him repose. No sooner was he at her side than she pampered and entwined him, cooing into his ear then brushing the length of his body with her scarlet lips.

'My subjects,' she whispered into his ear. 'All are yours.' Her pointed teeth nibbled at his earlobe. 'My riches ... yours too.' She licked his sweat-streaked neck. 'Long have we awaited you,' she oozed her poison breath. 'Bethalon needs a bad boy for a King!'

Eider raised the gauntlet-clad hand, warding off her waxen features and as the glove passed before her throat he saw its gemstones flash, saw her lips curl back in a snarl. He looked into her narrowed gaze and saw again the green eyes of the she-wolf! She grinned at him sensing the moment of recognition.

Eider turned away. 'This demon Queen craves All-Power,' his mind reeled with the ends and beginnings of thought. 'Yet the cloak cannot convey it ... without ... me!'

The sudden realisation sickened his heart and he groaned as she panted above him and he fell victim to her passion once again. As black silk enveloped him he fought to keep his thoughts fixed upon the glittering

173

towers of Rhye. The Black Queen's dark enchantments made no match for their soaring white heights and as his painted lips shuttered against her kisses, his head rang with the promise of his forefathers: 'Pledged forever to deliver Light and the gift of love and joy!' his mouth trembled as he tried to remember the ancient chant taught to him as a child, but he could do no more than groan in the baneful Queen's embrace. He gasped ... this Queen knew not of love, no ray of light or joy had ever entered this unseelie place, yet even as he felt disgust her torments forced him to enjoy her once again.

Soon the scarlet mouth drooled in delirious ecstasy and the eyes of the she-wolf flashed sadistic delight. As she soared to her climax, Eider struggled to keep his heart true, his mind's eye fixed upon Rhye's Ancients and their promise to protect their chosen one from Dark. 'Deliver ... Light!' he cried out at last and through the curtain of his wet hair he saw the cruel lips of his captor twist in sudden spite.

'Think not of it, my little King!' she commanded, smoothing his brow. 'Sleep again, take rest, for my King's days and nights shall be timeless! His duties rigorous and unending!'

'Never your King!' Eider cried out, clenching the gauntlet into a fist, his eyes smouldering with rebellion.

At his show of defiance the Black Queen cackled her contempt. 'Too late! The cloak is mine and now the glove!' she sang it loud and long as she strutted about his prostrate form. 'The little King is mine! And soon, so shall his kingdom be!' She brought the rod of iron crashing down, sparks showering from the granite steps. Eider flinched as one rap, then two and three silenced her revelling creatures until every face was turned upon their snarling monarch. 'The Kingdom is mine!' she screeched. 'Soon, Triad power ... then All-Power will be in the hands of the unseelie!'

Eider's eyes flashed as he watched her rally her subjects into a state of noisy hysteria. 'I curse with my left hand! I bless with my right!' she crowed, raising her arms as her creatures cheered her every dictate. 'I am King of Darkness and Queen of the Night!' The rhythm of her chant spread through the clearing as her obedient servants beat frenetic time with hand and goblet. 'Mine is the power!' she shrieked, thrusting one emphatic forefinger towards the gathering. 'March on with the Black Queen!'

The revellers leapt to their feet, marching in time to the rhythm of her curse and raising their frenzied voices in screams of wild delight. With a barbed grin she turned to Eider, her face made more terrible by the delirium of power, her eyes dazzling green enchantments into his dark gaze until he was numbed by their intensity. She spread out the silken black of the cloak, pacing the granite flagstones to parade before him like a peacock, her demented cries proclaiming victory as Eider fell at her feet in submission. She crowed her final triumph. 'See him kneel! He who held All-Power gives it to me!'

Eider crouched before her, feeling her hypnotic power course through him, yet still he clung to reason, watching with hooded eyes as she preened before her subjects. 'Yes, my queen,' he whispered as his thoughts unlocked. 'Here lies your strength.' He watched her fold and unfold the silk of the cloak like black wings. 'Yet here too lies your greatest weakness!' the faintest flicker of a smile played about his lips. Slowly he straightened his back, his hands clasped together in supplication. 'My life is in your hands,' he vowed into her hateful countenance. 'I shall foe and I shall fie!'

Her eyes smouldered as she drew him to her, lifting up his face with the tip of a single black nail. Eider lowered his eyes. 'I am what you make me. I am as you please,' he whispered, feigning submission as he kissed the hem of her cloak. 'I am your bad boy, forever to march in your wake!'

The demon Queen shivered with delight as he spoke, then heaving in a gasp of air she shrieked her victory to the highest branches. As she raised Eider to his feet, her entourage cheered lustily, their frenetic dance begun.

With the rod she bade him walk with her, and arms entwined they descended the steps of the edifice towards the raging pyre.

'Marching in their style! The evil and the royal!' chanted the spriggan youths as they followed in the footsteps of their monarch around the full perimeter of the clearing. 'Fie foe! The Black Queen!' her loyal creatures sang entranced. 'She cheats and she lies, she is ever in disguise!'

Edging closer to the fire, the Black Queen's visage began to glow with the heat and the flush of triumph. Demurely she rested the ebony claws upon Eider's leathered fist and bade him walk with her into the roaring flames. Soon their gaudy procession had encircled the leaping fire, and as they moved towards it Eider felt its supernatural heat. The churning flames set every gem in his glittering robes sparkling in its light, and he watched intently as the gauntlet began to pulse anew. About him the chanting crowd marched blindly on, heedless of the blistering heat, their pace quickening as they drew closer to the pyre.

Eider's senses screamed panic, but as he gasped for air the Black Queen thrust the rod of her majesty into his grip, bidding him beat time with the dance as she shrieked forth her curses. Eider bowed reverently, knowing her trust in his subjugation was misplaced. He raised the rod as he was bid, watching on incredulous as she sang on.

'Come, dance to Lucifer! In time with the song! To Hell with all of you! Now be gone!' Her words wove circles on the smoky air as every creature joined his hand to another's and stepped closer to the fire, caught in the rhythm of the dance.

Eider's body tightened as he felt the fire scorch his skin, while at his side the Black Queen swooned, taking pleasure from the heat as she lead him on to the curtain of blistering flame. 'Now is time to be gone!' she cried, throwing back her head in ecstatic worship of pyral demons.

'Forever!' cried the spriggans, as Eider gritted his teeth against the terrible heat.

'Forever!' cried the water nymphs, as he felt himself grow dizzy with the spinning rhythm of the dance.

'Forever!' cried the ape-goblins, as he clutched the jet black hem of the Black Queen's treasured cloak.

'Forever!' he cried aloud as the leathered fingers of his right hand fused about the rod and his body jolted abruptly. With a violent twist the rod became a manic spindle in the gauntlet's grip, reeling the cloak's vast train about his outstretched arm. Entranced, the Black Queen danced on towards the welcoming flames, until she felt the cloak ripped from her shoulders like the tearing of her skin. Her siren screams shattered the darkness and Eider clenched his teeth against its deafening pitch, feeling the rod propelled from his grip with a rush of gauntlet power. He saw the iron shaft fly straight and true, saw the tallow features contort and accuse, saw the rod embed itself in her demon heart! On impact the clearing blazed with a fountain of scarlet light, the raging heat blistered his cheekbones and erased his sight.

A searing flash, and the bloody corona rose up above the tree towers; the wizard halted and turned to meet the elfin's frown. 'What think you?' he asked.

Regor watched until the blaze of colour settled to vermilion, its fiery palette washing purple the gaunt trees and bracken-ferns. ''Tis fire,' he declared with a cursory sniff.

The mortal shook his head. 'Nay, yet neither is it sunset, we have not journeyed so far.'

Mystified, they watched the veil of colours rise and ripple, ebbing from mauve to delicate pink in the warm upper air, then finally to serene blue. A refreshing breeze had stirred about them, speeding away the mists and cleansing the sullied atmosphere.

Nairb started at the flap of wings; now there was birdsong on the wind and through the trees the purity of daylight seeped. He looked about him, the tangled undergrowth had given way to the saffron of crocuses, their gentle fragrance spilling out upon the crisp air.

Lehon was confounded. 'Spring has come to this strange place,' he exclaimed as they resumed their pace.

The vicious briars and bramble webs had shrunk away to reveal a narrow track to the forest's heart. They followed its well-marked line, marvelling at the fecundity of the flora as they moved effortlessly through tender grasses and flowering shrubs. Ahead, the dew-draped tangle of gossamer and lone petals hung from curved boughs as an intricate woodland tapestry.

'Be wary,' Lehon warned as the wizard made to part the veil.

Nairb's features creased in a tender smile and with silent gesture he bid the others look with him upon the scene: at the heart of the moss-strewn clearing Zephyr whinnied and rhythmically shook her ivory mane. Eider had woken. Gone the crumbling edifice of Dark. Gone the demon Queen. Gone her curses and vile perversions. Gone her courtiers and unseelie fire. All gone ... 'Forever!' Eider whispered the words of the distant dream.

About him the bright daylight streamed in upon the folds of silk clasped tightly in his hand. At sight of the unseelie trophy his keen eyes flashed, for no longer was the cloak an ink-black raiment of the Dark, but fell about him as a cascade of dazzling colour, of delicate tracery and silvered thread, and as shafts of sunlight caught its smooth surface, the light refracted as a magnificent rainbow. The pulse of an ancient weave had bestowed light and new life upon this darkbound place. At last Bethalon was free and the forest rang with Nature's joy. All gone the mouldering air and spike-filled tangle, in its place warm sunlight and spring-woken blooms.

Eider breathed in the richness of cleansed earth, watched jays fly in colourful display among the leafy boughs. His heart soared with them as he knelt to offer homage to the gods. He was safe, he and the ancient Cloak of Light. From its silken folds a rainbow aura broke forth, spreading upward to crown Bethalon in a shimmering arch of colour.

Regor caught his breath. 'The dark forest returned to life . . .' he stammered.

'By a Cloak of Light,' Nairb finished with a smile.

Eider turned at the sound of familiar voices and seeing the wizard, he stood to his feet, the dazzling silk held out to him.

Nairb bowed low in accordance with the Lore. 'The triumph of Light over Dark,' he announced reverently. 'The beauty of this unhallowed place freed by Triad power.' He clasped Eider to him. 'Be assured, Nature shall repay its debt.' He gently kissed the silken trim, whispering loric mantras as he draped the cloak about Eider's straight shoulders. As the wizard spoke, so the wounds inflicted on Eider's body were healed, their dark scars erased and health and vigour returned to him.

'Friend!' Regor cried as he and the mortal stepped into the light.

Eider strode to meet them, his hand extended in greeting.

'There was no forest made could keep my elfin shadow from your side,' Regor grinned grasping Eider's fist.

Eider's smile turned to a sigh of relief. 'Through all the days and nights, I thought myself lost forever to this place.'

'Forever?' Lehon shook his head. 'Why friend, you were gone but moments from our sight.'

Eider turned to the wizard in disbelief.

'It is so,' Nairb agreed with a secret smile.

Frost of autumn seeped across the valley floor, while on the meadow slopes the straggling line of peasants drove livestock to winter grazing. Edging the grey stone road on either side, the lowland village lay, its thatched roofs spiked with frost, its squat chimneys sending up spirals of grey smoke.

Within the dwellings there were voices, and the sounds of cluttered industry. Here, the icy air was warmed by the glow of peat fires, here the clay ovens filled the rooms with the smell of new-baked bread. From each window the washing lines of bunting were stretched, while upon the cobbled yards the Blacksmith beat time for the Woodman's axe. In their company the Hedger worked his twigs and boughs, whistling as he went about his task.

Celebrations were at hand, for this was a day of toasts and blessings, of prayers and litanies. A day of welcome return! Soon the lanes were filled with the smell of roast meat, of barley bread and spiced wine. With the bell of middle-day every man, woman and child jostled into the narrow streets, mingled songs and laughter rising to a happy chaos as they watched for sign of movement far away on the rough stone road.

The cry went up, and all eyes followed the thrust of the steady finger to the crest of the gentle hillock.

Atop the steep, Eider drew Zephyr to a halt, seeing the brightly decked village below and the clamour of people at its boundary hedge. 'A gathering of sorts?' he frowned as Lehon and Regor drew alongside.

'They welcome us,' Nairb smiled.

'Do they?' Regor scowled, the azure eyes narrowing.

'We cannot be sure,' Lehon warned. 'Stay close.' He led them forward at slow pace towards the cobbled trackway. Once upon its gentle gradient, he gave reassurance. 'They bear no arms!'

'Some feast day perhaps?' Nairb offered.

Regor grinned into the solemn face. 'If that is so, wizard, we are blessed with plenty!' he clicked his tongue and his steed moved on.

'Be wary!' Lehon frowned, and the three companions drew close about the white mare as they trod the grey stone to the village square. But they did not get so far, for no sooner had they passed the thorn hedge boundary than they were surrounded by peasant folk. Yet, though happy faces beamed up at them, and eyes were lit with joy, no sound was made. It was with awe that the simple folk watched the strangers' uneasy progress. Eider clutched the sword-hilt with a clammy palm, knowing Lehon and Regor did the same, until from the narrow windows, flowers showered down upon them.

'Hail! Heroes of Bethalon!' someone cried and soon riders and horses were bedecked with blooms.

Eider's dark eyes widened with surprise and his weary face spread with a smile. The people cheered his acceptance of their tributes, the air vibrant with shouts and cheers, with songs of welcoming and joy. Eider turned his laughing face to the wizad, 'What is happening?'

'It is welcome indeed!' Nairb smiled.

Regor said nothing, still watching close for any sudden or unexpected move.

'Keep close!' Lehon urged them, but even as he spoke the crowd pressed in on them forcing the horses to a halt. Eider reassured Zephyr as she whinnied low, yet she did not falter or panic as her master was lifted from her back and set upon the strong shoulders of the menfolk.

Soon Regor, Lehon and Nairb were seated in the same manner high above the singing crowd as the noisy procession wound away through every narow lane and village alleyway. Finally, adorned with gifts and flowers, the bemused guests were brought to rest before the open door of the inn.

There, the head-man of the village waited, a red-faced

innkeeper at his side. As Eider moved towards them, the innkeeper took up a great silver cup full to the brim with mulled wine. The head-man took it from him with a solemn bow and the crowd fell silent as he spoke: 'All hail and welcome, heroes of Bethalon! Our deliverers from Dark!' This said, he raised the shining cup aloft.

Aware of the seriousness of the man's deeds Eider took the cup with the reverence due to ancient ritual. Regor moved to give warning as Eider raised the cup to his lips, but the wizard prevented him, his peaceful expression giving silent reassurance and bidding him to give these good people no offence.

The crowd watched Eider drink from the cup, then pass it on to the wizard. Nairb raised his eyes to the skies, then, having supped, he passed the cup to the elfin. Regor held the cup in both hands, unsure, then copying the reverence of Eider and the wizard, he too drank, passing the cup on to the mortal. From Lehon the cup was passed to every person in the crowd until, as the last one wet his lips, a great cheer rose up.

As the head-man moved up to him, Eider extended his strong hand in friendship, yet his swarthy face flushed with surprise as the good man knelt in homage to kiss the gauntlet-clad fingers. 'Welcome, sire!' he said simply. 'To you, and to your brave company. I am Joff, and this, our proud innkeeper.'

Eider clasped the man's shoulders, 'Rise up, Joff,' he said taking the man's hand then in friendship. 'My company and I are honoured by these your words and deeds.'

The keeper of the inn bowed, making way for them, 'Enter, sire! You and all!'

Once within, Regor's fears vanished, his mischievous eyes grown wide with relish, for they were seated before a long bench decked with roasted meats, cakes, fruits and bread, and the finest of berry wines!

The innkeeper clapped his rough hands, and tankards were filled. Then, with the swift thump of a leather-clad foot on the wooden floor the happy fiddlers struck up their tune, setting the brim-full cups in circulation. Soon all within the ale-house, and without, ate and drank their fill. They danced and sang and raised their cups, gathering about the long bench to hear the stranger's talk of travel and adventures far beyond their understanding.

'Ogres!' Regor's eyes narrowed as the faces of his audience paled at the word. 'Both so tall ... they dwarfed the very peaks!' The elfin brow creased as his voice dropped to a whisper. 'Imagine ... one great eye ... focused in your direction!' he shoved a strong forefinger at one of the young men at his side. 'Imagine,' he said again, his trickster's eyes darting from face to face as he spread his upturned palm upon the wood, 'a hand ... so big your bones be crushed to dust!' The silent listeners winced as the elfin closed his hand in a fist.

'Regor!' Eider chided quietly from the other end of the table, but the elfin straightened his shoulders as he took fresh breath.

'Yet did we flee?' he smirked into the awestruck faces. 'We did not! Though my life was almost lost, I drew my dagger ...'

'Regor!' Eider warned again. Yet went unnoticed as the elfin submerged his listeners in the climax of his tale, '... and did plunge it into the brute! Thus!' Regor pointed to the centre of his forehead, a grin of triumph spreading across his oval face. The listeners gasped as one body, then their wonder turned to applause and Regor flushed, his slight shoulders soon aching beneath the slap of appreciative hands.

Eider shook his head in mirthful disapproval as he turned to the beaming innkeeper. 'Friend, your wines are potent stuff and make real the visions of the mind's eye!' he smiled.

The innkeeper laughed, 'Aye ... but sire, all here know the bravery of your deeds!' The look upon the goodly face was one of deep respect and awe and as he turned to refill the tankards Eider drew the wizard to him.

'It seems they think us heroes!' he smiled, clearly elated at the knowledge.

Lehon leaned forward between them, 'Aye, and many more may know of us,' he nodded. 'Reputation has proceeded us far!'

'Much more than that, my friends,' Nairb whispered to himself as Joff moved towards them through the noisy revellers.

With his arrival the elfin's tales ended abruptly, and the hectic chatter fell to whispers as room was made for him at the long bench. In his hand he held a silver carafe, and Eider watched as he refilled each man's cup. The dark eyes met the happy face as he took his cup. 'Good Joff,' Eider smiled, 'grant tolerance for elfin excess,' he nodded to Regor with a weary shrug.

The head-man raised both hands. 'Sire, 'tis well known elfin-kind do revel in the telling of the tale!' he laughed into Eider's apologetic face. At his words the company laughed aloud and Regor gave a sheepish wink as he raised the full cup to his lips and drank heartily.

Joff turned back to Eider with a frown, 'Every one of us knows fear of ogres! Some even go in search! Yet Bethalon . . .' the grey head shook in woeful recollection. 'Not even our bravest lads would enter there!' As Joff spoke sudden hush spread round the room, and Eider became aware that all eyes and ears were intent upon their talk.

'Dark of evil spread out from Rhye like a tangled web . . .' Joff exclaimed at last.

As the man talked Regor cast Lehon a look. 'Rhye, he said "Rhye"!' he whispered into the mortal's ear. But Lehon only waved him into silence, so intent was he on the head-man's speech.

'. . . black winds flew! Acid waters tainted all, withering man and beast alike!' Joff's gnarled hands whitened about his cup, his eyes filled with long-held grief. 'Long have we struggled to survive in its grip, nothing thriving save the black heart of Bethalon!' The sallow face scanned Eider's youthful countenance. 'Your time has seemed long in the coming, but now 'tis here . . .' the thin lips drew back in a trembling smile, '. . . and the spell of Bethalon is gone like a dream of old Mab's!' Joff snapped his fingers, his eyes alight with joy. 'Banished by your magic hand!'

The company cried, 'Aye!' at the head-man's words.

Eider looked at his gauntlet-clad fist. 'Magic hand?' he breathed, inspecting its leather contours and gem-studded back as if for the first time.

Joff drank deeply of his cup. ''Twas the prophecy!' he said. '. . . one passsed to me by my father's tongue.'

Eider watched intently as Joff's big eyes grew distant, as if he read the words upon the smoky air, '. . . he shall come, a shower of light from Bethalon's heart! His magic hand to banish Dark!' Regor shared an anxious look with Lehon as Joff flourished his wasted arm over the colourful array of food and drink, 'Look you sire, your deed released our bonds! See here the produce so long absent from our boards!' The man stood to his feet and raised his cup, 'Ever more, I say, this feast be kept! For he who freed Bethalon supped with us this day!'

Regor cast Lehon a second glance but the mortal had gone. He looked all about the crowd, but could not find him seated in the company. Soon his eyes met Nairb's gentle face but the glazed look in the wizard's eyes only made him more uneasy.

'Look upon it long,' Joff's voice had grown solemn once again, 'for here is the only colour in this land!' He sank back into his seat as if his heart were broken with unending sorrow.

Eider's face became solemn and he touched the man's forearm, 'This is the Kingdom's fate?' he prompted.

Joff's old face was ashen as he met Eider's determined look. 'Sire,' he shook his head, 'we live in shadow of the range . . . many's the rumour reaches us, but no sure truths.'

Eider frowned concern, 'Come, man, tell all to me now,' he urged.

Regor scanned the room once more as movement all

about him set the shuttered lamps aglow and a sallow-faced youth rose to shut the old inn door at their backs. He watched the head-man draw Eider close. ''Tis told us Rhye is lost!' he said. ''Tis told us all colour ran from it with the blood of the seelie line!'

Eider clenched his teeth as Joff spoke on: 'The seven sees were plundered by the Dark Lords, the Kingdom bled dry of all its splendour, or else ...' Joff glanced about him for safety's sake and whispered, '... unseelie hordes did raise it to the ground!' He crossed himself as a token against the dark nature of his words.

Silence fell on all gathered there, and Eider's head ached with the pain of grief. Joff looked to the wizard who gestured for him to continue. ''Tis said some seelie lords remain loyal to the Ancient Lore, though they needs must hold the candle to the devil to live on!' Eider's heart raced as Joff continued, 'Some say they are driven to secret ways, for those who oppose the King can be no match in number or in strength!'

'But the Lore!' Eider cried aloud. 'Does not the Lore withstand him?' he demanded glaring into the wizard's face. Nairb lowered his eyes, and the simple folk drew back, Eider's strange words beyond their comprehension.

Joff shook his head. 'You speak of magic. All trace of that seelie Lore is lost to Zarratt's spells!'

'King Rat!' Eider declared into the honest face. 'Call him vermin, for so he is!' The head-man drew back unnerved by Eider's fury.

Nairb laid a calming hand on Eider's shoulder and stood to address the company. 'Friends, the days and nights that brought us here were arduous indeed,' he breathed. 'I beg you all, take not this show of anger to your hearts.'

The innkeeper wrapped a blanket about Eider's shoulders, 'Nay sire, we know too well the hardships you all endured.'

'Forgiveness,' Joff frowned into Eider's weary face. 'We tax you with tales and spells so old they can be kept yet one more day.' He stood to his feet, 'Take rest sire, and blessings on your company.'

'Tomorrow,' Eider smiled, 'tomorrow we shall talk together long.' Joff bowed low, leading the revellers from the inn, out into the growing twilight.

The innkeeper had rebuilt the fire, poking at it as he set a pot of herb tea on the hot plate. 'Good even' to you both, sire,' he nodded in the lamplight, leaving Eider and Nairb to the glow of the fire and polished wood.

From his place at the end of the table Regor glanced at them seated before the hearth, each content in the other's company sharing their thoughts. Where could Lehon be he wondered, and taking quiet leave of them, he followed the inn's man through the door.

Eider drew the blanket tight about him and turned to the window where Nairb stood watching the deepening indigo of the night sky. 'What do you see?' he asked softly of the wizard.

The steady eyes silently appraised the jewelled sky. 'Orion sets forth,' Nairb announced, carefully rotating the barrel of the small night glass. 'Soon it shall dominate the southern skies.'

Eider rose quietly from his chair and as he moved towards him, the wizard smiled, proffering the telescope. 'A fine instrument,' Eider nodded, following the precision of the wizard's instructions as closely as he could, to find Andromeda set high amid the many shimmering orbs.

'A simple lens, an eye-glass made by father and son together,' Nairb explained, pressing a fingertip against the window glass and tracing the bone-white constellations there. His eyes grew wistful as he watched Eider rotate the lens. 'It has looked upon many things,' he breathed, his voice edged with regret.

Eider handed back the eye-glass, 'And now? What does it see now?' he asked.

Nairb shut the telescope. 'Half-forgotten ghosts,' he said with a strange smile, '. . . times past . . .' his voice trailed off to nothingness.

Eider caught his arm. 'And times to come?' he urged.

Nairb said nothing as he turned back to the cheering fire.

'You have said so little of late,' Eider frowned, '. . . yet, I know that you see more!' He watched as Nairb crouched down before the flames to warm his hands. 'You have looked into the crystal for guidance, haven't you?' he insisted kneeling beside the wizard.

Together they watched the flames leap and dance. Nairb shook the dark curls of his hair, 'The crystal does not consent to daily discourse,' he said, his tone one of quiet reprimand.

Eider swayed uncomfortably, regretting his lack of tact. 'Forgive me,' he said at last, 'I thought only of myself and overlooked the sacredness of the Sight.'

Nairb placed a hand on Eider's arm. 'Look into the fire,' he gestured. 'What do you see?'

His face grew sombre, 'Steel!' he said simply. 'A sword of dazzling steel!' He heard the wizard withhold a gasp. 'There is a gem at the hilt,' he pointed to the heart of the fire. 'Amethyst, I think.'

A slow smile flickered across the wizard's face, though it was short-lived as Eider jumped to his feet. 'But these are only fire pictures!' he cried. 'You know the truth of it. Yet tell it not!' he accused.

Nairb looked up into the anxious face. 'You no longer trust your own Sight?'

'Of course!' Eider's voice faltered as he ran his fingers impatiently through his hair.

'But you would have proof?' Nairb finished solemnly. He stood to his feet and reached for the saddle bags. From these he extracted the velvet cloth wherein the box of Horatious Thor lay. Eider watched with anticipation as the wizard produced several parchments from its depths. He brought out into the light with them, a compass, a sextant and a pentacle. These he set down upon the long bench, carefully flattening out the parchments as he bade Eider draw closer. Upon the parchment, a series of concentric circles were marked. These enclosed the celestial sphere of the constellations, the very one to which Nairb had drawn his attention in the night sky moments before. The wizard pointed to the centre of the circle. 'Pole star,' he said quietly, his fingers tracing clockwise about the nucleus. 'The zodiac, and the Sun's relative location.'

Eider leaned forward for a closer look. Upon the constellations the phases of the Moon were drawn, along with their calculated occurrences.

Nairb pointed to the first of the circles. 'The Moon's arrival in each of the astrological houses,' he explained. Then, moving on to the next circle he added, 'Calculations . . . the day and the date.'

Eider nodded, keen to understand yet baffled by the growing complexity of the chart and Nairb's explanations.

'The longitude of Moon and Sun appear in the third of these circles, and finally, significant aspects and events.' The wizard paused as if allowing the novice to assimilate all that had gone before. Eider gazed at the signs for long moments until Nairb said quietly, 'Friend, it is your chart we view. The time to come.'

Eider paled with the realisation.

The wizard pointed to the series of geometric shapes: square, circle, triangle, pentacle. 'The most powerful aspect is the conjunction,' he whispered, tracing the shape upon the chart. 'When two heavenly bodies fall together on the same degree.' He drew two further shapes. 'Trine, and sextile. These engender harmony and integration.' Finally he drew two circles joined together. 'The opposition, and the square, warn of tension and conflict.'

Eider cast his eyes over the faint shapes, and sought out their position on the parchment, trying to determine for himself the future drawn out before him.

Nairb's slender forefinger pressed upon the chart. 'Soon will you face Mars, conjunct with Venus, and much danger is shown. But here, the full Moon with Aries suggests successful combination.' Eider smiled at Nairb's

189

reassuring words, but the wizard did not stop there. 'Before the new Moon in Scorpio you must gain the Triad, and be ready to wield its power!' Nairb frowned and raised a slender finger in warning, 'Yet you must stay your hand, until the passing of that new Moon, for there is warning here! Irrational acts will bring self-destruction!'

Eider's brow creased in consternation and the wizard pointed at him emphatically. 'On the second day of its passing, the new Moon is conjunct with Mercury and your anger will be raised to a powerful weapon against your enemy!' the Wizard's voice trembled with emotion as he hurried on. 'Magic is loose! Here, Taurids mark your time with meteor-light, and in this phase Triad Power will be yours to command!'

Eider's face broke into a wide grin and he clasped the wizard to him, but Nairb's prediction ended on a sombre note of warning. 'Remember this: if the day be missed, so the Quest be lost! For the third day finds the Moon conjunct with Neptune, then chaos shall demand your life as forfeit!' He lowered his eyes, his head bowed in exhaustion and silent sorrow.

Eider took up the parchment, and silently counted off the days that Nairb had marked upon its surface. Less than twenty dawns would rise before his fate was sealed forever!

Regor descended the shallow steps, and took the straw scattered passage in one stride. Before the crooked beam of the narrow doorway he stopped, bending low to look within. There, in the peaceful glow of the fire, he saw the innkeeper, crouched before the flames. There too was Lehon, seated before the hearth in an old armchair that gleamed and creaked as it rocked him to and fro. The inn's man ignited the long taper at the fire and, rising, lit the oil lamp, smiling as he glimpsed the elfin standing in the doorway, 'Come in, sir, and welcome. Sit yourself down by the warm, while I bid ye both goodnight.'

'Goodnight,' Lehon replied, turning his solemn face to

meet Regor's in the wash of the firelight. He bid the elfin join him as the innkeeper made his way up the creaking staircase.

Regor watched the arc of lamplight vanish to the rooms above and strode towards the mortal and the dancing flames. The fireglow burnished his golden hair to copper as he pulled off his worn boots and stretched his legs out upon the hearth. 'More wine?' he extended the carafe to his quiet comrade.

Lehon smiled into the oval face as Regor refilled his cup. 'Hold!' he gave a short laugh as wine overflowed onto the heated flagstones. 'Do elfins never have their fill?' he chided playfully.

'Never!' Regor grinned replenishing his own cup. 'Take sustenance, say I. Yonder we shall lack many a thing found in plenty here!'

'True enough,' Lehon agreed quietly pulling the worn tobacco pouch from his jerkin. He prepared his clay pipe, conscious of the elfin gaze fixed firmly on his task. 'Help yourself,' he nodded without looking up.

'Blessings, mortal!' Regor grinned, scooping tobacco into the bowl of his own pipe. Moments later the taper was lit and as the smoke rose in sweet blue curls the two of them took their comforts before the bright flames.

'What do you think we shall find?' Regor asked, staring absently at their shadows on the ceiling.

Lehon exhaled the warm smoke. 'Yonder?'

'Aye. Those ranges look colder and more hazardous than crags!' the elfin frowned wriggling his toes in the warmth of the fire.

Lehon nodded agreement as Regor leaned closer across the hearth. 'Mortal, do you know what waits there? Or any other place beyond?'

Lehon drew long upon the pipe. 'I only know what the maps tell.'

Regor gave him a sideways glance. 'Come man, your kin spoke well of it!' Lehon shook his head and Regor fell silent, chewing the pipe-stalk. 'Left to me, we would leave mountains well alone!' he said, shuffling in his chair. 'No kin of mine ever interfered with mountains!' he looked sternly at the silent Lehon. 'Left to me, we would all turn back now!'

The two of them smoked on, Regor glancing at the mortal from time to time until he could remain quiet no longer. 'Would you not go back? With me?' he asked.

Lehon sighed. 'Friend, 'tis not so easy,' he said simply.

'No.' Regor frowned, falling into despondency. He watched Lehon's face flicker in the fireglow, its expression changing from contentment to deep sorrow. 'What is it that you seek?' he asked of him. 'Your kinsman?'

Lehon shrugged. 'Nay, he is long gone.'

'Some remnant of him then?' Regor insisted diplomatically. 'Some news of him?'

'Aye,' Lehon relented with a sad smile, 'something of the kind . . .'

The elfin eyes shone as he turned back to the fire. 'I seek the seelie kingdom,' he said proudly.

'And its treasures!' Lehon added ruefully.

Regor frowned aggrieved by the very suggestion. 'I would see the minstrel gain his rightful place!'

Lehon smiled, but then his brow creased in puzzlement. 'Is Eider the lost Prince?' he asked quietly.

'He has always said 'tis so,' Regor shrugged, snatching a spill from the hearth and relighting his pipe.

'These good folk would have it so,' Lehon nodded, remembering again the look of hope on the faces of the village folk.

'Aye,' Regor agreed.

Lehon's placid gaze met the elfin's look in a thoughtful frown. 'And if he is not?'

Regor shrugged at the question.

'Does he have any proof of it?' Lehon pointed at Regor with the stalk of his pipe.

Regor frowned, then suddenly remembered, 'He has a gem. One he calls "Firestone",' he explained hesitantly.

'You have seen this stone?' the mortal queried.

'Aye,' Regor grinned. 'Big as the palm of your hand it is!' He shook his fist as if he held it there.

192

Lehon drew smoke from his pipe, his mind caught up in thought.

Regor leaned forward across the hearth. 'He will not part with it. Told the wise man it was found with him as a child, by his mortal guardians.'

'Foundling?' Lehon questioned and stated all at once, his eyes still fixed upon the fire.

'Aye,' Regor nodded returning to his pipe.

Lehon turned to look at the elfin. ''Twas wise he kept it.'

'It was?' Regor frowned.

'Aye, the thing could be his proof,' Lehon mused, rocking back and forth in the chair.

Regor's eyes widened at the mortal's reasoning. He gave a weary shrug. 'We have to find the place first!' he said, kicking at the scorched flagstones. 'If it still exists! If it ever did!' He raised the carafe and refilled their cups. 'Your kinsman, Lehon, did he ever come close to that realm?' he asked quietly.

'I do not know,' Lehon replied as Regor drank deeply of yet more wine.

The elfin wiped his mouth upon his cuff. 'Your folk told us Rhye was lost. These here say the same.'

'Clothed in Dark, my kinsman said. Lost to the Sight,' Lehon corrected.

Regor shrugged wearily. 'Riddles!' he swore leaping to his feet. 'Signs and rumours! Nothing real!' He turned on Lehon. 'Friend, we risk our lives for stories!' Lehon looked up at him, but the man's bereft expression was too much for the elfin to bear. 'I go to my bed!' he glowered. 'Take rest while you can, mortal!' he advised as he paced away.

'I shall stay a while,' Lehon replied quietly, 'finish the pipe.'

As the door closed at his back, Lehon settled before the flames, the distant green eyes watching their dance as he thought of home. When the coals had dwindled to embers he still remained there wakeful, the wooden chair on which he sat scraping the flagstones as he rocked to and fro. But then, quite abruptly, he stopped his rocking and turned his head to listen. He frowned and shook his head, no sound came to him now, yet still inquisitive he lay down his pipe and rose from his chair. Quietly he moved towards the window and looked outside. There the indigo sky was spread, and he gazed up at it naming in whispers each bright star. On the distant horizon the thin grey line of dawn was etched, but here, on the cobble-stones of the yard, all was stillness. Yet . . .

Lehon felt his senses strain. Had that been the grate of a stealthy step upon stone? He listened intently. The sound was lost and he blinked against the dark. Was that shifting an illusion of the night? Some trick of the light? Or a man like himself, watchful and obedient, but to some other master?

The impure glow of tallow reflected on the glossy black walls of the chamber, its sickly light seeping into huge shadows across the marble floor. The candle-fat sputtered. A wheeze and then a snigger rattled against the stillness and the slit eyes of Lord Taekhor glinted with delight. 'My rare beauty,' the knotty fingers stroked the bejewelled sword-hilt. 'How you gleam.' The purple-tinged lips drew back in a savage smile, baring the diamond-studded teeth. 'Soon my beauty, very soon!' he promised, caressing the shaft of smooth steel. How the blade dazzled in the torchlight. How the solitary gem-stone at the centre of the hilt oscillated with viridian power.

The sudden twist of the door handle caused the knarled limbs to stiffen and the puce lips shuttered. 'Enter!' Lord Taekhor screeched. The heavy door eased open and in its arc a rotund figure was silhouetted, teetering reluctantly on the dark threshold. 'Come hither, Charone!' Taekhor groaned and the gnome scuttled across the smooth floor, his shiny bald head bobbing erratically as he effected one grovelling bow after another.

Upon the lowest step of the dais, the heavy body fell to

its knees. 'My Lord!' he gasped. 'Most 'onourable, most worthy of monarchs, master of the subter . . .'

'Yes, yes!' Taekhor yawned, wafting a twiggy claw. 'What news, toad?' he glared into the frightened face.

'Worshipful 'ighness . . .' the gnome began again, casting a long look at the splendour in which Lord Taekhor reclined. 'Important news, sire . . .' his sweaty face glistened as the piggish eyes fed upon opulent beauty.

'Well?' Taekhor sneered, the predatory stare fixed upon the trembling gnome at last.

Charone cowered visibly. 'Majesty, they 'ave survived!'

'Good,' Taekhor's sugary tones melted on the hot air and the yellowed skin flushed sickly green in the flickering light. 'Good, good, good!' he exclaimed louder still, rapping the marble arms of the throne with tight fists. 'I knew Bethalon's demon Queen would not resist the brat! Ignorance!' he spat. 'Her ignorance forfeited all – to me!'

'To you, sire!' Charone gibbered.

Taekhor's eyes bulged with visions. 'The Black Queen knew what it was,' he oozed, his thin fingers clawing the air with the swivelling of a skeletal wrist.

Charone nodded excitedly. 'Oh, she knew all right!' he agreed.

Taekhor wriggled with contempt. 'She could have had it!' he spat viciously. 'Could have used it!' the scaly skin glistened with the sweetest of imagined fears.

Charone dithered, concerned that his master's anger grew with every dark thought. 'But, sire,' he offered smugly, 'she was ignor . . .'

'Weak!' Taekhor screeched. 'All that power,' the flexible throat rippled with suppressed mirth. 'All lost . . . to me!' His wild delight threw him into a fit of protracted laughter and the protruding shoulder bones jerked in spasm.

Charone gave a polite cough. 'But 'e is considered somewhat 'andsome, master,' he said quietly.

Taekhor became silent. The bead black eyes narrowed in sudden hatred of the word. 'Handsome?' the thin mouth tightened.

Charone bit his lip. 'The people of Urmion say 'tis so, yet my lord,' the gnome let out a desperate laugh. 'I myself saw no rival for the beauty of your own, dear, countenance . . . none at all!'

'Urmion?' Taekhor's voice had become clipped and incisive.

'They shelter there,' Charone nodded, eager to please.

'And Zarratt?' Taekhor's reptilian tongue rolled the enemy's name upon its tip.

The gnome smirked. ''E suspects nothing, sire.'

Taekhor grasped Charone's rough cloak and yanked the fat face close to his. 'I will slit that greasy throat if he ever does!' the innocent tones seeped from the purple lips as a poisonous threat.

'Yes, my lord!' Charone agreed wholeheartedly.

Taekhor pushed him away, the smell of an underling too much for his sensitive nose. 'So the brat survived unseelie massacre?' he mused, smoothing the pointed chin with the tip of the baton.

'I 'ave 'eard it said,' Charone bobbed up and down at his master's side, eager to tell all.

'Survived cruel waters and a youth spent among strange races.' Taekhor considered, drumming his fingertips upon the marble arm of the throne.

'Strange races?' Charone agreed and questioned simultaneously.

Taekhor's thin lips twitched with sardonic mirth. 'Zarratt knew it not, he thought him dead.' The smile vanished abruptly. 'We all did!' he spat.

The gnome's fleshy lips trembled. 'And now 'e comes . . . our way,' Charone reminded with a manic gurgle.

'Let him come, let him come,' Taekhor's smooth tones rolled upon the chamber's heat. 'He shall never pass beyond this point!' The sickly face set with firm resolve. 'By rite of Dark Lore the brat should be dead, yet has

196

survived and now brings All-Power within my grasp!' A whimper of delight escaped the long throat.

''E did 'ave 'elp, sire,' Charone offered, a forced smile setting the flabby cheeks aquiver.

'Helpers?' Taekhor snapped, his mouth twisting into a sneer. 'A feeble seer and an elfin?'

'And a mortal, sire,' Charone reminded, wringing his hands nervously.

'Mortal?' Taekhor scowled into the sweat-streaked face. 'What kind of creature is that?'

Aware that his master had grown severely disgruntled, Charone raised a squared forefinger. 'But 'e does come our way!' he emphasised.

Taekhor grimaced and tapped the marble arm of the throne with impatient fingers. 'Charone,' he croaked wearily. 'He comes our way because we insist upon it!' he finished with an arrogant nod.

The gnome nervously bobbed his head in agreement.

Taekhor's yellowed face gashed with a savage smile. 'I shall have it all!' his lips drooled over every word.

'Take all, master, take all!' Charone chanted in the darksome light.

Taekhor's bead black eyes narrowed with spite. 'Zarratt pays his allies well to rid him of this brat, and so we shall!'

'Indeed we shall, sire!' Charone gurgled, revelling in the charisma of his master's power.

'But Zarratt ...' Taekhor reminded with a sneer. 'He too is ignorant!'

'Ignorant,' Charone chimed instinctively.

'He thinks I will kill the brat to save his precious skin,' Taekhor mused.

'When in fact ...' Charone prompted.

'It is Zarratt who shall die!' Taekhor gave a shudder of delight.

Charone's smile had turned to a confused frown. 'We do not kill the brat?' he scratched the pink head in contemplation.

Taekhor's voice had dropped to the gentlest whisper. 'Eventually, but I might keep him ... for awhile.'

197

Charone sniggered but the leering expression vanished abruptly as he saw his monarch stiffen in a cobra pose.

'But Zarratt dies!' The vow struck, he pushed the gnome from him with such force that Charone's flabby face found itself in sudden contact with the marble floor. 'Long has this Dark Lord been denied the taste of Triad power,' Taekhor growled.

'But they shall see . . .' Charone whispered, pre-empting a speech he had heard a thousand times before.

'But they shall see it live again, shall see All-Power wielded by me!'

'With such knowledge . . .' Charone spluttered, his head now aligned with his master's arthritic feet.

'With such knowledge as this boy brings, with the Triad in my grip, we shall rid this realm of his wretched line forever!' Taekhor's wizened body trembled with resolve. 'Then Taekhor shall possess Rhye and all its sees – shall possess All!' he said rapturously.

At his feet Charone gathered breath. 'Zarratt's head upon a pike . . .' he whispered at last.

'Zarratt's head upon a pike!' Taekhor raved.

'And I . . .' Charone's eyes had clouded with the most daring of thoughts.

'Emperor of the realm!' Taekhor exclaimed aloud, his hand raised in triumph.

'Of the entire realm!' Charone muttered to himself. From the corner of his eye he glanced at his master attempting to rise from the confines of the throne.

'Then shall I stand erect,' Taekhor strained, forcing the wasted limbs to take the weight of the hollow, mis-shapen torso and the heavy head. 'Monarch of my race!' he finished weakly and tried to straighten.

Charone fidgeted. 'Sire?' he hesitated.

Taekhor wavered unsteadily. 'What is it, worm?' he snapped, preoccupied.

'What might a Triad be, 'xactly?'

Taekhor's face turned sour and failing to stand tall, he

fell back exhausted into the fur-layered confines of the throne. 'Never mind,' he groaned wearily into the servile face.

Charone scuttled to bestow attentions on his ailing lord but the scrawny fingers were swift as they snatched at the gnome's rough cloak once more.

'When do they depart from Urmion?' Taekhor demanded.

'This day, my lord,' Charone gulped for breath. 'And they are heading our way!' he reminded, releasing a desperate snicker into the cruel features.

'Send word to my dear Zarratt,' Taekhor's limp tones oozed into the greasy face. 'Tell him my armies shall aid him as we have done in the past. Tell him . . .'

'Yes, my lord?' Charone nodded compulsively.

'Tell him, he can rely on us.' Taekhor pushed the gnome away, scowling as he wafted fresher air to the sensitive nostrils. 'When that is done, meet Rhye's brat and bring him here to me!'

The gnomish features wrinkled. 'Me, my lord? But 'ow?'

Taekhor's brow arched with disdain. 'Is that a problem for your Emperor to solve?' The twiggy paw darted out and slapped Charone's fleshy cheeks. 'Go to!'

Clutching his face, Charone stumbled down the marble steps of the dais. 'It shall be done, my lord!' he vowed. 'All of it, straight away, master!' he grovelled, bowing profusely as he scuttled backwards across the chamber floor.

Taekhor glanced up momentarily from his preening. 'And see no harm befall that . . . precious boy,' he whimpered. The reptilian grin spread across the bony face from one pointed ear to the other.

With a final obeisance Charone gathered his cloak to him and stole from the chamber as quickly as his fat legs could carry him.

In solitude once more Taekhor looked again upon the great sword and traced its unqualified beauty. 'Soon . . .' he drooled excitedly, appraising the razor-sharp cutting edge. 'Soon you shall do my will, keen blade,' he hissed. The large head fell back in ecstasy as slowly he drew close to the sword and pressed his clammy body against the cool steel. 'My rare beauty,' he croaked.

— 18 —

Regor grumbled in his sleep, brushing from beneath his nose the copper-coloured strands of hair belonging to the serving wench with whom he had shared his bed. He gave a long, contented yawn, his keen nose sniffing the sweet fragrances that wafted to him on the morning breeze. He opened his eyes to see the window agape and in its frame the distant mountain range glistened like sugar crystal in the weak sunlight. Regor eased himself free of the girl's sleeping form and threw on his clothes. Below he saw horses in the yard and soon the sound of voices drifted up from the back room of the ale-house.

As he entered into the brindled light of the tavern, Regor saw his three companions seated at the long table with the head-man, Joff, and three other of the village men, all eating a breakfast of bread and cheese and fresh goat's milk.

'Tam and Ilam have both gone beyond the first level,' Joff said, nodding at the two youths on his right, the likeness of kin struck in their faces. 'And Rowan here has been higher still.'

'Aye!' the ruddy-faced man gave a nod. 'As a youth I went with the hermit to the level of caves.'

'Hermit?' Nairb was suddenly interested.

'One who came amongst us,' Joff explained dismissively.

'One of them mystics,' Tam corrected, his corn-coloured hair sticking out in every direction.

'Wanted to dwell on his own,' added Ilam. 'We carried his belongings up there, but was frighted off by blizzards.' He gave a shudder of remembrance.

'And the hermit?' Nairb asked quietly. 'What of him?'

Joff finished his breakfast. 'Still there as far as any of us knows.'

'How long ago?' Lehon questioned, pursuing an interest of his own.

Rowan looked to Tam, and Tam to Ilam but none could recollect.

''Twas a long time 'fore the Dark,' offered Ilam at last.

'Aye,' said Joff, setting fruit upon the table. 'Before Rhye's cruel deceiver claimed the throne.'

Regor stopped supping at his ale, meeting Lehon's wink.

'Well 'fore those poor wretches fled to us from beyond the range,' Rowan was more specific.

'Folk from beyond the range – but how did they get here?' Lehon frowned, eager to learn of the route and match it with his own.

Rowan shrugged. 'Fear can bring about the impossible,' he said with simple logic.

'As can love,' Nairb breathed.

'Aye, so did the seer speak,' Joff recalled. 'Said good and evil have like power to stir the soul.'

Tam took a bite from his apple. 'So did good and evil rage to claim Rhye and its power,' he mumbled.

'What power?' Regor's eyes twinkled at the tale.

Joff shook his head. ''Tis the word you spoke, sire,' he said turning to look at Eider. ''Tis what is called Lore, though what that is and what it's not none of us has the wit to tell.'

'Why 'tis what Zarratt has,' Ilam nodded with certainty. 'A jet orb of it.'

'Jet orb?' snorted Tam. 'No, 'tis a monstrous bird with giant wings I was told.'

'I heard it said,' Ilam insisted. 'A black orb that does spin and rise of itself into the air.'

'What is "orb"?' Rowan frowned, confused by words he had no knowledge of.

Tam and Ilam shook their heads unable to explain.

'But Lore is what was lost,' Joff interrupted. 'That I know! All these other things we only heard and have no understanding of.'

'And these folk who escaped from Zarratt's clutches?' Eider questioned. 'Did any survive?'

Joff shook his head. 'Though what they witnessed was in their faces, 'twas enough to tell us blood royal had been spilt and offspring of the unseelie held Rhye at last!'

Rowan refilled his cup. 'Then came Zarratt's hordes,' he shuddered with the memory. 'Our land was plundered, burned and brought to ruin!' his grey eyes were tearful.

Tam shook his head in sorrow. 'Then we folk suffered.'

Ilam bristled with anger. 'I did see Zarratt's men sever the hands of starving children who stole bread.'

An aching silence fell upon the gathering as Ilam covered his face with his rough farm hands and his brother comforted him. Upset by their common grief, Rowan bowed his head and looked away.

'They tortured and murdered many and imprisoned those who would not yield,' Joff said bitterly, his old face wrinkled with remembered pain. He turned to Eider. 'Yet still we clung to hope, awaiting the new light as the prophecy foretold.'

Tam looked up. 'We never lost faith in the forefathers and the words that they passed on,' he said proudly.

''Twas I saw the rainbow arc when Bethalon was freed, we knew then you came,' Joff smiled into Eider's unflinching gaze.

'You knew me?' Eider was incredulous. 'That I would come to this place?'

The head-man grinned and pointed towards the window. 'Beyond that range lie seven sees and at their apex the royal see and the throne of Rhye.'

Regor looked up from his ale at mention of the Kingdom's name.

Joff's face coloured with excitement. 'That throne shall be yours!' he knelt on one knee to kiss Eider's gauntlet-clad hand. 'And his hand shall banish Dark!' the good man breathed, closing tear-filled eyes.

Eider clasped his shoulders and raised him to his feet.

Joff's voice fell to a whisper of warning. 'Yet be wary,

sire, for beyond that range no colour is. There Zarratt holds sway and nought is safe to trust.'

Eider cast a look at the wizard, yet it was Lehon who spoke out. 'These dispossessed?' he frowned. 'Did they make new route through the range or round it?'

Tam shrugged. 'We cannot tell, as those who climb and then return can never recollect a path.'

'Yet I have parchments,' Lehon explained reaching inside his jerkin, 'given to me by my kin.'

'Maps?' Rowan frowned, looking to Tam and Ilam as the mortal eagerly spread out his parchments for the men to see.

Ilam shook his head. 'These paths are but half drawn,' he dismissed.

'We have maps,' Rowan offered, nodding to Ilam and Tam. At his approval the two youths lay their tattered parchments on the table and the gathered company looked upon them as the four good men compared their charts with Lehon's.

'Yet look, our maps agree!' said Ilam at last. 'There where lower steeps stretch, and here where rock and snow levels climb.'

'And there, where your faint line does stop, mine goes on to ice and hidden caves,' said Tam, his dulcet tones edged with excitement.

An agreeable smile had begun to spread across Lehon's sombre face as he watched the rough fingernails trace each new line.

With a sniff the elfin leaned forward. 'And this?' he said, drawing Lehon's eyes back to the faded red stain on his own torn parchment.

Lehon gave a sigh. 'It brings my father's tracing to an end.'

Regor squinted at the patch of red, then still squinting he looked into the mortal's thoughtful face. ''Tis a dead end!' he said with a scowl.

Lehon tightened at the insinuation. The elfin leaned closer, 'If we had not found Urmion our path was lost for good!'

Eider drew the elfin away. 'The parchment is unfinished, the mortal has always told us so,' he reprimanded.

Regor spat at the sawdust-covered floor. 'An untimely end, say I!'

Lehon turned upon him, his face flushed with sudden anger. 'So 'twas said!' he glowered. 'My father left the map with me, then was lost forever, never to complete the task.'

Joff clasped Lehon's arm in comfort. 'Many good folk have been lost, your kin are mortal so 'twas Fate.'

Lehon frowned at his words yet he did not take the man to task, for his half-constructed knowledge struck him deep.

Eider glanced at the wizard whose patient face was wrinkled with the complexity of thought. Then, in silence, he watched him rise from his chair and move quietly over to stand beside the window, there to look out and say nought. Eider turned back to Joff. 'These folk who trekked the range,' he mused, 'they must have found some passage, some safe route?'

Joff nodded. 'Aye, a route exists, but no safe one, sire. 'Tis none of what it seems, 'tis treacherous and at its heart the mountain our ancestors called Sham.'

Tam leaned across the table. 'Some call it Trap Mountain!' he added under his breath.

'Its snares are well concealed,' reminded Ilam.

'Invisible webs,' Rowan chimed.

Joff raised his hands for quiet. 'Hearsay in part, yet 'tis a place against all life we know.'

''Tis riddled with bore-holes and the like,' said Tam.

'Aye, and sharp with needles and spindrift,' shivered Ilam, as if feeling the cruelty of the range once again.

'Needles?' Regor scowled, looking at Tam. 'Spindrift?' he turned to Ilam.

'Sharp peaks,' said Tam.

'Snow-smoothed razor sharp by the bitter winds,' explained Ilam.

Rowan traced his finger across the parchments, drawing Lehon's attention to the terrain. 'Scree slopes shift underfoot, rock and rubble shower from glaciers above,' he looked up into Lehon's face. 'Rock slides block the dwindling paths and cairns are few.'

'Most halt at the second level, from then on sparse wands may be found, put down by the hermit ... till the blizzard blew.' Ilam's voice trailed off, his eyes grown moist. Tam gripped his shoulder in comfort.

Rowan looked at Lehon. 'We never went back after that day,' he said flatly.

'None of us ever goes to Sham,' Joff said again.

Regor put aside his ale having lost the joy to consume.

Lehon's eyes had never left the curl-edged parchments. 'These maps make a route far into the range,' he looked to Eider.

'It is enough?' Eider's tone was half question, half statement.

Lehon nodded hesitantly. 'Yet from the level of ice we are alone,' he warned.

'And probably lost,' Regor added his doubts.

'Trust in the Lore, it is enough!' Eider flared, his fist striking hard upon the table.

The four village men started at sight and sound of his vehemence, yet Joff's eyes softened as he saw the desire in Eider's face. 'Sire,' he said softly, ''tis the reason I brought Rowan and my sons ... we shall go to Sham again ... together, and for your sake.'

Eider's black eyes flashed, yet at their darkest point compassion sparkled. 'Risk not your lives for mere adventure,' he said rising from his chair.

Joff shook his head, his voice tremulous with joy and sorrow. 'Sire, none traverses Sham without good purpose,' he looked Eider in the face. 'If you must do so, then 'tis our duty to give aid as far as we can go.'

Rowan stood at Joff's side and nodded. 'Sire, 'tis the least, and 'tis the most that we can do.'

'Aye,' said Tam and Ilam as one voice, folding their arms either side of their father's shoulders.

Joff bade them fill their tankards with ale. 'For the

kingdom and Rhye's crown!' he proposed and all drank deep.

'For the kingdom,' Eider breathed and raised his tankard in new toast. 'To your goodness,' he nodded to the village men, 'the plume in Rhye's crown!'

As they drank, Nairb turned back from the window to smile into Eider's happy face. Yet at the table's end the elfin sat unmoved, his mouth turned down in sullen discontent.

So they worked with the villagers, preparing the horses and gathering together the provisions necessary for the trek. Tam and Ilam brought with them climbing tackle, while Rowan made sure that each had warm furs to wear against the bitter winds. All was loaded onto the strong backs of the horses and as the village folk gathered in the yard to see them off, Joff appeared with rowan staves to serve as talismans for safety and support. He handed one to each of the party and smiled as Eider, Regor and the wizard tested the staves for weight and wieldiness. Only Lehon politely refused the head-man's gift, holding to him the ancient staff that he had carried with him from the stone house of his kin.

Seeing the mortal's quiet sadness, Eider drew close. 'Do not be sad,' he said.

Lehon shook his head. ''Tis but a sudden homesickness and will pass as quickly as it came.'

Eider nodded understanding. 'It seems your kinsman may have come this way,' he offered a smile of hope.

Lehon nodded. 'I know now he was here,' he glanced towards the dark range of mountains high above the village. 'Perhaps I may know too how he died.'

Eider clasped the mortal to him. 'Your presence here, with us, is a sign his sacrifice was not for nought,' he insisted.

Lehon nodded silent agreement but their quiet reflections were disturbed by a loud belly laugh and they turned to look out across the yard. Ilam was bent double with mirth. Before him the elfin stood, his diminutive frame buried beneath weighty layers of fur.

'Be sure you do not die of the cold, elfin!' Eider taunted, but Regor did not see the joke and merely scowled as he went about his tasks.

'He is unhappy with the route,' Lehon remarked, tightening his horse's girth and testing the saddle.

Eider shrugged. 'He was discontented from the first, yet what choice have we?' he shook his head. 'He knows he could not survive the return journey on his own.' He smiled to see the wizard moving towards them through the morning mist, his wiry frame gracefully draped by the folds of a fur cloak.

'Are we ready to depart?' Nairb asked, the placid brow raised in expectation.

Eider nodded. 'Though the elfin . . .' he gestured.

'Fear not,' Nairb assured him. 'He shall not stray from us.'

'I hope not,' Eider frowned, watching Tam and Ilam help the elfin to load his horse.

By the time the bell had chimed the tenth hour they had rechecked garb and tackle and made certain that all provisions were well packed.

Joff raised his rowan stave. 'All is done!' he cried and the chattering crowd made a way for them from the cobbled yard of the inn to the boundary gate.

So the four companions and their new-found guides moved out into the first day of their mountain trek. At their head, Joff pointed to the heavens. 'Blue sky and the morning's bright!' he said cheerily. 'Good speed be made this day!'

Mist seeped from the sun-warmed bracken as they followed the stone path until it began to narrow after several miles and then to dwindle to scattered stones. At last they reached the place where no frequent footfall had been left upon the earth and the pathway disappeared completely.

Now they were moving through coarse grasses, thickened out by barbs and tares; a cruel, inhospitable stretch of land, unwanted and untamed, its irregular hills and ditches gradually giving way to gorse and savage briars. Soon strong thickets garrisoned the silent trees and as the tireless party topped the jagged ridge, they saw flood water spreading out below, its glossy sheen stretched across the hardy grasses like slivers of glass. In minutes they were treading the sodden fields, the over-burdened horses struggling in the waterlogged earth, their hoofs churning deep furrows in the mud.

Among these lovelorn fields, small islets of land sat in the free spreading water. Eider stopped to point out broken fencing and derelict buildings. Men had once worked this land, yet had given up the struggle, retreating in long times past, to firmer soil. Many of the trees were death-black, though a few thrived on islets or clung to life bough deep in water. By evening the rich brown mud had given way to solid packed clay and shale and the weary horses had regained their even pace. Above them the sky had grown heavy and flint-grey and the first snowflake had melted on Eider's cheek.

By mid-morning on the third day, the snow had taken grip, flurrying in their faces and clinging to fur and hair like a sprinkling of fine dust. Beneath the yellowing sky, the mountain loomed like some dark tormentor who sowed their pathway with frost hollows and brittle shale. The snowflakes had grown in size and soon the contours of the land were obscured and transformed.

Joff watched the racing sky and turned an anxious look upon his kin. 'We're in for a 'eavy fall!' he warned.

Regor shivered at his words and pulled the fur cap well down over his ears. He cast a glance at Eider but his determined friend paced on through the silent snow. By late afternoon the fall was settling rapidly and the travel-lers began to tire, for neither they nor the horses could keep their balance as they struggled through the gradients of soft snow.

Eider gritted his teeth and determinedly thrust his stave into the ground for support, his feet slithering beneath his weight. At his side, the wizard and the elfin gasped, losing their footing whilst Tam and Lehon helped each regain his balance and the party halted to gather energy and air. They had made good progress despite the weather and now stood almost at the top of the lower level.

'Soon we cross the crevasse and ascend the range itself,' said Joff

Tam called to them from atop the steep and they climbed up to him. His arm stretched out across a vast white valley and Regor's heart sank at the sight of the awesome snowfield ahead.

The elfin threw his stave to the ground. 'No more!' he was adamant. 'No further, already we are spent. How fit shall we be to climb mountains, if we ever get to them, that is!'

'We shall reach them,' Joff reassured, recovering the discarded stave and returning it to the elfin.

'And we shall climb them,' Eider insisted.

'You shall climb them!' Regor swore, moving towards his mount and throwing from its back all things not his own.

Lehon made to stop him, but Eider held him back. 'Return then!' Eider told the disgruntled elfin. 'We go on without you.' His eyes met those of Joff and they turned to face the flint ridge.

In angry silence Regor watched them move off, watched them climb steadily until they reached the gentle summit. Then he saw their silhouettes against the stark sky as one by one they disappeared over the brow. None looked back.

On the other side, the nervous mounts slid down the slope, their masters prodding the soft snow for bore-holes or obstructions until at last they reached the level plat-form of the valley floor. Joff pointed to the rising steep. Above it a vast overhang loomed between them and the central peak, a curving buttress of smooth, solid ice. As Joff described its awesome dimensions, Eider glanced back over his shoulder at the trail they had etched in the virgin snow. Any who came after might find their way if the snows did not flurry and conceal the path. He turned back to the wizard, but neither spoke his thoughts.

They had covered only half of the snowfield when a harsh wind rose up, ice-laced and raw it whipped up the wet top snow, freezing it to bone hard crystals and soon they could hear the dull crunch of their footfall as they made towards the upper level of steeps. Now the wind was gusting and the afternoon sky had begun to darken rapidly. At the base of the steep they halted.

'Snowstorms brew,' Tam told them. 'We must shelter, sit it out.'

Joff dismounted. 'We'll dig in, come let's make a start, the boy will show you how.' He herded the mounts into a hide beneath a roof of tall, ice-fused boulders, while Tam showed the others how to dig out a small cave from the frozen snow.

As Eider broke the solid earth with his shovel, his instincts drew him back to the elfin. He could be lost by now, frozen to death in the snowstorm. His head hung low with sudden grief.

Soon they were within the dug out, wrapped in canvas and lying on the heavy hemp ropes for insulation. Nairb had coaxed the fragile flame of the candle-stub, spreading fire through a structure of bracken and twigs, and keeping this fed, they managed to make broth. Yet they ate in silence, noting every sound without, every howling wind and drumming snow flurry. Now the storm heaped snow against their dug out and the meagre fire guttered. Ilam caught the rhythmic clank of metal upon metal and looked up to see the same intent gaze on the faces of the others as they listened. The crunching of snow crystals without sent Eider sprawling for the opening, leaving those within to gasp relief as they heard his cry: 'Regor! Thank the gods you are safe!'

The ice air gusted about the dug out as Eider brought the elfin inside, his face and hands stiff with the cold. 'The light of your fire saved me,' Regor could barely speak as they took it in turns to rub the bloodflow back into his hands and feet. 'Without it, I was lost!'

''Tis no place to be alone,' Joff frowned, pressing a cup of hot broth into the elfin's frozen fingers.

'The ranges grow more treacherous beyond this place,' Tam warned. 'You'll do no such madness up there and live!'

Regor's teeth chattered so much that he could give neither quarrel nor reply. Without dry fuel the fire soon dwindled and extinguished and they sat out the bitter night huddled together for warmth.

With the dawn the horses were repacked and plans made to traverse the next section of the snowcapped terrain.

'We take the steep,' Rowan pointed. 'From thereon cairns guide us to the crevasse.'

Lehon looked at the icy contours stretched far ahead. 'The snow seems frozen well enough,' he said to Joff, trying to offer comfort to them.

Joff agreed as he squinted into the watery eye of the winter sun. 'But them fresh drifts won't support our weight, to be safe we tread the firm stuff.'

The icy wind had dropped to a flurry as they set out on the morning of the fourth day, guiding their horses over thick impacted snows and up towards the valley ridge. From there they would track to the base of the range. Yet keeping to the firmer terrain forced them away from the pathway of cairns and Eider grew anxious that their changed route would cost them dear in time and effort. Desperate to make faster progress he led them on at break-neck pace, his face set with grim determination. Beside him Tam grew weary as he constantly tested the snow-veiled hollows with his stave.

Ilam clasped Lehon's arm. 'Mortal, we must take rest,' he said, out of breath. 'My father is grown weary and cannot keep the pace.' Lehon could see Joff struggling with the horses at the rear of the party and he cried out to those ahead to halt.

The wizard turned and waited on the slope while the

212

elfin slithered back, helping Lehon to steady Ilam and Rowan as they gave the older man a strong hand of support. Suddenly Joff released the reins of the elfin's mount and lurched forward to grab at Rowan's out-stretched hand ... the fall of snow roared like thunder and the spray from it was pure ice. They heard agonised cries as the great drift ran under their feet and a crevice gaped open.

'Ilam!' Joff cried out, seeing Regor's mare plummet to the depths, his son and Rowan sliding away after it.

'A rope!' came the frantic cry, and as the ice particles settled they saw the elfin stagger towards them, pointing almost hysterically to the gaping jaws of ice. Below them Rowan clung on to the frozen debris and as they held fast the rope, Tam edged his way down through the powdered snow. Silence seemed to hold him by a thread, yet with every step Rowan slithered further from Tam's grasp. Again and again, the rope was cast but the trembling fingers could not grip it. Then, a sudden cry was heard, 'I have it!' But the snow on which Rowan lay spreadeagled, groaned and fell away and he too was lost to the waiting jaws of the crevice.

Clouds of snow flew up as Tam staggered back to safety and as they took his weight upon the rope, so the elfin looked fearfully beneath him at the changed slopes. Deep within he saw the ice, its octagonal crystals like brittle webs cascading away to the frozen depths. Deeper still, a white and gruesome criss-cross of bones laying in haphazard heaps told him that two good men had found their graves as countless others had before.

'Trap Mountain!' Regor growled into the freezing wind.

'Tie yourselves to the rope!' Tam commanded and they obeyed by instinct alone. Soon on the upper part of the slope they were each clasped tight in Eider's arms, while the wizard gave quiet solace to the tear-stained Joff and his sole surviving son. They moved from the crevice in silence, trudging up the final section of the slope to reach the point at which the overhang loomed up before them, a massive citadel of ice, the last and greatest obstacle to the central peak. Tam told them that behind it lay a hidden crevasse, full open to the elements and fluted with icicles thrice taller than a man. They made camp in its ice-blue shadow, digging in as before ... tomorrow they would climb on and set foot on the central peak itself.

Their fire flared vibrant and alien in the pitch black of the winter night. They watched it in silence, its rippling colours echoed in the glistening fingers of ice, their thoughts frozen. Nairb melted snow crystals and mixed their pure water with herbs for tea. Meanwhile, Tam thawed out the dried meats and fruits and mixed a thick warming paste of oatmeal. They ate mechanically, their energies almost spent, their hearts choked with the dual pain of loss and fear. As Regor stacked the bowls and the wizard poured the warming brew, Eider saw the anguish in Joff's tired eyes. He gripped the man about the shoulders in a hug of empathy and affection.

'Good Joff,' he breathed. 'Such a man as you deserves a kinder hand from fate.'

'Nay, sire,' Joff shook his head. ''Twas not fate took the boy but the hand of Dark. 'Twas the mountain being true to its purpose.'

Eider looked at him, touched by his faith.

'Aye,' Tam agreed. ''Tis but a boundary line 'twixt the lowlands and the seven sees ... the seven dark sees 'tis said.'

''Tis fate brought you all here,' Joff grasped Eider's arm, his sad eyes glistening with tears.

'I am here because I know no better,' Eider chided his own selfish heart. 'From hereon Joff, I and my companions go alone.'

Regor's brow arched at Eider's words yet he settled down among furs and canvas to sleep without a word.

'Nay,' Tam said proudly. 'We came only for thy sake ... now Ilam and Rowan are gone we must find the route to the seventh see.'

Nairb placed a hand on Tam's shoulder. 'What of your father, he may not manage the climb.'

Tam glanced at Joff, then cast Eider an urgent look. 'Then let my father return to the lowlands, I shall be the one to take you on.'

Eider shook his head. 'Tam you are all that's left for him.'

'Aye, stay with him,' Lehon agreed softly. 'Stay lad, he needs you with him on the land.'

Tam glanced at each of them in turn. 'Then I'm not to go ...' he said sadly. 'Not even for Ilam's sake.' A sob caught in his throat and he looked away.

'Not even for the Kingdom's sake,' Eider told him firmly. 'Your sacrifice is already great enough.'

'Never,' Joff said quietly. 'No sacrifice could be enough for Rhye.'

Eider placed the gauntlet-clad hand on Joff's shoulder. 'Yes friend, but that sacrifice is mine, not yours. Do as I bid you.' He drew them close about him. 'With daylight go together, back the way we came.'

'But sire,' Joff protested, tears falling to the flames.

'I say again, return,' Eider commanded gently. 'Take the horses to safety and all we do not have the strength to carry, take that too.'

'You shall have need of tackle and food,' Tam noted.

'We shall divide the supplies between us,' Lehon said resolutely.

'Nay, I'll not have that,' Joff argued. 'We can walk towards food, ye cannot.'

'No quarrels,' Nairb said calmly. 'We shall divide food according to needs.' Joff and Tam nodded reluctantly.

'Then it is agreed,' Eider slapped Joff upon the shoulder. 'You and Tam head for home with the horses.' He turned anxious eyes on the youth. 'Mind you guard the white mare well, for she is rare and precious to me as breath itself.'

'She is rare indeed, sire,' Tam agreed. 'None of her kind has seen the light since the time of banishing.'

'The banishing?' Nairb quizzed.

'The Dark Lords did banish all things white, said they were tainted by Ancient Lore, yet still they cannot blot out the moon's bright face,' said Joff with a smile of hope.

'Some say that white orb shall turn black in time,' Tam touched his father's arm worriedly.

'Nay, not now,' assured Joff and hugged Tam to him.

'Indeed not,' echoed his son as together they settled down before the fire.

None saw the embers of the fire die out for sleep overcame them all, shutting out the cold and the roar of the relentless wind.

With the fresh bite of morning air they awakened, Nairb brewing up before dividing up the food stocks. Lehon and Regor packed the mounts whilst Eider took from Tam the tackle needed to complete the climb.

Regor clenched his teeth as he adjusted the chestnut's girth. 'Would that we were returning with them,' he told Lehon, casting Eider a sideways glare. 'He tells them to return to safety, never a thought for us!'

'Nor for himself!' Lehon snapped, turning on his companion. 'Elfin, if you must, then go with them. 'Tis better we are free of your discontent on such a climb.'

Stunned by the mortal's harsh tone, Regor fell silent and watched him pace off to where Eider inspected the tackle. Meanwhile, Nairb had made up the food packs and stood in the bright morning light surrounded by the individual loads. He smiled as the elfin approached. 'Give one each to Tam and Joff, the rest are ours and can easily be carried on our backs.'

Regor scrutinised the packs. 'I hope we have enough . . . who knows how long before we find anything to hunt or trap.' Nairb did not reply as he helped Regor with the packs. 'I said to Lehon,' the elfin shrugged absently. 'We all should see sense and descend.' Nairb wiped his brow, hardly seeming to hear the elfin speak. ''Tis madness,' Regor grumbled. 'Climbing to who knows where for the sake of a dream, some remnants of an ancient tale!'

'Elfin it is enough!' the wizard swore, his eyes narrowing to slits as he thrust a single food pack at him. 'Here, take your ration! Go with Joff and leave us all in peace!'

'Go?' Regor was hesitant.

The wizard nodded emphatically. 'Decide once and for all. Either pull your weight or go from my sight!' Regor drew back, his mouth agape, unable to believe the placid man could speak so. Then realising his plight, the elfin paced away towards the dug out, there to sulk.

All done, Joff stood before Eider, his solemn face caught between respect for a King and love of a son. 'The gods speed you on, sire,' he said quietly.

Eider held the man to him in an embrace of farewell. 'And you, Joff. The gods protect your folk and the crops of your fields.'

'Sire, I beg you, for the sake of light and life, free Rhye,' Joff urged him.

'I shall give my life to it,' Eider pledged. 'For light and for those we have lost.'

The old man's eyes were wet with tears as he parted from them. He turned to Tam and saw the horses and packs made ready for their journey.

Zephyr whinnied and tossed her proud head, her wild eye reflecting Eider's form as he paced towards her. The gauntlet-clad hand smoothed the velvet neck, 'Sweet lady,' he breathed into the hollow of her ear, 'we shall not be parted long. Fate shall bring you to me when the time is right.' The white mare nuzzled him, her noble head nodding to the rhythm of his speech. She whinnied low, her voice anxious as he turned from her.

As the sun gilded the snow contours, Tam and Joff set off along the trail, towards the path of cairns. From the top of the sheer slope, Eider and his two companions watched them go, the tiny caravan having barely moved off before Regor reappeared and took his place at Eider's side. 'The gods grant you safety and all speed!' he cried through cupped hands. As Joff and his son turned to wave a final farewell, Lehon glanced at the wizard, their shared half smiles telling all they had to say.

By mid-day they were trudging ever closer to the treacherous overhang which barricaded the mountain face. Beyond it the vast crevasse yawned revealing the frozen crystals of the glacier. Following Tam's instructions Lehon led them to where the upper snows and the ice of the range met to form a narrow dyke, a bridge between the upper and lower lips of snow.

'It is a risk,' Eider frowned his concern into Lehon's face.

'Aye, but it is our only chance,' he replied. 'Tam was right, there is no other way across.'

Regor and Nairb scanned the dyke, narrowing their snow-sore eyes against the luminous glare. Lehon turned to them. 'We take it one by one,' he decided, then beckoning Regor to him, instructed. 'Take the rope, feed it as I pass across.'

'Careful, friend,' the wizard warned as Lehon prepared to walk the dyke.

Regor took firm stance, threading the rope through his belt as instructed.

'Follow my lead,' Lehon commanded. 'Pay out the rope till Eider and the wizard be safe across.' Regor nodded dubious agreement, seeing Lehon set off over collapsing snow, high above the ice-toothed crevasse.

For minutes at a time the mortal vanished from sight and the elfin closed his eyes, fearful that the ice mouth had swallowed the mortal whole. But the rhythmic running, then tightening of the rope gave him assurance of Lehon's survival, until at last they saw him, standing on the farthest side waving them on.

Regor grinned into the blustering wind and Eider urged him to take the dyke whilst he fed the line, but the elfin shook his head, allowing him and then the wizard to go ahead. Thus, one by one, they edged across the fragile bridge, the snow miraculously bearing their weight, remaining intact until as Regor set foot on the firm base of the central peak, the edge of the snow bridge slipped and fell away. Eider and Lehon gripped the elfin's arm and hauled him to safety, gasping as the impacted crystals cascaded, a thousand glistening snowdrop feet below. Regor shuddered, aware of how fragile had been his grip on life. Lehon turned him about and together they viewed the mauve and blue face of the central peak.

They climbed on to where Tam had said protruding rocks would offer secure anchors, aiding them up the rugged ice face. But the climb halted abruptly as they found themselves confronted by a wide gully which cut across the face, dark and impassable. For long moments they looked at it disheartened then Lehon turned them westward. When they reached the topmost end of the gully, they discovered a route leading directly to the summit. Now the winds raged anew and fine snow savaged their faces. At their backs the gully plunged wide and deep. Exhausted, they reached the edge of the snowfield, where the chiselled face of the central peak rose before them. They found themselves on the edge of a rising snow crescent where fresh snowfall lay upon a treacherous layer of ice and Lehon bade them move with care. As the unstable surface cracked and shifted beneath their weight, they were forced to cower beneath the fall of dislodged ice.

Soon they were in sight of the vast steep of firm ice which led to the summit and the edge of the range. Lehon gasped for air. 'Tomorrow we reach the pinnacle and walk across the chain,' he pointed to the flat roof of the range. 'But for now, dig in, we'll make our final camp.' As they crawled inside their makeshift shelter, the fine ice flurries gave way to heavy snowfall and as the temperature dropped, severe weather set in.

When Lehon climbed out into the morning light he gasped: the range and all its contours were buried beneath the night's blizzard. Now all was flawless white, save the summit which gleamed blue and silver in the thin air. Eider clasped Lehon's shoulder, 'What trouble, friend!'

Lehon drew his hand across the scene. 'The snowfield and its signs are lost. I can no longer tell direction by Tam's route,' he explained.

Eider pointed on. 'We shall take the straight line to the summit,' he said simply.

Lehon shook his head. 'Eider, all is not what it seems, the way has chasms, clefts and boulder traps, without landmarks it could take days.'

Eider nodded understanding. 'No word of this to the others,' he turned a dark look on the mortal.

After the warming bowl of oatmeal and tea they set off. The sky was clear blue now and the snow layers dazzling white in the sunlight, yet it was as if they walked through a blizzard still, for their guide was blind to the accuracy of the way ahead. Lehon led them cautiously on, aware of the dangers underfoot as he tested the deep snows with his staff and bid his companions do the same. Again and again he scanned the vistas of infinite whiteness, their shadows cruelly deceptive to the eye, seeming constantly to shift and change.

So the day wore on and weariness throbbed through every vein as they struggled across the relentless expanse of snow and ice, gasping in the thin air, seeming barely able to move at all. By late afternoon it had begun to snow again and as the sky darkened they stumbled to a halt, exhausted and despondent.

'Lehon, we must take rest,' Eider called out, leaning on his stave to catch his breath.

Lehon shook his head. 'Let us push on!'

'Push on? To where?' Regor glared at him, then pointed to the zenith. 'See the sun?'

His friends looked at the setting orb, then watched as the elfin pointed to the snow at their feet. There a straggling line of footprints was cast in the ice crystals. 'Those footprints are our own,' he declared 'We have come full circle, not for the first time this day, I'll wager!' He glowered into Lehon's taut face as Eider and the wizard inspected the prints, their silence conceding that Regor was correct in his assumption.

Lehon wearily wiped his eyes. 'The snow makes all look the same,' he explained.

His companions said nothing, too exhausted to quarrel, their white faces merely watching the sky as the clouds thickened and the winds stirred afresh. Lehon led them in silence towards the shadow of slabs, barely able to find the energy to help them dig out their shelter for the night.

The spark of the tinderbox lit up their worried faces as they sat close to the flames to dry out boots and clothing. The fire barely kept alight, hungrily devouring the meagre twigs and lichen that they had found to sustain it. Eider took from his sodden pack the shimmering cloak and huddled close together they wrapped themselves within its voluminous folds, gaining some comfort from its gentle heat.

Eider was lost in thought, unable to understand his plight, feeling himself betrayed by the ancient tale, deserted by the Triad power that he had fought so hard to gain. If he were its chosen wielder then why had it not aided him in his hour of need, why had it not enabled him to save Rowan and Ilam, to save them all? Outside the winds battled upon the slopes and gusted about the opening of their hide.

Nairb had put together their dwindling foodstocks. 'Enough for two more days,' he announced quietly.

Regor gave the packs a cursory look. 'Two more days of circles,' he growled. 'Then we perish!'

Eider glared at the elfin. 'Silence! Or I swear your tongue shall be first meat when rations fail!' Regor's face whitened at Eider's vehemence.

Nairb placed a reassuring hand on Eider's arm. 'Fear not,' he urged. 'None shall perish in this place.'

Regor frowned into Nairb's calm features. 'If not here, then higher up! Friends, we are lost and soon we shall . . .'

'We are not lost!' Eider shook a determined fist. 'When the snows cease we shall find Tam's route again.'

Lehon nodded into the elfin's anxious face. 'There are small birds and animals in this place that we can trap.'

'Your eyes are fast shut in dreams!' Regor barked.

'Reality is the mountain, the snow, no direction, no food, no hope!'

'Enough!' Eider lunged out at him, but before he could release his anger the sudden crunch of ice echoed in the darkness beyond the entrance, setting his teeth on edge. It could not be Joff and his son, they would have called out at their approach. Some mountainous creature perhaps, lost and hungry as themselves? Daggers drawn they crawled to the entrance of the dug out.

'Who goes!' Eider demanded, his voice steady. No sound came back, save the howling of the wind and the crackle of their ebbing fire. But there, in the erratic dance of its flames, Eider saw a shadow grow and scrambled out through the ice arch. Lehon and Regor crawled close on his heels, blinking against the dark until finally they were able to make out the rotund figure standing before the entrance, hunched and hooded against the bitter cold.

Noticing that the figure clasped a heavy staff, Eider tightened his grip on the dagger hilt, marking the stranger's contours in the dim firelight.

'Who goes?' Regor shouted warning. The stranger stopped, suddenly aware of the three blades that marked him.

'Friend or foe?' Lehon demanded, edging forward.

''Tis neither!' Regor spat, snatching at the intruder and dragging him with the strength of hatred through the ice arch and into the firelight. ''Tis a gnome!' he snarled, pulling off the stranger's hood.

'Friend, sire,' the gnome blurted, his bald head shining in the dappled light. The piggish eyes darted about the dug out, glancing at the weary faces of its occupants as they closed in upon him. From the silence of his dark corner the wizard saw the fat face glisten with sweat as three daggertips were pressed against the well-fed paunch.

'Hold,' Nairb said at last. 'Stranger, your name and business will suffice,' he assured the trembling gnome.

'Charone,' the creature squirmed. ''Umble traveller, like yourselves.'

Lehon poked at him with the blade. 'To where do you travel?' he questioned.

'Why, across these ranges,' Charone gave a quiet and well-timed cough. 'Back and forth . . .'

Eider cast a glance at Lehon. 'Back and forth?' he repeated.

Charone nodded, a sickly smile creeping across his jowls. 'West to East,' he said with exactitude. 'Then back again . . . often.'

'For what purpose?' the wizard's tone was incisive.

'Trade,' Charone gave a bob of the shiny pink head. 'Sometimes to barter, or to buy. Sometimes to beg . . . when times are 'ard.' The constantly shifting eyeballs fixed momentarily upon the meagre food set upon the hot stones to warm.

Eider's silent command withdrew the glinting blades and quietly the wizard reapportioned the rations to include the stranger's need. Soon the fat layered face was in full view and all four watched as Charone gorged himself, grunting like a starving beast, occasionally pausing to give cursory thanks, the fleshy mouth gaping in a grin as he crammed his mouth to overflowing. So hungry was he that he took a second portion, then a third while stomachs turned at the sight of his unremitting greed. Nairb was the first to take heart and speak, 'You journey alone?' he began as he poured herb tea for everyone present.

The shining pate bobbed agreement. 'Quite alone,' Charone said cleaning the bowl with the edge of his thumb. When the last morsel had been neatly mopped up, the gnome threw down the bowl and after wiping his mouth upon his sleeve, gave out a long belch of contentment.

'Disgusting,' Regor growled as he turned away.

Charone scanned each silent face with fresh interest. 'You too would traverse the range?' he squinted as he warmed his greasy hands before the fire. He shook his head. 'No easy task,' he mused, cleaning the gaps between the square teeth with a dirty fingernail. 'Many take the risk and are soon lost.'

223

The wizard's eyebrows arched. 'So it is with us, yet . . .' his speech halted as he caught sight of Regor glowering at him across the flames.

Charone's keen eyes missed nothing.

Lehon leaned towards the newcomer. 'There is a route through these ranges, is there not?'

'Indeed!' Charone nodded with a gnomish grin. He took up the warm brew and slurped at it, setting his cup down with another belch. 'None 'as ever been marked, mind,' he said at last. 'That parchment for 'xample . . . that can 'ave no route here traced.' The gnome nodded towards Lehon's jerkin pocket and the edges of the maps poking out into the dim light.

Lehon shoved the parchments deeper into his jerkin, but Eider had nodded agreement. 'Indeed it has not.'

'Yet we do have astronomic guides,' Nairb added quickly. 'Pole star is our sign, as is fate.'

'Ha!' Charone's fleshy wet lips curled back smugly. 'Then truly you *are* lost, and fate 'as 'ad an 'and in our meeting.'

Regor cast the minstrel a doubtful look, but Eider was staring at the gnome in their midst. 'How so?' he demanded.

Charone gave a careless shrug. 'I am the one can direct you through the range,' he said carefully into Eider's determined face.

'Direct us?' Eider echoed. 'You could do that?'

'Of course – for the right price.' The gnome gave a cough that was almost a snigger. 'Why friends,' he said glancing at each face in turn. 'I could even take you through myself.'

'Then name your price,' Eider said quickly, his eyes bright with new hope.

'Eider, wait on this,' Nairb warned quietly but Eider cast the gentle hand from his sleeve.

The gnomish face grew bright with greed. 'Silver pieces,' Charone grinned at last. 'They never go amiss in 'ard times.'

Eider reached inside his jerkin for the leather purse,

feeling all eyes upon him as he counted silver out upon his palm. 'I have ten,' he told the gnome.

'Ten will do,' Charone nodded, reaching out a grubby hand.

Eider withheld the purse. 'Half the sum now,' he frowned into the eager eyes, 'the rest at journey's end.'

Charone's mouth twitched as the coins trickled into his square palm. Feeling Eider's gaze upon him he gave a diplomatic bow. 'Most gracious I'm sure,' he said.

'Let us seal the bargain,' Eider insisted, extending a strong hand.

Charone hesitated, but as all eyes focused on him he clasped Eider's hand. ''Tis done,' he said, the clammy palm gripped tight in Eider's own.

Lehon said no more that night, only watched the well-rounded newcomer snuggle down in the rock hollow to sleep. Regor too was wakeful, shivering as he eyed the fitful snow flurries and drew irritably on his pipe.

Closer to the dying flames, the wizard turned to Eider. 'Friend, I bid you think carefully on this,' he pleaded.

Eider searched the anxious face. 'Wizard, we are lost!' he exclaimed beneath his breath. 'Unless you can lead us by your magic from this place, I see no other choice!'

'The Pole star will guide us. Given time we . . .'

'Time!' Eider whispered urgently. 'You know 'tis time we cannot spare!'

'Eider, where is your faith? Fate will not fail you now. Only watch and wait . . .'

'Watch, wait?' Eider threw his hands up in despair. 'I no longer care for speculation! The quickest route across this range is all that I desire!'

Nairb's heart raced as they glared at each other across the smouldering embers. 'You trust this stranger above a friend?' he said at last.

Eider lowered his eyes at the words. 'These ranges are the gateway to Rhye,' he murmured and looking up he reached out in desperate supplication. 'Destiny demands all speed, you yourself have told me so, yet now you deny

225

guidance from this place.' The swarthy features grew taut with resolve. 'We must follow the gnome, the sooner we leave this ice and cold the closer we are to Rhye and to triumph!'

Nairb shook his head in silent disagreement, seeing Lehon and Regor look away, both now aware of the hopelessness of argument. They were lost and because the deal was struck were now forced to trust the sly-looking gnome for better or for worse.

Soon all burrowed down for warmth and comfort, yet long into the night the corpulent gnome clutched tight the silver in his sweaty palm, his quiet snickers seeping out into the impenetrable dark.

— 19 —

At first light they moved out into the fresh snowfall, following closely the rotund figure who scurried ahead oblivious to the snow-clad terrain, uncaring of its softness or its firmness underfoot.

Now the mighty face of the range towered over them and as they topped the final glittering ledge, Charone halted. He pointed to the gape of an awesome cavity worn away in the granite. Through its jagged eye they could see vertical steeps plunging down on every side, the granite contours smoothed away to form a conical bore-hole cutting deep into the heart of the range.

Regor gave a low whistle of amazement and turned to meet the awestruck face of his companions. Nairb's eyes narrowed as he traced the spiral of the cone, wondering at the perfection of the excavation and the awesome force necessary for its creation. Regor caught the gnome's arm. 'What place is this?' he demanded.

Charone bared the squared teeth in a grin, 'My friends, 'tis the route.'

Regor held him fast and turned to Eider. ''Tis a trap!' he growled. Nairb nodded agreement. ''Tis a strange structure built in a manner uncommon in Nature!'

Eider moved towards Charone. 'Who was it worked this winding way?' he demanded.

Charone glanced at each in turn, fat fingers caressing the many folds of his chin as he spoke. 'Some say it was carved by an ancient race. But, no matter, friends,' he offered, the hairy brow knotted in a frown. 'You would travel with all speed, would you not?'

Eider glanced at the faces of his companions, yet none gave vent to his feelings.

'Truly, this is the quickest route,' Charone persuaded as Regor's fingers tightened about his fleshy forearm.

''Tis safer than clambering up the ice ledges,' he wheezed.

Eider gave an impatient sigh. 'What choice have we?'

Regor scowled. 'Chilled to the bone, or buried alive! No choice at all!'

With a grin Charone snatched his arm free of the elfin's grip and rummaging inside his cloak and tunic he pulled out two sticks of tallow. These he broke into smaller pieces, handing them out, yet saving the larger for himself. In the shelter of the ledge he lit the tallow from a tinder box, cupping his hands about the windblown flame and bidding them follow suit.

They crowded about Charone's slender flame and one by one ignited their stumps of wax, the meagre light seeming insignificant amid the vastness of the peak. Without a word the gnome scurried from them, beckoning to them with his chubby hand, yet never looking back, so certain was he that they followed.

Eider paced on after him anxious not to lose sight of their new guide, but Lehon halted him. 'Wait, take the rope,' he insisted.

Eider did as he was bid, watching the mortal scan the rock for an anchor point. There were several solid slabs and wedges at easy reach, firmly packed and rooted, capable of taking the strain of a careless footfall. Lehon drew the palm of his hand across the chosen spike of rock, it was weathered smooth, unlikely to cause the rope to chafe or tear. Himself the anchor-man, Lehon would belay the rope and bear responsibility for the weight of any fall. In silence they each adjusted rope and packs, then, with a final testing of the line, they set off, hands cupped about the fluttering tallow flames.

So began the perilous descent, Eider leading them in pursuit of the gnome whose rolling gait and bobbing bald head could only be glimpsed as he stepped along the uneven pathway with the confidence of one who knows every twist and turn, every stone and ledge by heart.

The outer rim of the shaft was straightforward enough, the path wide, its gradient not unusually steep, and they moved with relative ease and growing confidence that the rest of the shaft would be likewise. It was not. Once clear of the outer track and the ridge, they found themselves moving into deep shadow, the path becoming abrupt in its descent – a tight narrow spiral, which swept down to the black heart of the mountain.

At first, the regiment of tallow flames threw elongated shadows on the opposite wall of the shaft, then, in a deeper section, their shadows vanished where the dismal light was unable to cross the expanse that lay between them and the opposite wall of the spiral. The rope had begun to tighten as the descent grew more severe, and they were often forced to steady themselves against the rough-hewn shaft to draw a trembling breath.

'This is madness!' Regor's curse echoed in the blackness.

Eider wiped his brow and looked up to see the taut elfin face haloed by the guttering flame of his candle. Beyond him, the patch of daylight had almost gone and he felt his heart race with fear. He turned back to find the gnome's guiding light. Yes, it was still there! A disembodied tear of light several feet, or seventy, below him. Or ahead of him? Or above? He frowned and could not tell, for the fissures in the rock-face poured thin lines of daylight on the uneven stones disturbing his perception of width and depth, as if chiselled by some malign force to confuse unwanted wanderers in this place.

The slack in the rope grew less and less with each new section of the shaft. Soon there was nothing to see but the guttering tallow and Eider halted as he felt part of the rock fall away beneath his feet. He listened intently for its fall, but the moment of impact was barely audible. Eider rocked unsteadily, suddenly aware of the terrible void and the fragile borderline on which he stood! He felt choked by the erratic throb of his own pulse, and he fell back against the slime-streaked wall of the shaft.

With the slithering and scraping of boots at his back the rope tightened, and he realised he was not alone in

229

the darkness as the grunts and groans of anguish echoed and his companions drew close.

'Friend Eider,' Nairb's voice was a concerned whisper.

Eider braced himself against the rock as he felt the wizard's hand steady him. 'Thank the gods you did not fall!' He heard the soft voice say.

'I am safe,' Eider managed, filling his lungs with as much air as he could.

Below a glimmer of ochre light sputtered and Eider saw again Charone's pink head glistening in the damp air. The fat fingers still held the lighted stub and the piggish eyes squinted up at him. 'Nought to fear,' he said, his mildly taunting tone of voice setting Eider's teeth on edge. The squared hand beckoned him on.

'Eider!' Lehon called from above. 'The rope nears its end. We must retrace or give it up!'

'Follow the gnome!' Eider rallied them. 'He would have his silver and so will not leave us stranded in this place.' Eider did not heed the whispered protests that followed his decision but began the descent, his very momentum forcing the others to comply for fear of losing him.

They had negotiated several metres more when Regor's tallow fire sizzled and was extinguished. With it a little more of their courage ebbed away. Eider urged them on, yet they had not moved much further when their lifeline finally reached its end. 'What now!' Regor growled.

'Onward!' Eider gave stern reply.

Below him the gnome halted. 'A few more steps and we are safe,' he promised.

'A matter of opinion!' Regor muttered. 'And what if . . .'

'Nought to fear.' Charone's voice drifted up to them. 'Almost there, friends.'

Untying the lifeline they followed on, one slow hesitant step at a time, their knees stiff, their backs pressed against the damp rock for balance. At the bottom of the shaft the grinning Charone waited. 'I told you, nought to fear.' He reminded with a sardonic smile.

Lehon wiped his brow. 'You know the route well,' he frowned.

'Indeed I do!' Charone wheezed smugly.

Regor spat rock-dust from his mouth. 'Then you can tell us where you are taking us!' he frowned in annoyance.

'By the safest route,' Charone answered with the same sickly smile.

Regor grabbed the gnome's rough collar from above, twisting it like a noose. 'Remember, friend,' he growled. ''Tis more than silver hangs on your words!'

'Regor!' Eider warned, prising the squirming Charone free of the elfin's grasp.

Their red-faced guide spluttered for air. 'What? Bite the 'and that feeds?' The fat face trembled in a forced smile as he backed off from the angry elfin.

Regor glared into Eider's face. 'I smell a trap!' he swore.

Eider shook his head.

Lehon watched the gnome move off. 'He knows the route too well. All is in his favour!'

Eider turned a look on the wizard awaiting his opinion. Nairb shrugged, 'I too sense danger and so cannot be sure.'

'You are fearful of your own shadows!' Eider swore contempt, 'If we are lost then so is he!' He looked into their worried faces, 'What choice, friends? Perish in the cold above, or take our chances here?'

None had time to voice his thoughts before a brighter flame appeared and they saw Charone, his fat hands clutching a blazing torch. In the sudden light-flare they were quickly aware of their surroundings. They stood on the threshold of a vast cave system, honeycombed with tunnels. The gnome grinned, but before they could quiz him he set off, taking the passageway to their right, his bright torch bobbing and weaving as he strode assuredly ahead of them. Their candle flames almost spent, the

231

gnome now had the only source of light, and Eider, anxious not to lose sight of it, followed on.

From friendship and fear the others chased after him, yet even as they gained upon the torch its flare dipped abruptly and vanished! Eider fell awkwardly in the sudden dark, fingernails scraping fungus from the damp rock wall. There followed the slither of steel as Lehon and Regor armed themselves instinctively, yet as suddenly the torch flame reappeared haloeing the gnome's rotund form against a low archway. 'Come, friends,' he said, his fat-layered features creasing in a smile as he ducked through the arch and on along a low-roofed tunnel.

They saw him push then pull his round body between the narrow sections of rock and followed him close, hearing him mutter curses as the ceiling of the passage plunged lower still. Forced to their knees they stumbled and crawled in his wake, limbs grazed by the jagged formations, their lungs drumtight with dust and stale air. The intermittent shifting of loose shale revealed the presence of vermin and Regor and Lehon clutched their daggers in self-defence. Yet soon the tunnel opened out and they were able to stand upright once more. In their ears the monotonous drip of water echoed on, and the bitter stench of sump-pools filled the heavy air as they trudged wearily in Charone's footsteps.

Now the walls were running with rivulets of water which formed shallow pools beneath their tread. Here too the route was strewn with rock debris, the ceiling and walls heavily stained with old mud tidelines.

Regor frowned certain that the tunnel system was a death-trap, from its look it regularly held fast-flowing water. The smallest melting of ice, or flash-flood, would ensure a sudden and most horrible death!

Lehon was close on the elfin's heels. 'Listen,' he whispered into the pointed ear. Over the constant dripping and splashing of their own feet came another, more distant rhythm. A dull, almost mechanical pulse-beat.

Regor nodded agreement. 'What do you think, mortal?'

Lehon frowned. 'Waterfall?'

Regor shook his head, pressing his ear against the rock wall. He listened intently. ''Tis no sound of nature, friend,' he said. He snatched at Eider's arm keen to draw his attention to the noise.

'I hear only your eternal protests, and the footsteps of the gnome!' Eider grimaced into their concerned faces.

Regor would not accept his companion's insult as an answer. ''Tis more than water and the gnome, I say!'

Eider's mouth drew to a thin line but the wizard stopped their quarrel. 'Eider, it is not an echo,' he said in the elfin's defence.

Eider listened hard. 'I hear nothing,' he concluded.

Regor spat into the blackness. 'You see what you want to see! Hear what you want to hear!' he sneered into the tired face. 'And like fools, we stumble after you, to who knows where, at the word of a cut-throat gnome!'

Eider pushed Regor aside. 'Elfin fears! Should I take those more seriously than the word of a gnome?'

'I care for your safety! Let us flee this place!' Regor urged.

'You care for no one's safety but your own!' Eider growled.

Regor gritted his teeth. 'I shall despatch that gnome right now!' he vowed clutching the dagger-hilt.

Eider snatched at his sword-hilt. 'Walk on!' he commanded the elfin. 'We cannot move without his light for guidance.'

'Look!' Lehon exclaimed, seeing the torchlight gutter in the distance.

Fearful, they raced on to catch the gnome and soon they were wading knee-deep in icy water. Its temperature numbed their limbs and worsened their fatigue. Then as the route ascended the tunnel widened forming a vast cave of fluted rock. Here, the eerie light of a colony of glow-worms shimmered in the dark recesses like a million tiny stars.

The distant rhythm had grown by now into a heavier, more regular throbbing, and Eider glanced at the elfin apologetically. He called to Charone, 'What makes that noise?' but the gnome kept safe distance. He grinned at Eider then moved on into the cavern. 'Echoes, no more than echoes!' he called over his shoulder.

The gnome scrambled up the rough-hewn ledges, knowing precisely the location of helpful footholds in the poor light. The ascent was steep, almost vertical, and as he neared the mid-point of the climb, he lit up a new-found torch waiting in the shadowed sconce.

'Convenient!' Regor scowled into Eider's face.

Eider trembled knowing in his heart the truth of the elfin's fears.

At the very summit of the climb Charone raised the torch triumphantly. He stood now before a vast hand-crafted archway beckoning to them to follow on.

Eider clambered along the uneven slabs in pursuit eager to question the gnome. The footholds were well worn, and as he neared the upper reaches of the climb he became increasingly aware of the mechanical rhythms of constant industry. His face set in a frown as he opened his mouth to ask his question but the gnome had gone and he found himself on the edge of a giant walkway. It stretched out across a vast and splendorous cavern, lit up by a thousand flaring torches. The vaulted roof was a mass of stalactites of every size and colour, glistening in the amber light and conjuring gigantic shadow-play across the plunging expanse of the gemrock walls. Eider's awestruck gaze took in at once the terrifying drop from the walkway to the forest of stalagmites below. Those gleaming formations thrust upward as petrified architecture, their prongs clasping the descending stumps in places to form lofty towers and slender turrets.

As Regor and Lehon joined him on the walkway he pointed to the strange structures, seeing in their rough design, doors and portals, and here and there narrow staircases spiralling either to the pinnacle or the ground below. He gasped, suddenly aware that he was as much observed as the observer. 'The formations,' he said, 'they are alive with people!' As he turned to share the discovery with his companions he found they all were marked by the lethal blades of a small battalion of soldiers.

He snatched recklessly for the sword-hilt but was disarmed with speed and ease, and though Regor tried to aid him he was constrained by his companions lest the guard be less accommodating a second time! They turned as one hearing a snigger at their backs and saw Charone step from the safety of the shadows. Regor lunged at him with a well-aimed fist, but was again withheld, this time by the gnome's bodyguard.

Charone wagged a dirty finger in the elfin face. 'No more tricks elfin, or you fall to certain death!' He turned a glower upon the guard. 'To the stone galleries!' he commanded. The soldiers took up their positions at front and rear of their captives, while Charone lead the procession out across the walkway. 'Nought to fear!' he cackled turning back with a toothy grin. As he led them on they heard his whining voice rehearse the words of triumph he would use to greet his master.

'What chance escape?' Regor murmured into Lehon's ear as they marched along.

'Too many of them,' the mortal grimaced.

Regor edged closer. 'I still have my dagger.' He lowered his eyes, indicating his left boot. Lehon smiled acknowledgement as the guard moved them along.

Soon the monotonous rhythm which they had heard long before grew to an intolerable pitch, which reverberated through the rock like some vast unseelie heartbeat. The walkway took them beneath the overhang and on into larger caverns where the volume of the chaos became visible as the leaden echo of hammers on stone. There, above and below, hundreds of sweaty bodies toiled at the mine, excavating the very stuff of the cavern itself, hewing gleaming fragments from seams of dull red and glossy black gemrock. The mining work had carved endless stairways through the mountain's heart, which scaled the sheer walls on a multitude of different levels.

There appeared to be two distinct groups at work: those hewing at the rock-base were black haired and sinewy, their shoulders hunched from the inhuman effort of their toil. Between the clatter of hammer and chisel their voices droned, weary and guttural. Their skin, untouched by light of day, was ash-white and veined, and though they worked in groups, few moved from their allotted space without hesitation, their vision seemingly poor. In contrast, those who worked high up on the rock-face were skeletal, with pale stringy hair which stood out from their heads in violent spikes. They climbed spider-like across the stone contours, making short bursts of movement back and forth, searching out the smallest cleft and foothold. Having gouged the glossy black deposits from inaccessible places, they would emit high-pitched shrieks of triumph and throw the gemstone to the ground below.

Nairb's attention focused on the small carts, heavy with mineral deposits which the creatures manoeuvred along the narrow ledges towards the loading bays. On every level of activity the guards watched, silent and menacing.

'What is this place?' Eider whispered into the wizard's ear.

'Stone galleries the gnome said,' Nairb frowned. He shuddered, his eyes measuring the organisation of manpower, the provision of taskmasters. 'A terrible place,' he murmured. 'Yet the source of great wealth!' He pointed to the glistening seams of pink and red. 'Agate, and carnelian. And there – onyx.'

Within earshot the elfin gasped at the sight of so much potential wealth!

'So many of these creatures.' Eider was incredulous. 'Yet none resists the labour!'

Nairb gestured silence as one of the guards closed in on them, halting the gnome with gruff respect.

'No concern of mine, my man,' Charone's smug tone

236

drifted back to them on the dusty air. 'We've 'ad trouble with Grykes before!'

The guard's response was barely audible but the gnome appeared to be losing his patience. 'Then make an example of 'em!' Charone sneered hands on hips. 'A few days without lirium and like the Runnels below, they'll work until they drop!'

Nairb's placid brow arched. 'Lirium,' he frowned knowing the word had once been familiar to him. 'Lirium . . .' he repeated quietly. He fancied he had read about it somewhere, yet could not recall its properties or its usage.

Meanwhile, Charone turned arrogantly to his captive followers. 'This way, good friends,' he sniggered. 'I would 'ave you see the upper levels of my domain.'

Regor exchanged a look of disgust with Lehon, but before they could share a word on the repulsiveness of gnomes the cavern rang with a terrifying death-shriek. The Gryke fell to the cavern floor squirming in the debris until it let go of life, whilst the Runnels that surrounded it toiled on oblivious to its fate.

Eider looked away, while Nairb silently cursed the creatures for their mindless obedience.

At the end of the walkway, wedges of rock formed an impregnable barrier which, at Charone's bidding, inched slowly apart granting admittance to a series of smaller chambers. Here, a wooden cage was suspended from thick iron chains. Charone ordered them all inside, taking two of the guards for his own protection. Regor and Lehon eyed each other, soon their moment would come.

Creaking like a galleon the structure rattled upwards in slow ascent through the tracery of a tall turret to the upper levels of which Charone had spoken. As the cage shuddered to a halt, the gnome ushered them out into a corridor awash with blood-red light. Here was warmth and the sudden easing of the senses that made the elfin forget all notion of escape. Soothing music mingled with the smell of sweets and perfumes and soon the walls of chiselled rock gave way to an enclosed walkway fronted

237

by ornately worked grilles and windows. Within these small chambers all manner of creatures reposed. Slim-limbed and androgynous they were neither mortal nor fay, but a curious hybrid of unions long past. All were tastefully attired in loose-fitting velvet or silk, all lounged on cushions or divans, some playing board games, others engaged in idle chatter. Some fashioned gemrock into ring or phallic ornament, while others whispered gossip behind perfectly manicured talons. Their sleepy eyes half closed they made gestures of studied boredom, their smiles fixed, their minds empty.

Charone spat contempt. 'Mopustrata,' he cursed. 'No good ever came out of 'ere!' he swore as he led them on through a catacomb of small rooms and corridors, here and there stopping to peer through a narrow portal, his face flushing momentarily as he gave them all a lecherous grin. 'Dark rooms of delight,' he snickered. 'Wombs of indolence wherein all sorts of lustful excess goes on, unchecked!' he drooled.

Eider sickened at his tone as they paced on, the heady atmosphere pulsing now to the rhythm of drum and tambourine, the frenetic jangle of fingerbells and the tinkle of chandeliers. On they sped through the widening hall where beautiful and hideous libertines preened before handglasses. In the alcoves others of their kind tumbled in coital embrace or revelled momentarily in music or banqueting. Here too were secret closets, dark red recesses where observers become the observed and the dispensers of pleasure are also the dispensers of pain. Here grapes were peeled and scattered, delicacies fingered and devoured, perfumes and juices smoothed over naked limbs, while barefoot harlots tossed flower heads upon the orgiastic tangle. They smelt the musk of desire and saw the smoke rise from bowls and hookah pipes and watched all enrapt, their faces flushed in the sticky heat, their senses confused by sensory delight and the miasma of heady vapours.

Charone turned to them, a globule of saliva trickling down his chin, his sweaty palm beckoning them on. Soon they had closed the door on the senses and found themselves in a corridor of cold silence. At the end of the corridor, leather-clad guards armed with halberds stood before great oak doors. Eider hesitated, but the sword point in the small of his back forced him on. Charone rapped thrice upon the wood, and the door was opened from within.

They found themselves atop a staircase which swept down in a majestic arc to a floor of marble. The walls of this great hall were glossy black and studded with garish lights. The aisles were set with long jet tables, while the floor between was scattered with a sea of damask cushions. At the farthest end, narrow steps ascended to a marble dais whereon stood an ornately carved throne, festooned with furs and silks.

Eider measured the grandeur of it all and mused upon the power of the throne's occupant. He narrowed his eyes, watching as Charone scuttled across the polished floor, head bent low in respectful homage. Barely able to see the deity ensconced amid the sumptuous furnishing, Eider took a hesitant step forward. The insistent prod of a sword blade urged him on and he descended the staircase towards his captor. He took the floor in measured strides, an expression of determined calm etched upon his face. The others followed close upon his heels, fearful, saying no words as he paced to the dais.

As Eider halted at the base of the steps, the gnome shrank away into Taekhor's shadow, his bald head bowed low in cowering submission. The yellow-skinned monarch prodded him in the stomach with his silver baton. 'Too close, dog!' Taekhor grimaced, snatching a pomander from amid the furs and waving its perfumed ball disdainfully. Charone edged away, apologising profusely.

Eider's skin bristled at sound of the monarch's voice of sweet poison and he watched him intently, noting the hunched shoulders, the knotted joints and wasted limbs. Thick black ringlets of hair fell about the pointed shoulders as Taekhor leaned forward, craning his slender neck to see the captive who stood silent before him. The thin lips drew back in a hungry smile and Eider caught the diamond-glint of sharp incisors.

Taekhor took a slow, asthmatic breath. 'Welcome to my kingdom, Prince Eider of Rhye,' he wheezed. The slant eyes were like glossy black beads, flickering in their narrow slits as they appraised all within their sight. 'How pleasing to have you here among us.' The thin smile had reappeared.

Eider tightened. 'How is it you know my name?' he demanded.

Taekhor wriggled amid the furs, delighted by Eider's aggressive tone. 'So fragile in my great empire, yet so proud!' he whispered, amused. Coyly he leaned forward. 'My dear boy, whole kingdoms know your name!' The twiggy fingers made girlish flurries on the smoky air. 'Whole kingdoms await your coming! Why, you are a hero.' The sickly face squinted as he sought Eider's companions in the perfumed mists. 'Come forth, you are all heroes!'

'Heroes?' Regor repeated softly into Lehon's ear.

Taekkhor's grin had stretched to wolfish proportions. 'We have waited so long.'

Eider flushed, embarrassed and angry at the insinuating tone. 'Then know too that I am true heir to Rhye's throne. Come to take my birthright from the usurper Zarratt!' he said, his eyes ablaze.

Taekhor smiled, absently he drew the silver baton from hollow cheek to pointed jaw. 'Delightful,' he cooed, noting Eider's strong frame, the straight limbs, the beauty of the face.

Eider raised his head in arrogance. 'And you?' he demanded. 'What title do you give yourself?'

At his words the silently gathered court erupted into noisy laughter and the four captives looked about, knowing themselves ridiculed. The monarch laughed through his rail of fangs, wheezing with the effort, then at a wave of his knotty hand, the court fell silent. Ten twiggy fingers pressed against the sunken chest. 'My dear, I am Taekhor. Lord of all you survey! Master of the Under-kingdoms!'

241

He glared at Eider, awaiting the customary courtly obeisance, but his young captive barely nodded as he confronted the monarch with steely-eyed defiance. 'In my life I never heard your name or mention of your kingdom!'

In the shadow of the throne Charone almost choked on his laughter and as Taekhor aimed a goblet in the gnome's direction, the elfin touched Eider's arm. 'The fellow is mad!' he breathed.

Spangles of light flashed across their sombre faces as they watched the pinch-faced monarch concede Eider's verbal victory, circling the knotty hands in a seated bow and setting the jewelled bracelets at his wrists a-jangle. The elfin watched the gaudy reflections, noting every precious gemstone and all in plenty.

Taekhor's lips had begun to twitch, the smile having faded to controlled annoyance. 'Mine is an introverted race, not given to wandering beyond familiar boundaries,' he gave Charone a cursory glance. 'But to aid you on your way, my dear Prince, is our honour.' The tones were honeyed but there was venom in his look.

'You think me a fool?' Eider growled, hands on hips. 'You send the gnome to trick us. You take us captive and speak of honour!'

'Tricks?' Taekhor's thin mouth rippled as he threw back his head in mock hurt. 'My dear, you are not prisoners. You were brought here for your own good! You would have perished in those icy climes.'

Eider flourished a hand at the bulky guards who manned every portal and door. 'Not prisoners?'

The solitary pearl that hung from Taekhor's earlobe swung back and forth as he shook his head. 'Merely ceremonial,' he explained, then frowned. 'Though it is not hard to see how the misunderstanding ...'

'I misunderstand nothing!' Eider interrupted. 'Or if I do, return our weapons.'

Taekhor stiffened at Eider's arrogance, yet practising patience he called Charone to him. 'Do as he says, worm!' he smiled through gritted teeth.

The gnome dithered in the shadows, confused.

Taekhor turned to Eider, a look of exasperation on his face. 'An idiot!' he confided. 'Such impertinence! Tomorrow you shall see him flogged!'

'That will not be necessary,' Eider frowned, deferring the dubious honour.

'Necessary? Oh, but it is very necessary,' Taekhor echoed. He flourished his hands and a brown-limbed servant carried forth a tray bearing goblets and a carafe of wine. Taekhor snapped his fingers and food of every taste and texture was brought before them; he clapped his hands and the entire court erupted into a frenzy of delights. The thin lips stretched in a vindictive smile. 'Partake of the hospitality, if only for the smallest portion of time,' he insisted demurely.

'The weapons, we would have them in our grasp,' Eider reminded. His immovable glare prompted the monarch's mouth to ripple.

The skeletal fingers stretched out into the shadows and snatched Charone by the collar. 'The gnome shall see no harm befall,' Taekhor assured. 'And tomorrow he shall take you by the quickest and safest of routes,' he vowed. Charone's bulbous head nodded in vigorous agreement.

'Return the weapons!' Eider's voice had become strained with the flush of anger.

Taekhor's eyes met his, cold as the hunter's. He rapped the marble arm of the throne with his baton, his fragile patience almost spent.

'I demand ...' Eider cried above the clamour of the revelling courtiers and turned to see the guards move in upon his friends. Two of the soldiers seated Nairb abruptly before a table set with sweets and wine, while Regor and Lehon were led firmly to the sea of cushions and the array of strange delights that lay in wait. Surrounded and unsure, each did as he was bid, captive partakers in the feast.

Eider, meanwhile, had been coerced towards the throne, a goblet of ruby liquid pressed firmly into his hand. He saw the gleam of a thousand glittering baubles and the throne decked on either side by low gilded tables spread to overflowing with food and wine. Next to these, a silk-draped divan lay empty and inviting.

Taekhor wriggled in anticipation as the young man drew closer. His eyes grew bright as they caught sight of the jewel-encrusted gauntlet on Eider's right hand. 'There it is,' the cretin monarch whispered, the throb of desire caught in his throat. 'There is the Triad gauntlet.'

'Yes, my lord,' Charone agreed from his place at his master's shoulder. 'A most rare and beautiful thing.'

'A powerful thing,' Taekhor narrowed his eyes. 'Won't come off, you say?'

Charone leaned closer. ''Ighness, that night upon the ridge I tried yet though I was stealthy and quick, their pockets were empty and the laces of the glove would not yield.' Taekhor gave a grunt and the gnome shrank back, flinching as if expecting a slap from the wizened paw. This time he escaped the blow for his master was engrossed by the youthful prince who strode towards him.

'I shall have it!' Taekhor vowed, beneath his breath. 'And he shall give it to me himself!'

... Seated upon the divan, Eider felt the heat grow more intense, the ruby red wine and the heady perfumed air having dulled his senses. Soon he lounged, dishevelled and exhausted upon the bed of cushions. Taekhor smoothed the youthful brow with the tip of a peacock plume. 'You have had such rare adventures,' he whispered admiration into Eider's sleepy face. 'It is our desire to honour you thus . . .'

Eider pushed Taekhor's hand away. 'I seek passage to Rhye, no more!'

'Of course,' Taekhor agreed. 'My dear, you are not alone in your hatred of the usurper.' Eider listened with new interest as Taekhor continued. 'Indeed, your passing through my kingdom is no mere coincidence,' Taekhor chose his words with care. 'Why, it is fate!' he smirked. 'Be assured, in these days ahead you shall have great need of allies.'

In the ensuing silence, Taekhor cracked his knuckles one by one, awaiting Eider's response, but none came. He snatched up the goblet from the table. 'Come, let us seal our alliance in the sharing of the cup,' he said irritably, raising the goblet to his narrow mouth. Eider watched the yellow throat stretch, saw the ruby liquid seep through the purpled lips. He raised the goblet to his lips and feigned the toast. 'Tell me,' his wily host persuaded. 'You have gained much for all your trials?'

Eider wiped the sweat from his brow, his senses now whirling in the sticky heat.

'Treasures ...' Taekhor prompted again. 'You must all carry with you tokens? Precious objects? Things gained, or won, upon the journey?' As he spoke, he teased the thongs of the leather gauntlet.

Eider nodded wearily. 'A noble mare,' he sighed sadly. 'Left in the lowlands for sake of safety.' Taekhor's smile turned to a sneer, deploring Eider's sentimentality. Eider snatched his hand from Taekhor's grip. 'And my lute,' he smiled, taking up the instrument laid at his side. 'Bringer of joy and good living along the way.'

Taekhor's teeth clenched, the twiggy fingers clawing fur as Eider brushed the lute strings in tuneful harmony. The music halted as Eider cast a long look at his gauntlet-clad hand, its pulsing gemlight seemed to call to him and he flexed his fingers. 'And this,' he said, proudly raising the gloved fist. 'Token of victory over the Ogre King!' Taekhor's eyes glinted as he watched the oscillating light of the gauntlet.

In a sudden flurry of laughter and sport, a crowd of gaudy courtiers stole the lute from Eider's grip and as the puvvering vapours of incense and perfume rose up from the floor of the hall, a distant chiming filtered in upon the balmy air. Taekhor grew taut, the yellow-tinged features now set in a grimace of expectancy.

The gnome at his side drew close. 'My lord, it is the hour,' he whispered. Flicking the silken switch, Charone summoned forth the litter-bearers who raised their now impassive monarch to its velvet seat.

'Stay among them,' Taekhor charged the gnome and as the great oak doors swung open and then closed, Eider sank down into the silken folds of the divan.

. . . It was a chamber set apart from the rest, low and alcoved, a shadowed place where blood-red drapes cascaded from the ceiling to form voluminous arches of shot silk. A kaleidoscope of colour was set in motion by regiments of lit tapers ranged about the faceted walls. There were hangings of crimson velvet, figures with erotic design and lacquered tables set with grapes and dark wine. A tall upright mirror reflected charts of the heavens strewn across a fur-draped settle. At the centre of the silken arcade, a cushioned divan was set before an altar of onyx whereon, on a plinth of stone, was held aloft the symbol of subterranean reverence: a sword of burnished beauty. The pommel was of silver, acorn-shaped with gold filigree, whilst the hilt was long and slender, fashioned for the grip of two strong hands. At centre of the hilt was set a large round stone, faceted and domed, which pulsed rich emerald in the smoke-layered light. On either side of the stone, handguards tapered to prongs of solid silver whilst the double-edged blade was awesome in both length and grandeur. The naked steel gleamed with delicate tracery, pentacle and sphere were woven with laurel leaves, culminating in the majestic rays of solar fire. A weapon of breathtaking beauty, reverenced in this secret place, found by chance. Yet the Lore proclaimed that nought was by chance and Nairb felt satisfied that all was as it should be. Nevertheless, when voices sounded without, the wizard was at odds to make his escape and could do no more than fold himself within the darkest shadows and wait.

First to enter was a solemn-faced courtier who carried with him all manner of ritual paraphernalia. This he placed on a small table close to the dark altar. At his back, red-faced bearers carried in the litter upon which their monarch reposed flicking his silken switch at naked shoulders to quicken the pace. Deposited with care upon the divan, Taekhor waved a hand of dismissal and the bearers hastened away. Amid the sensuous textures the shrivelled creature lounged, absently tracing a painted fingernail along the neat folds of his robes and lingering about the V-shaped expanse of his hollow chest. He gazed with greedy eyes upon the proud sword, a trickle of sweat glistening on his upper lip.

At the foot of the divan, the courtier, Agvar, filled a silver goblet with wine and handed it to his master who drank long and deep. Returning to the table, Agvar put flame to the contents of a pewter bowl and the room filled quickly with spiced vapours. Taekhor threw back his head and inhaled, his eyes drooping as he took from Agvar the bone hookah. He slipped the gold-tipped stem between his purple lips and sucked until his jaundiced features were tinged with pink and the pupils of his eyes dilated. Taekhor wriggled in a spasm of ecstasy and sinking back amid the cushions, nodded for the silent courtier to continue.

From the tray, Agvar took an onyx jar and with great deliberation unscrewed the scalloped lid, aware that his master's eyes sparkled with every delicate twist of thumb and forefinger. As the lid was lifted and the glistening contents revealed, Taekhor released a low moan of anticipation. Agvar hesitated momentarily but then glimpsing the undulating motion of his master's ribcage, he leaned forward. Taekhor caught the thin wrist in his grip but as the courtier brushed the edge of his master's velvet robes, Taekhor released him, allowing him to touch the protruding breastbone.

The monarch's skin was cold and as thin as muslin, the knotty throat trembled in a groan and the tremor wracked the rigid body, setting the pearl droplet swinging like a frenetic pendulum from his ear. Agvar knelt before his master and dipping the tips of his slender fingers into the smooth golden liquid, he gave a nod of commencement.

Taekhor's mouth twisted, bony fingers fumbling with the folds of his robes until they were parted to reveal the wizened chest. The left nipple lay like a small blotch of dried blood whilst the right surmounted a fleshy teat which sagged like that of an old bitch wearied from too much suck. Agvar oiled his hands and cupping the flaccid appendage between his palms, gently rubbed until it grew firm beneath his touch. Taekhor shuddered with delight, a fine patina of sweat covering his face and chest. With each caress Taekhor thrilled to the roots, his head rolled back in silent ecstasies until finally his back arched in a violent spasm. A milky droplet oozed from the pulsing nipple and Agvar caught it in the silver chalice.

Now sweat poured profusely from the monarch's body as he fought to control the spasms, secreted milkdew now dripping rhythmically into the waiting vessel. Agvar's eyes grew wider still and he held his hand steady as the curious juice dribbled forth and collected in the chalice. Taekhor trembled, wracked with fevers, his pleasure turned to pain until at last the flow was staunched and he fell back against the cushions, spent, his body like a dried up root. Agvar set down the chalice and quickly draped the fur-lined cloak about his master's shoulders.

Taekhor revived. 'Touch me not, dog!' he thrust the hand away. Agvar bowed obediently and withdrew. 'Quickly, take it!' Taekhor commanded, his voice a hoarse whisper. 'Make certain it is prepared for our honoured guest.' Agvar nodded and secreting the chalice beneath a heavy coverlet, carried it from the chamber as he was bid.

After he had gone, Taekhor climbed unsteadily to his feet and dragged himself across the flagstones to kneel before the powerful blade. The viridian eye stared back at him from the centre of the hilt and he smoothed arthritic fingers over the length of the blade. At his touch an intensity of colour flooded the heart of the gem and Taekhor sighed. 'Soon I shall be your wielder,' a laugh of insanity escaped the yellow throat.

A loud rap upon the chamber door announced the return of the litter and Taekhor, his calm demeanour restored, gave orders to be taken to the great hall. 'We must not keep our little prince waiting!' he sneered, clapping his hands emphatically.

As the footsteps faded into the distance, the wizard emerged from the shadowed recess. He glimpsed the solitary globule glistening like a pearl upon the silken cushion, and turned away, spitting the bile from his mouth. 'Lirium!' he announced his disquiet.

Taekhor surveyed himself in the handglass, the sagging skin bore new wrinkles and the mauve shadows were darker still about the eyes. He shuddered and draped cool linen about the thin-skinned shoulders. At his back the door inched open and Taekhor turned, 'Yes? What do you want, toad?' he glared annoyance at the gnome.

Charone tipped a cursory bow and scuttled to his master's side. With squared fingers he took up the cloak of fur and draped it about his master's emaciated form. 'Easy, easy!' Taekhor squirmed, staring into the handglass and Charone's unsightly face. Charone complied with new-found gentleness, carefully eyeing his monarch's sullen expression in the glass. 'Damn the furs!' Taekhor swore, trying to wriggle himself free. 'Give me velvet!' The gnome hurriedly snatched up the requested robes. 'Soon I shall have a cloak of pure silk!' Taekhor breathed, feeling the soft texture of wine-red velvet against the wafer-thin tissue of his backbone.

'A cloak is but a cloak, my lord, and this is a fine raiment,' Charone said, attempting to placate.

'Not this one, worm!' the glinting teeth showed in a wily grin. ''Tis a Cloak of Light ... know what that is?' Charone shook his bald head. Taekhor pouted. ''Tis a relic of old Lore ... a healing thing.'

'I thought that things of Light destroyed Dark Lords and all their power?' the gnome said, trying to recall the tales told to him as an infant.

Taekhor rapped the baton hard upon the onyx tabletop, just missing the gnome's squared fingers. 'In my hands this Cloak of Light shall do my bidding! Shall make this haggard form of mine whole again!' Charone shrank back, bowing silent apology for his stupidity. Taekhor turned a haughty look upon the gnome. 'With strength of body returned I shall take up that great sword, and that gauntlet of the boy's shall help me wield it!'

'A joyous day, master!' Charone grovelled.

'All-Power shall be mine!' Taekhor's face grew bright with imaginings. 'Those seelie lords shall be wiped out for good!' Charone giggled hysterically. Taekhor made to stand on his feet. 'And the Dark Lords,' he gasped with the effort. 'All shall jump to my tune!'

The gnome quietly scoffed at his master's words yet Taekhor was no sooner upright on his trembling legs than he had fallen back into his seat, lacking the strength to stand a moment longer.

'Zarratt shall die!' Charone declared, eager to avert Taekhor's anger at his frailty.

'He shall indeed!' Taekhor hissed, gasping for air.

Charone's face was lit with murderous desire. 'Let me go now, my lord, and slit the travellers' throats?'

'Not yet!' Taekhor seized his collar and pulled him near. 'Not until I have the Cloak . . . you discovered its . . .'

'Whereabouts, 'ighness?' Charone finished with an evil chuckle. 'The pretty one 'ad wandered into the orifice of sensual delights, yet the elfin's tongue was loose enough,' he rocked with remembrance of the deed. 'Elfins have no morals!' he leered. 'I do love their wicked ways!'

'Where is it?' Taekhor spat, losing patience.

Charone gagged as the grip upon his collar tightened abruptly. 'The box. 'Tis in the box 'eld by the tall one,' he spluttered.

'Get it! Bring it to me!' Taekhor commanded as he relinquished his hold.

'The two cannot be parted,' Charone rubbed at his bruised neck. 'We must wait, the merest fraction of time, till alco-dew has done its work.'

'Yes, yes,' Taekhor wafted a limp hand.

'The tall one is called "wizard", was my lord aware?'

Charone offered the titbit, casting his master a sideways glance.

'Ha!' Taekhor sneered. 'A wizard is he? I see no spells! No strange enchantments!' he glared into the gnome's grinning face. 'No escape!' The cackling laughter joined with Charone's as they shared the joke.

'No escape at all, master!' Charone echoed. 'Let me kill them, master?' he pleaded.

Taekhor's laughter stopped abruptly. 'The tall one called "wizard" we give to the alchemist for ... experiments,' the yellow knuckles were cracked. 'You can have the other two.'

Charone bobbed up and down with excitement. 'Thank you, 'ighness!' he grovelled, but then a sudden frown met in the middle of his forehead. 'Should I 'ang 'em master, or torture 'em, or both?'

The bony forefinger prodded him in the chest. 'I don't care, do as you will! But remember, the young prince is mine!'

Charone made towards the chamber door. 'I'll 'ave 'em all taken to the cells straight away!' he blurted.

Yet Taekhor held him fast with dark command. 'First, bring that box to me!'

Charone gave a brisk bow, barely able to contain his eagerness to draw the travellers' blood. Taekhor fixed him with his snake eyes. 'Then the phial of lirium, bring both to the Hall of Feasts – go to!' Charone scuttled away.

'I shall have him for all time, and lirium shall make the beauty fulfil my every whim.' The purple lids drooped over cruel visions and the emaciated frame shuddered in anticipation. Taekhor eyed the handglass. 'Now my plan begins and sweet revenge gives my woeful exile meaning.' He closed his eyes in ecstasy. 'As I would destroy all claimants to that throne of Rhye, so will I destroy you, youthful prince returned!' The wasted body arched, yet the sudden draught made the yellow skin shiver as the chamber door slammed shut: the gnome had scurried to his tasks, and to his own delights.

— 21 —

'To the cells!' Charone ordered as the guards hauled the elfin and the mortal from the hall like lifeless marionettes. The gnome turned. 'Hurry! Search the passageways!' he barked command, and a second battalion of soldiers clanked away into the dim light. ''E can't 'ave got far!' Charone cried after them. The sound of armour and weaponry grew faint on the heavy air as he turned with a scowl to his escort. 'Can't 'ave got far!' he wheezed almost to himself, squared hands clutching Nairb's box to his paunch.

Charone had begun to sweat. Should he tell his master of the wizard's absence from the sea of cushions? He shook his head. 'The guard will net 'im,' he assured himself. The flabby cheeks trembled in a smug grin, he, Charone, would now take unto his master all that he desired. He alone would reap reward. But even as he turned to scuttle across the glossy floor, curiosity pressed in upon him and he eyed the red wood of the box with suspicion. Did it not seem much smaller than when he had first laid eyes on it? He inspected it for long moments, then shrugged, perhaps all new things seemed large until the eye has grown accustomed to them. He smoothed the ornate latch with a stubby finger. Perhaps the Triad was within? Charone had long contemplated this particular mystery with no result, yet here was his chance to see that which his master desired so much. See it for himself. He glanced about before trying to flick the latch but in that moment the fan-bearers pushed through the heavy doors and in their wake came the litter.

Charone swore under his breath, he had not been trusted to do the deed! His fat face paled as Taekhor's finger pointed at him. 'That box, bring it to me!' he commanded as the litter-bearers wafted him away to the

252

shining dais. Charone scurried after them, tripping as he took the steps, still clutching the box as if to life itself.

. . . The gloved hand fell with the suddenness of death, releasing a wedge of pain that tore through skin and bone. The wizard felt the trickle of warm blood and the yawning silence that precedes unconsciousness.

When he came to he found himself gripped by the arms, saw the blur of corridors skid by and felt the sickening friction of his boots as they scraped the flagstones. The guards said nothing as they dragged him down the winding stairs, their breath escaping in icy grunts on the damp air. They threw their dazed captive into the waiting cell, slamming the door and sliding the heavy bolts.

Nairb lay for several moments half stunned before he saw the chequered light that seeped from the iron grille above him. He dragged himself unsteadily towards it, the door was cold and solid, and its locks and bolts were without. His temple throbbed with the pain of the blow, a pain which seemed to erase all pattern of thought until the insistent scratch of flint on flint drew his attention back to the heavy dark. A meagre spark pirouetted in the blackness, then a sliver of flame lit up the bruised faces of the elfin and his mortal comrade.

'Friends, you are safe,' Nairb smiled weakly as they embraced.

'Eider is not with you?' Regor questioned as they crowded around the tallow flame.

The wizard raised a brow. 'I thought you all together?'

Regor shook his head. 'Cleverly parted and taken by surprise!' he said bitterly, his skinned knuckles tightening about the candle nub.

Lehon gave a heavy sigh. 'Our own foolishness brought this about.'

The wizard touched his arm in a gesture of comfort. 'Friend, this was a trap well sprung. Taekhor would have the Triad amulets for his own and would stop at nothing.'

Regor bared his teeth. 'And we no more than willing victims!' he spat.

The flickering light etched the frown on Lehon's brow. 'If that is so, then why not kill us and be done?' he stated his reasoning.

Nairb nodded calmly. 'Oh, that will be, but first the subterranean lord must seize the Triad and cannot do so without Eider's help.'

Regor stiffened. 'Eider will never surrender.'

The wizard smiled quiet reassurance. 'Indeed he cannot,' he shook his head. 'For the gauntlet has claimed him for its master.' Regor screwed up his nose, not sure of the meaning of the wizard's words.

Lehon eyed Nairb critically. 'But what of the Cloak?' he asked.

Nairb smiled a holy smile and extracted from the folds of his gown a tiny pill box which fitted exactly into the palm of his hand. He lightly tapped the lid. ''Tis safe,' he announced.

Regor's brow wrinkled disbelief but he said nothing, feeling the gravity of the situation and of their plight. He raised his arms in a gesture of hopelessness. 'Then Taekhor will kill us all and be damned!'

The wizard cupped his hands about the flickering tallow, encasing the flame as a globe of amber. He searched the reflected glow, felt the fragile pulse. 'The Triad must be gained intact, or will not confer All-Power,' he stated as if reading from some ancient text. 'And since Eider will not freely give, the gauntlet must be persuaded from him or taken!'

Regor narrowed his eyes, hardly daring to ask the question. 'And how might that be done?'

Nairb drew them close, his face tight and wan. 'This baneful lord has the power of lirium at his disposal.'

Regor frowned ignorance but Lehon rubbed his chin thoughtfully. 'I heard that word spoken before,' he said.

The wizard nodded and explained. ''Tis the stuff those poor creatures in the Stone Galleries are addicted to,' he shook his head sadly.

'What is this lirium,' Regor asked.   •

'Culled from viper's milk and datura stramomium,' Nairb whispered the unseelie potion.

The elfin caught his breath as if arrested by some spell. 'Devil's Apple!' he remembered with a shudder.

The wizard nodded. 'The tincture concocted is lirium. 'Tis said it has the power to make joy . . . and madness.'

'Viper's milk?' Lehon scratched his head, unable to follow the connection.

The corners of the wizard's mouth turned down in distaste, recalling the scene of revelation. 'Trust they have it in plenty,' he said with a nod. 'Lirium makes of folk mere ciphers for their master's bidding!'

Regor's understanding was now clear. 'The stuff becomes the lifeblood . . . without it . . .'

'Pain most terrible and visions foul!' Nairb finished.

Lehon looked to them both, irritated by their shared knowledge of such mysteries. 'But what of the upper levels?' he questioned. 'What use have those?'

Nairb gave a resigned smile. 'Centres of indolence where every need is catered for. Seeming joy dulls the need to rebel, the power is retained.'

Lehon shook his head, clearly amazed by the wizard's assessment. 'Then this Taekhor is a powerful enemy indeed,' he surmised.

'That is why we must escape before Eider falls victim to his evil devices,' Nairb urged.

'Escape?' Regor gave an incredulous laugh. 'Wizard do you not see the thickness of the walls, the stoutness of the locks and bolts?'

The wizard blinked his birdlike eyes. 'But we must!' he insisted. 'Lirium corrupts true nature, taints reason,' he explained. 'Whilst the wielder cleaves to good, none can remove the gauntlet without his bidding. But Taekhor's corruption will free the amulet, deliver it to Dark.' He turned desperate eyes upon them. 'We must escape!'

So they huddled together, the candle-flame bobbing erratically as Regor and Lehon whispered plans of escape.

. . . The guard had changed for the nightwatch and Lehon peered from the iron grille as their jailer walked his weary route from one intersection to another. As he neared the cell door, Lehon nodded to the wizard who on cue released a terrible wail.

Outside the door the guard hesitated, then prompted by further cries, he pressed his face against the grille. Before he could peer inside, Lehon's quick hands had shot through the bars and grabbed him by the throat, yanking him full force against the door and stunning him. He slumped against the wood and Lehon struggled to hold him, but the inert body slid the length of the cell door to the flagstones.

Regor hauled himself up to the grille to look. 'Mother of Hecate!' he swore, turning blazing eyes upon the mortal. 'You've knocked him senseless! Now he is beyond our reach and the keys with him!' Lehon fell back against the door, angry at his mistake. 'Now we shall never get out!' the elfin scowled at the wizard who had watched their attempt with silent interest.

'Come now, elfin,' Nairb flourished a hand. 'Give me the blade you conceal.'

Regor sneered. 'Friend, the door is solid! Would you turn every screw? It will take hours!'.

The wizard extended his hand still further. With a scowl the elfin retrieved the small stiletto blade from the inside of his boot. Nairb admired its slender shaft then drew his fingertips softly from hilt to tip. Passing his hand from west to east above the blade, he pointed it as a steady arrow towards the door of their cell. Beneath his breath the incantations flew, only their rhythms discernible as word and mystic union became consort to the deed. The wizard moved soundlessly to the door, slipping the blade into the lock and turning it as one would a key.

The elfin gave a laugh of sarcasm which changed quickly to an audible gasp as the mechanism clicked. Together with Lehon, he scrambled closer seeing the wizard at his rite and the dagger-blade charged with the force of Nairb's mystical divination.

Slipping the thin shaft between the slit of the door, the wizard exerted the faintest pressure upon the hilt and the heavy iron bolts eased back as if drawn by strong hands. Regor's eyes were as wide as saucers and he was struck silent, uncertain of what he had just witnessed. He swallowed hard as the wizard turned and offered him the blade. 'Most fortunate,' Nairb smiled benignly as the elfin took the dagger from him, grinning awkwardly.

Lehon pushed at the cell door and together they dragged the unconscious guard within. 'Get his sword!' he urged the elfin as they tied their captive's hands and feet. Soon they were in pursuit of the wizard who had hurried on ahead, leading the way up the narrow steps to the waiting chambers.

... The guard slumped beneath Eider's blow. Now free he scanned the orifice of delights, within, the gaudy creatures lay in tangled sleep amid the silken sheets. Eider crept towards the contracted iris of the opening, it dilated as he drew near, its silver shutters folding back to let him pass. Cautiously, Eider stepped through its inviting centre.

Before him the sea of cushions lay as he had left it hours before, though the courtiers had all departed and his companions were nowhere to be seen. Eider's heart raced, what fate had befallen them in his absence? Was he the only one alive? On the edge of the silken sea lay Regor's cap, there too Lehon's pipe and his own lute. Barely a hand's grasp away a mislaid dagger glinted and he reached to take it up. It was then he saw the distant procession winding its way towards the dais. He saw the fan-bearers, the sombre guards, and the sumptuous litter, and then he saw Charone. Eider looked in consternation, for in the gnome's sweaty grasp was the wizard's precious box. He watched the procession halt momentarily before ascending the many steps to the throne. Taking advantage of their preoccupation, Eider darted to safety, pressing himself into the shadows before making his own way to the dais. Soon he drew close enough to see the yellow-skinned monarch preening before the handglass.

The faithful gnome struggled to mount the steps, his legs buckling beneath the sudden weight of the wizard's box. At last the panting Charone took his place before the throne, forced to wait in silence until his master's eyes settled upon him.

The fan-bearers lit the dim purple lamps whilst the litter-bearers draped their master in royal furs. That done, Taekhor fussed before his handglass for what seemed an eternity until finally he stretched out a scrawny hand as if to clasp the box. Eider heard him speak. 'Well? Open it!' Taekhor snapped irritably.

'Yes, master,' Charone gibbered, fumbling for the ornate latch.

Taekhor wriggled with excitement. 'Now the Triad is mine! Everything is mine! Power eternal over the land is mine!' he chanted deliriously.

'Yours indeed, master,' Charone echoed, trying to force the lock.

'And the precious little prince,' Taekhor giggled behind the crooked claw. 'He shall be . . .'

'Murdered?' Charone prompted.

'Enslaved!' Taekhor corrected with a glare as Charone struggled on with the silver latch.

Taekhor gave a shudder of ecstasy, imagining the delights of such sport. 'So many things to do with such a beauty as he!'

Charone gave a careless laugh in reply, yet the smile faded as his master shoved a black fingernail under the latch and yanked it free. As the lid flew back their heads cracked together, so eager were they to push their faces into its gape.

Within, they saw an unfathomable deepness. They eyed each other confusedly until Taekhor thrust his thin hand inside the red wood shell. The shadow sacks under his eyes twisted as his hand attached itself to some mysterious object. As he gained a grip on it, Taekhor's pointed teeth gleamed in a grin and with a sharp tug he

258

extracted the object. The solitary rune fell silently into his lap.

Charone eyed it cautiously . . . was this the Triad? He looked to his master for confirmation . . . clearly it was not.

'The travellers, they are in safe keeping?' Taekhor growled into the flabby face.

Charone nodded zealously. 'Chained like beasts to the cell walls, even as we speak!'

Taekhor cracked his knuckles. 'The one called "wizard" – bring him here!'

Charone quivered, knowing he could not deliver. 'But first, my lord,' he grimaced, 'should we not examine this precious thing more closely?'

'Yes, yes,' Taekhor gave a sneer of boredom and thrust his wizened paw deeper still into the box. The silky texture that met his fingers' touch forced the thin lips into a grin once more. 'The Cloak!' he exclaimed, giving a firm tug. A bright ripple of colour flew up into the light and the two of them watched the perfect triangle of red silk flutter to drape the rune in Taekhor's lap. Taekhor glared at it in contempt.

Charone saw his master's mouth tighten with angry discontent and he dared not speak as Taekhor's pointed features thrust into the box's gape once more. What he saw was a perfect square of nothingness. Nothing to be seen, nothing to be touched. Nothing to be prized. The mouth curled in a spasm of rage. 'A worthless stone! A 'kerchief!' he screamed, the very colour of the silk inciting his wrath.

'Not the Triad?' Charone questioned politely.

The yellow hand slapped hard against the flabby cheek. 'Triad?!' Traekhor's dreadful wail pierced the stillness. 'That boy! Bring him to me!' Charone bobbed instant obedience. Taekhor's fury raged unabated. 'Make me a fool would he? Make a joke?' he cracked the knotty fingers, joint by joint. 'Well, I shall have that gauntlet if I have to cut it off!' he shrieked.

'And the Cloak, master?' Charone insinuated.

'That wizard shall tell all. I shall have the Triad out of them if it is the last thing I do!' he screamed.

Eider's stomach churned to see the tincture of the monarch's skin ripple and change as quickly as the colours of a chameleon. However, his disgust was as quickly overcome by his indignation. 'And it would be your last act!' he cried, stepping out into the purple light.

'Seize him!' Taekhor waved his arms hysterically and the vast hall rang to the sound of weaponry as the guards ran forth. Eider whipped at the candles with the dagger-blade, extinguishing light on every side. With the soldiers' advance he ran from them, casting everything that he could lift to throw into their path.

Upon the dais Charone armed himself while Taekhor shouted garbled orders to his men.

Eider snatched a torch from its sconce, keeping the bulky guards at bay with fire and the dagger. Soon their shining swords marked him on every side and he could do no more than duck and weave as lethal steel skimmed past him and hacked the pungent air. He leapt over the long table, kicking at it as he landed and levering it onto its side to act as a barrier. He grinned into the chaos of arms and legs as the guards fell in on one another, but others gave chase as Eider plunged into the sea of cushions. As they closed on him, he cast down the blazing torch and raced for the marble floor. Sudden combustion filled the hall with powerful heat; wisps of silk flew up on the fiery currents and in the scarlet flare, Taekhor watched in horror as Eider ran towards him clutching now both sword and dagger.

'Seize the villain!' Taekhor gave frantic command, but the captains and their men were now preoccupied with fire and unable to reach their threatened monarch. 'Seize that meddler!' Taekhor coughed in the puvvering smoke. The fan-bearers ran to obey, meeting Eider upon the upper steps. He struck their leader with the sword and the others fled, fearful they would meet the same fate.

Eider turned, a new battalion of guards had entered

260

and were running through the billowing smoke like a solid mass towards him.

'Get me a sword!' Taekhor screeched, struggling amid the trappings of his throne. Charone had vanished and the litter-bearers were trying desperately to do their master's bidding and help him to his feet. Deft as a shadow, Eider was upon them, striking out at the dithering servants and scattering them. Taekhor cried out as they fled from him and Eider clasped the monarch's bony shoulders in his strong grip, turning him about to use as a shield against the advancing guard.

Regor darted from the shadow of the doorway, his blond head bobbing in the torchlight, then lost once more to the safety of the nearest alcove. Lehon watched him go, then prodded Nairb to run forward and take up the elfin's old position whilst he guarded the rear. He waited until Regor had found another shadowed niche before making his own move in the wizard's wake.

So they made their way along corridor after corridor until at last they crouched together in the deep shadow of the great arch that began the long corridor up to the Great Hall. Regor screwed up his nose. 'I smell smoke!' he frowned.

'I see it!' the wizard pointed to the squared junction where corridors met and where the smoke veil drifted like a ghostly shade. They watched it slip through the corridors, glimpsing soldiers race across their vision and vanish into the choking vapours. Soon the heavy doors rumbled open and the corridor flooded with mauve light.

'Follow on,' Nairb insisted. 'We have found the Great Hall of Delights!'

They raced the length of the passageway in the wake of the guard, holding their breath and wrapping their neckerchiefs about their faces as the smoke grew thicker. Upon the threshold of the Great Hall they pressed themselves against the door and one by one crept unnoticed into the chaos.

Fire ate at the silken expanse of cushions while servants

and guards tried frantically to put it out. Sword-wielding captains ran towards the marble dais where Eider held the skeletal monarch hostage, the brittle neck and jaw clasped tight in the gauntlet-clad hand.

'Hold!' Eider warned the marauding soldiers. 'Or I snap his neck!'

'Do as he says!' Taekhor ordered, gasping in Eider's grip, feeling the power of the gem-studded glove. The captains held back and Eider glanced across at the heavy doors intent on dragging his hostage with him.

'You shall not get so far!' Taekhor spluttered.

Eider shook him into silence but before he had taken his first step from the throne's shadow, sudden pain wracked his skull and he fell headlong.

'Help me!' Taekhor cried out, pinned beneath Eider's stunned frame. 'Hurry worm!' he growled, glimpsing Charone as he scuttled from the shadows. In his hand was clutched the candlestick, the one with which he had struck the creator of this havoc. The one with which he had loyally defended his master.

The gnome bobbed up and down in thanksgiving for his master's safety, raising Taekhor to his unsteady feet then leaning him against the throne for support. Exhausted, Taekhor heard not one word of Charone's deeds or thanks, his shocked features still intent upon Eider who lay prostrate before him. 'So beautiful,' he wheezed sadly. 'So dangerous.''

'Dangerous, my lord,' Charone echoed. 'Very dangerous indeed!'

In the shadows the wizard's deft hand held Regor back. The elfin's temper flared. 'What are we waiting for?'

'Not yet,' Nairb told him, anxiously surveying the smoke-filled hall and the dais where Charone stood over their unconscious friend.

The fat arms of the gnome flailed in all directions. 'To the cells!' he commanded. 'Fetch the collar and chain! Fetch the cage! Our master would have 'im kept close by for 'is sport!'

'No,' Taekhor waved a dismissive hand.

'No, master?' Charone stammered.

'I dare not let such power live,' Taekhor whimpered regret even as he seethed with hatred.

Charone's face split into a wide grin and he knelt down to place his dagger at Eider's throat. 'Shall I kill it, master?' he offered delicately.

'I shall kill it!' Taekhor snarled, reaching out for a weapon with which to do the deed. The captain stepped forward with his sword to oblige, while Charone lent his bulk to steady his fragile master upon the two steps needed to reach his victim. The brittle arms trembled violently as Taekhor held the sword. Once again he contemplated the handsome form and face, the gauntlet-clad hand; he swallowed hard remembering its strength about his neck. He turned to Charone. 'First I shall take that glove!' he vowed. 'Then, go to, fetch the captive wizard. He shall see the meddler prince die and gladly give up the rest.' The sword wavered as strength faded from the feeble arms. Taekhor cried out. 'Summon the court into my presence. All shall witness my winning of the Triad glove!'

Charone nodded obediently. The fan-bearers ran through the open doors at his bidding and moments later the sleepy-eyed courtiers were thronging the corridors and pressing into the smoke-draped hall to witness their monarch's deed.

Within the deep shadows of aisles and recesses, the wizard bid his friends keep silent as they inched their way unnoticed in the wake of court activity.

Atop the dais Charone dithered, waiting for the blade to rise. Its fall would bring about the severing of the hand, and the gush of Eider's blood at last.

As Taekhor shifted his stance to deliver the blow, he caught some reflection on the marble floor and stopped. Charone had seen it and so had the captain who bent to take it up. The leather-covered hand passed it on to Taekhor who peered at it for long moments before curling his lip in disgust. 'Some discarded bauble!' he said, tossing it in Charone's direction.

The gnome clutched the oval stone in his sweaty palm and held it up for a better look. ''Tis a beauty, master,' he snickered. 'Red as fire.' The squared teeth showed in a grin. 'Red as blood!'

'Firestone!' Regor started as the gnome pocketed the gem. The wizard pressed a finger to his lips and led them on.

Charone bowed profusely for his master's gift, but Taekhor pushed him aside, too intent upon his task to care. 'Move aside, worm!' he scowled, the yellow arms straining to lift the blade.

In the darkness, Eider's anxious companions saw the blade slowly rise, saw the dark captain step on Eider's arm, steadying it for the cruel blow. In the yawning silence, Regor and the mortal lowered their heads in utter despair. The wizard watched on, a crystal tear forming on his cheek as he began to whisper the words of the sacred mantra of Horatious Thor. The placid face set, the limbs began to shake and the slender fingers vibrated to the very tips. Suddenly his eyes widened, transfixed by the gleam of rosewood on the edge of the sea of cushions. Nairb stretched out his arms and the power of the mantra drew the lute to him. It floated silently on the smoke veil and came finally to rest within his hands.

Regor and Lehon were silent as they watched the wizard stroke each fragile string and give it voice. Soon the gemrock hall flooded with the echo song, in pitch and melody as ancient as the magic Lore from which it sprang, woven anew by the wizard's mystic hand.

The captains stood with daggers drawn, awaiting their monarch's command, yet below the dais, courtiers and servants alike had been seized by the power of the music and had begun to rock unsteadily, and then to dance. Taekhor stood stock-still, the sword held in readiness, his ears twitching to the mystic sound as frantically he scanned every orifice of the hall for the perpetrator of such melodies. The mystic music soared to the cavern roof then fell, its flying notes weaving in networks of silken twine, shining threads that spread from the gemrock roof to the marble floor in geometric structures that edged the cavern round.

Taekhor watched each twisting strand, the tiny pin-points of his eyes at last sighting Nairb's shimmering form. 'Stop him!' he shrieked, thrusting a twiggy claw in the direction of the alcove. 'Stop that white enchanter!' he commanded.

As the dark captains charged across the marble floor, Nairb's gaunt shape stepped into the candlelight. He held the lute before him as a shield and took his stance afresh, attacking the fine tension of the strings until harmonies merged with discords and soaring pitch climbed helter skelter up the scale. In the backlash, bass timbres reverberated to the very core of the rock, and upon the dais Taekhor's sword clattered to the marble steps as he lost his grip upon it, desperate to protect his throbbing eardrums with thin fingers. The dark captains paid no heed to music, moving ever closer through the smoke but the wizard tossed the dark curls in defiance, his nimble fingers bending the shimmering strings. In an instant deep resounding chords echoed themselves in complex counterpoint and the silken strands twisted, spreading out their cords and rungs until a giant web took shape.

As tempo and melody entwined in endless variation, so the web was woven finer still, until the lute song rose to fevered crescendo and gossamer shot through with the vibrant power of Light. Now the web hung in glittering and multicoloured splendour, consuming the Great Hall from marble floor to vaulted roof. Now all was still for the creatures of the court, the servants, the dark captains and the guard were all entrapped within its delicate design.

Upon the dais Taekhor shook with fury and fear of the spell as Nairb's haloed form moved towards him across the glossy floor.

'Master, let us be gone!' Charone urged picking up the sword in their defence.

Taekhor stiffened with determination. 'I shall have that gauntlet!' he hissed snatching at the sword-hilt. Though both master and servant put all their effort to the task they could not raise the blade fast enough as the lute's frenzied pitch echoed on and Nairb's white form drew closer still.

'Curse it!' Taekhor spat, his face flushed green with rage.

Nairb held the lute in outstretched arms, the magical instrument now playing of itself as the final cords of the web attached in perfect lines and strands to the dais.

'To the labyrinth!' Taekhor commanded at full cry but Charone had already gone. Taekhor struggled to turn but had hardly moved before the magic notes had clutched him with silver fingers and bound him fast. One final growl of anger throbbed in Taekhor's scaly throat as the sticky web encased him and he was forced to drop the sword.

Nairb sighted the silk-trapped lord and all his court and ceased to play, yet still the lute song echoed on as he moved calmly towards the dais.

Meanwhile, Regor had watched Charone descend the narrow side-steps of the dais and had darted after him, zigzagging the still spreading strands of silk to grip the thief.

'Not so fast, gnome!' he growled into the fearstruck face.

Charone gabbled unintelligibly upon the topic of mercy as Regor pushed the dagger tip firmly against flabby flesh.

'You hold on your most hideous person that which belongs to me!' Regor snarled, searching the fat-layered frame, through cuffs and linings, hems and pockets until finally he clutched the Firestone in his fist.

At last Eider awoke and as his eyes focused he heard the drifting notes of an ancient melody. He glanced about him, gasping as he saw the intricate network of the magic web. Below he saw Taekhor's court enchanted and transfixed whilst beside him on the dais their spellbound lord was held fast by silken tracery. Eider drew close to the motionless features and raised the gauntlet-clad hand. He flexed his fingers before the transfixed gaze and laughed aloud as his diamond-studded fist cast spangles on the yellow skin. He turned, laughing still as he descended the shining steps to where the wizard stood.

Nairb clasped Eider to him. 'Thank the gods no harm be done!' he smiled relief.

'Thank the gods for music!' Eider grinned into the blood-drained face.

'Your magic notes saved all our lives,' Lehon marvelled, stroking the rose-coloured wood of the lute.

At their backs, spiralled notes resounded as the final rungs and ropes of the vast web joined. The gnome stood transfixed and Regor ducked and weaved to escape the sticky thread stretched out behind him as he raced down the steps.

'Good friend,' Eider cried as the elfin ran towards him through the clinging gossamer.

Regor clasped him tight. 'Music has strong magic so you always said!' he reminded, his face alight with joy.

Eider grinned. ''Tis thanks to the wizard's magic we are free.'

'Not free yet,' Lehon warned, scanning the smoky hall for an exit.

'Come,' Nairb urged, bidding them to follow him. 'Quickly! Already the echo song dies away.'

Eider, Regor and Lehon gazed about in awe as the wizard found the low door adjacent to the dais and led them silently into the inner sanctum.

'How do you know this place?' Eider gasped, taking in every detail of the silk-draped chamber.

'It was here I found the vile source of Taekhor's power,' Nairb explained.

The elfin touched the faceted walls and gilded tables whilst Lehon moved over to the tapestries, finding in their complex design the progress of a sensuous life.

Eider had found the marble table whereupon were set talismans and instruments of navigation and there upon the trestle were parchments inscribed with spheres and bisecting lines. He beckoned the wizard. 'Celestial maps,' he said anxiously. 'These are like your zodiacs.'

Nairb cast long fingers over the parchments. 'Indeed, these are solar charts,' he agreed. 'Your coming was expected.'

'Then you are not alone in your wisdom,' Eider's eyes met his. 'The unseelie lords knew of my coming and thus Zarratt too may know.'

'Perhaps,' Nairb said distractedly.

'You know he does!' Eider glared into the impassive face.

'I cannot be certain,' the wizard frowned.

Eider turned from him in sudden rage, the flare of torchlight at the farthest end of the chamber arresting his gaze. He saw the stone altar set in the darkest corner; upon it black candles were arranged and between them was set the stone plinth on which the mighty double-edged sword stood reverenced. Eider's heart-beat quickened. 'Such beauty,' he gasped as he drew close, appraising the figured blade and pommel, the dense green of the gem set at centre of the hilt.

'I never saw the like!' he murmured, enthralled.

''Tis an ancient relic . . . of the Lore,' the wizard said quietly.

Eider turned to him. 'Of seelie Lore?'

The wizard nodded and as their eyes met, their thoughts fused as one.

'Then it is the Triad blade!' Eider gasped.

'The sword of your destiny,' Nairb said with calm certainty.

Eider looked to the sword and knelt in homage.

'Honour not the corrupted blade,' the wizard breathed, raising him to his feet. 'Yet make that which is yours, your own!' he commanded.

Eider flexed the gauntlet-clad hand and nodded in silent reply. He turned again to the altar where the jewelled hilt cast its viridian rays about the blade. Regor drew close to the mortal and they watched together as Eider took the steps to the altar, silk black hair cascading the taut back. As he drew closer the torches flared into the blackness and Eider's heart beat heavy in his chest. The sword stood in all its magnificence but inches from his grip, and before it, upon the flat table of the altar, lay its belt and scabbard. The belt was of broad leather embroidered in red silk. Eider touched the soft tassels with a fingertip as he inspected the scabbard of leather and ivory, inlaid with gold. He glanced at the watchful blade, then cautiously took up the belt. This he fastened about his waist, feeling the scabbard hang heavily at his side. Yet again the great sword recalled his gaze, the keen blade emitting a deep green spear of light as if in retaliation for his deed. Eider's eyes gleamed with his intention and he thrust out the gauntlet-clad hand, his fingers flexing to clasp the ornate hilt.

At fingers touch the torches flared anew and Eider felt his leathered hand fasten tight about the hilt, felt the dead weight of the sword as he tried to lift it from its allotted place. The ancient relic did not move and the stone at its hilt began to transform before his eyes until it throbbed like a tiny molten pool at the sword's heart. Eider's brow was laced with sweat and he heaved for breath as the gauntlet's grip fused ever tighter.

A sudden jolt and power coursed through his forearm. He shuddered with its primal force but as he gritted his teeth he found himself able to raise the weapon free of the plinth. Arm and hand trembled under the sword's great weight and as he clasped his left hand to the gauntlet's aid he turned his back upon the dark altar. Now the blade emitted fiery shafts, rapidly turning to pure heat as Eider descended the altar steps. By the time he had taken the final step to the jet floor, the hilt was a molten mass and the blade flushed blood red.

Eider was gripped by fear and pain as he paced slowly towards the wizard, yet at the floor's centre he was forced to halt as the sword moved of itself, the bloodshot blade arcing first left then right as if in combat with some imaginary foe. Eider cried out, almost cast to the floor by the force of the whiplash. As he struggled to regain his feet, the sword arced again, but this time he stayed its rebound. His eyes fixed on nothingness as will-power alone tightened the gauntlet's grip upon the hilt.

'It makes combat with the air!' Lehon whispered, marking the red-hot weals in the blackness.

'It fights Eider!' Regor frowned. 'Hold to, friend,' he growled beneath his breath, round face set with grim determination as he saw Eider halt the sword's aggressive display.

Now the blade pulsed deep magenta as Eider held it parallel to his solar plexus. He drew breath to calm himself, but at once the blade swept to and fro like a pendulum, its fiery steel scraping the jet floor on the downward stroke. The sparks that it cast up chequered Eider's features as he took fresh stance. He had hardly mastered the blade's rhythmic marking of time before the sword whipped upwards into the air casting him left then right as it drew its red arcs anew.

The mortal clasped his ears as the great blade struck the onyx walls on every side, its metallic echoes reverberating through the heavy shaft. Fire brands shot about

Eider's taut frame as he tried to arrest the ancient weapon's malevolent attack.

'Hagdarth . . . Horam . . . ' Nairb quickly whispered the incantation, gazing at the lethal blade.

Eider gasped for air, trying to recoup his strength in the moment of the blade's inertia. He cried out as the sword sighed and plummeted like a diviner, cleaving in two the marble table near his feet. Eider stooped beneath the awesome weight of the shaft, his gauntleted hand welded to the hilt. 'Triad blade shall relinquish Dark!' he growled, his white face fixed with immovable command. At his words the gems of the gauntlet shot through with sparks of ice blue, freezing leather and stiffening the molten metal of the hilt. 'Aksharat!' Eider cried aloud, his fingers frozen inside the glove, the muscles of his arms and legs pulsing with new vigour. He felt his shoulders strain, his spine straighten and he lifted the great blade high against its will!

The sword hissed as the ice-diamonds of the gauntlet hardened the hilt. Now the opaque gem ebbed to vibrant cerise and then to lilac as Eider forced the blade vertical. Gritting his teeth he pressed the hilt to his lips and kissed the stone. With the deed the blade shot through with dazzling silver and Eider's heart raced. Slowly he raised the hilt again, this time to press the oval gem to his forehead. As it passed before his eyes he saw the gemstone change from unseeing agate to translucent amethyst and with a prayer of thanksgiving he pressed it softly to his forehead in ritual acceptance of the sword's obeisance. The cool hilt eased his brow and he felt the warm pulse of the gemstone's power against his skin. The blood rushed through Eider's veins and immediately he was able to withstand the blade's awesome weight. Now he set himself in combat stance, feeling the sword grant him control as he prepared to wield the blade in ritual display.

First, he swept the shaft in a wide arc above his head to east and then to west, next he turned, drawing deft and lethal weals to his left and to his right. He gave a silent

271

sigh as he completed the ritual arcs but then the spirit of the blade returned, its power pulsed through his arm, his gloved hand whipping involuntarily at the hilt and casting the sword downward in a pattern of tight circles. Eider was seized by panic yet the great blade whispered as it slid magically to rest within the scabbard. He gasped for the sword was set at his hip as if it had always been there. His hand now ached with the effort and he flexed his fingers, seeing the gems upon the gauntlet's back shimmer their multicoloured beauty once again. Stunned and weary, Eider looked to his companions.

The wizard's eyes had not once left the blade until this moment and he paced towards Eider, shaking with emotion. 'Good friend!' he cried as he clasped Eider to him and fastened the Triad Cloak about his shoulders. 'I kept all safe,' he told him. 'Now 'tis complete! The final amulet is won!' he exclaimed, his face alight with joy.

'Then wise man we are close!' Eider gripped his arm tightly. 'Close to Rhye!'

'Indeed,' the wizard smiled. 'And with these three amulets the land is saved!'

Regor and Lehon embraced Eider, their joy in his triumph reforging the bonds of friendship.

'Yet come,' Lehon reminded. 'We must escape these tunnels.'

They turned to see Nairb testing the gemrock walls and taking a torch in his grip Lehon set to and added light to the wizard's task. Eider made to follow, but Regor held him fast. 'Friend, I willed you strength to win,' he said in earnest.

Eider made to shake his hand, but Regor took off his cap and fell to his knee in homage as he kissed the gauntlet-clad hand. Eider flushed but before he could raise the elfin to his feet, Regor had turned over his hand. 'And this ...' he said, dropping the Firestone onto the leather palm. 'I saved it ... for you.'

Eider helped him to his feet and clasped his forearm in firm embrace. 'The gods walk always with you for this deed,' he nodded emphatically.

'This way!' Lehon urged them as he raised the torch and together all three followed on in the wizard's footsteps through the narrow opening.

Pitch blackness met them beyond the low door and in the flare of the torches they saw tunnels running off in every direction. 'Which way?' Lehon's brow creased. Regor sniffed the musty air.

Eider took one decisive step forward, but the wizard held him back. 'I take the lead, my friend,' Nairb said. 'Better follow one with knowledge than enter unprepared.'

'You know these passages?' Eider questioned.

Nairb shook his head. 'I know not the paths, but have knowledge of the key.'

'What key is that?' Lehon frowned.

Regor scowled into the mortal's face. 'Riddles!'

Nairb shook his head. 'Not quite,' he said patiently. 'Yet what we enter is very similar – 'tis a labyrinth.'

'I heard tales of such things as a child,' Eider mused thoughtfully.

'And I,' Lehon added. 'Why, such places trap the unwary!'

''Tis a testing ground,' Nairb breathed, his birdlike eyes intent upon the endless dark before them.

'Have we not been tested enough?' Regor spat.

'A proving of the soul,' Nairb frowned into Eider's face. 'Fate brought us here, together, that I might make the passage easy.'

Regor raised the torch. 'But which passage?' he implored.

As he spoke, Nairb drew a square on the air and all three watched, amazed to see the ornate box appear. Nairb placed it on the ground, extracting from it a perfect sphere of wood. This he broke into fragments and pressed them into Eider's hands. Eider's face paled. 'What shall I do with these?'

'Triangle. Pentacle!' Nairb smiled, closing his eyes.

The elfin shook his head. 'Games!' he whispered into Lehon's ear.

Eider looked hard at the wooden pieces, but then with a blink of his eyes he saw the movement of a child's hands. 'The girl-child!' he exclaimed into Nairb's beaming face. 'She solved the puzzle!'

'She trusted to herself,' Nairb reminded gently. 'Now, close your eyes and watch again the girl-child's hands,' he breathed. Regor shrugged his shoulders uneasily, yet neither he nor the mortal could take their eyes from the irregular shapes of wood.

Eider's face changed from panic to serenity as his eyes shuttered and the vision returned. A glimmer of light in the mind's eye and the child's hands worked fast, testing and gripping, the fragments squeaking and sliding, then snap! Eider followed sight and sound, joining the fragments in his grip. 'Triangle!' he cried at last, holding out the fragile construction.

'Good,' Nairb laughed. 'Hold up the lattice to the dark,' he instructed. Eider obeyed and watched enrapt as the torchlight cast a shadowed design upon the rock. 'See . . . the shadow of the pentacle,' Nairb drew the shape. All three nodded silent appraisal. 'Where the apex of four triangles fall, four tunnels weave, each leading to impasse,' Nairb explained.

'What of the fifth?' Lehon frowned.

'That points to the surface,' Nairb whispered and thrust his bony forefinger to the core of the central passageway. 'We take the way of the soul.'

'The middle way,' Eider noted with a smile.

The wizard nodded reassurance and led them on. Lehon and Eider followed close in Nairb's footfall while the elfin guarded the rear, his acute sense of hearing tuned for sounds of pursuit. On they trod, their long shadows racing ahead of them until they were halted by the rising wedges of a vast staircase. At Nairb's signal they began to climb, the deep steps seeming to ascend forever.

'Listen,' Regor whispered in the dim light.

All strained their ears, hearing nothing but the distant trickle of water, the steady heaving of their lungs. So they climbed on, but at the sight of the yawning abyss that spread below, Eider felt compelled to stop, to press his back against the damp wall of rock, to cling to the fragments of wood still in his grip. The lids of his eyes flickered in spasm as the flash of memory-light brought with it sight of the small hands working the wood. Eider responded, he tested and teased, the fragments squeaking and sliding together, then, snap! 'Ka-aba' he cried and Nairb turned to him, seeing in his trembling hands the now half-constructed puzzle.

'Cube,' he smiled in happy reply.

In that moment Regor slipped and lost his balance, teetering on the edge of the stairway. Lehon snatched at him, pulling him back to safety by the edge of his ragged jerkin, but the elfin's cap was lost. They watched its flight, seeing it shrink to a pinpoint then vanish into the blackness. They turned as one, noting the intricate design of squares cut into the rock as a flight of steps. Regor blinked hard, for the steps appeared both to climb and to descend though they grew smaller in size with distance. The elfin shuddered, disoriented.

'Do we climb up?' Lehon questioned making no sense of the inverted design. 'Or do we climb down?'

The wizard held out a reassuring hand. 'Fear not . . . we climb,' he said simply.

The damp walls echoed to the snap of wood and Lehon held aloft the torch. In its flare all three saw the perfect sphere set upon Eider's palm. 'Circle!' he smiled triumphantly into their solemn faces as he handed Nairb the complete puzzle. The wizard looked up, yet nothing could be seen but endless dark.

'Put out the torches,' he ordered.

Lehon started anxiously. 'We cannot.'

''Tis madness, without light we shall fall!' Regor argued.

'Put out the fire, our trust must be in the Triad now,' the wizard persuaded.

'Do as he says,' Eider insisted, casting Regor's flare into the abyss. Lehon looked long into the dark eyes before following Eider's example.

They stood consumed by the blackness for what felt like eternity itself, none daring to move or make a sound until Eider cried out, 'I see it! A sphere of light!'

The wizard smiled in relief as all made out the perfect pinpoint of daylight shining far above. 'Praise the gods,' Nairb breathed his thanks.

'And pray they tell us how to reach it!' Regor scowled, bound to the spot by fear.

'We cannot move without light,' Lehon reasoned.

'The Triad shall give us light,' Nairb answered.

Eider's heart raced as he understood the wizard's words and drew the sword from its scabbard. As it met the waiting dark, the broad blade gleamed, its soft light making all things clear. So they moved on, up towards the circle of light; above them rose a funnel of rock, the eye of daylight grown more distinct at its farthest point. At last they felt the rush of cold air on their faces and knew this sphere to be their exit.

'The shaft is treacherous,' Eider handed the wizard the Triad sword and bent down so that Lehon could climb up into the funnel.

'There are wedges, narrow and well spread,' the mortal gasped as he grappled with the dusty rock. With a groan of effort he began to climb towards the light.

'Press your back to the rock, your feet to the opposite rock for support!' Eider instructed.

Lehon did as he was bid, sharp fingers of granite piercing his shirt as he edged his way up the shaft. Here and there gnarled roots protruded from the compressed rock and earth and Lehon stretched out for them but failed to grip.

'Try again,' Eider urged amid the dust fall.

Lehon lunged for the twisted root and snatched it up, testing its strength as he pressed against the walls with legs astraddle. Soon he was standing on the sturdy root and reaching above to use others as a ladder to the surface.

Sure of his progress, Eider shinned up after him, gasping with the effort, rock-dust spiralling about him and clogging his eyes and mouth. He glanced below, Regor had begun to climb after him, his golden hair coated with the dustfall. Eider clutched the thick root now firmly in his grasp and pulled himself up upon it as Lehon had done, but the root slithered with the shifting duststream, the force of its shift flinging Eider away from the rock face. He cried out, feeling himself fall, yet managed to hang on, careering back against the fluted wall as loose shale rained down upon him. Below, the elfin curled himself up for protection as the debris showered forth.

'Hold on!' the wizard cried from below.

Eider raised his legs and halted the swinging motion by tightening his grip on the root. Meanwhile, Regor had gripped the new-formed ledges of the shaft and pulled himself upward, supporting Eider's weight with his back and shoulders. Eider glanced down to see the glow of Triad light, held safe within the wizard's grip, and carved out beyond, the intricate design of the mystic puzzle, as if it formed the heart of the mountain. Sweat trickled down his brow and he shuddered with memory. 'Trap Mountain,' he spat.

Lehon clasped Eider's hand and pulled him up after him; together they pulled upon the strong tuberous root which hung from the craggy opening high above. It ran through their fingers like strong yarn. 'Our lifeline,' he whispered to Eider beneath his breath, threading it down to the others as a coarse rope to aid their climb. The wizard had begun to climb, the Triad sword held firmly in his belt. He followed the elfin's route and soon had his grip upon the knotty cords, climbing on in the footsteps of his companions.

'The way is clearly marked!' Lehon shouted out as he secured the next leathery rung, his senses now alerted to a low, distant rumble issuing forth from the core of the rock itself. He flattened himself against the moss-smeared face, his fingers hooked into time-worn hollows, and listened intently. Shifting his position, he pressed his ear against the damp stone: a throaty roar echoed through the rock. They all had heard it.

''Tis the thunder of heart-beats!' Regor shouted, his keen ears attuned to the alien sounds. He wound his fingers about the strong roots and pulled himself up onto the ledge beside Eider. 'What joys do the gods prepare to welcome us this time?' his voice grated.

A few seconds elapsed before the wizard's dust-caked head was seen and he clambered up into a position of safety. ''Tis a natural force at work,' he pronounced, fingertips pressed against the rock face. 'And one close at hand.'

Eider gazed up at the disc of light above them and taking hold of the tangled skeins, he called out to Lehon to climb on. They continued to ascend, feeling for finger-grooves in the rock, pressing their toes into the narrowest of fissures and hauling themselves laboriously up towards the spreading circle of daylight. Time and again they were forced to press themselves against the wet stones as slivers of rock showered down, carved free by those above.

Lehon climbed higher, the disc of light grown into a dome until with each tired manoeuvre it changed from cold white to the watery blue of a winter sky. His enthusiasm rallied as his mouth moistened with the first taste of sweet, sharp air and he pulled himself on with renewed vigour.

The once distant rumble had now grown to a deep, sonorous roar, and wrapping the blackened coils about his fist, Lehon moved determinedly upwards taking the final stage of the climb, hand over hand, his muscular legs powering him on towards the jagged rim. With an emphatic push he was free of the shaft, his eager hands groping dry rock and soft earth. He fell exhausted onto the springy turf, filling his lungs with the taste of clean air. His mortal eyes applauded the blueness of the heavens so long unseen, and he tingled as the breeze touched his cheeks, blowing his hair about his face. But contemplation turned to consternation as he felt the earth tremble beneath him and he rolled over onto his stomach, searching out the source.

'Friend, your hand?' Eider's anxious voice shook him from thought and he crawled back to the opening, extending strong arms to his comrade's aid.

'Look on,' Lehon urged as Eider eased himself from the shaft.

They stood on a rocky promontory which hung precariously above a yawning chasm of bone-white rock. The snows had disappeared and in their place bleached stone swept upward in majestic towers, whilst to the right a hairline pathway threaded the craggy profile, unravelling itself across the impassive face. Where the pathway ceased, the source of the deafening roar could be seen. From the heart of the east face, a torrent of water gushed forth to form a dazzling curtain of fine spray. Millions of crystal globes danced above the bubbling foam, surrendering themselves to the ice air, and where the torrent smashed against the rocks, a shimmering cloak of mist rose up, trapping a watery rainbow in its folds. At the base of the falls a lake churned with the impact of the torrent, reflecting in the water gold sunlight and the azure blue of the sky.

Eider led them on along the hairline path and soon amid the curtain of fine spray they glimpsed the water-splashed walkway that etched its narrow path behind the falls and across to the opposite bank. He moved on impulsively, but Regor caught his arm. 'Friend, you are too rash,' he warned.

Eider spread out his arms to encompass their surroundings. 'There is no way but this,' he said simply. 'The falls wait here for us and cross we must.'

Regor scowled in silence, his eyes meeting Eider's in a reproachful glare. Eider tightened, then wheeled about, his swarthy features glistening with the spray. Suddenly he was gone, stepping briskly over the wet stones towards the shimmering curtain of water and mist.

Nairb called out to him but his voice was lost to the

279

frenzy of the falls and he turned back to his anxious companions. 'Be strong of heart,' he said calmly and reached out to clasp Lehon's wrist. 'Believe in what you hold most dear,' he urged, his voice bright with certainty.

Lehon felt a stab of fear as he looked hesitantly beyond the wizard and into the raging waters. He inhaled deeply as if partaking of the wizard's calm, then tightening his belt with firm resolve, he took to the rocks and onto the dripping walkway. Nairb watched him go before turning to the elfin who stood transfixed before the thunderfall, his mouth frozen half agape. The wizard extended a hand of encouragement, but Regor stepped back, unsure. He scanned the rocky towers, the churning waters and the moving sky. Regor shook his head and turned away, but the wizard reached for him. 'Come, we follow,' he said quietly.

Regor stretched out a trembling hand, then as their fingers locked he felt the wise man's calm flood through him and felt courage stand beside him. Together they stepped over the water-smoothed stones, their clothes soon heavy with the spray as they peered through the fine mist to glimpse the dark drenched forms ahead of them.

Halfway across, Eider halted, his hand cupped the back of his head in despair for the walkway had been swept away by Nature's force and a perilous gap had opened between its end and its resumption. He turned anxiously to the wizard, his face streaming with the spray, his shoulders studded with crystal gems. The rage of the falls was so deafening that they were forced to yell until their lungs ached and as Eider gestured towards the awesome gap, all hung their heads in solemn despair.

Eider leaned upon the sword, devoid of means to straddle the gulf. The figured blade glistened in the filtered light and he watched its shadow reflected in the glassy curtain. He narrowed his eyes, within the water sheen it looked solid and strong, a twin blade so real that he fancied he could reach out and take it up.

The wizard touched his arm lightly, 'Look beyond what you perceive.' Though he strained to be heard, Nairb's voice was distant, time ancient. Eider shook his head unable to understand the meaning of the wizard's words. Nairb pointed to the crumbled walkway and to the swirling waters beneath. 'The water divides,' he turned to Eider and clasped his forearm firmly. 'In you is the power to unite.'

Eider wiped the spray from his eyes and stared afresh at the yawning gap, seeing no way of traversing the spacelessness. 'Yet how?' he challenged.

The wizard spread his hand towards the sword. 'Transcend the physical,' he said with a smile of calm. 'Herein lies the bridge to your destiny.'

Eider's brow was furrowed with uncertainties, yet his instincts compelled him to take up the Triad blade and move to the edge of the crumbled pathway. Regor made to stop him, but Lehon held him back. The water wailed like some terrible banshee as Eider sank to his knees, the dripping locks of his hair hanging limply over the water-filled abyss. At his back, the elfin turned away, unable to look.

The blade upon his flattened palm, Eider took the pommel between his fingers and placed it gently upon the last stone of the walkway. Carefully he slipped his hand from beneath the blade, the weight tempered by a solitary finger on the pommel. The blade trembled slightly, then steadied. Eider watched on enrapt as rivulets of water ran the length of the shaft, on and on until they reached the tip to form a globe of crystal. Captured within the glassy eye, sunlight was held in rainbow hues and Eider's heart leapt with hope. From the crystal core was the blade reflected on until the steel had stretched far across the divide and united both sides of the walkway as one. From crystal had formed a bridge of steel and as Eider carefully withdrew his fingertips from the pommel, the Triad sword was still and horizontal, supported it seemed by the very air itself.

He turned an uneasy look upon the wizard. Nairb's eyes were closed in holy communion with the gods, yet he spoke as if he had seen all. 'Walk with mind and spirit,' he said calmly.

Eider looked fearfully at the sword-span and tentatively he placed his foot upon the flat steel, testing its stability – it held firm beneath his weight. In the spacelessness, the blade seemed narrower than a hair but when next he looked, he did not see the quivering steel or glassy reflection but looked upon a walkway of gleaming silver. He felt his heart burst with courage and took the first steps out onto the shaft, his soul freed by the knowledge that the Triad would not falter nor pitch him to the depths. He walked the bridge of steel as pure spirit, his physical form exerting no more weight than ether, seeing himself reach safety and turn in joy to beckon his comrades on.

Regor and Lehon were dumbstruck at the sight. 'What magic is this you perform?' the elfin demanded of the wizard.

Nairb shook his head. 'The magic is within us all,' he smiled, flourishing a hand towards the newly formed walkway.

Regor pushed away. 'Not I!' he stated.

Nairb drew close to him. 'Regor, my friend, 'tis fear will harm and hope that will save,' he told him. 'The Triad will not fail those who would aid its wielder.'

The elfin looked up at him with narrowed eyes. Beyond the walkway, Eider stood arms outstretched, urging them on. Regor lowered his head, 'Wizard, I am afraid,' he said solemnly.

'And I,' Lehon added, his eyes strained against the fine spray, his face white with terror.

Nairb took their hands in turn and bound them together with his own. 'I will not see thee lost,' he assured tightening his grip in a pledge. 'Trust in the goodness of your heart, believe not in what you see, but what you wish to be.'

They moved slowly towards the argent span, the wizard leading on, his hand holding firm to Lehon's and the guide to that of the trembling elfin. As Nairb took the first step, his face bore the serenity of knowing and he moved out across the chasm, his wet hair streaming from him like glossy black pennants. Lehon crossed himself and followed on, whilst the elfin darted a look at Eider and wished him triumph and the fulfilment of his dream.

'Dreams,' Regor smiled to himself. Why none could dream such dreams as these, nor see the like of them in becoming. This was more than sleep and the Triad more than mere adornment, and Eider, whatever he be, had proved himself worthy wielder of the power. Regor tightened his mouth with resolve; if he, a mere elfin perished now, then so be it, for he had followed in the path of dreams and knew them to be far more. He closed his eyes and grabbed Lehon's forearm, stepping closer to the edge of the crumbled walkway.

From the other side, Eider watched them move as a ghostly apparition across the bridge of blade, Nairb leading on. Eider praised the gods for their benevolence and vowed his allegiance to Triad Lore. Whatever had been designed for him in days to come, he would be the instrument of Triad power, there for the gods to do with as they bid. Soon the wizard's bony fingers wrapped about Eider's fist and he knew them safe, knew that the Triad Lore had claimed him for its own.

— 23 —

Eider rose with first light, longing for the gleaming towers of Rhye but knowing they still had miles to trek before he would have sight of them. Silently he watched the rising cloud-veil and saw the land revealed, a land so grey and damp that only skeletal ferns and sparse grasses survived. The dark eyes followed the line of tangled hedgerows and blackened trees, all wasted, all starved of warmth and light. He smelt the air, tinged with the bitter-sweet of linseed and decaying bark. Winter had surely overtaken autumn's fire, and now the forlorn earth laboured wet and dull beneath a brooding sky.

He turned back to the camp, rallying his companions and bidding them gather their belongings for the walk. Carefully he wrapped the Triad sword in the silken folds of the Cloak and placed them within his canvas bag.

Together they ploughed on through soggy meadow-land, through waist-high grasses and decaying bracken.

'What plan, friend?' the elfin asked as he drew alongside Eider. He did not reply and so Regor extracted the clay pipe from the pocket of his jerkin and pointed with it. 'We must have a plan,' he frowned, 'or will Zarratt welcome us with the affection of a long lost uncle?'

Eider still made no reply, continuing on his way with steady pace.

'Where do we go?' Regor urged. 'How do we know we go the right way?' The wizard cast the elfin a glare of warning but Regor continued to pester, 'No favours await us in Rhye!'

Eider turned a frown upon him, 'Triad shall aid us.'

'So he says!' Regor frowned dropping his voice as he cocked a glance at the wizard. 'But one sword, against armies? I cannot see that at all!' The elfin wrinkled up his nose. 'Friend, you are deceived!' he said sadly.

Eider halted in his tracks, ''Tis you who are deceived, good Regor, not I!'

Silenced by Eider's tone, the elfin paced on ahead mumbling curses.

''Tis natural apprehension grips him,' Nairb reassured Eider as he and Lehon drew close. 'He shall see all in time.'

'So shall we all, I hope!' Lehon frowned.

Before Eider could speak Regor's cries were heard and drawing his sword Eider raced with Lehon through the bracken. But then Nairb heard laughter and as he drew close saw their faces were bright with mirth, for there caught in a rope snare hung the elfin. Red-faced and cursing he flailed his arms in the air in a desperate fury. His three companions shook their heads in mock woe as Regor's contortions succeeded only in scattering the contents of his pockets to the earth below.

'Friends,' Regor wheezed as they laughed on, 'release me! Give me the solid earth!'

Eider stood hands on hips surveying the sorry sight, 'Why Lehon, is it not an elfin?' he taunted pushing the helpless Regor in Lehon's direction.

'Aye, so it is! And I thought it our supper caught at last!' Lehon laughed pushing the swinging torso of the elfin back in Eider's direction. Regor struggled and cursed.

'Come now, Regor!' Eider cajoled. 'What elfin sport is this?'

Regor's face burned with rage as he swung back towards Lehon, 'Let me down!' he commanded with a growl. 'Or by the pointed ears of my ancestors I swear I'll . . .' But the elfin curse was lost to the thundering of hoofs as riders closed in upon them from every side.

In a flash Eider had severed the rope, and Regor plummeted to the coin-strewn earth swearing aloud even as he snatched for sword and dagger. He took his stance beside Eider as the riders closed in, yet they knew they were outnumbered and vulnerable within the sparse woodland.

Eider motioned them to run for cover, but retreat was barred by the second group of horsemen who approached at greater speed. Regor tossed his dagger to Nairb trying to arm him, but the wizard merely fumbled with the weapon panic-stricken. Eider's fear-filled eyes flashed with sudden decision and taking the pack from his back he tossed it to safety among the tall ferns.

'Friend!' Regor cried desperately. 'The time has come to defend us all with fate's amulets!'

'The gods dictate their time, not I!' Eider shouted in hurried reply.

The riders were upon them and the woodland echoed to the heavy clank of steel and stave.

'The dogs wear Zarratt's livery!' Eider cried unleashing long held venom upon each burly attacker, forcing every ounce of strength behind the hilt as blades locked and his opponent stumbled in the bracken.

Meanwhile, Regor and Lehon ran between the rearing horses, felling riders with blows from sword and fist. Nairb threw down the dagger despatching two of the riders with his walking stave, the recipients of its blows stunned most effectively he thought!

Eider rallied as each visored rider fell to the sheer fury of his attack, and soon he found himself astride another of them, sword poised to deal a fatal blow. Yet, before he could deliver it he himself was felled and his attacker pinioned him to the ground.

Eider gasped as the dagger pressed against his throat, with a tightening of his limbs he wrenched the heavy visor and flung his assailant from him. They soon were locked in battle, and though Eider was the master in skill and strength, his wiry opponent was fleet of foot and fought with the fury of a regiment!

Eider wheeled about, hauling the man over his shoulder and sending him crashing to the damp earth. Though dazed, his opponent landed a glancing blow to Eider's thigh which sent him sprawling, but as he fell,

Eider pushed his boot firmly into his stomach and thrust him backwards through the air. Snatching up his discarded dagger, Eider dived upon him. 'Prepare to die, Zarratt's cur!' he growled, bearing down upon the wiry frame with all his might. With one forceful wrench he pulled away the helmet and pressed the blade to the naked flesh of the throat. But then he stopped abruptly, for his attacker was a mere boy, no more than fourteen years old! The youthful features were struck with fear as Eider's eyes fixed on him.

'Kill me not in the name of the usurper,' the youth gasped in defiance.

Eider frowned, 'Then in whose name will you die?' he demanded, tracing the youthful jaw-line with the dagger-tip.

'Rhye's name!' the youth cried. 'I serve the seelie realm!'

Eider clutched at the fair hair. 'Then you serve the usurper!' he growled.

'Not so!' the youth gasped. 'My kinsmen swore allegiance to the rightful heir! Long live the King!' the boy cried, eyes closed prepared for death.

Eider pressed his face into the pale features, 'Where is this rightful heir?'

'He comes! Soon he shall claim his throne!' the boy blurted, '. . . and we to aid him!'

Eider withdrew the dagger-blade. 'Who are you?' he demanded, but before he had his answer Eider heard the slither of steel at his back, felt the sudden ice of cold steel between his shoulder blades. His taut limbs relaxed then, and he dropped the dagger.

Quickly on his feet, the boy snatched up his sword marking Eider with its tip, 'I am Pantul, son of Gaunt!' he declared, 'and you are my prisoner!' He motioned to the soldiers left and right, 'Bind them, we take them with us.'

While he and his companions were tied and hoisted to the backs of the mounts, the rest of the battalion of men, fearing that more of Eider's allies were at large, searched the undergrowth with boot and sword. Eider stiffened as the youth emerged from the tangled bracken holding the canvas bag aloft in triumph. Eider clenched his teeth, angry that the Triad was no longer in his possession, confused at the sudden impotence of the gauntlet about his hand.

The soldiers and their captives left the clearing in solemn convoy, journeying in silence by the fallow fields and roughly built walls. Eider noted the sad grey landscape, the meagreness of light, the sparseness of the flora. How dark this land of Rhye was, how bleak the lives of its people must be. Finally, they reached the garrison. It stood on a sandstone hill overlooking the bend of the narrow river. The walls that surrounded the courtyard were protected by a moat, and behind the heavy entrance doors stood a portcullis. At intervals the curtain wall was strengthened by towers and Eider realised that this was no mere outpost but the fortress of some noble.

As they approached, the portcullis was hauled up and the horses clattered over the drawbridge and passed within. 'Inform my father I return safe, and with prisoners!' the boy grinned as he paced through the archway. At his back the guards carried Nairb's wooden box and the canvas bag.

'But my son you disobeyed!' the voice of Lord Gaunt rose in reprimand. 'Your hunt was for the taking of boar, not prisoners!'

'But father . . . four of Zarratt's spies were on our land!' the youth extended both arms in desperate explanation. 'We could not let it pass!'

The old man shook his head, 'Zarratt's spies! You know this to be true?'

Pantul frowned. 'They were dressed for mountain climes! If not spies then they are bandits!'

Gaunt raised a silencing hand, 'My son, your judgements are too hasty.'

'Father, here is proof! These are no ordinary travellers!' Pantul placed Nairb's wooden box on the oak table.

The old man looked at it quizzically as his son struggled with the latch. 'The lid is held fast!' Pantul exclaimed. 'Nought but a vice will open it.' The boy placed Eider's pack beside the box. 'But this ...' the arched brows accentuated joy-filled eyes as he unwrapped the canvas to show the glittering cloak. From its folds he brought forth the sword. ''Tis plunder!' he nodded emphatically, 'of bandits ... or mercenaries!'

At the sight of the sword Gaunt rose to his feet, his old eyes scanning its intricate beauty, the glowing amethyst at its hilt.

'Father ...?' Pantul urged seeing the old man's face turn pale.

Lord Gaunt stroked the cloak's fine silk. 'Have your prisoners brought here.'

Pantul bowed at his command.

'I would have them tell the origin of these things,' Gaunt murmured as his son paced from the room.

Lord Gaunt stood watchful at his window, his brow deeply furrowed until at last the doors of the hall swung open and Eider and his companions were led inside. On seeing the great sword Eider's heart leapt and as the gaze of the noble lord met his he stood erect and proud, feeling the old man scan his features and his form.

The Lord Gaunt wondered at Eider's swarthy features, his strange garb. He turned to look at Nairb, frowning at the length of his curly hair, the flowing white robes. The elfin's mischievous face and darting eyes unnerved him for he knew well the way of elves. He frowned upon the mortal, his skin colour and his bone structure so alien to seelie kind. He turned back to Eider and as their eyes met again Gaunt almost smiled. He flourished a wrinkled hand over the amulets, 'What know you of these?' he demanded.

'The objects you have stolen are my own,' Eider glared. 'Mine and the good wizard's.'

At his last word Pantul stepped forward but his father halted him with a look. Gaunt turned steady eyes upon Nairb, 'You are a wizard?'

'Of the seelie Lore,' Nairb qualified with a slight bow of his head.

Lord Gaunt raised a hand. 'Then it is fortunate that you were found on my lands ...' He turned to Eider, 'Young man, what is your business that you travel with such as he?'

Eider frowned, 'I seek the kingdom's seat,' he said simply.

'Liar!' Pantul accused.

Lord Gaunt silenced him once more. 'Traveller, make no light jest! 'Tis barely tolerated here, but would seal your fate if you stray further!'

Eider's dark eyes flashed at the old man's tone, 'Sir, I do not jest and know well the dangers that I face!' He glanced about him, 'yet the lowlanders told me of men of war, loyal to the seelie cause!'

'Father!' Pantul cried. 'Speak no more!'

Gaunt glared at his son, but cast the same look on Eider, 'Sir, leave us now for you shall find no vestige of seelie Lore in this place!'

'Not even for the wielder of its amulets?' Nairb questioned.

The silence was heavy as all eyes looked upon the sword.

'They fear us,' Regor whispered into Lehon's ear.

'Many have laid claim to that most arduous of thrones, yet none with such a sword as this.' Gaunt looked into Eider's face again, 'Not since Eyre.'

Eider's face set, 'The name of my ancestor and the name of my father.' He looked to the wizard who with silent gesture gave him his cue. Slipping his hand inside his jerkin Eider found the leather pouch, and Gaunt watched intent as the Firestone slid onto Eider's palm. 'The gift of my father, the King, on the eve of his death.'

The aged man gasped as he fell to his knees in homage.

Regor and Lehon watched him amazed, but the youthful Pantul was confused. He took a solitary pace forward but was halted by Eider's immovable glare.

Once upon his feet, Lord Gaunt nodded solemnly into

Eider's face, 'Your voice and face came to me as if from the past when we first met . . . but this . . .' The old voice trembled into silence and Eider clasped his arm seeing the old man overcome with emotion. The grey eyes met his again, 'Sire, we have waited long.' At his words the room filled with the sound of clattering armour as Pantul and all his men at arms fell to their knees in homage to their King.

Lord Gaunt looked again upon the perfect gemstone, 'Sire, your father asked my kinsman to wait upon this very stone, as a proof of your return.'

Eider held the old man to him, 'I have returned, and with All-Power!' He smiled into the weary face. Gaunt clasped the gauntlet-clad hand and looked with joy upon the rippling silk of the cloak.

'Yet still their combined power has not been granted,' Nairb reminded quietly.

'But Prince, it is clear to all, you are the chosen wielder!'

Eider nodded his thanks for the old man's faith, 'Yet it is as the wizard said. The Triad's full power is still unknown to me.'

Nairb raised the hourglass from the table. 'With fall of night the crescent Moon shall rise, and Mercury begins his cycle of All-Power.'

Lord Gaunt turned to Pantul, 'Send word! Summon the loyal men of the five sees!'

24

They came in the shifting light of dusk, the loyal lords and captains of the five sees, wrapped in their heavy cloaks and bearing the gift of weaponry for their King. Beneath their winter garb all wore the livery of the seelie realm, their leather doublets embossed with the spreading wings of the royal phoenix insignia.

Pantul led them one by one into the great hall, where shuttered windows kept all light within. The oak table now served for their conference, its gleaming wood reflecting candleglow where scrolls and parchments did not cover the surface. As each man took his seat, his standard was unfurled and raised about the walls. Then came the time and as Eider and his entourage entered the hall, Pantul gave out their names in turn: 'Be upstanding for Eider, son of Eyre, Prince of Rhye! Nairb Horatious seelie wizard, of Hairb Horatious and Horatious Thor! Good Regor and the mortal, Lehon, Knights of the Prince's Guard! And Lord Gaunt, master of the first see!'

At his words the lords and captains rose to their feet as Gaunt led each of his company to their seats. Now Lord Gaunt spoke of Eider's likeness to Eyre, and Eider retold his memories of infancy, and of his escape from the blazing castle-town. The eldest of the lords, he of the third see, spoke of that same time with perfect clarity. He told of the ancient Kings of seelie Lore who were the ancestors of Eyre, and whose likeness Eider bore in face and demeanour. The company listened intently, yet still seemed unsure until Gaunt bid Eider show the stone.

Eider glanced at the wizard, and seeing it was well, he brought the Firestone out into the light. At sight of it the loyal men went down upon their knees, knowing the stone had once belonged to Eyre and all his line before him. 'All hail Rhye's King!' they cried as one, and rising to their feet they filed to the head of the table, there to kiss Eider's sword-hand. Yet, though each of them marvelled at the sight of the gauntlet, none dared speak of it before the elder in their midst had acknowledged its presence.

Regor and Lehon watched all intent and silent, alert to every nuance of sight and sound as the men filed past Rhye's heir and back to the seats allotted to them.

Eider spread out his arms, 'Let this first session of the seelie court commence.' At his words the loyal men resumed their seats and wine was brought to them. Eider looked into their proud faces. 'The usurper,' he frowned, 'does he still live?'

One open-faced captain nodded, 'Though by alchemies alone, they say.'

Gaunt frowned, 'We hear many rumours, yet there is no proof.'

'His armies are divided still,' the captain added. 'We here bear witness to that fact.'

Eider nodded, smiling as the aged lord of the third see made to speak, 'Those of us who have remained loyal to seelie Lore have willed your return by day and night.'

Eider looked at him, 'Who among you has command?'

The wet eyes lowered respectfully, 'None, sire. All wait on Your Majesty's command.'

Eider felt a surge of anger. 'In all this time you have done nought but wait?!'

Gaunt trembled at Eider's displeasure, yet the honest captain took his part, 'Sire, we undermine the usurper's schemes where we can, yet dare not . . . '

'Dare not!' Eider snapped.

'Sire, we are so few,' Gaunt interjected. 'And without us, who keeps the Lore safe? Who awaits the heir? Who gives him aid?'

Eider clasped the gauntlet-clad hand into a fist, 'But to wait so long! To allow Zarratt to thrive!'

'Sire,' Gaunt poured calm on Eider's anger, 'none

could free Rhye of this unseelie scourge . . .' he looked into Eider's youthful face. 'Not without the Triad's aid.'

Eider's face whitened with sudden realisation of the responsibility he bore, 'Then it is true!' He frowned turning to Nairb, 'The earth-mirror spoke true!' Nairb's placid features softened as he nodded in silent reply. Eider searched the weary faces of the old lords, the hopeful faces of the captains. He clasped Gaunt's wrinkled hands in his own. 'Forgive me,' he said softly.

The aged lord of the third see spoke then of the gauntlet, 'Sire, do I truly see the glove of the ancient myth?' The white brows met in a frown.

The wizard stood to his feet, 'Honoured elder of the third see it is indeed that ancient glove. The third amulet of Triad power.'

The lords and captains raised their hands and eyes to the heavens at his words 'The gods be praised!' said the elder. 'I, and my forefathers before, thought it lost on the winds! Yet, its image was never lost from our Lore!'

Nairb met the old man's piercing gaze, 'It was so, until Eider reclaimed it for us from the Dark!'

Gaunt rose to his feet. 'Friends, His Majesty holds the Triad of All-Power!' he said joyously. 'All three of the amulets are in his hands!'

The words were repeated around the oak table from whence the last man looked back to the head, ''Tis said Zarratt has created a match for that archaic Lore!'

Eider's brow clouded, 'Then the Triad shall do combat with that force!'

'It is said he can change his appearance to suit,' said one. 'That his needs and appetites are gross and insatiable!'

'He killed every one of his concubines,' another man whispered.

The gentle lord of the second see nodded, 'Twice a year tributes must be paid him by every man, woman and child in the realm. Their value raised every time.'

The lord of the fourth see frowned, 'Little wonder the people starve!'

294

Lord Gaunt shook his head in sorrow. 'Many have lost kin to his murderous whims.'

'We see it every day in the castle-town,' the honest captain nodded. 'The streets are clogged with beggars and the blood of innocents.'

'Since the death of your father, blood has not ceased to flow,' the lord of the third see finished.

Eider's mouth turned dry as the bile of vengeance rose in his throat, yet he fixed his gaze upon the elder. 'And what of the orb?' he questioned. 'The lowlanders spoke to me of a black orb charged by the power of unseelie alchemies.'

Pantul nodded with the exaggeration of youth. 'Some say it levitates.'

'Demons fly from it at Zarratt's bidding, I hear tell,' said the second of the lords.

The face of the honest captain grew pale. 'I know a man who entered Zarratt's court and never left. Spies among the guard spoke of a man eaten by a sphere of blackness.'

'Then Darkness protects its own,' Eider mused, then frowning he looked to the wizard. 'The black orb is the source of Zarratt's power?'

The wizard nodded.

''Tis a formidable foe,' Lord Gaunt warned.

Eider turned to the company. 'Send for your battalions! Zarratt is flesh and blood and like any other man, he can be fought and beaten!'

His words cast silence on the gathering and as all eyes were drawn to the Triad gauntlet, the wizard rose to his feet. Peering through the shutters he saw the crescent moon hanging in the night sky. 'It is time,' he whispered softly.

In the black room, Zarratt's eyes flared demon red as the gleaming crown rotated slowly on the plinth. The servant filled the goblet but the leathered fist smote it to the dust-layered floor. The bearded mouth drew back in a toothy sneer. 'I know what he'll do!' In the still chamber, the deep voice bellowed like the chesty call of a bull.

'He'll seek a battle. It is all they know, these sons of Rhion!' the black leather of the hand clenched tight. 'I shall destroy him utterly, he and his seelie kind!' The blazing eyes turned upon the councillor who stood silently in shadow. 'No quarter!' Zarratt commanded. 'There shall be no mercy!' he vowed.

The fearful councillor bowed low as his brutish master threw back his head. 'Alchemist!' he bellowed. The terrified man rose like a green flame in the dark. Zarratt's predatory eyes set on him. 'More of that stuff!' he demanded. 'I shall have more.'

The alchemist's fingers trembled as Zarratt took the delicate phial of liquid from him, consuming it in one gulp. The heat of the potion made Zarratt wince. 'That son of Eyre is close, and he shall die at my hand!' he threw down the phial and crushed it. 'And when he comes, I shall be ready. Ready for that collection of loric gems.' Zarratt moved towards the black orb set atop the pedestal of jet. 'Astronomer!' he bellowed.

A wiry-haired man ran from the shadows with a litter of scrolls and measuring instruments. Zarratt bade him spread them on the floor for his inspection. He looked to the black orb. 'Arch-wizard!' he roared as the astronomer worked at his feet.

The hooded shape threaded towards him as a fragment of Dark itself. Bone-white arms protruded from the black velvet sleeves and cupped the black sphere. At his touch the orb rotated, oscillating from jet to red, then to malachite as it sped on in demon flight. Zarratt gave a primal groan, his body arching, silver talons breaking from the leather fingertips of the gloves. Across the wall of the chamber, a horned shadow stalked, then wrapped within the forcefield of unseelie power, the figure transformed. Wild-eyed, sleek black, the panther bared its teeth, prowling the darkness, blood lust in its throat.

Zarratt snarled his pleasure in the orb's demon potency, conferring any shape on him that he desired. The wild red eyes flashed. 'How close?' he growled through the black velvet muzzle.

'The first see harbours him,' the Arch-wizard replied in a low whisper.

The snarl of the great cat resounded, the teeth locked.

'He will come alone ... by night,' the Arch-wizard predicted from the shadow of the wide hood.

The beast snorted. Cloven hoofs pounded the chequered floor. 'He shall die by my hand!' Zarratt swore, his voice decelerated to the low braying of a bull. A strong tail lashed the warm air.

The Arch-wizard turned to the solar charts. 'Mercury has begun its cycle. Seelie Lore completes its phase in six dawns, the Lore of the unseelie reckons it in eight dark nights.'

The orb ceased to rotate. The shape of a man transformed amid the shadows. 'All is well,' Zarratt stroked his beard, his eyes intent upon the black perfection of the still sphere. 'When the son of Eyre comes looking for a fight, I shall delay him. The hour will be lost and Dark will seize Triad for its own.' The eyes of a madman stared at the studded door, silver talons pointed.

'A shield of steel,' Zarratt bellowed across the chamber. 'Make me a shield which no army can breach to aid its leader ... steel,' he murmured. 'Steel that will smash his crystal heart!' He turned cruel eyes upon the Arch-wizard. 'Let him come ... alone.' Zarratt looked to the solar charts. 'On the sixth day the Triad shall fall out of his hand, into mine,' he vowed, his eyes fixed upon the demon orb. 'I shall cheat Rhye's heir of all he owns.'

None dared move as Zarratt revelled in his imaginings, his laughter echoing through the chamber, setting the fire aflare, and rattling doors in every corridor and chamber beyond.

Far below the castle keep, the windows of every dwelling in the town reverberated with the power of dark mirth and the people of Rhye knew their King would sleep no more this night.

... Midnight. The old moon slumbered in the new moon's embrace and the ramparts of the castle were

297

silvered with lunar sighs. It was bitter cold and as night's frosty fingers clasped him in tight embrace, Eider drew his cloak about him. Above garlands of stars and galaxies embroidered the firmament and he marvelled at the haloed moon aswirl with variegated colours.

'You stand as if on watch,' the wizard's voice drifted to him and Eider turned to see the billowing robes and long tousled curls.

'I wait for signs,' Eider said solemnly, feeling the icy air brush his cheek. He pointed up at the night sky where stars fell one by one in fiery trails towards the horizon.

Nairb stood beside him and together they watched the luminous streaks of starfire shower the indigo sky in vivid arcs of white light. 'Taurids,' the wizard named them, then turning to the west, his slender finger pointed out a glimmering constellation. 'Aquarius,' he whispered, guiding Eider's gaze to its principal star. 'Some call it sadal melik,' he explained as if divulging a holy secret. ''Tis said to be the fortunate star of kings.'

Eider's face was taut as he surveyed the turning sky. He trembled slightly. 'The moment is close,' he said in a quiet voice.

Nairb touched his shoulder in reassurance. 'As the clock ticks, so time moves to its measured beat.'

Eider turned to him. 'Does the Eye see my Fate?' he asked hesitantly, half afraid to hear the answer.

The wizard smiled and looked again upon the star-fretted canopy. He raised his hands towards its network of designs. 'The heavens turn and Mercury is conjunct with Venus, revelling is at hand!' he flourished an arm in the direction of the Great Hall and the sounds of happy celebration. 'But soon the lunar face has Pluto in conjunction and the hatred of wives and mothers will be avenged!' he predicted.

Eider frowned at the words but remained silent as the wizard traced astrological designs upon the sky. 'Before the new moon proper, Sol squares Jupiter and those given to conceit and arrogance will stir against you,' he

298

warned and Eider read the meaning there, his body tight with hatred for his adversary.

Nairb held him at arm's length and spoke clearly. 'On the sixth night the planets align to do your bidding.'

Eider gripped his forearms. 'Six days hence?' he gasped, his eyes frantic at the news. 'It cannot be so soon, our allies may not have joined us and how can we gain victory without them?' he demanded, urging Nairb to offer hope.

The wizard lowered his head. 'I read only time-steps and have told you all I see.'

Eider turned from him, reluctant to let the wizard see his fear.

Nairb touched his shoulder. 'The Triad has chosen, trust and it will not fail you,' he assured, taking silent leave.

Alone, Eider stared on into the fathomless indigo of night, watching the star clusters and the meteor light, his hand clenched into a fist of resolve.

25

The touch of a hand upon his shoulder roused the elfin from thought, he turned to see the mortal and at his back, Lord Gaunt and his son Pantul.

'Friend, the messenger has flown,' Lehon's eyes glinted.

The aged man nodded. 'News of our King's return shall spread within Rhye's walls this night,' he assured.

Regor grasped his forearm. 'This day marks the meaning of our trek,' he smiled.

'A day too long in coming, friend,' Gaunt sighed as he seated himself wearily before the table and glanced across at his son. 'Yet I am thankful he and his offspring shall see Rhye's pure light cast colour over these lands again.'

'Father,' Pantul chided. 'We all shall see it, the time is come.'

The elfin raised his goblet high and the company joined him in the toast. ''Tis to yourself, my lord and to your loyal men we drink,' he cast a grin into the aged face.

Gaunt flushed with joy. 'Drink up!' he urged. 'Yet in moderation, for this night sees the plotting of our deeds and tomorrow, preparations for the fight!' At his bidding, Pantul cleared space upon the table, while his captains spread their parchment maps before the gathering.

Lehon raised a critical brow. 'Such charts!' he enthused moving closer to the table.

Regor made way for him and flourished a beckoning hand. 'Come, map-maker,' he grinned and together they viewed the ink drawn parchments, scanning every detail of the terrain and asking questions of the military men.

Gaunt, bemused by Lehon's keen interest, drew the

elfin to one side. 'A man of earth,' he whispered into the pointed ear. 'Yet one of few words,' he noted.

Regor laughed. 'And one of unmatched skill concerning maps,' he finished proudly.

The company haggled over routes and tactics long into the night. Time and again Lehon cast an authoritative finger on the parchment, Gaunt and his men looking to him as he calmly forged order from a chaos of opinion.

'You say you have the oath of two hundred or more peasants, all loyal to the cause?' Lehon questioned.

'Aye,' the first captain agreed, 'as well as our own infantry.'

Regor nodded, 'And there are men at arms ... and some cavalry?'

'Five hundred men all told,' the second captain added.

Lord Gaunt frowned, 'Our army is not great, yet those within add to our number.'

'Then we must rely upon surprise,' Regor growled.

Lehon placed both hands upon the parchment's edge, 'We must attack just before first light, when all sleep and the night-watch is ill-prepared!'

Pantul refilled Regor's cup, 'Your guide speaks as a veteran might,' he frowned nodding towards Lehon.

'Indeed, 'tis ancestry makes him so,' Regor agreed, proud to be friend to a mortal so respected of seelie lords.

From atop the battlements Lehon gazed down in wonder upon the blossoming trees of the arbour, its spread of white flowers making stark contrast with the blackened trees of the landscape beyond, where battling crows clung to the lethal twigs and staves.

Yet the sun cast warming rays upon the frosted land and soon the silence of the courtyard was broken by the clattering hoofs as horses were made ready by the farrier. By the time frost had begun to drip as water from the grey stone walls, the courtyard rang with the sound of voices and the clank of steel as soldiers gathered, donning armour and testing weaponry.

Regor shivered and turned about, his golden hair

buffeted by the winds. At the far end of the battlements Lehon stood, scanning the lands to the west. Regor moved up to him. 'All is activity below,' he said squinting against the wind.

'Then the plans are approved,' Lehon frowned.

Regor nodded, 'Come, we must to the Great Hall.'

As the doors swung open, Eider and Nairb glanced up from the parchments. Eider smiled, striding to meet them, his face pale yet radiating strength and peace. He gripped their hands in turn as he spoke, 'The night's toil has born its fruit, friends, your plotted progress has my seal.'

He led them to the table and together they glanced over the parchments. Eider nodded, 'We ride this night, with two of Lord Gaunt's trusted captains.'

Regor and Lehon frowned, confused as Gaunt moved towards them, 'Word has come, you shall be given secret entrance at the North Gate.'

'A party of six? You will not head the troops?' Regor looked confusedly into Eider's face.

Gaunt traced a line upon the map, 'Our gathered forces follow in your wake, attacking the citadel shortly before the dawn on two flanks . . . here and here.'

Regor's anger rose in his throat as he darted a glance at Lehon.

Eider clasped his fist tight within the gauntlet-clad palm, 'By then we are hidden within the walls.'

Regor bristled at Eider's words, yet it was Lehon who spoke, 'Friend, this is a foolish risk! Where is your defence!'

Eider glared into the placid face, ''Tis time dictates the risk, not I.'

Regor threw up his hands in disbelief, turning from the company in silent anger.

Eider leaned over the maps with calm resolve.

Lehon looked to the silent wizard, then paced towards the elfin, 'Return to table . . . the matter must be agreed,' he pleaded.

'Agreed?' Regor swore through gritted teeth. 'To meet an enemy thus, with no defence, with no army at your back, 'Tis madness!'

Lehon frowned, ''Tis lack of time makes Eider suffer no delay.'

''Tis lack of patience, nothing more!' Regor seethed.

Gaunt moved towards them clasping Regor's shoulder, 'Friends, the task awaiting is too grave to have Rhye's heir lost in battle before the gates!' Silently Regor and the mortal followed Gaunt back to the table, unsure of the ploy, but trusting to the old man's wisdom.

Amid the stone and wooded panels of the armoury, heavy silence prevailed, the four companions making their preparations, minds concentrated on the night ahead. Nairb sat upon a stool before the fire, watching the flames dance and flicker in the hearth. Close by, Eider pulled on the gauntlet, while a servant buckled up his boots, another tying the leather thongs of sleeves and tunic. At either end of the room Lehon and Regor carried out their tasks. Regor shining the deadly blades of sword and dagger, while Lehon secured ropes and grappling irons.

At length a page-boy entered with news that their mounts were made ready in the courtyard. Eider rose quickly from his chair, his three companions watching as he gathered up the amulets from the table. Reversing the cloak, he wrapped its vibrant colours about his frame, the black silk of its lining providing useful camouflage for the night's deeds. Sheathing the great sword, he nodded and together they paced out into the lower corridor.

At the door to the courtyard, they were met by Lord Gaunt, 'All is ready, sire,' he bowed, flourishing a hand towards the waiting captains and the mounts.

Lehon tied ropes and tackle to his saddle, while Regor helped the wizard to his horse, their cloaks wrapped close about them against the harsh winds.

'Go safely and the gods protect you all,' the aged man breathed as he and Pantul kissed the young King's hand.

'The gods bring you speedily to the castle gates and

grant us victory!' Eider replied, drawing himself up proudly in the saddle.

Gaunt's men flanked his steed on either side, there to remain, ready and watchful for their King's protection. The wizard drew in line close at Eider's back, while Regor and Lehon protected the rear. At Gaunt's signal the great gates of the keep swung open and Eider raised his hand, leading the company into the frosted landscape.

So they rode out against night's bitter chill, draped in long shadows of the luna glow. Silent and steady was their progress, each man pondering the deeds ahead. Yet Eider's heart grew heavier at every step, for the lands through which they passed were barren, their grasses hollow and parched, mournfully chafing beneath the cruel wind. The shrublands and spinneys through which they trekked bore no leafage, but scraped at earth and sky with their lethal spikes.

Eider shuddered, aching for light, for the growth and warmth of spring. The might of an evil hand had brought all that once was life to nought, here, as at Bethalon. He narrowed his eyes against the sight, kicking hard at the stirrups as vengeance moved within his breast.

Their quickened pace carried them speedily through the barren meadowlands and lifeless woods until Gaunt's men brought them to a halt and Nairb thrust a tapering finger out towards the horizon.

Eider's eyes gleamed as he scanned the brooding walls and towers of Rhye, its pinnacles and turrets etched in the frost-glow.

'We skirt the castle-town,' Lehon said as he pointed to mossy climes and the dark woodlands ranged high above. 'The undergrowth is sparse, yet shall protect our passage to the north wall.'

Each man nodded agreement and they forked left, the horses scrambling upwards through the coarse shrubs of the steep. Reaching the wooded brow, they threaded their way through charred and blackened trees, every footfall sounding with the crack of brittle debris.

Soon the dwindling path led them clear of undergrowth

and Eider's heart raced at sight of the great stone wall thrusting sheer and immovable against the night sky.

Dismounting they hid their horses among shrubs and dead bracken, keeping close, as silently they raced over parched turf to the unrelenting buttresses of the north wall. In moments they were in the shadow of the fosse, Lehon and Gaunt's men casting their lines and grappling hooks high against the frost-coated ramparts. Yet though one of their hooks made grip, two more did not and they each clattered noisily earthward. Every man dived to his belly, waiting and watching, hidden among the muddy bracken of the ditch, but no sound came from the nightwatch and so, scrambling to their feet, they cast the hooks once more.

Gaunt's man was the first upon the rope, shinning the ice-cold structure. Once aloft he reached out to aid the King. Eider struggled upwards, legs braced, slithering against the granite, yet he too gained his foothold and hauled himself onto the narrow ledge of the battlements.

Soon the second of Gaunt's men had stretched out his hand, bringing Nairb's wiry frame to the safety of the ledge. Lehon gave a wince of pain as he gripped Regor's forearm in the darkness, but soon the agile pixie was grinning into their faces atop the rampart. Gaunt's man nodded and one by one they edged forward, balancing on the walkway.

To their left, blackness and the force of the blast; to their right the silver-grey slates of the spreading roofs and piercing turrets.

Suddenly they were descending the deep-cut stairway, boots grating against its frosted slabs. Once at their base, they darted into giant shadow-wedges projecting from the towers and outhouses of the castle keep. Exhausted they pressed their bodies against the pitted walls, sweat trickling down face and limbs, their breath drifting upwards in warm spirals.

In moments they were racing out again across the cobbles of the quadrangle, their hearts pounding as they chased in line, then turned sharp left into the long shadows of a colonnade. Like wing-clad demons they ran beneath the carved archways, swift and silent, their silken cloaks billowing in darkness then light as they darted between the ornate pillars of the portico.

At length, they were brought to a halt against a crumbling wall, the low oaken door set within it worn with age, grown about with ivy and moss. Gaunt's man motioned silence, 'Make no stir,' he whispered. 'Await the signal.'

With three raps of his bony knuckles upon the wood, the attentive captain waited and at the gentle repetition of his rhythm, he nodded to the company. Suddenly the door creaked softly as one by one they pushed inside.

They found themselves standing before a tall man, flaxen haired, draped in heavy chain-mail and captain's livery, bearing Rhye's insignia.

Gaunt's man took the captain's hand in greeting, yet as Eider's eyes met his, the soldier paced forward. 'Hail Majesty!' he breathed, the steely eyes and honest face meeting Eider's in steadfast gaze.

Eider nodded acknowledgement as the soldier glanced about, then drew them close, 'Zarratt awaits your formal entry into Rhye.'

Eider's eyes glinted, 'He waits in vain.'

The soldier grinned, 'Men at arms fortify the western battlements, while regiments and cavalry prepare to meet your gathered armies at the main gates.'

'This night the Triad reclaims Rhye,' Eider growled, the gauntlet fingers clasping to a fist.

The soldier nodded to Gaunt's men, 'Take your places at the gate. Prepare to open to Gaunt and lead Rhye's loyal men in counter-attack!'

Gaunt's men nodded in unison then pacing to the door, they darted out into the dark night once more. The captain beckoned them towards a second door, 'To the inner chambers,' he breathed, leading them over the threshold.

Soon they were creeping along a corridor of polished wood. At intervals their leader halted them, pressing into the shadows until, convinced of safety, he lead them on. Eider and his companions kept constant vigil glancing left and right as new passageways appeared, twisting and turning into the blackness. With every step, dust clung in thick layers to their boots and clothing, their darting forms causing more dust flurries as they brushed against heavy tapestries.

In this manner they negotiated the lower level, attentive of every sound, forced time and again to retrace their steps as guards pounded the interconnecting corridors, oblivious of their presence.

At one such moment, Eider saved them from discovery, leading them to safety up a winding stairway. At the top of the flight they were forced to a halt, unsure of direction. 'Who goes?!' a gruff voice demanded from the darkness beyond and the rattle of steel shook them all as once again they pressed into the shadows. The curious guard marched in their direction, passing too close as he scanned the passageway. In an instant, the captain had drawn his dagger, silently despatching the guard and hiding the lifeless form behind the doorway.

Nairb shuddered, glancing down the darkened corridors which ran in all directions from this point. The distant clank of steel echoed from an adjoining passageway, throwing them into confusion and sending them hurtling towards the first dark orifice that presented itself as a would-be hide.

Yet as they ran they marked the dwindling sequence of torches and how, with the turning of each corner, the wood carvings grew more ornate. Here dust on the crazed slabs billowed upwards in choking clouds and soon only blackness loomed ahead. They halted, the captain quick to turn about retracing their steps, but the sudden clank of iron drew their curiosity to the low door, its wood so black with age, they could scarcely make it out in the gloom. Now it stood open, a shaft of yellow light streaming from its gape.

Regor moved closer, but Eider held him back, each of them curious yet afraid to venture further, watching intently for stir of life. The distant torch flame flickered. 'A draught,' Lehon nodded. 'It caused the slipping of the latch.'

'Yet beyond is light!' Regor frowned, drawing steel from scabbard and pushing at the blackened wood with the blade's tip.

'Careful friend!' Eider warned, as with a glance and a nod, Regor slipped through the narrow gap. Anxious not to lose sight of him, the others followed close.

In the light of a solitary candle they saw the chaos of the chamber. Shelves from floor to ceiling, crammed with phials and jars, books and binders. Tables worn with age buckled under the weight of boxes and books, ledgers and papers, all draped in dust and a tangle of spiders' webs.

Eider and his companions gazed upon the scene in silent awe, the chaos seemed to stretch on and on into the dark. Eider cast a glance at Nairb yet found no trace of fear in the placid face.

'Enter,' a weary voice invited.

Panic-stricken, they turned about, yet saw no one.

The command drifted to them a second time and all eyes focused on the shadowed alcove at the farthest point in the chamber. In the ebbing light, they glimpsed the outline of an aged man, seated before a small table, his back to their company, his arms spread out, enveloping a crystal sphere which sat at the table's centre. White hair cascaded down the narrow shoulders and back, while silken robes flowed in perfect folds to the stone flags.

'Seer!' Nairb breathed aghast.

'A wizard?' Regor whispered into Lehon's ear.

Fearful, Eider gripped Nairb's arm but he could not prevent him as he paced into the chamber.

'Welcome Nairb Horatious of Hairb and of Horatious Thor,' the voice drifted on the dusty air.

Nairb turned deathly pale as he tried to control his quaking limbs.

Eider paced forward, clutching at his sword in Nairb's defence, but a sudden fine and piercing shaft of light sprang from the amethyst, locking the blade firmly into scabbard. Eider frowned, struggling to unsheath the great sword, yet the repeated slither of steel at his back as Regor and Lehon took their stance provided reassurance as he followed at a distance, drawing closer to the alcove.

The white-haired form did not turn, but remained intent upon the glistening sphere as he spoke, 'Hail Eider! Heir to the throne of Rhye.'

Eider gasped, turning fearful eyes upon his companions who suddenly and simultaneously sheathed their blades once more.

'Sire,' the ancient breathed, 'you were guided here and so are safe. Few have knowledge of the chamber.'

Eider clutched at the immovable hilt, but the aged man was keen of wit, 'But for the Triad's grace you may not have lived ... or come so far!' Eider halted as the aged man continued, 'Be wary. The usurper waits on your return.'

Eider steeled himself against fear. 'You know of Triad Power?' he questioned.

The seer nodded slowly. 'Triad and the One who wields it.' The time-worn hands traced invisible designs about the sphere. As he did so, an image made of light poured forth into the chamber. The company gasped, for the image was Eider's and it relived his every trial until at last the Triad sword gleamed in his grip.

The ancient nodded, white hair flowing on the air. 'Long have the people waited, long have I grieved for the kingdom,' his voice ebbed and flowed like a powerful sea. 'So much done, so much undone.'

Eider cast a glance at Nairb whose peaceful gaze remained fixed upon the pulsing sphere.

'Triad is our means,' the seer breathed. 'Our only hope, but see ...' the bony finger pointed to the centre of the sphere, 'the time is late!'

Eider gasped to see a myriad of stars speed by within the gleaming orb.

'The phase of Moon and Mercury has begun. Now Triad Power is yours to wield for good ... or ill!'

'For Good.' Nairb's distant whisper gave reply, his crescent features meeting Eider's in a gentle smile.

Eider drew closer to the alcove, but the aged man knew his question in advance, 'The chamber is well sealed. The best of soldiery protect it night and day.'

'Guards are of no matter!' Regor growled but Lehon frowned silence into the elfin face.

'Even Triad's Power may not suffice.'

Eider glanced at Nairb's face but it had been the seer who had spoken and Eider looked back to see the ancient man clasp the sphere in both cupped hands. In that moment the misted surface cast new lights into the room, projecting images of smoke-grey.

'A veil!' Eider gasped.

'Of Dark and of Fear ...', the seer breathed, '... the spell of the Black Enchanter ...'

Eider frowned, 'Zarratt would make himself invisible?'

'He can make of himself many things,' the seer breathed. 'Beautiful and bestial alike ...' the trembling finger traced the shape of a dimly lit chamber. 'See ... there the phoenix throne ... there the bright gem-crystals of the crown.'

Eider strained his eyes but could see nothing beyond the veiled surface.

The white hair shimmered as the ancient lowered his head in grief, 'None has passed beyond the darkening screen.'

Eider clutched the Triad's hilt, his mind racing with a thousand questions, yet he remained silent as the seer cried out in woeful supplication, 'Sire, the spell denies me foresight! Your fate is our only strength, though cast before all time!'

Eider's face paled, dark eyes reading no sign from the seer's actions, finding no assurance in the whispered words. A multiplicity of meanings circled in his mind until suddenly his body became taut, his thoughts spinning with vague realisation as he watched the flickering colours of the sphere return, 'Then ... he has waited ...

long.' Eider's words faltered upon his lips, the young King barely understanding the meaning of his utterance.

An ice-cold finger ran the length of the elfin's back. 'How long?' Regor whispered into the mortal's whitened face.

The ancient heard the elfin speech and read the same question in every heart. He touched the sphere and set it spinning. 'Time has carried you far ...' he said simply. Eider shielded his eyes as the crystal lights dazzled the chamber walls, washing every awestruck face with a cavalcade of colours.

Suddenly the ancient raised his skeletal hands. 'Enough!' he cried aloud and turned to gaze upon them all. In that moment, Nairb released a gasp, his youthful features meeting his own likeness full-on. He held up his hands to halt the apparition, saw the crescent features drift and merge, waxing and waning, on and on, like the time-old phases of the moon through all the ages of his line. At last the eye of time was still and Nairb gazed in profound awe upon the vibrant and benevolent features of Grand Arch-wizard, Horatious Thor.

The grandson gasped, reaching out to touch the kindly vision, yet though the ancient name rose upon his tongue, he could not speak the sudden truth or halt the moving time-step as the great man vanished in a cloud of glittering dust.

All gathered there could neither speak nor move a muscle, watching on until the smallest pinpoint of mystic dust had shimmered its last.

Nairb had turned ghastly white. 'Be gone from here,' he commanded Eider and the others.

Eider's heart ached to comfort him but the wizard had already seated himself before the whirling sphere of Horatious Thor, intent upon the deed.

'Sire,' the captain said at his back, shaking Eider from trance. 'Sire, we must be gone,' he urged.

Eider wrapped the cloak about him and beckoned the others to follow on. At the door, the captain raised a warning hand. 'Watch well the passageways,' he cried. 'The King must first be hid.'

Regor flashed a worried look at the mortal, concerned that they should be separated from one another. The captain frowned. 'News comes slowly from the spy.' Lehon and the elfin marked the captain's speech, unmoved until the steely eyes met theirs with dark insistence. 'Zarratt does not play the fool!' the military man glared angrily. 'He tells no one of his plan!'

Eider moved towards them and placed a calming hand upon their shoulders. 'Do as you are bid,' he commanded.

Regor met the captain's face in silent defiance, until the mortal took Eider's hand in his strong grip. 'The Triad protect you, sire,' Lehon breathed, urging the elfin to do likewise.

'Victory be ours this glorious day!' Eider vowed, gripping the elfin's outstretched hand. Darting a final glance towards the trance-taken wizard, he turned to the captain. 'Where would you have me hide?' he frowned.

— 26 —

In the shadow of the corridor, Eider watched the captain clasp the page-boy's hand and send him on his way. 'Go safely,' the soldier murmured as the young boy vanished into the darkness of the intersection.

The captain turned to Eider with a smile. 'Sire, Gaunt's signal has been sighted and the regiments' positions as arranged. Zarratt waits . . . well guarded in the east wing.' He led Eider onto the stair well. 'These stairs lead to that place, you must find the turret chamber beyond. None shall discover you hidden here,' the soldier explained. 'As battle begins, take the steps, from there the passage left where are tapestries and a single light.'

Eider nodded drawing the cloak's black folds about him.

'Be wary of the guard,' the captain warned gripping Eider's forearm. 'Victory to the King of Rhye,' he added, his glinting eyes riveting Eider's gaze.

'And to the kingdom, peace.' Eider made solemn reply.

As the man turned to depart Eider clasped his shoulder. 'Friend, your name,' he urged.

''Tis Hariss,' the honest face beamed in reply and Eider smiled watching him pace quickly away into the shadows.

Alone within the dark Eider gripped Triad's hilt, girding himself against panic, sights firmly set upon the dark wood of the staircase. Soon the spreading warmth of sword steel fused through palm to fingertips, but then, a sudden piercing jolt forced Eider to glance at the hilt. His grip tightened as he watched the pinpoint of light flicker and grow strong at the amethyst's heart.

'The time is close,' he gasped beneath his breath, glancing down the corridor to left then right. He felt his pulse begin to race and he yearned to take the stairs. Yet still no signal came or sound of stir. He looked at the stairs once more, the pulsing heat of the amethyst echoing his pounding heart as time and again he held himself back, pressing into the shadows.

Suddenly his heart leapt, a flurry of activity setting his nerves on edge as first one then another group of soldiers ran past him in the gloom. Eider held his breath, yet they were gone as suddenly as they had appeared. He shuddered. 'Patience, friend,' he warned himself in a whisper, taking grip upon impulse once again.

On and on he waited, yet still no signal came. Then loud cries without stirred his blood and moments later the clank of steel and the grating of the gates against their ratchets forced his decision and sent him striding up the wooden stairs in giant leaps to the summit. Before the low door he halted, hardly breathing as he watched for a sign of movement.

The corridor beyond was low and narrow, draped with tapestries, its only light a solitary candlestick, perched upon a carved table. Eider ventured onto the flagstones, yet some strange quality of the shadows held him back and he retreated, peering once more from the protective shield of the door. He scanned the spreading blackness, sweat breaking out on his brow as part of the blackness seemed to move, flowing to and fro.

Eider frowned, for as the wedge grew larger he caught sight of the stiffened features of a fighting man clothed entirely in black: his boots and gloves gleamed in unison with his pace, his shining helmet echoing the rhythmic glint of sword and dagger. He held his breath as the soldier passed close by, but before he could brace himself for combat the form had merged back into the darkness of the passageway beyond.

Eider's heart raced as he slipped from his hide once more, checking left before darting right, causing the candle-flame to flicker as he flew past it, pressing himself into the shadows of the wall hangings on its farther side. He listened and watched intently for the soldier's return, a wry smile spreading across his lips as he realised he was alone. He had outfoxed the treacherous guard. Soon he would be in the presence of the usurper!

He had taken but one pace eastwards when the slither of steel alerted him to a second iron-chested guard pacing rapidly towards him through the gloom. 'Triad protect me now!' Eider breathed drawing the great sword, taking his stance and blocking the passageway.

With a silver flash their blades met, Eider's body straining behind the hilt as the guard lunged forward. Eider gasped, barely able to counter the heaving bulk of his opponent, yet as he battled the gauntlet grip fastened tight about the hilt, the blade vibrating its response. Eider dodged and dived, forced backward by the guard until the sudden jolt of life within the Triad blade thrust the soldier back upon his heels.

The great blade scythed the air, slashing ink-black chain-mail, landing blows with lethal accuracy. Suddenly Eider was forced forward, drawn on by pulsing steel, and he clenched his teeth, struggling to keep his grip upon the hilt. He clung desperately to it with both hands, his face grim as with one forceful blow he ran the soldier through, and watched him fall black and silent to the dusty flags.

Eider ran on into the dark, darting along the winding passageway until his lungs ached for air. How far Zarratt's chamber? How many such guardians along the way?

Reaching the corridor's end he wheeled about unsure of direction, he veered sharply left but was forced to a halt, the way ahead was unlit! He waited, considering the length of the passage, then in the murky atmosphere his ears caught the rhythmic breathing of a sleeper. He watched and listened for long moments, waiting until his eyes had grown accustomed to the dark. Soon he traced the outline of the sleeping guard and the faintest flicker of light seeping beneath the black door.

Eider held his breath, the guard blocked the doorway to the east wing and he knew he could neither reach nor pass through without raising the alarm. He frowned unsure, until a sudden cool draught took up his hair and he turned. At his back an open archway framed the night sky and he nodded determinedly, climbing fearlessly over the sill. The icy draught took his breath away for he found himself atop the battlements. Before him lay the vast black sky protecting its crystal stars from the dawn. In his mind's eye Eider saw the whirling planets of the seer's sphere and gripped the sword-hilt with firm resolve.

Battle-cries flew upward on the fierce winds and Eider's mouth turned dry. He glanced down, suddenly aware of a sea of horses and men clamouring within the deep shadow of the walls. Desperately he scanned the surging grey of their legions for sign of Gaunt or his own brave companions, but the guttering torches cast only fleeting glimpses of limb and flank. Eider winced as swords and lances clashed in combat, lethal blades flashing silver in the blackness.

Yet a sudden pulse of jagged light drew his eyes to the night sky, shafts of lightning penetrating the cloud banks. Moments later he felt the earth tremor, the thunderbolt reverberating through the very foundations of the castle.

Eider shivered as he surveyed the battlements and towers that spread before him, but suddenly the dark eyes glinted, for there, at the far eastern corner of the keep, a turret thrust its slender pinnacle upwards into night. Intent upon the sparkling wall, Eider searched out its tiny window, his teeth on edge as his gaze pierced its yellow light for sight of the chamber's occupant.

'Now I have you!' Eider growled, his vengeful words echoing with the thunder across the stone expanse. A sudden rush of energy, and he had leapt onto the narrow parapet which snaked its way eastward towards the turret tower. The force of the blast took his breath and he almost lost his balance, but the great sword gave him balance and he remained firm and upright as he inched along the narrow ledge. Beneath him, sections of the ancient stonework began to crumble, scattering onto the shining roofs and battlements. Soon the ledge vanished and a terrible void stretched out to where the remains of the parapet stood. Eider caught his breath, knowing he must traverse the span. He stretched out his arms. 'Aksharat!' he cried, and threw himself across.

Lightning shimmered its flare as he landed atop the jagged fluting of the bulwark and raced from the walkway towards the carved stone of the heavy arch. Beyond he saw the ancient spiral of a stone stairway, unused and weatherworn, it clung to the outside of the turret like the grey flesh on ancient bones, only to vanish into the narrow portal adjacent to the window of Zarratt's chamber. A light reflected from within, the sight of which made Eider grip the Triad hilt tighter still, revenge maddening him. As he paced forward, intent upon the flickering light, the grate of leather upon granite quickened his pulse. He halted and the crunch of armour and weaponry announced the sinister presence.

The lightning fork illuminated the archway and Eider clasped the sword tight. Before him stood a monolith of fighting strength. Half in shadow beneath the granite tower, the knight met Eider full on, draped in black leather and silvered steel, heavy helmet surmounted by a metal spike. At the trim of the helmet, three metal flaps hung to the iron-moulded shoulders, while steel and strong silk bindings formed resilient protection about the muscular limbs.

Eider's heart raced with terror as he raised the Triad sword, his keen eyes scanning the moving shadow, yet reading no plan of attack in its stance, the metal grid of the faceguard glinted, expressionless in the lightning flash. They watched each other, silent and intent. Eider's gauntlet-clad hand locked about the hilt and he stood firm, his determined gaze fixing the narrow slits of the faceguard.

A low growl seeped from the metal grille and the ancient turret walls echoed to the crunch of armour as the massive bulk lumbered towards Eider from the shadow of the arch. He stiffened as gleaming steel was swung aloft and, as Eider raised the Triad steel, he felt the backlash course through his body as the dark knight smashed his sword against the figured blade. His opponent swung the sword again but Eider side-stepped the blow, watching the steel fall but inches from his frame, setting the granite alight with sparks on impact.

Eider gripped the Triad hilt with both hands, gritting his teeth as he swung the blade upwards, then brought it earthward in a power dive. With a deafening crack, the razor steel dented the dark knight's breastplate, yet he merely grunted as he shifted his stance. The massive arms swung the sword once more, slicing the air about Eider's head.

Eider retreated, forcing the Triad blade upwards, parrying the hail of strokes, but the knight's powerful torso forced him back against the fluted wall of the battlements. Eider winced, feeling steel graze his upper arm as the blade cracked against stone at his side. He darted to safety seeing the sky torn with silver forks of light, outlining the massive bulk as it strode relentlessly towards him. Growling behind the face-grid, the knight swung his blade high, smashing rythmically at Triad steel, bearing down with immovable force until Eider was forced to his knees beneath the weight.

Desperately Eider dodged left and right, avoiding fatal contact, but though he managed to scramble to his feet he was compelled to retreat as the tower of muscle and steel lunged at him in unceasing attack. Eider gripped the Triad sword as life itself, the gauntlet almost welded to its hilt as he swung the silver blade high, gritting his teeth as the blow fell, scoring a deep gash at his opponent's shoulder.

Eider shuddered, for still the knight paced forward, the stroke having merely cleaved the protective bindings at the joint. Once again, forced to retreat, Eider trembled with exhaustion, heart racing as he glanced at the sky, then he turned upon the knight, his face alight with hatred. He must deal one fatal blow or miss Triad's appointed hour, losing forever his heritage. Yet as he watched the double-edged sword rise he gasped knowing he might not survive.

Trembling in the windrush Eider felt the death draught as the knight's blade sliced the air. Helpless, he raised both arms in defence and in that moment the hidden colours of the cloak furled outward, reflecting the forks of white light. With a blinding flash the power of the Triad cloak fused, a shower of light shafts hurtling towards the knight like silver arrowheads. Caught within the shower of light the knight lurched back upon his heels, protecting his eyes against the attacking shafts. Eider exulted at the sight of the amethyst burning at the Triad's hilt and trembling with the strain he spread his weight.

The great sword scythed the air, dealing blow after blow as Eider stood protected at the still-centre of the Triad's bloody arc. The dark knight's leaden form plummeted from the battlements to the jagged crenellations of the lower ramparts, then further to the cobbles of the courtyard far below.

When at last he returned the Triad blade to the scabbard, Eider's heart soared with victory and the folds of the silken cloak furled about his shoulders in protective embrace. Soon he renewed his flight, darting on towards the spiral steps. He took them two by two, glancing up at the turret pinnacle. Now the glittering sky was alight with storm and silver spearheads of rain showered the granite wall. In the shimmering glow he set his sights upon the round-arched doorway at the stone flight's summit and the window light of the Usurper's chamber close by.

Eider gritted his teeth, clambering up the final time-worn steps to where they vanished into the turret wall. He pressed himself against the moss-coated door, careful to make no sound, watchful of the yellow light shimmering from the adjacent window. Gripping the rusted handle he pressed himself to it once more, but still the swollen wood of the door would not give. As stone crumbled underfoot Eider glanced down, his head spinning as he watched the fires of battle raging far below. Desperately he clung to the rough metal of the ring while rain lashed at his body. He closed his eyes in silent prayer, trembling in the ice-cold draught, fearful he might follow the knight to the cruel courtyard below.

Yet as he grappled with the rusted latch, the Triad sword vibrated in his grip, the flickering amethyst echoing the lightning flash. Suddenly his leather-coated palm fused with the hilt and Eider raised the sword, its shaft of cerise light coursing the length of the blade to its tip. As the gemstone's light made contact with the wood, the latch clanked open granting him admittance. Eider drew the flapping cloak to him and clasping the great sword to his heart he stepped over the threshold towards his heritage.

Below the loyal men of Rhye fought on, their strength and vigour thwarting every onslaught and wily strategy of the royal guard. The main gate and all four of the watchtowers were now unmanned, and Gaunt's men had swarmed across the courtyards to the castle apartments, despatching all who blocked their way from the deepest dungeon to the tallest tower!

White silk billowed against the dark as Nairb Horatious struggled along the rampart's edge, his eyes fixed on the moon's white disc, his hand outstretched in invocation:

> Mercury kiss the white Queen's face
> Light the Eye, and free the Mace
> Blend before the hour has flown
> Grant Rhye's untainted Heir his throne.

The lightning force sprang up, its vibrant white spangles reverencing the good man's presence, forming an aura of electric blue and white about his form as he waited there, watching the narrow portal for the sign.

Zarratt looked at the window, its rectangle bright with the lightning flash. He unlocked the chest, and from its depths removed the elongated box wrapped in black silk. He carried it to the table at the centre of the room and broke open the seals. The arrogant mouth turned down in a sardonic smile as he lifted the lid, appraising the identical weapons that lay before him. Sword and dagger, their lethal blades encased in ebony scabbards. Zarratt fingered the silver vipers embossed upon their sheen then, catching his breath, he slithered the weapons from their casings, eyes glinting as he lay them on the polished table.

Without, battle-cries flew upwards on the wind and he started, glancing at the orb with a toothy grin. The core of blackness gleamed and as he moved towards it he saw upon its metallic screen the castle gatehouse and the battle raging far below.

'Soon he will be here,' Zarratt seethed. He paced the room and at the doors of the adjoining Hall of Monuments he stopped, turning the keys in their locks. This done he pressed his back against the doors, pleased to have raised a further obstacle in Triad's path. 'He comes ... but he shall not pass through!' He swore through gritted teeth. 'He shall not light Triad's Power!'

The shimmer of the lightning fork unnerved him and he looked again at the window. Thunder followed, rattling the doors like eager hands and shaking the granite foundations. Zarratt drew the heavy black robes about his muscular frame and returned to view the orb. Now he saw horses floundering in the courtyard as men fought hand-to-hand. The orb pulsed blackest black, then oscillated showing the bleak tower and the stone stairway. Zarratt frowned, where was this son of Eyre?

At his back the leaded window rattled and he turned with the thunder crack to see lightning tracers. An ice-draught flew into the chamber and Zarratt stiffened, his keen eyes darting to every dusty corner, eager to catch air's flight. The torches had not flickered. Zarratt smiled well pleased and poured himself wine from the jug. He raised his cup, content in the knowledge that no little prince, or his army of rebels, could do harm against Dark Lore!

'To that son of Eyre ... where'er he be!' he sneered, but the wine of the toast had not passed his lips before he felt the ice-draught stir anew.

'Here I stand!' the whisper came from the shadowed walls.

Zarratt glanced round the chamber uneasily.

'Look around,' the whisper flew. 'Can you not see me?!'

The cup fell from Zarratt's hand as a flash of pure white light illuminated the chamber, then was gone.

'I am here!' the echo-whisper pronounced as Zarratt wheeled about in the glow of a second flash.

The usurper glanced at the window again. Was this light within or without? He turned back, his swarthy features aghast as he faced the form of a youth draped in folds of light! The lithe shape flew from him as if on winged heels!

'I am here!' the whisper flurried on the air. 'I am there!' the chant came back from the opposite wall.

Zarratt twisted and turned until his head was spinning. Then sudden stillness and Zarratt's brow beaded with sweat. He paced towards the table, but even as his fingers touched the sword's hilt a rush of white lit up the room, dipped, then seemed to fly the length and breadth of the chamber. Zarratt snatched at his weapons, yet could not fix the light-veiled figure as it rushed at him, then stopped abruptly in battle-stance. Zarratt scowled, seeing the figured blade of an ancient sword.

'Zarratt!' Eider growled.

'Son of Eyre!' Zarratt seethed as their eyes met in cold recognition.

'Aye, and true King of Rhye!' Eider pronounced.

'Where is the proof?' Zarratt's lips drew back in hatred.

'I need show a thief no proof! I shall have all that is mine!'

Zarratt hit the shaft of his sword with the dagger blade, 'Be gone, wastrel!' he commanded, his neck reddening with desire for the fight.

Eider's eyes narrowed, 'Out of my way, deceiver! The kingdom lies in ruin by your hand!'

'You are your father's son! Like Eyre, you are a fool!' Zarratt mocked.

'You, Zarratt, have the look of my line, yet your soul is dead!' Eider spat at the usurper's feet, but Zarratt's bellowed laughter turned his stomach.

'You have the tongue of the father, but the beauty of the mother,' Zarratt retorted. He groaned long and low, 'That dark-eyed beauty was mine in her last hour!'

Eider's heart ached for vengeance. 'You shall pay in full for that stolen pleasure!' he swore.

Zarratt drooled, clasping at the sword-hilt, beckoning Eider to him, drawing him into combat.

Eider raised the Triad sword and kissed the amethyst at its hilt. 'For my mother,' he whispered.

'Be gone, outcast!' Zarratt clashed dagger-blade against sword once again. 'See the tools that defeated Eyre! Your own death etched upon each blade!'

Quick as lightning Eider whipped the Triad's blade to left and right drawing silver arcs upon the air. 'I fear you not, King Rat,' he hissed, unsheathing his dagger and rapping the blades as Zarratt had done, thus accepting his challenge to duel.

Zarratt stood his ground.

Cautiously Eider approached, setting Zarratt's heart with the sword's tip as they circled each other in the torch-glow. He marked Zarratt's every move, stepping close enough to smooth the steel of his blades across Zarratt's. The four hilts locked and Eider taunted his adversary with an insolent smile.

Zarratt stiffened at the insult and drew his blades away, steel licking steel in murderous ritual. Silent rage tightened his face as he made a sudden lunge, his razor blade resounding as it clashed with the Triad shaft. For each of Zarratt's blows Eider leapt to safety, sure-footed and unruffled by the flurry of reckless strokes as he warded off each thrust and cut. 'Come, come, King Rat!' he mocked the usurper. 'Royal titles warrant more skilful swordplay!'

Zarratt lunged at him again as Eider ducked and side-stepped, tantalising his ungainly adversary until, with a flick of the Triad shaft, he forced Zarratt off balance. The usurper recoiled, stumbling backwards as Eider rushed him once again. Spitting curses, Zarratt parried then dived, thrusting out with dagger then sword-blade. Each time Eider dodged the shaft, thrusting Triad to within inches of Zarratt's heart, yet always withholding the tip.

Zarratt staggered between lunging attack and sudden retreat, while the youthful prince danced and darted between the glancing blade pirouetting to left then right, well out of harm's way. For every advance that Zarratt made he was forced back twice as far by Triad's keen tip until at last, glancing over his shoulder, Zarratt found his back to the wall.

Sensing victory Eider pushed forward with renewed vigour, Triad sword poised to deal the final blow. Zarratt was forced to one knee, both blades raised as a shield against attack, their united strength taking the full force of the great blade. The three shafts clashed, slithered, then locked as both men concentrated his full weight behind the hilt. Eider growled and bore down harder, feeling Zarratt's arms tremble with the strain, but still the usurper managed to block him, and Eider was thrown back, gasping as he struggled to keep his feet.

Zarratt seized his chance and lurching forward he whipped at Eider's legs with his lethal blades. Yet still the lithe prince flew from him, swift feet skipping the glancing blades to left and right. Breathless, Zarratt chased on, forced low as he tried in vain to wound and halt the darting spectre. Jumping higher still Eider lashed out with the Triad blade, kicking at Zarratt's sword-arm in his flight and sending him sprawling to the flagstones.

Dagger lost, Zarratt stooped, visibly shaken, pressing a wounded hand to his mouth as he clutched at the sword-hilt with impatient wrath. As their eyes met Eider heaved the great blade with such force that Zarratt staggered backwards barely countering the rapid succession of blows that rained in upon him through the silver arc. He gulped air, parrying and weaving, seeing murder in the young prince's determined face.

In an instant the Triad blade had cleaved the space between them and Zarratt's aching wrist twisted, his sword wrested from his grip and sent spinning to the dusty floor. Helpless, Zarratt cowered before the gleaming shaft, his terror-stricken face riveted to Eider's implacable gaze.

As their eyes met, Eider cast a savage grin into the Usurper's face, brandishing the Triad blade yet halting again the lethal tip inches from Zarratt's heart. Taking silent pleasure from his deadly sport, Eider traced imaginary weals upon the black velvet of Zarratt's chest, again and again repeating the thrust of death in mimed gesture while Zarratt's face whitened each time the blade-point drew closer to its mark. Eider laughed aloud: 'Come, traitor!' Eider mocked him bringing the blade to rest against the velvet black. 'Take fair chance of life! A benefit not afforded my kinsmen!' With that Eider paced from him, catching up Zarratt's discarded sword with Triad's tip and sending it spinning into the air.

Zarratt stiffened, incensed at Eider's sport, and as the glinting shaft plummeted from the heights, his face set and he leapt forward halting the sword's downward flight as he caught it in his grip.

Eider laughed on, striding from his humiliated opponent, tempting him to cowardly attack. In his rage the usurper hurled himself at the straight back of his adversary, but the young prince heard the rattle of steel as

325

Zarratt approached and turned, meeting the challenge afresh. Zarratt waited, mere paces from him and Eider's face broke into a demonic grin as he marked Zarratt's heart once more.

Zarratt's rage had turned to evil laughter. 'Little prince, the time will soon be past! . . . See . . .' The usurper pointed the dagger-tip towards the alcove. There, upon a plinth the perfect circle of the black orb had begun to spin. As it rotated the orb was haloed with silver which gradually eclipsed the sphere to form a screen upon its surface. There, the heavens and all the speeding constellations were held in the black eye.

The gauntlet tightened about the Triad's hilt as Eider forced aside his opponent's blade, but Zarratt's strength had doubled even as his own had diminished. 'Triad aid me now,' Eider gasped but his plea went unheard as with one powerful blow Zarratt threw him to the marble floor.

'Homage to Rhye's King, wastrel!' the low voice boomed. Zarratt threw back his head and in the dim light the shadow cast bore horns like crescent moons.

Eider's heart raced, could this be real or some Dark trick?

'Come, son of Eyre, confront me now!' Zarratt provoked, pointing a silver talon towards the orb and drawing demon life-force from its core.

Eider saw the monstrous face flush red then sulphurous green, saw the cloven hoof scrape marble, saw the thick whip of the tail lash out, felt its sting across his shoulders. He floundered, suddenly aware that he was crawling across the cold black floor, pursued by the pounding hoofs. The tail whipped his back and he cried out in pain. He felt the shadow of the beast consume him, until at last the Triad blade shuddered in his hand and with sudden vigour, Eider was on his feet again to lunge at the menacing form.

Zarratt's laughter reverberated, his skin glossy with body heat. The menacing eyes glanced at the carved doors of the Monument Hall and knew that his demon power kept all without.

Eider grew agitated. Zarratt read his thoughts.

'Soon the power of the planets will wane and Eider, last of the seelie line, shall die!' he taunted.

Eider dived for the doors, a sudden high-pitched yowling echoing in his ears. He felt the draught of speed, the heat of hot breath, the texture of fur, saw sleek blackness glide over him. He heard the dull thud of feline paws and saw the panther set itself in challenge between him and the carved doors. The black back arched, the sharp teeth bared and the lethal paw was poised to strike. Eider knew well the blazing hatred of the eyes. The Triad blade raised slowly of itself.

Feline eyes bulged and its ears flattened, the guttural warning of attack underlined by a violent flicking of the powerful tail.

'The gods protect me now,' Eider gasped, his eyes fixed upon the demon beast as he tried to match its unflinching gaze. In that moment the door of the ante-room burst open at his back, Lehon and Regor filling its gape, their bloodied swords held in readiness.

'Eider!' Lehon cried, darting forward in his defence. The great cat growled and spat, its lethal talons flailing the air as it sprang upon the mortal, inflicting wounds with claw and tooth.

'Go to!' Regor cried as Eider joined him in the defence of their wounded friend.

'The wizard . . . ,' Regor snatched up a torch as the beast prepared to strike. 'He bids you go to!' he yelled at Eider in desperation.

Eider ran for the carved doors of the Monument Hall, hearing the venomous yowling of the great cat held at bay. The Triad sword smashed the locks with one fell swoop and the doors swung open. Upon the threshold, Eider saw the Monument Hall, now an expanse of endless monochrome; from the black and dull white of the chequered floor, to the ebony drapes, and all between a monotonous wash of pewter grey. The gauntlet-clad hand pulsed about the sword-hilt and he entered in, an apparition of pure white light. He did not feel the dark

327

presence as it slipped in behind him, nor see the pinpoint of black dart past his shoulder.

Now within, Eider saw the tincture of his skin change to ivory. The Triad sword had become his only source of light and he trembled as the rainbow hues of the cloak began to dim until its crystalline lights were almost extinguished. He pulled its drained folds about him and they clung like a leaden patchwork. From behind, he heard the ear-piercing screech of the panther and he shivered, knowing his true friends did battle with the beast for his sake. He raised the Triad sword, scanning the vast hall by its omnipotent glow.

Three tall windows spanned the eastern wall, their ink-black drapes hanging heavy with dust to the chequered floor. He moved towards them knowing he must part the drapes and break open the shutters, but his fingers had barely brushed them when a low drone echoed within the dark expanse. Eider turned aghast to see the black orb, see it shudder as it spread its mass. He took his stance, his sword awaiting the demon Zarratt, but the form of beast or man did not appear. Instead, the orb of Dark homed in on him and Eider was forced to jump clear of its speeding flight. It hit the wall but did not smash on impact . . . it simply vanished.

Eider gulped air, keen to bring light to this unholy place and set to shinning up the drapes and frame of the central window. He wrenched the rusted latches and the broken shutters crashed back, knocking him off balance. He had barely found his feet when the darksome sphere, grown larger still, was hurtling towards him once again. Whatever direction he took, the orb followed suit and as its blackness closed in upon him, Eider encircled himself with the Triad cloak, awaiting the pain of impact. The orb rolled to his feet as a shiny black bead. He bent down to pick it up and looking at it closely, he caught in its sheen the reflection of his own black eye. With a growl he cast it from him to the farthest corner of the hall.

Desperate, Eider threw himself at the window and began to climb its frame. It would not yield and he clenched his teeth, yanking hard at the sash until finally the panel shuddered and as the window swung open each small square of glass flashed with the reflected light of the moon.

Eider gasped as the night air clawed at his dust-filled lungs. Above him the black sky, vast and calm, the spread of ice-cold stars and the moon, full and round in their midst. He looked out over a zigzag of roofs and turret towers. Atop the battlements he saw the wizard, his silken robes billowing in the speeding wind. The skeletal arms were stretched taut and skyward, ice zephyrs carrying Nairb's words to Eider's ears, 'The throne!' he cried. 'Look to the throne!'

Eider turned back to view the hall. The rush of air had shifted debris and drapes. The orb was nowhere to be seen and as he searched for it in the shadows, his eye was caught by the edge of something pale and white. He climbed down to the chequered floor, his inquisitive eye following the contours of ivory steps leading upward into a shadowed recess. As his eyes made their ascent, his heart raced ... at last he had found Rhye's seat of majesty. It stood atop the marble dais, neglected and dwarfed by Darkness. Eider saddened at its plight, yet though it stood entwined in the shroud of Time, still he sensed a mystic presence there. He saw it in the marble seat itself and in the dust-draped instruments of an ancient lore still set in ritual upon the low table. Tears welled up in his dark eyes for all lay as it had on that last terrible day. As his heart dwelt on his sorrow, the cries of the wild cat screeched from without and Eider knew that he must act quickly or lose the throne again, this time forever! He peered into the deep recess and caught his breath. His sight had focused upon the shape of wings outspread in marble majesty above the throne. Eider followed their outline, the curve of the slender neck and head, the edge of the cruel beak, the diamond-shaped hollow of the eye. He smiled, the vast sculpture was the emblem of his ancient line. 'The royal phoenix,' he whispered, appraising the beauty of its form. Yet he frowned, the eye of the bird was sightless.

The realisation hit him hard. Frantically, Eider searched inside the cloak and then into the deepest pockets of his jerkin. 'Firestone,' he breathed, dropping the almond-shaped gemstone into his palm. He placed his foot upon the first step of the staircase. The rush of an awesome force slammed against his back and he toppled. The orb's black shadow had returned to enfold him and hold him from his deed.

The gauntlet shut tight about the Firestone as Eider ran up the six remaining steps, seeing his own white foot-prints in the dust. Now his only thought was the almond hollow of the phoenix eye as he clambered up the claw feet and marble wingspan to reach it. Dark gravity pulled at his back but the white shield of the cloak held him firm, the gauntlet never weakening its grip upon the gem until it had been slotted into the socket.

Eider raced with elation and he turned to see the orb's baneful shadow recede. He looked to the mighty bird, its red eye the only hint of colour in the vast hall, yet why did it not gleam? He held up the Triad blade, it shimmered with reflected light. There in the broken frame of the window, the perfect white disc of the moon was hung and Eider felt compelled to greet it. The sudden lightning halted him, its ice-white tracer showering the chequered floor. Upon those same flagstones crept black on black and Eider knew the war of Light and Dark was begun.

He paced forward, taking his stance upon the white square and raising the Triad blade to waist height. The shadow of Dark moved in unison, spreading out from the black square to consume him. Eider pulsed with fear as he raised the hilt, his eyes searching out Triad light at its centre. The gemstone core remained dim.

'Darkness!' Eider took determined stance. 'I banish you from this hallowed place!' he commanded, but Dark-ness made silent reply, rising to encircle him chest high.

He held the Triad sword higher still, brushing the amethyst with his lips as he pressed the shaft to his forehead. Now the sharp tip pierced the seething blackness above and Eider trembled beneath the weight of the blade. He waited . . . The lightning sheet was momentary, yet had ignited steel within his grip, the blade had begun to pulse and Eider's fingers throbbed with the first tremor of Triad power. His face turned ash white as he watched lunar shafts dart the hall to criss-cross his form in violent display. He braced himself for contact as they surrounded him but it was not he they attacked, but the lengthening mass of Darkness.

Eider clenched his teeth. ''Tis the orb, 'tis Zarratt's black heart,' he gasped as the suffocating shadow ringed his chest. Fear twisted Eider's stomach as the lunar glow burned out in the dense black of the orb's power. He clung to the Triad hilt, fighting off the magnetic pull of the unseelie and its shadow host. The keen blade carved steel arcs in the encroaching blackness, yet came to nought against the forcefield of Dark power.

'Light!' Eider cried out. 'Reclaim this hallowed place!'

As he spoke the new moon flew, matching the circle of Darkness with a circle of pure Light. Eider's midnight hair whipped about his face in the sudden backlash and the Triad cloak beat at his back like wings, raising him inches from the floor. The powers of White and Black began to duel, while he at still-centre, clung to the Triad's hilt, waiting for the glimmer of a purple flame at the amethyst's heart.

At last the dazzle of meteor light ripped through the window smashing every pane, and lightning arced, conducted by the Triad blade. A surge of electric power hit Eider's body and he cried out, 'Gemfire!' against the spasm. Now the circle of black was spiralling about his whole body, he gasped for air but his lungs were clasped tight. He felt the Darkness sucking him into its core and his eyes ran with tears as they implored life into the weak flame at Triad's hilt. As the forcefield of Dark throbbed with new intensity, Eider groaned, feeling his entire being fixed to the sword-hilt, his limbs wracked by the increasing tension as he hovered at the centre of the battleground, trapped between stasis and motion.

'The gods help me!' he yelled, now so weak he was barely able to cling on to the Triad hilt.

Brighter than lightning the line of ice fire sped from the lunar heart, zigzagging the blackness to hit the amethyst gem with the purity of light, then as if directed by some ancient hand it raced on, hitting the Firestone at its centre. In an instant it had doubled back upon itself, now vibrant red, then mauve, then blue as it evoked a curtain of crystal light. Caught in its shimmer, the Triad cloak added its faceted colour until every variation of every hue hung above the chequered floor. Lunar shafts criss-crossed the spectrum foregrounding the black orb, its shape and onyx density now clearly visible to Eider's eye. His body wrenched with a mighty force as the Triad blade raised of itself, its razor steel dazzling as it fell and smashed the eye of Darkness to a million ebony fragments. They hovered about Eider as if he were the axis and he, the still centre of All-Power, raised the Triad sword absorbing all Darkness in an orbit of fragments until he had created of them a whirling vortex.

He spoke his seelie judgement. 'All Dark be banished to the wastes!' The doors of the great hall burst open and the vortex drew to it all Dark days and all Dark nights, all Dark hearts and all Dark souls, all Dark lore and all Dark spells. His head reeled with the motion of the curse and his heart raced to see the great cat fly from the door's gape, its sharp claws falling velvet soft upon the chequered floor. Yet as it approached him its size diminished and as it flew at him the Triad gauntlet clasped it by the scruff of the neck. Eider looked into its face, seeing nought now but a small black cat; it bared its teeth, it swore, it spat, its insignificant yowling all that remained of Zarratt's wrath, of Zarratt's power.

Eider glanced at the carved doors where his two companions had halted in the chase. Lehon's bloodied sword was held in readiness, while the elfin still clutched the blazing torch. As their eyes met, Eider gave a

332

sardonic smile, he shook the struggling feline, then tossed it in disgust to the heart of the vortex.

He raised the Triad blade and the whirling core of Darkness rose up, following the blade point to the open window. Before the draughty portal it bobbed like a spinning top upon its point. Faster still it flew until the Triad force that manipulated it, cast it out at high velocity.

Atop the ramparts, Nairb's heart filled with joy as he stretched both arms to the zenith. 'Go, black enchanter and familiars all! Be banished to the wastes of Time. For while the seelie line reside, you shall not thrive within these walls.'

So all watched evil fly from Rhye, shrinking to a small triangle then to a pinpoint . . . lost to time and the desert wastes.

In that moment the throne room flooded with the dazzling white aura within which Eider stood. He gasped as the primary colours flew from the tip of the Triad blade, spanning the chamber in a rainbow of vivid bands. The radiance of colour took his breath, and feeling his limbs tremble, Eider brought the great blade to rest against his chest, dark eyes dancing as he surveyed the vast crystal prism in which he stood. Still his body tensed as he felt fresh agonies twist his sinews and the arc of mystic power clash against the Triad steel.

Upon impact a cloud of sparkling light particles showered the vast chamber, drenching the throne in a spectacle of colour. In that moment Eider's anxious features softened, before him he saw the silver-white of the ivory throne, and nestling upon the silken cushion, the regalia of Rhye's monarch. The glittering display of Rhye's treasures brought childhood memories of regal ritual flooding to his mind's eye and he breathed deeply, perfecting his stance. He raised the Triad sword high in invocation as once his ancestors had done and pressing the amethyst to his heart he touched the noble blade with his lips. Closing his eyes he gave himself wholeheartedly to the worship of the Ancient Lore.

The Triad steel emitted a searing flash which hit the Firestone like an electric impulse, its intensity giving birth to pure flame. Eider watched the flames ripple, their vibrant glow illuminating at last the majesty of the firebird.

'The royal phoenix,' he breathed, falling upon one knee in reverence.

From talon's tip to elegant neck, from noble head to sharp, bright eye, the luxurious plumage unfolded before him in a splendour of scarlet and gold. Enrapt within the glowing embodiment of Rhye's sacred emblem, Eider whispered ritual thanks, his head bowed low before the powerful symbol of his trial. In that moment, shrill trumpets sounded without marking the end of battle and heralding the newly woken dawn. With the first note of birdsong the great blade surged with awesome power and Eider stood to his feet: from his taut, straight shoulders the cloak of light cascaded in dazzling folds, whilst from his gauntlet-clad fingers diamond claws shimmered. Eider tossed his midnight hair in a proud gesture and pressing the sword-hilt to his lips, humbly received the blessing of the gods: he was one with its power and the living heart of the Triad's mystical corona.

—— Epilogue ——

The shrill fanfare of trumpet and clarion echoed long and loud as the heavy studded doors of the gatehouse, so long bolted against revolt and a kingdom's misery, swung open. The people of Rhye proclaimed a King.

Above the entrance arch to the barbican, the brooding portcullis was woven with flowers and from the castle towers the flags of every noble see rippled colour on a land so long austere and grey. From every fluted wall and soaring gable royal standards were draped and the great courtyard festooned with newly woken blooms, until it seemed that every tower and turret was forged of delicate blossoms and scions of tender green.

The long nightmare had ended and at the sight of Rhye's loyal soldiers, the townsfolk cheered for life itself had been restored to them. The loyal champions of the sees followed on, resplendent in their black and scarlet liveries, their horses bearing the Phoenix crest emblazoned upon caparisoned flanks. The majestic wingspan of the firebird echoed on in the fluttering silk of banners and upon the proud chests of every marching battalion.

The upright lances of the infantry cut sharp silver lines against the bright blue of the sky as Captain Hariss led them in brisk step to the beating drum. They halted at the centre of the courtyard and as every jostling onlooker fell silent, a fanfare of trumpets blared and the captain raised his sword in proud command: 'Armies of the seven sees, surrender up your honours to your King and loyal people.'

At his words, standard bearers stepped forth from the ranks, each holding aloft the banner of a royal see. Hariss dismounted and moving to the head of the procession, he ordered them on towards the crenellated west tower with its round-headed door. The serious-faced captain struck the aged wood thrice with the hilt of his parade sword and admission of the battle honours was granted. Glinting steel rattled in unison as the procession wound through the dim passageways of the lower storey and ascended the sweep of stone steps beyond.

At the intersection of the third level their numbers swelled as peers and councillors filed in at the rear of the standard bearers and their guardians. Upon the fourth storey, courtiers and velvet-draped pages moved to head the slow-marching company, carrying tall candles, symbolic of the light restored.

And so from every compass point they came, threading their way towards the call of a long trumpet, to the Throne Room at the castle's heart. Before the great oak doors, halberdiers stood to attention as the procession halted, declaring itself thus:

'We, the liege lords, councillors and citizens of this realm do proclaim with one voice our faith and loyalty to the throne and hereby offer up our royal colours. Stand aside, that we may bear witness to the coronation and do homage to our King.'

The doors swung open and the procession entered in.

The Throne Room so long shuttered from the purity of natural light was now ablaze with colour, from the delicate tracery of stained glass windows to the rich heraldic tapestries which hung the length and breadth of the oak panelled walls. The ceiling, rich in gold leaf, was embellished with the phoenix insignia, while from the stone corbels flags and banners were draped in dazzling lines. On either side of the ivory throne, ceremonial swords were hung alongside elegant shields of courage, whilst behind and above, the majestic phoenix spread its marble wings reborn of Triad power.

Before the dais the wizard stood in silence alongside the gold-robed Arch-elder who placed the sacred talismans and ceremonial regalia upon the marble altar. At the centre of the altar the great sword stood reverenced, awaiting the chosen heir.

At the sound of the clarion, the senators and pages came bearing caskets, seals and sacred scrolls. In their turn, Rhye's seven elders walked forth, white-haired and holding aloft their ivory wands of knowledge. Pages carried the ancestral treasures of orb and baton, sceptre and swords, sacred ring and golden keys. And there, held high in solemn praise, Rhye's resplendent crown rested upon a velvet blue cushion, its turreted frame of gold sparkling with gems of sapphire and ruby.

The noble lords and statesmen, the captains and courtiers, silently took their allotted places alongside Regor and the awestruck mortal, until at last the chequered floor was lost beneath the gathering.

A solitary trumpeter played the voluntary and all eyes turned to see their King proclaimed, as Eider walked down the aisle in slow time towards the waiting throne. Crimson robed, he halted before the dais, bowed silently to the Arch-elder, then took his place. The trumpet was lowered and in the stillness the silk-robed elders shuffled forward, each lightly touching Eider's shoulders with their sacred wands. Climbing the steps of the dais they took their places on each side of the throne alongside Nairb and the Arch-elder.

The most revered of Rhye's loric elders began the ancient rite, turning to every compass point within the hushed chamber. Eider mirrored his moves as the old one announced in a voice of sung litany:

'I offer unto you, King Eider, true monarch. Those who come to do him service and homage, announce your vowed intent.'

The gathering cried as one. 'The gods save our King,' and the trumpet fanfare echoed their response.

Eider stood sombre and erect before the throne watching intently as the Arch-elder called forth his helper who placed at Eider's side a pedestal of ivory whereon a large black volume lay inscribed in the ancient tongue.

The Arch-elder stepped forward. 'As Rhye's King now pledge loyalty to the Kingdom and to its people.'

Eider rested his hand upon the ancient book and spoke

in a clear, steady voice. 'I swear allegiance to Rhye and its crown, to uphold law and justice, to be merciful and to show humility. By the grace of the Gods I commit my life to Rhye, its people and to Triad Lore.'

The wizard, Nairb Horatious, moved forth and took up the ancient text, returning it to its honoured place upon the altar.

Eider bowed his head as he was divested of his crimson robes and now in the white linen of a simple gown he moved silently towards the throne, seating himself beneath the fiery eye and awesome wingspan of the phoenix.

The Arch-elder stood before him and dipped his forefinger into the silver chalice. 'With Phoenix blood I bless thee, Eider, King of Rhye.' He drew upon the high forehead the sign of the mystic pentacle. 'Born of flame to flame return, pure of heart, in whom the gods have placed their trust. I name thee King and Wielder of the Lore.'

Eider bowed his head. The Elder bade him rise and pages walked forward to drape him in the Triad cloak of sovereignty which they held at his shoulder with a gilded clasp, while about his waist a girdle of gold was fastened.

The Arch-elder nodded and Eider walked towards the dais and ascending the steps he touched the golden keys upon the altar, then, his taut back towards the gathering, he raised the ceremonial swords in dedication to the gods. Upon his left wrist, Nairb Horatious clasped a gold bracelet of wisdom whilst upon his right the Triad gauntlet was fastened.

'The gods give you wisdom and strength,' the wizard pronounced. 'These are the bonds that unite you with your people.'

Onto the fourth finger of Eider's right hand was slipped the sacred ring and into his left hand the baton of justice.

Nairb stepped back as the Arch-elder moved towards the altar and took up the majestic crown. Holding aloft the symbol of kingship, he turned to place the crown reverently on Eider's head. At his bidding, Eider moved to the altar and stretching out the gauntlet-clad hand, took up the great Triad sword. It radiated in recognition of its wielder, casting its argent light about his swarthy face as he lifted it vertical and steady.

At his back the congregation rose as one and Eider turned, the shimmering blade held parallel to his chest. A rainbow of refracted light arced above the congregation who raised their caps in joy. 'The gods save our King!' they cried as one.

Trumpets declared his coronation as Eider received homage from his subjects who knelt before him to kiss his hand and pledge allegiance. To the accompaniment of drum and clarion, he walked from the chamber in triumph, King of Rhye and Wielder of Triad Lore. The dream had been fulfilled, a new page would be written in the ancient book, and the Throne Room rang to the sound of sung blessings.

... Atop the battlements Lehon looked out across the newly woken colours of spring. Still his mortal eyes scanned the contours of the land for sign of the shimmering boundary, set between the realm of enchantment and that of mortal men. The green eyes grew heavy with sorrow as he shook his head. 'Nevermore,' he said softly. A warm breeze caught up his hair and carried in its flight the sound of brisk footsteps on the wall walk. He turned to meet the elfin's broad grin.

Regor clasped Lehon's shoulder. 'Such activity! Such splendour!' he enthused. 'Come, join me in the feast below!'

Lehon smiled, his watchful eyes returning to the horizon.

Regor leaned against the fluted stone wall. 'What do your mortal eyes behold in seelie climes?' he frowned.

Lehon sighed, 'Blackened wastelands blossoming into spring.' He turned to the elfin, ''Tis truly an enchanted place.'

Regor laughed and slapped him on the back. 'Minstrels become Kings!'

'Aye,' Lehon nodded with a gentle smile. 'You had your wish and more.'

Regor's eyes were saddened. 'But you, my friend, you did not find your kinsman.'

Lehon looked at him. 'Yes I did for I found myself along the way. I am my kinsman,' he answered quietly.

Regor grinned into the solemn face. 'Then magic enfolds all and all is well!' he caught Lehon's arm. 'Come, let us leave these blustery heights and join the festivities.'

Lehon shook his head. 'Let those who have waited long make celebration on this day.' He gripped the hilt of his sword. 'Good Regor, stay awhile, for trusted friends upon the battlements prove greater service to our King.'

Joyful cheers flew upward on the warm spring breeze, the symbol of life returned and hope for better days, while across the landscape the vibrant colours of Triad Light shone on, even to the shimmering borders of Time.

Also available from Unwin Paperbacks

Continuing from *Crystal and Steel*:

BLOODSEED
Book Two of *The Eye of Time*
Lyndan Darby

With Eider as its King, Rhye basks once more in a summer of joy and celebration. The gates of the palace are thrown open; yet among the guests is a masked actor and his troupe, whose dumbshow brings the first bite of autumn frost.

Mystics or tricksters? Truth or illusion? A shadow falls across the halls of Rhye, but the eye of the Crystal is blind to its progress.

The Dark Lords have regrouped: vengeance has spawned a vile alliance, and from the bloodseed comes the instrument for the Triad's destruction.

PHOENIX FIRE
Book Three of *The Eye of Time*
Lyndan Darby

These are strangely troubled days of rumour and omen, of failing light and dark winter.

Now is the time for Rhye's elders to perform their ancient rite atop the barrow-grave of Kings. Here the destiny of the Triad's wielder is revealed, and when the Dearth Hand rises Eider is condemned to the Shadow-Land and to his Fate.

Yet can he find Phoenix Fire and bring about his final redemption?

Also available from Unwin Paperbacks

All these books are available at your local bookshop or newsagent, or can be ordered direct by post. Just tick the titles you want and fill in the form below.

Name ....

Address ....

....

....

Write to Unwin Cash Sales, PO Box 11, Falmouth, Cornwall TR10 9EN.

Please enclose remittance to the value of the cover price plus:

UK: 60p for the first book plus 25p for the second book, thereafter 15p for each additional book ordered to a maximum charge of £1.90.

BFPO and EIRE: 60p for the first book plus 25p for the second book and 15p per copy for the next 7 books and thereafter 9p per book.

OVERSEAS INCLUDING EIRE: £1.25 for the first book plus 75p for the second book and 28p for each additional book.

Unwin Paperbacks reserve the right to show new retail prices on covers, which may differ from those previously advertised in the text or elsewhere. Postage rates are also subject to revision.